RESURRECTION BONES

© 2023 NC LEWIS

All rights reserved. No part of this publication may be reproduced, distributed, or transmitted in any form or by any means, including photocopying, recording, or other electronic or mechanical methods, without the prior written permission of the author, except with brief quotations embodied in critical reviews and certain other non-commercial uses permitted by copyright law.

This is a work of fiction. The characters, organizations, and events portrayed in this novel are the product of the author's imagination or are used fictitiously, and any resemblance to actual persons, living or dead, businesses, companies or events, or locales is entirely coincidental.

CHAPTER 1

Shirley Bickham woke from a terrifying dream and knew the day would be hell. She stared at the water-stained ceiling, blinking away the night terrors. Today was the day she prayed would never come.

"To hell with it," she said to the dark bedroom, then slid from the bed and padded barefoot and nude to the window.

She gazed at the thick curtains, sewn from scraps of cloth by her mam and hung on giant brass rods by her dad. A patchwork of greens and browns with reds and purples thrown in. Drawn tight, they blocked the faintest trace of light. Just as Shirley liked it.

A dizzying jolt of pain pounded behind her eyes. How much did she drink last night? She recalled the first shot of gin, but after that it was a blur. She half turned to glance at her naked body in the dressing table mirror, eyes lingering on her face. Like a plum turned into a prune, she'd not aged well. Sunken cheeks and swollen eyes and loose skin which collapsed in deep hollows. The years had pockmarked her body with the vigour of a garden mole.

Another shard of pain twisted in her skull, and a slow creep of shame crawled along her neck. What did she say last night? What did she do?

"To hell with it all."

She yanked the curtains wide and squinted. The afternoon sun glared through the glass. She swore the bleedin' thing got brighter every day. Something to do with global warming. Well, this was England not the Costa Brava, the bugger could go back behind the clouds where it belonged and leave her eyes in peace.

"Shirley, you awake yet?"

Shirley turned to face the door, did not answer, and staggered back to the bed. As she sank beneath the bedsheets, the bedroom door swung open.

"Today's the big one," her mam said, skipping into the room. "Forty years today. Happy birthday, darling. My, how the time flies."

Shirley's mam, Ida Bickham, was short and slender with narrow shoulders under a frizzy black wig, pale grey eyes and a broad smile that, despite the chemotherapy, never slipped from her face.

Too upbeat for Shirley first thing in the afternoon. Too cheerful for a freshly minted forty-year-old still living at home. Too optimistic for a single mum with a twenty-one-year-old daughter in tow. Forty years with nothing to show. Shirley felt acid churning in her stomach.

"Party, party, party," Ida said, waving her arms in the air. "Come honey, get your glad rags on. We're having your birthday do downstairs in ten minutes."

It was a simple homemade cake with icing whipped and dolloped in sweet peaks on a firm brown crust. Four pink candles clustered in the centre. Three generations of Bickham women sat around the scrubbed pine table in the kitchen, eyeing the cake. Ida, Shirley, and Shirley's daughter, Ginger.

It was a crowded kitchen with hard tile floors and cream walls. Pots and pans hung from giant hooks. Photos and notes were stuck on the fridge door. It hummed. A battered iron kettle hissed on the stove. Shoes by the door. A cricket bat leaned on the wall next to a vegetable rack. A stone jar used for fermenting beer stood disused in the corner. A broom, dustpan, brush, mop and bucket leaned in the other corner. The kitchen window, heavy with net curtains, looked out onto the back garden, wild with foliage in bloom.

"One candle for each decade of your beautiful life," Shirley's mam said, smile a mile wide.

She did not mention Shirley's lack of friends or trouble keeping a job or the gin. Mam always stayed on the positive side, always hoped for better to come. No matter how bad things got.

"I'll kill myself when I get to thirty-nine," Ginger said, picking a speck from her tight black t-shirt.

Shirley's jaw tightened. Why was Ginger so difficult? Her daughter might have long legs, a thin waist, big breasts and swirls of wavy black hair, but she was still a child.

"Forty is ancient," Ginger said, fixing her mam with a sour look. "An antique, really. Like those old mobile phones that looked like bricks. No longer of much use. Old. Past it. Best tossed on the scrap heap and left to rot."

Shirley said nothing. She wouldn't let her daughter needle her. Not today.

"Most drunks have at least one friend," Ginger said, watching her mam for a reaction. "We would have invited them for a slice of cake if they existed. Mam, you need to up your game."

Shirley didn't want to argue. Not with her head still thudding from last night's gin and God knew what else. There was her birthday party to endure and she did not want her mam to get upset. She kept her gaze on the candles, quietly seething.

Ginger scrunched up her face. "Mam, did you know most drunks don't live past fifty?"

"Let's not spoil your mam's big day," Ida said, her voice soft. "Forty is a slip of a lass. Wait until you get to my age. Now, one, two, three..."

They sang the birthday song with Ida's deep voice keeping the harmony.

"Blow out the candles and make a wish," Ida said in an excited sing-song tone.

Shirley blew and made her birthday wish. The same wish she made every year. For money.

As they were eating the cake and proclaiming how moist and sweet it tasted, Ginger rose to her feet, her t-shirt rising and exposing her belly. "I know it is my mam's birthday and I don't want to spoil it but I've got an announcement."

"Here we go," Shirley said, pushing her plate away. "Little Miss Centre Stage wants to share a secret."

"Tell her to stop with the spite, Gran," Ginger said, pulling her t-shirt a touch higher so her full belly was exposed.

Ida sighed, placing her hand together as if in prayer. "Let's all be thankful that we are alive and well, eh?"

"She started it," Ginger replied, lips twisting into a pout.

Shirley took a steadying breath. She didn't want another blowout argument with her daughter. "Why can't your drama queen act wait until we've finished the cake? Better yet, tell us tomorrow, we'll be all ears."

Ginger dashed to the sink, sobbing into her hands. "Mam, why don't you ever listen to me?"

Shirley rolled her eyes. "Here we go again."

"What is it, darling?" Ida said, following her granddaughter to the sink and placing her arms around her.

"I wish Grandad was here," Ginger said, clinging to her gran.

"We all wish it was different," Ida replied, and kissed her on the forehead.

"Gran, he needs to know too."

"Know what, honey?"

"I'm three months pregnant. I'm going to have a baby."

Shirley was on her feet, shouting. "You are twenty-one. What about college and your exams?"

"Oh come off it, I don't care about college," Ginger replied, eyes blazing. "I'll get a job."

"I want the name of the lad," Shirley said, screaming. "I'll tear a strip out of his hide."

"Mam, grow up." Ginger eased from the grip of her gran. "Anyway, his name is none of your business."

Shirley raced across the kitchen, was at the sink with her hands around Ginger's shoulders, shaking the child. "You will tell me his name."

Ida raised both hands, palms out. "Leave her be. Have you forgotten how the hormones made you feel? She'll tell us in her own sweet time. Just like you told me when you were carrying Ginger."

Shirley's hands dropped to her side. "But—"

"It was all hush-hush with you," Ida said with a hint of disappointment. "I wasn't even there for Ginger's birth. You didn't tell me which hospital you were having her in, so give her a break."

Shirley felt pathetic and powerless and angry, but managed a weak smile. "I want to help you, Ginger."

Ginger glared. It was the look she always gave Shirley when she wanted her to bugger off so she could natter in peace with her gran. The defiant look of a young woman who had outgrown her mam's power.

"I want to help," Shirley repeated. "I'm your mam. I'm here for you."

"Yeah, and a monkey will fly out of my butt," Ginger hissed. "Mam, you stink of booze. I can't talk with you here. Sling your hook."

"Now, Ginger, don't be mean." Ida glanced at Shirley and flashed her mile wide smile. "Shirl, why don't you take your dad a slice of cake? He'll want to wish you a happy birthday and hug you. The landlady turfs them out in the day so he will be at the allotment working his turnips."

CHAPTER 2

Shirley Bickham's day lurched in a sickening downward spiral as she trudged down a narrow lane boarded on one side by a dry-stone wall and hedgerows on the other. Seaview Allotments were on the edge of town. She shuffled along the sodden path, slick from morning rain with a cloth bag in her left hand. It contained a carton with a slice of cake for her dad.

The sun radiated from a cloudless sky. Wild honeysuckle twisted around the trees, plunging from branches in spidery fingers. The air smelled of damp grass. Rain all morning. Sun after noon. Fog at night. Typical of Cumbria in late May. A normal day. Except for the strange sensation that overcame Shirley. A sense of inevitable doom.

With every step, Shirley's heart screamed. Was it normal for a mother and her teenage daughter to fight? The rift with Ginger had plunged them into a bottomless void. Why didn't Ginger talk to her? Shirley brooded over the question. She needed a drink, would stop by the pub on her way home. Only one shot of gin with a large splash of soda water to weaken its strength. *Promise.* She crossed her heart as though it were her last day on Earth.

The trail swung uphill. At a turn in the lane, the view opened across the valley. Green fields dotted with sheep and hedgerows and trees in full bloom. In the distance, the pier and, at the end, the abandoned lighthouse. It had protected the Port St Giles shore for hundreds of years. A scene from a postcard. Shirley paused to take in the view and listen to the growl of the sea. If she had her phone, she would have taken a picture, but she left the house in such a hurry she forgot it.

Over the hilltops, a pair of crows uttered a raucous scream. They wheeled and tumbled, mercilessly mobbing a buzzard. Below in the fields, sheep bleated, their fleeces a dirt stained grey. Shirley watched without seeing. She wanted to know the name of the lad who got her daughter pregnant. They would be nattering now. Ginger and her mam. Sharing secrets. Not much good for Shirley, though. Her mam kept Ginger's secrets, would take them to her grave. Shirley's jaw stiffened.

"To hell with it."

She glared at the grime-stained sheep and the distant lighthouse and the crows mobbing the buzzard. Once she got a sniff of the lad's name, she'd teach Pretty Boy a lesson. With a cricket bat.

She felt her lips twitch into a smile. What would the lad say when she cornered him? She pictured herself screaming at Pretty Boy—and then she pictured her hands around the neck of the cricket bat that leaned by the kitchen door. Swinging it. Again and again. Until Pretty Boy's face squelched like mush and his frightened eyes went blank. She jerked alert when she realised she was swinging the cloth bag like a bat.

The crows continued to mob the buzzard, screaming their warning cry, beaks stretched wide. Shirley was about to hurry on when ice crept along her neck. She was being watched. Someone had their eyes on her.

She tightened her grip on the cloth bag and turned to look back along the path. Ash and hawthorn and gnarled oak. Hedgerows and sheep. Pier and lighthouse and groan of the sea. She turned back to face the allotments. They were at the end of the dead-end lane. Half a mile at most.

"Hello, is anyone there?"

Furtive movements came from the bushes. Something rocketed from the hedgerow, hissing and screaming. It moved fast. Arrow fired from a bow fast. Blink and you missed it fast. Straight at Shirley's pockmarked face. A black dart aimed at her eyes. She blinked, ducked and spun as it scraped past her ear.

A blackbird.

Shirley stumbled back three steps, then staggered back four more. What was it her dad said about blackbirds? Something to do with seeing three of them and death.

Another bird hissed from the bushes. A high-pitched, unsettling, warning squawk.

What the hell was she doing in this Godforsaken place on her birthday? She picked up the pace, breaking out into a shambling trot. Ten yards on she stopped, doubled over, catching her breath, gazing behind, watching for the birds. A third bird hopped onto the ground, its black eyes watching her. *Christ, she really needed a drink now.*

She started along the trail. The quicker she moved, the sooner she'd be chatting with her dad. He'd be up for a festive drink down the pub. She peered at her pockmarked hands, gazed at the cloth bag, and sighed. At least her dad would get a birthday surprise. He would insist on filling the bag with turnips for her to take home and cook with her dinner. Recycling. He was big into saving the Earth.

As she crossed a disused tramline which snaked to a defunct quarry, a man's voice called out.

"How do, lucky lady."

A wizened figure scrambled from the bushes. He had thick sideburns and wore a flat cap tilted so it shaded his face and a rumpled brown short-sleeve shirt. His leathered face was all hard angles and a sharp gleam shone in his deep-set eyes.

Shirley stumbled back three paces. "Where the hell did you spring from?"

"That is no way to talk to a war veteran," he replied, rubbing his left elbow.

"Didn't they teach you not to jump out on ladies?"

"Aye, they did, but I'd hardly put you in that class, Shirley."

"Cheeky sod."

"That's what the ladies like about me, darling,"

he said, right hand still rubbing his elbow. "That and the size of me turnips."

George Rouge sold award winning vegetables from his stall in the town market. Shirley's mam shopped at the stall. He had a habit of lurking in the shadows and seemed to enjoy leaping from nowhere to frighten folks.

Shirley studied him. He was slightly winded, with a sheen of sweat on his face. "Have you seen my dad on your travels?"

His face reddened, eyes shafts of dark. "Why would I be looking for your old man?"

Shirley did not want to set him off. He had a temper on him. Everyone knew the man suffered from rage. A sort of madness brought on by too much contact with the chemicals used to work the soil, Shirley thought. She changed the subject. "What is that rash on your arm?"

"It's nowt."

"It looks nasty."

"I said it is nowt."

Shirley didn't like the look of the red splotches bubbling and spreading from his elbow. Was it contagious?

She took a step back. "You need to see a doctor."

"I'd rather see a nurse."

"Randy sod." She looked at him, smiling. "I'm forty today. Wish me a happy birthday."

"Well done, lass. I remember when I was that age. I thought my life was over. Downhill is what they say."

"Sounds like me right now," Shirley admitted. "I'm so far past it my daughter treats me like I'm already dead."

He laughed with a donkey's bray, exposing crooked yellow teeth with wide gaps and black gums. "Not to worry, lass. My life wasn't over at your age. Not when I found out the ladies still fancied me turnips."

Shirley grinned. "We've got to watch you. Thought you'd be at your market stall today."

"Me boys run the stall on Saturdays. I retired from that lark five years back, but I still like to keep my hand at the allotment." He rubbed his left elbow. "Me work is done here. Time to sink a pint. Want to get in early, fog tonight."

Again he laughed with a donkey's bray. He shuffled away with surprisingly quick bandy steps.

"Watch out for the blackbirds," Shirley called after him. "They go for the eyes."

She didn't think he heard until his reply drifted back on the breeze.

"Keeping us safe, eh? I like that."

CHAPTER 3

Shirley waited until George Rouge disappeared around a bend, then walked on, cloth bag swinging. The lane narrowed into a single dirt track. The trees formed a canopy of shade. They called this part Dead Man's Walk. Shirley didn't know why. She stopped.

Although she had visited the allotments before, the stillness made her uneasy. Was someone following her? She watched to see if anyone was there. As she scanned the darkness ahead, the donkey bray laugh of George Rouge rattled in her head. *Keeping us safe, eh? I like that.* She took a step, once again stopped and peered into the gloom.

"Who's there?"

The wind carried with it the rustle of leaves and bleats of sheep. A soft scurrying noise came from the bushes.

"George, is that you?"

George Rouge had a habit of lurking in the shadows and leaping from nowhere to frighten folks, and she swore she heard sinister laughter carried on the stiff breeze. Might have been the call of a crow or a blackbird or the bleat of a lost lamb. Might have been gin playing tricks on her mind from the night before. Might have come from a man hiding deep in the bushes. Might be George Rouge. Might not.

She listened.

Heard nothing.

"I know you are there."

No answer.

She waited a full minute.

Nothing but the wail of the breeze.

With growing trepidation, Shirley started down Dead Man's Walk. A gull screamed from somewhere unseen. Her walk became a trot.

At the iron gate that led to the plots, panic seized her. Someone lurked in the shadows and they were coming to get her. She dare not turn around; knew they were two paces behind; felt their hot breath on the back of her neck.

The rusted latch took a twiddle at the best of times. Her hands trembled as she seized it, yanked and shoved. A clang of rusted metal squealed. The gate swung inward. Shirley went with it, stumbling, skinning her knee on the moist soil. She lay there, chest heaving, cloth bag clutched to her chest.

She blinked. There was no one behind her. No one was following her. Nothing bad was going to happen. *Gin and tonic twice at the pub. Stuff the sodding soda water.*

Agitated by her foolishness, she stood and steadied herself. It was her birthday after all, and the argument with her daughter was more than enough bad luck for the day. It had made her jumpy. Heap on the baby and the way Ginger flounced about and flaunted the news as they ate cake. Well, was it any wonder she felt consumed by doom?

"To hell with it all," Shirley said as she gazed around, trying to get her bearings.

Seaview Allotments covered a vast area. "Thirty acres," her dad had said. From what Shirley could see, most of the lots were overgrown—bindweed, ground elder, and thistle. A ragged sheet of plastic flapped in the breeze. It was attached to the rotted wooden skeleton of a greenhouse overtaken by brambles. There was a Victorian iron hand water pump, black with age, with a rusted jerrycan at its side, and a red phone box, coin-operated. A ramshackle collection of allotments stretched to an unkempt orchard.

There was no one in the place. No villagers working the soil. A desolate land. Her dad must be mad, she thought. She shopped at Fresco for veg and watched the telly in her spare time. No way would she dig and weed in the filth plants grew in. She tramped along a dirt trail to the orchard. Her dad's plot was on the other side of the wild fruit trees.

A robin sang a haunting song as she picked her way through the apple, pear, and peach trees. More bindweed, thistle and stands of nettles. She passed along a grassy bank, then down a dip and her dad's plot came into sight. She paused to look. No tell-tale signs of pipe smoke, or the bobbing of his flat cap as he prodded a garden fork into the soil. Was he in the potting shed? It was made from slats of scrounged wood and corrugated iron.

"Dad," she called, approaching the shed. "Got some birthday cake for you."

No reply.

Shirley knocked and entered. It was a small space with a bench piled with tools and two wood crates used as makeshift chairs. It smelled of cigarettes and sweat and moist earth. There were no windows, but a slither of light came through a crack in the walls. A thin layer of sawdust covered the bare ground.

No sign of her dad, though.

She left the shed and leaned against the door, watching for the flat cap of her dad as he crouched low between the raised beds. For about thirty seconds, Shirley stared at the patchwork of green plants and black soil. A creeping sense that something, somewhere, was terribly wrong, slowly formed in a chill along her spine.

When she turned to her left, she glimpsed a flash of metal, then grinning yellowed teeth and a manic stare.

"No," she cried, falling to her knees. "Please God, no."

His flat cap tilted over his face, brown short-sleeved shirt rumpled, lips in a taut grin with a trowel clutched in his right hand. Owl-eyed and terrified, legs too weak to stand, Shirley scrambled on all fours toward the man. A swarm of flies took flight in the odious, sweet-scented air. That is when she saw the trickle of blackened blood at the side of his head. She knew then, her dad, Fred Bickham, was dead.

CHAPTER 4

Detective Inspector Fenella Sallow was deep in the potted vegetable aisle. Saturdays at Johnny Dew's Organic Garden Centre always came with surprises. Today, the clematis was out in full bloom, a riot of white across the trellis at the entrance of the store. There was a glorious range of spring plants arranged in row upon row of luscious shades of green. Framed photos of the winners of Johnny Dew's Organic Garden Centre gold medal hung on the walls. The winning veg, that is, not the people who tended them. Each winner received a real gold coin imprinted with the Johnny Dew logo at a festival on the beach. It was the highlight of the year for serious gardeners and hobbyists. Fenella considered herself the latter.

She picked up a tray of baby aubergine plants, put it down and picked up another, then stepped back and stared at them both. Which tray? Last year the tray she planted shrivelled and died. This year she would grow them in the greenhouse, pray for a long hot summer and hope they'd thrive.

"Daddy says you must always buy two trays."

Fenella spun to face a girl of about eight with auburn hair tied in two pink ribbons.

"And who are you, pet?" Fenella asked, placing the tray back on the rack.

The girl cocked her head to one side. "Daddy says I'm not to talk to strangers."

"You spoke to me first, remember?"

The girl's lips turned up and she smiled with a mouth crowded with small white teeth. "Only because you picked up one tray. I wouldn't have said anything if you had taken two."

"Two trays, eh?"

"Daddy says so." She glanced up at Fenella again, looking her over more carefully this time. "Two or three trays."

Fenella had a soft spot for bairns. She'd had five, all grown. She liked the idea of buying two trays. If anything went wrong, they'd be back up vegetables for the kitchen table. And if both trays did well, they'd be a deluge of fresh veg to give as gifts and for the freezer. She placed both trays into her basket with a soft clunk. She'd get Eduardo, her husband, to plant them. He needed the exercise. When they were ripe, she'd send him to pick and Nan, her mam, would make a delicious grilled salad.

The girl nodded her approval. "They call them eggplants in America. Aubergine is from the French. In Swahili, they are known as mbilingani."

"Learn that in school, eh?" Fenella asked.

Again she nodded. "My daddy told me two are not guaranteed to work, but it is worth a try, isn't it?" Again came the mouth crowded with small white teeth. "Do you have lots of friends? Mbilingani make great gifts."

Fenella looked at the plants in her basket and she looked at the girl with pink ribbons. She hesitated. Something wasn't right. "You didn't tell me your name."

"Why?"

"So, I can thank you for your excellent advice."

A blackbird landed on a sack of bedding soil, cocked its head to one side and gazed at them. It let out a shrill squawk and flitted away when the girl spoke.

"My name is Cherry Dew."

Fenella was about to ask if her daddy's name was Johnny when she heard a male voice. "Oh, there you are Cherry; I was looking for you."

A beanstalk thin man hurried from the end of the aisle. He had a head too big for his thin shoulders and a ponytail flecked with grey. He wore black boots, blue jeans and a brown short-sleeved shirt. Johnny Dew, the owner.

"This lady is buying two trays, Daddy," Cherry said, grinning. "We were getting to how many friends she has so she can buy a few more."

Johnny Dew winked. "Good lass." He turned to Fenella. "Don't forget potting soil. You'll need a couple of bags. Buy three to be on the safe side. Always wise to have a spare. Never know when it will come in handy."

"Aye, I'll add it to my list," Fenella said, eyeing the smiling face of the young girl with renewed suspicion.

Johnny Dew turned to his daughter; voice low. "Got an extra delivery of wheelbarrows to push to the punters. How about you stand near them and help? Two barrows are better than one, remember that, lass. Remember that."

He plucked Cherry into his arms and strode off, muttering about how great she was at sales.

On her way to the potting soil, Fenella stopped at a display of intelligent lawnmowers. An engine thrummed. The lawnmower at the front trembled. She read the display:

Fancy a mowed lawn whilst you drink tea in your favourite armchair? Yes. Yes. Yes. This tireless machine will work while you snooze.

Fenella regarded the lawnmower as it shuddered and shook. It was the size of two push mowers and resembled an alien spacecraft. She wondered if it would be of much use on the rough land surrounding her cottage on Cleaton Bluff. She pictured it shredding her rose bushes and smashing into the greenhouse. She'd not trust the thing out of her sight, but her husband would want to give it a try. He hated physical work. She hurried on.

"Don't forget to get runner beans."

Fenella recognised Nan's voice and turned to see her mam with Eduardo, her husband.

"I don't like runner beans," Eduardo said.

"I'll toss them in butter and garlic," Nan replied.

Eduardo wrinkled his nose. He wasn't keen on vegetables or salads or green anything. "Pity they don't have an organic ice cream plant. I'd love to have one of them growing in our garden. Next to the apple pie tree."

"You'll never lose weight if you think like that," Fenella said, smiling at her husband.

He drew cartoons for a living. It involved lots of tea drinking and munching on digestive biscuits. Over the years, he'd put on a glut of pounds and needed to shake them off. Doctor's orders.

Nan said, "The lazy bugger wriggled out of the park run this morning and now he's talking about apple pie trees."

"I'm a comic artist," Eduardo said. "I'm allowed to dream, aren't I?"

Nan clicked her teeth.

Fenella saw a pair of small eyes watching from between the stack and burst out laughing. Nan followed her gaze and did the same.

"What are you peeping at you silly sod?" Nan said, her voice directed at the pair of eyes.

Cherry Dew stepped between a gap in the shelves. She stared at Fenella's shopping basket and gave an approving nod. She turned to Eduardo and put her hands on her hips. "Runner beans are good for you. You'll need three trays of beans. Daddy always says it is best to keep one spare."

"Don't like beans that much," Eduardo replied.

Cherry shook her head.

Everyone laughed.

When Fenella looked back many weeks from now, she thought the soft creak alerted her to trouble. A faint groan, low, at the edge of her hearing. An instant later everything slowed to a crawl. The crowded tooth smile of Cherry. Another creak. Louder. An elongated groan and a slight wobble at the edge of Fenella's vision.

Then time sped up.

Fenella sprinted into the gap between the shelves. She grabbed the child into her arms, holding her tight. A high whine shrieked as a lawnmower burst free from its display and raced along the aisle. It spun hard right into the shelves. A boom shattered the air. The shelves buckled with a piercing growl spewing a deluge of lawn feed, bird feeders and hose reels to the floor.

Fenella crouched low, child covered by her body, as cartons and hose reels bounced off her back. A moment later she felt a sharp pain at the base of her spine and swallowed hard to fight it back.

It went quiet, and she heard Eduardo's voice. "Oh my God, are you alright?"

"Think so," Fenella said, easing to her feet, releasing Cherry from her grip and rubbing the base of her spine. Bruised she thought, and hoped there was nothing else wrong.

Eduardo had his arms around her. Nan was checking Cherry. The child blinked, face pale, but was otherwise unhurt.

Eduardo said, "We'd better get you to the hospital."

"I'm fine," Fenella replied, trying not to wince, and smiling at Cherry.

Cherry extended her hand. "This is for you."

She dropped a silver brooch into Fenella's palm.

"It's an eggplant," Cherry said, returning the smile. "It will bring you luck."

Fenella slipped it into her pocket. "I hope it helps me grow my trays of veg so I have lots of eggplants to share."

Cherry nodded with approval.

Johnny Dew arrived a split second later, a horrified expression on his face. He snatched Cherry into his arms. "We'll send those bloody robotic lawnmowers back. The bleedin' machines are deadly."

"Can I have a dog, Daddy?" Cherry said in a baby voice, eye's watching her dad. "A big dog to protect me."

"Anything you want, girl. Anything." Johnny Dew turned to Fenella. "You'll never know how grateful I am. Listen, your basket of goods is on the house. Fill another, if you like, it is free and I'll be—"

His voice faded as a policeman bustled along the aisle. It wasn't so much the speed at which the officer moved as his jerky wobble that caught the eye. You could pick PC Woods from a crowd of thousands.

PC Woods gasped with a loud sucking sound as though he'd run a hundred-metre sprint in record time. "Came here as fast as my legs would take me, ma'am. There's been an incident in Seaview Allotments. Superintendent Jeffery said it requires your urgent attention."

CHAPTER 5

The woman stopped screaming thirty seconds after the paramedic gave the injection. It was then that Fenella started screaming inside.

"She must be shell-shocked," Fenella said, as she stood on a patch of dirt surrounded by bindweed in Seaview Allotments. "Do you have her name?"

"Miss Shirley Bickham, guv," Detective Sergeant Robert Dexter replied.

He was her second in command and kept his ears close to the ground. So close, Fenella wondered whether he spent his free time listening to police radio.

Dexter was still speaking. "The lass called it in from the payphone. She is the daughter of the victim, Mr Fred Bickham."

They watched the paramedics guide Shirley Bickham to the waiting ambulance. A howl rang out in the warm air. Shirley burst free, took three steps and collapsed in a pitiful wail. The paramedics eased her to her feet, and hustled her through the ambulance door, leaving it open.

"Hell of a thing to happen amongst the veg, guv," Dexter said, rolling up his shirt sleeves. "If it were my old man, it'd send me into a manic mania too."

Fenella said nothing.

It was three thirty on Saturday afternoon, and warm for May. The air held the tang of the sea. Oak and ash trees shimmered in the soft breeze. The shrubs were in full bloom, their foliage thick with life. From high on a branch of an oak tree, a blackbird whistled its alarm. And a man lay dead amongst all this beauty.

"Miss Bickham found him over there, guv," Dexter said, pointing at a shed rotted with age.

A crime scene forensics team had arrived and were setting up a tent.

Dexter continued. "She found him in a patch of weeds, near the turnips. It ain't nice."

The blackbird whistled again. Shrill and wild. They turned to look.

"Me grandad was always going on about blackbirds." Dexter pointed at the tree. "He'd sing a rhythm about sixpence and a pocket full of rye."

"Aye," Fenella said, trying to remember the words.

Dexter was ahead of her. "Sing a song of sixpence. A pocket full of rye. Four and twenty blackbirds baked in a pie. Lovely, one that."

"Aye, but remember how it ends?" Fenella said, recalling the poem in full. "The maid was in the garden. Hanging out the clothes. When down came a blackbird and pecked off her nose!"

"Me grandad always said they can be vicious buggers, guv. He said if three hop near you, your days are through. Strange birds, he said, because they bring good luck and death."

They turned back to the crime scene.

A mournful voice wailed from the open doors of the ambulance. Shirley Bickham held her head in her hands. "How am I going to tell Ginger? What will I say to my mam?"

The doors shut with a solid clunk.

Dexter raked a hand over his grim face. He swore. "Ain't a nice one, guv. I feel sorry for the lass."

"Time for me to take a peep," Fenella said, eyes glued on the closed ambulance door. "Is Lisa Levon on site?"

Lisa Levon headed the forensic team.

"Aye, guv, saw her suit up. She is with the body."

Fenella set out toward the crime scene tape, mind preparing for what she would see. She noticed Dexter hanging back, which meant one look was enough for him. *The first look seared the deepest.*

"Ma'am?"

Fenella spun. A fiery spasm seized her tailbone. She gripped her back. *I have to be more careful*, she told herself, recalling the lawnmower accident at Johnny Dew's Organic Garden Centre.

PC Woods waddled along a dirt path, arms raised, waving and gesturing. "Ma'am?"

He stopped at the police tape, sucked in a ragged breath, speaking as he exhaled. "Superintendent Jeffery has asked you to visit her at the station. She said it was urgent, ma'am, and left you a message."

Fenella reached into her handbag and retrieved her phone. She turned if off on the weekends. She had expected a comfort shop in Johnny Dew's Organic Garden Centre and a quiet weekend with her family. She switched it on. It pinged filling the screen with messages. Five. All from Superintendent Jeffery's assistant.

"Like I say, the boss said it was urgent, ma'am," PC Woods said, casting a nervous glance at the figures in white suits.

He was an office cop. The doughnut and cream bun type who snatched a quiet smoke when no one was watching and got his excitement from a flutter on the horses. Crime scenes were not his thing. Too gruesome.

Fenella glanced at the crime scene and she glanced at her phone and she glanced at the ambulance as it drove away. "Jeffery can wait."

"The boss said it was urgent, ma'am," PC Woods repeated.

"So is the situation here."

PC Woods shifted from foot to foot. "I'm to drive you back to the station, ma'am."

"Aye, well you can join me in that tent. When we are done, we can head out."

PC Woods glanced at the white tent and the patch of weeds where figures in white suits flitted between the rows of vegetables. Again, he shifted from foot to foot, his pallor turning two shades paler. "In there with the body, ma'am?"

Fenella said, "Tell you what, find out who was

the responding officer. Let them know I want their report before they knock off."

"Yes, ma'am," he said, bustling away before she changed her mind.

The sun blazed down. A black-headed gull hovered. White suits moved between the rows of vegetables searching for clues. Dexter was back at Fenella's side.

She said, "We'll have a team briefing. Me, you, Jones, Detective Sergeant Ria Leigh, and invite PC Beth Finn and PC Woods."

"What time, guv?"

"About an hour."

"Sorted."

Fenella put on shoe protectors and gloves and passed through the police tape. The black-headed gull screamed as she entered the flap of the tent.

It was much worse than she expected.

The hot air, sweet with the stench of death, watered her eyes. She snatched a tub of vapour rub from her handbag and slathered a dollop under her nose. It helped. A little.

"Ah, Detective Inspector Sallow, wondered if you'd be on call."

Lisa Levon, the head crime scene tech, strode toward Fenella. She flashed a dazzling smile, the type you'd expect to see on the big screen not in a crime tent with a rotting corpse.

"What have you got for me?" Fenella said.

Lisa shook her head. "This way so you can get a full view, and be careful, that is poison ivy."

They made their way to the body. A photographer worked every angle. Two figures in white suits crawled around the corpse in an expanding circle. Fred Bickham lay in a patch of bindweed and poison ivy. He wore a flat cap, brown short-sleeved shirt and green corduroy trousers. His feet were small for a man, size seven moccasins with socks which might have once been white. His right hand clutched a garden trowel and his head was twisted away from view.

"This will be ugly," Lisa Levon said, kneeling at the side of the body.

She swished her hand. A cloud of flies rose in the air. Fenella was telling herself it might not be too bad when Lisa Levon tilted his head.

Fenella stared for a moment then looked away.
The first look seared the deepest.

His face was a blackened blob of pulp with two dark sockets where the eyes should have been. A blast of wind battered the side of the tent. *Bam. Bam. Bam.* The cloying reek intensified.

Fenella said, "Why did they smash his face in?"

"I'm not a detective, so I can't speculate why anyone would do such a vile act," Lisa Levon replied. "There are signs the animals have been at him. I reckon the gulls had his eyes."

Fenella dragged another dollop of vapour rub across her upper lip. "How long has he been here like this?"

Lisa shrugged. "In this heat? From the number of flies, I'd say two or three days. We'll have a better idea once we get samples of larvae to the lab."

Fenella gazed at the patch of poison ivy. "Any footprints?"

Lisa slowly shook her head. "The killer was light on their feet, plus the rains not been helpful."

A photographer zoomed in on Fred Bickham's face.

Click. Click. Click.

A cold shiver of dread crept along Fenella's neck. "What caused that much damage?"

"Dr MacKay is best placed to tell you about that," Lisa replied.

Dr MacKay was the pathologist. He loved to speculate about the cause of death, had turned it into high art.

Fenella turned away. She'd not look at Fred Bickham's face again until she had to. "What is your best guess?"

"Off the record."

"Aye."

"Blunt instrument. The shape of the crushed skull suggests a bat; cricket, most probably." Lisa tilted Fred Bickham's head and prodded an eye socket. "Swung multiple times with vicious force."

CHAPTER 6

Den Ogden needed money and he needed it fast.

After fruitless hours searching for work, he declared the day a lost cause and slumped onto a bench at the bus stop. His age counted against him, that was the crux of the problem. At forty-nine the clocked ticked at double speed. He considered himself a farmer. Till the soil and plant the seed, tender and reap the harvest. But more and more these days they laughed in his face when he showed up, and his dome shaped double chin didn't help. Soon they would call him grandpa. Anger ran over him like rain. He felt hot with rage. He'd show them. Den Ogden was far from finished. All he needed was a fresh angle.

He took the bus to the Port St Giles animal shelter and spent a good—and heartbreaking—ninety minutes wandering from cage to cage, reading each animal's tragic story. Barks and yaps erupted as he approached. He stopped at a grim cage with a black dog. It had pointed ears and a green headscarf tied around its neck. The dog shuffled to the bars. It gaped at him with a snout so filled with teeth it gave the appearance of smiling.

"He's a right softie looking for someone to adore."

Den turned to face a stocky woman—white hair, bright brown eyes and skin as thick as leather. Seventy-five was his guess. She wore the uniform of a shelter worker. That she crept up on him with the soft paws of a cat, didn't bother Den as much as perhaps it should.

She regarded him with a pleasant smile, but he thought he saw the devil dancing in her eyes.

She said, "Elfrid. That is his name."

"Strange name for a dog."

"He's knocking on in years."

"An old hound like me," Den said, rubbing his dome shaped double chin. "We old-timers have picked up a lot from life. We know what works. I'll take care of me, if you will please take care of you. I lived my life by it, and now I'd like to share my philosophy with a dog."

She laughed, craning her neck so it stretched, long and thin like a turkey. "Are you new to town?"

It had been over twenty years since Den was last in Port St Giles. A lifetime. His last port of call had been Whitehaven. He changed the subject. "I live in a flat. Does he bark much?"

"He was a prize dog in his youth," the woman replied. "A joy for his owner."

"And where is his owner?"

"Dead. Alas, Elfrid had nowhere else to go and came here."

Den stared through the bars at the dog. "What's

wrong with his tail?"

"Nothing."

"It isn't wagging."

"He's an old dog." She looked hard at Den, the devil dancing in her eyes. "Elfrid likes you."

"Does he bite?"

"Looks like he is smiling with all those teeth, doesn't he?"

"What about kids?"

"Elfrid has never met a child who is not a friend."

Den waited a heartbeat then asked the all-important question. "Does he get on with teenage girls?"

"Girls and boys both."

"Amazing," Den said.

"Interested?"

Den gazed at Elfrid. He needed money and he needed it fast and he needed a new angle. But a dog?

He said, "I'm sure he will find a nice home."

"He has been here four months."

Again, Den gazed at the dog. It smiled back. He said, "What will happen if I don't take him?"

"He is down to meet..." Her face twisted in anguish. " ... the vet next Friday."

"Is he sick?"

She shook her head and went into a blow-by-blow account of what awaited Elfrid on Friday if he didn't find a home. Bone-chilling detail. She stopped at times to weep into a handkerchief and watch him with sharp eyes.

Den left the animal shelter with Elfrid trotting at his side. When he was sure no one was watching, he did a little cockerel strut, puffing out his chest, his slit of a mouth stretched into a smile over his crooked teeth. He looked at the dog, it stared back, snout looking as though it was smiling.

"Best thing I've done since I woke up," Den said, doing a chicken jig.

Elfrid gazed at him, grinning.

"Look at my landlady like that and she might give you a ham bone and knock a few quid off my rent," Den said, pausing for breath.

They wandered through the broad streets and narrow lanes of Port St Giles with nowhere in mind. It was too early to go back to his bedsit. It was a cheap room in a rotten neighbourhood with bugs which sprang from the bedsheets. The landlady expected him to spend a full day on the hunt for a job. He pictured her on the doorstep yelling, telling him he was a waste of space. It was her swearing that got under his skin. She knew more foul words than a drunken sailor. She called him a loner and seedy and a stain on town life. But he performed a valuable service. It wasn't his fault pickings were slim. Den swore and went to the canal.

Although the sun was up, puddles of water pockmarked the towpath. The dregs of the morning downpour slowly shrinking in the warm sun. Den sat on a bench and watched the ducks. Three ducks waddled from the water, squawking as they went. Elfrid's dark eyes fixed on the birds but he did not bark.

"You and I are going to get along like a house on fire," Den said. "Man's best friend, eh?"

Elfrid turned from the ducks and stared at Den. A glint of sunlight bounced off his sharp teeth. The ducks squawked. A narrowboat chugged into view. The engine fumed coughing up plumes of black smoke. A middle-aged woman, plump running to lard, with a tangle of bleached blonde hair steered from the rear.

The boat slowed.

Den became aware of her watching him. She leaned forward, muttering with a quiet intensity. She cut the engine.

Silence, besides the squeals of the ducks as they dashed back into the canal and paddled away.

It took Den some moments to realise that the woman's mutterings contained a question.

The woman spoke again. "Don't I know you?"

Den twitched, heart skipping three beats. He pulled out his mirrored sunglasses, but it was too late.

The woman said, "Den. Den Ogden?"

"Come on boy," Den said to Elfrid.

He walked with fast steps in the opposite direction, breaking out into a trot.

"Come back here you filthy sod," yelled the woman.

But Den didn't go back. He darted along a dirt track that snaked past a derelict warehouse. When he was sure the woman wasn't following, he slowed to a walk and for the first time noticed the limp. He watched Elfrid for several paces. The dog's left hind leg was noticeably shorter.

He stopped. The dog looked at him and he looked at the dog. Elfrid's doleful gaze stirred something deep inside.

"To hell with this," he said, rubbing his domed shaped double chin. "We are going home so you can get a bite to eat, curl up in a dog basket and have a long sleep."

It was four o'clock when they arrived at the bedsit. Elfrid climbed the steps to the front door at a crawl. He sat on his hind legs panting. Den patted the dog's head. "We'll have you inside in a jiffy. Nice bowl of water and a plate of dog chow, eh? The landlady will have some fine scraps."

He turned to look both ways along the street. He had already checked no one was following him. But as he slouched by the door, he checked once more. Satisfied, he took out his door key then bent to scan the list of names beside the bell buttons. They were scrawled on a strip of white paper in blue ink. The names were always changing, and it was important he knew who else lived in the place.

Den leaned closer, staring in stupefied horror at the blank where his name had appeared when he left to look for work. Leaning in close, he examined the spot, and yes, there were faint traces of paper where someone had ripped it off. Running a finger over the blank space, he felt the stickiness of glue.

"Vandals," he muttered, looking up and down

the glum street. Why did the hooligans always pick on him?

He jabbed the lowest button, stepped back and looked up to where the landlady's hidden camera watched. She'd be at the kitchen table, fag in hand, sipping from a chipped mug of milky tea, watching him with the app on her mobile phone.

He heard a click from the speaker and glared at the camera. "Mrs Fassnidge, vandals have ripped my name tag from the plate. Can you kindly see to it?"

The landlady's gruff voice crackled through the speaker. "Mr Ogden, I have changed the front door lock. Your junk is in the alley by the bins. I have evicted you for non-payment of rent. Now, sod off else I'll have the police after you."

CHAPTER 7

Detective Constable Ria Leigh raced around her house looking for the scrap of paper. She had searched the two bedrooms, bathroom and linen closet. Twenty minutes of her lunch break wasted. In ten minutes she had to head back to the station.

Ria shoved open the kitchen door. On the pine table were a coffee mug with lipstick on the rim, a plate with crumbs and her burner phone. She picked up the mug and looked beneath; same with the plate. No scrap of paper.

Where was it?

She snatched a glance at her watch, fumed as the second hand ticked. This was agony. What a fool she had been to lose it. She recalled writing each letter with a slow hand. She had folded the paper so it formed a neat white square. Then she had put it ... where?

The slip of paper had the password to her bank account. The bank account which paid for the house. The bank account from her side hustle. Her secret bank account.

A sharp pain jabbed her gut and for an instant she thought she might be ill. Stress. At work and now at home. Hands on hips, she scanned the room, taking it all in, seeing nothing.

"Why did I buy such a bloody big house?"

She recalled scrawling a crazy line of digits and letters with a blue pen. Sixteen at least. Random. To deter anyone from cracking the code. And now it had her stumped. She bent over her knees, fighting to keep the howl of frustration from blurring her mind.

The alarm call of a blackbird screeched from the garden. A raspy, venom-laced croak. Ria went to the sink, gazed through the window and let out a groan. Yes, she was on the patio with her laptop when she wrote the note. Upset at only now recalling, she slammed through the door into the garden.

A blackbird stormed from a birch tree on the tail of a fleeing jackdaw. Ria turned to watch the bird fight. The jackdaw spiralled high, silhouetted against the white clouds. She lost track of it, but, a minute later, caught sight of the blackbird on the garden wall whistling a sulky tune.

Ria went to the patio table and peered under the chairs. Nothing. She walked along the path, head down, scanning left to right. She stopped at the garden wall and turned to look back at the house. The blackbird's whistle turned gruff. Ria cursed. The note with her password wasn't in the garden.

She stomped along the side of the house and in through the front door. The hallway was short and dark. Grubby green wallpaper peeled from the walls. The air smelled of boiled cabbage. Ria had played hard on the price. When the seller agreed, she lowered her offer by five percent. Again, they agreed. Ria knew then the owner was desperate to sell. *Beat 'em down and beat 'em down again.* She dropped her bid by twenty-five percent, told them to take it or leave it.

They took it.

It was such a sweet deal she bought the house without an inspection. Her dream home. Cash from her secret bank account paid for the deposit on the house and the mortgage. It would pay for the painter, due to start next week. A Polish bloke willing to work for ten percent of the going rate. Cash only. *Beat 'em down and beat 'em down again.*

Back in the kitchen she snatched up her burner phone and re-read the message that had started the hunt:

Low funds in your account. Please top up to avoid an overdraft fee.

Ria had to know how much money was in the account, but didn't want to log in from work. Now she couldn't log in from home because of that idiot slip of paper. Where had she put it? She slumped at the pine table, head in her hands, thoughts slamming her mind for the answer.

The kitchen clock ticked off the seconds. Time stretched to eternity. Above the constant tick-tock, a melodic jingle forced itself into Ria's brain. She tried to focus on the note with her password and where she had put it. The jingle played again. Her doorbell.

She fumbled out her work mobile phone,

swiping until she found the app linked to the camera at the front door. She gasped at the face staring back.

"Oh crap. What the hell does that cow want?"

When Ria opened the door, PC Beth Finn said, "Good afternoon. Detective Inspector Sallow is looking for you. Someone told her you left the station to go home. She sent me here to pick you up."

Ria was certain PC Beth Finn had it in for her. The woman had been anything but friendly since Ria joined the Port St Giles police station. "What's the rush?"

"Briefing about an elderly man found dead in Seaview Allotments. Detective Sallow wants the entire team at the first briefing." She paused as if trying to decide how to put the next few words together. "I don't suppose Detective Constable Jones is here?"

Neither woman spoke for ten strained seconds. The blackbird whistled from the garden. An angry squeal. Ready for a fight.

Ria said, "Why would he be here?"

"Mind if I come in?"

"Give me five minutes," Ria replied slamming the door shut and dashing to the kitchen.

That damn tart gets right up my nose. No way is she coming into my house. Ria stopped and clapped her hands to her head. She remembered now. She had scribbled the password on the back of a Fresco till receipt. For a second, she basked in a pleasant glow, luck was on her side at last, then she scrambled to the cupboard under the sink and snatched out her shopping bag. There it was, folded in a square at the bottom. Her woes were over. A quick log in on her side business laptop and she would know where she stood.

A fist pounded on the kitchen window.

Bang. Bang. Bang.

Ria jumped.

PC Beth Finn peered through the glass, eyes scanning the room as if searching for someone. "We have to go now."

"Righto," Ria said, slipping the receipt into her purse. "I'm ready now."

CHAPTER 8

Den Ogden shambled down the steps of Mrs Fassnidge's guest house. The alley where she dumped his things was on the left. He turned right.

"Mrs Fassnidge is a terror on two legs," he said to the dog. "But I've got her number."

He was no fool. This was not his first time around the track. If he scoured the alley for his things, Mrs Fassnidge would call the police on him. Out of spite. He imagined her at the window, phone in hand, bony fingers twitching to make the call. If the police found him rummaging between the black bin bags in the back alley, they would nick him.

"Better to flee than to fight on her doorstep," Den said to Elfrid. "Never let the buggers in blue cross your path."

With haste, he shuffled along the street for fifty yards. Elfrid panted at his side. Den stopped, stared back at the bedsit, pulled out a bag of tobacco and rolled a cigarette. He lit it with a match and inhaled nicotine deep into his lungs. He puffed out a plume of smoke, dropped the burning match, smothered it with his shoe, and felt a sharp sense of relief. He travelled light and kept nothing of value in his room. His things could rot in the alley. He was lucky to escape the toxic swill of Mrs Fassnidge's pigsty. The woman had eyed him like he was her toy boy. When he refused her advances, she turned nasty. Started kicking up a fuss about his late rent. *Greedy cow.*

"Our best bet is to find a place where we can bed down for the night," he said, head tilted to look at the dog.

Elfrid stared back with a grim face. His tooth filled snout looked less like a smile. Den was struck by the size of the dog's teeth. They were gigantic. He gawked at the knife-sharp gnashers in a kind of stupefied wonder.

Elfrid held his gaze.

Den stepped back, suddenly dubious of the animal shelter worker's claim the dog did not bite. What did he really know about the hound? Elfrid's dark soulless gaze was freaking him out. He had not liked the gleam in the eyes of the animal shelter worker, either. He sensed something unnerving when she gave him the leash. A slither of dread chilled his blood as he pictured the dog in a bad horror movie, prowling in the shadows on the verge of a mad killing spree. Was Elfrid a killer devil dog?

Don't be ridiculous.

He wasn't in any danger. There would be no violence from the dog. No massacre. A lot of his grim thoughts were driven by his need for cash. He and the dog were friends.

Elfrid doesn't bite.

Den growled to see if the dog would at least

whine.

Not even a yap.

Still, he wondered why Elfrid's tail never wagged. He said, "Don't stare at me like that, I sprang you from dog prison. We work as a team, eh?"

For a long while Den brooded over his next move, riveted by the savage fangs and cold stare of the dog. Maybe he needed a different angle?

He was thinking about what to do when he heard the clack of a door. He turned. Fifty yards away, Mrs Fassnidge leaned on the railings, eyes fixed on him. A cigarette dangled from the side of her mouth.

He rubbed Elfrid's ear, his voice dropping to a hiss. "I should never have mentioned fine scraps. I swear the manic hag has it in for us."

Elfrid cocked his head to one side. Den turned back to look at the guest house. Mrs Fassnidge held her mobile phone in her left hand, dragged the cigarette from her lips and spat.

"Pizza," Den said to the dog, jerking on the lead and breaking out into a fast trot. "I know a place where the slices are as big as your face. Not far from here."

Do dogs eat pizza? Den felt guilty for not knowing the answer. He'd order pepperoni so they could share the salty meat. He tugged on the leash. Elfrid limped with frail steps, panting hard.

When Den rounded the bend, he stopped, peeved at Elfrid's hobble. He glared at the dog, bent to examine the hind leg but jerked back. That wasn't a smile on the end of its snout. It was a scowl.

"Come on boy, pizza awaits."

Elfrid sat.

"Okay, you win. I'll order a meat feast. Come on boy."

The dog did not move.

Den was telling Elfrid how they would gorge on pizza piled high with meat when he heard a car throttling back. A brown Ford. The sun caught on the windscreen as it crawled to a stop.

The driver side window lowered.

A thin-faced, sharp-eyed man with hair cropped short at the sides leaned out. He wore a green raincoat and a brown trilby hat. Beads of sweat shimmered on his forehead.

"Excuse me," the man said. "I need your help."

There was something odd about his voice. Not a local. American. A hard accent like you hear in movies about the mob. All shards of glass and jagged edges. Chicago or New York City or somewhere in between.

Curious, Den approached the car. "Yes?"

The man shuffled to the passenger side and waved a fifty pound note. "I'm looking for a boarding house."

"This street is full of glorious hovels, each passing itself off as a fine place to rest your head for the night," Den replied, eyeing the cash. "I know every guest house this side of Port St Giles. What is your pleasure?"

"I'm looking for a very specific place."

Den grinned. "I'm sure I can be of help."

Again, the man waved the fifty pound note, this time extending his arm out of the window.

Den moved closer; snatched the cash. "Fire away."

"I'm looking for a place run by a Mrs Fassnidge. Any idea where it is?"

Den peered into the car. "Mrs Fassnidge?"

"That is right. I want to know where she lives." The man wiped his brow. "My contact tells me her place is around here."

"What do you want with her?"

"A friendly chat." The man in the brown trilby flashed a slow smile. "I've got a gift for her."

Den was a betting man and the odds were in his favour he'd never see Trilby Hat again. "Never heard of that name and I know all the landlords on this street. You sure you got the right town? Try Whitehaven, I think you will find what you are looking for there."

"I see," the man said, starting the engine. "Looks like I've been given bad information. Not the first time."

Den watched as the car pulled away. He touched his double chin. Something felt off about the man in the brown trilby, but he didn't know what.

"Fifty quid for nowt," he said to Elfrid. "We dine on pizza within the hour."

He started along the street as a black cat slunk low to the ground and vanished in an alley. After five paces he realised what was odd about the man in the brown trilby hat. It was in the man's car, on the back seat. A pair of binoculars, two cricket bats and a box of cricket balls. No matter, lots of people play the game. But the bloke was American. Baseball was their thing. What the hell did the man want with a pair of English cricket bats?

CHAPTER 9

Ten minutes later, Den reached the parade of shops. They lined a narrow street of buildings with boarded windows and pubs with shuttered doors. The lights from a grocery store were the only sign of life. During the day the street remained quiet. At night, it sprang to life. The air smelled of decay.

Den bustled down a side alley which led to the front door of the pizza shop. He grabbed the door handle and noticed the large note pinned to the glass:

CLOSED FOR GOOD. LEASE AVAILABLE.

Bile bubbled sour and hot in Den's gut. He turned to Elfrid. "Crap. Another blow but it ain't my fault."

The dog's head drooped. Den stared at its withered hind leg then tugged the door handle. Locked. He took a penknife and fiddled in the keyhole. He twisted the knife one way, then another hoping to hear a clunk and pop.

"Come on honey. Let Den boy in."

He didn't hear the footsteps at first. Solid, heavy footfalls. Deliberate and slow. Someone was moving along the street. Taking their time.

Den stopped fiddling with the lock, ears keen.

The crisp crack of boots halted, then moved on. A clear determined clip clop.

Den shuffled to the end of the alley, crouched and peered into the street.

A figure stopped, kicked at a pile of black bin bags and moved on, head turning this way and that. An icy tingle crawled down Den's neck and he shrank back in shock. It was the American bloke in the brown trilby. And he didn't look happy.

CHAPTER 10

It was after five when Fenella's team gathered in Incident Room A. She ordered pizza and ice cream. Who wants to be stuck in a briefing on a sunny Saturday? At least the food sweetened the deal. They ate, relaxing and chatting, their minds never far from the grim task ahead.

"Can't beat pepperoni on a crisp crust dough," Dexter said, munching on his fourth slice.

"Tried them all." PC Woods looked at his plate and frowned. It contained five slices of pizza, one from each box. Two bowls of ice cream rested at his side. "Don't know which I like best."

"I like the ham and pineapple," Detective Constable Jones said.

He was thirty-five, joined Fenella's team straight from the National Detective Programme, had lived in London, and was still finding his feet in Cumbria. Fenella worried he'd soon get bored with the sleepy seaside town.

"You would be a ham and pineapple man," PC Beth Finn replied, shooting Jones a sour look.

Fenella ignored the sparks. The relationship between PC Beth Finn and Jones blazed on and off. She'd keep an eye on it.

"Ham and pineapple are my fav too," added Detective Constable Ria Leigh with a broad smile. "Enjoyed it. Thank you for feeding us, ma'am."

Fenella gave a cute curtsy. Everyone loved Ria, the newest member of the team. The lass had won Civic Officer of the year three years straight and was on track for her fourth. A record that would put her in the history books.

Start with the positive, Fenella told herself. Lift the mood before the grim stuff. "Shirley Bickham had a nasty shock today. The good news? She is out of the hospital and back at home."

Everyone clapped. Dexter punched a fist in the air. PC Woods grinned. Ria blew a kiss and cooed. Even PC Beth Finn managed a smile. The room thrummed with energy.

Delighted, Fenella said, "What have we got so far on Fred Bickham? Clubbed to death in Seaview Allotments. The attack happened two or three days ago. The killer left Fred Bickham's body in the open. Why?"

"Too heavy to move, guv." Dexter always got the ball rolling.

"Mr Bickham wasn't a large man," Jones countered. "Easy to drag or cover with sticks, so there must be a reason he was left for all to see."

"The attacker might be of slight build," added PC Beth Finn. "A passion killing."

"Are we talking about a woman?" PC Woods took a bite of pizza, munched and continued. "She might not have had the strength to haul dead weight and left Fred Bickham where he fell."

"The wrath of a lass ain't a thing to mess with," Dexter said. "I heard of a mother who shifted a tree trunk when her bairn was pinned to the ground."

"Yeah, but it might be a bloke," Ria said. She flashed Jones a sly grin. "Mr Bickham might have got in a fight over the size of his carrots."

Jones grinned.

PC Beth Finn scowled.

"We are going around in circles, lad," Dexter said, eyeing Jones with a manly gleam. "If it weren't a man, it were a woman."

Something niggled at the back of Fenella's mind. She went back to her original question. "Why leave the body in the open where it would be seen?"

Ria was first to speak. "Panic. Or as a warning."

"Like a horse's head left in your bed by the mafia." Jones said, voice thrilled. "Could be we are in for a wave of rival gangs fighting over turf. Mr Fred Bickham must have stirred up their wrath."

"Come off it, lad," Dexter said. "Them allotments are half empty, folks are fighting to leave. Ain't no turf war to get into that place."

"But what if it is drugs?" Jones replied, his eyes glittering at the idea. "This might be the first shot in an all-out war like they have in London."

No one spoke. A mob murder seemed too far-fetched for a little Cumbrian seaside town.

Fenella paced at the front of the room, placing a hand on her back to ease the dull throbbing pain. That lawn feed, bird feeders and hose reels packed a punch. Straight at her back. She'd see a doctor if it persisted, but hoped it was just badly bruised. Next time she visited Johnny Dew's Organic Garden Centre she'd stay well clear of robotic lawnmowers.

She pushed the dull throb to the back of her mind. "We will have a tighter grip on the time of death once we have Dr MacKay's report." She paused, scanned the grim faces and knew they were with her. "Gardening creates community. Someone must have seen something—heard an argument, cries for help, a scream. Dexter, you do a spot of garden work, don't you?"

"Not so much now my Priscilla is in the States, guv." He sniffed.

His long-term girlfriend recently moved to New York City for a once-in-a-lifetime opportunity —backup singer in a touring band. Dexter encouraged her to go although Fenella knew he wanted her to stay and marry him.

Dexter was still speaking. "We have a garden at my block of flats and I work a small plot. You see the same people, have a quiet chat and share tips. Might quarrel about the best way to keep the bugs down, but nowt to kill a bloke over."

Fenella stopped pacing and placed her hands on her hips. "Jones get a list of the allotment owners then you and PC Beth Finn do the rounds. We need to know their movements over the last few days. Tomorrow is Sunday, they will be chatty, excited and shocked at what has happened. Soothe their nerves and ask questions—rumours, gossip and facts. We want it all."

Jones was already on his laptop, tapping the keys hard. PC Beth Finn had her notebook out, pen moving fast across the page.

Fenella turned to Dexter. "Work the Fred Bickham angle. Who were his friends? Any form?" She glanced at Jones. "Any gangland connections? I want the works. I'll speak with his daughter, Shirley Bickham, and the rest of his family myself."

"Got it, guv."

Fenella nodded at PC Woods. "We need your help"

He sat up, aware the room watched. "Do what it takes Woods is what they call me, ma'am. Happy to be part of the team."

"Go back to the crime scene and find out the status of the forensic search," Fenella said.

She knew he'd keep his ear to the ground and pick up any unofficial news.

"Now?" PC Woods suddenly sounded defensive.

"Aye, and you are on night crime scene duty."

He rocked back in his chair, mouth wide. "Thought they'd be some files that needed sorting."

"Excellent," Fenella said, "That is your Sunday morning task. Report here for eight."

"Oh." PC Woods clasped the chair handle. "At eight?"

There was a moment of silence. Someone snickered. It might have been Dexter. PC Woods scowled.

Ria Leigh raised her hand. "What do you want

me to do, ma'am?"

Fenella opened her mouth to reply when the door flew open and Superintendent Jeffery marched in. She wore grass-stained cricket whites and carried a cricket bat under her arm. A delighted glow shone from her wolfish face. "I had an inning with the ladies' eleven. I haven't lost the knack. Jolly good game."

"Nice to see you, ma'am," Fenella said, noticing the Newbery logo on the cricket bat—top tier, expensive. "They found Mr Fred Bickham's body in Seaview Allotments. I will fill you in after the briefing."

Jeffery waved an irritated hand. She wasn't interested in death amongst the turnips. "Chief Constable Rae was at the game. He gave me praise for our limited use of search warrants. I told him I was watching their use like a hawk." She smiled, bearing wolfish teeth. "Now, what I am going to tell you is hot off the press, so lips sealed until the announcement on Monday, please."

Everyone mumbled their agreement. Monday wasn't long, but Fenella, like her team, wanted to know the big news now. She stood next to the boss, ears straining.

Jeffery spread her arms as a priest might when giving a blessing. "I am now in charge of the Barrow-in-Furness station until they hire a new superintendent. 'Two stations under my superb command.' Chief Rae's words not mine."

Fenella couldn't believe the boss barged her

briefing to crow about climbing a notch up the greased monkey career pole. She clenched her jaw. Dexter cleared his throat. Feet shuffled. They knew what came next—the motivational speech.

Jeffery lowered her arms. "Both stations must work as a team, pull together. There will be tough days ahead but we shall climb the mountain peak in full—"

"We get the point, ma'am," Fenella said. "But we've not got time for a speech. Is there anything else?"

Another snicker. Definitely Dexter, although he threw his voice so it sounded like Jones.

Jeffery flashed a wolfish glare at Jones. He shrank back in his seat. Someone snorted. There was no mistake it was Dexter.

Fenella said, "You were saying, ma'am."

"A case from the Barrow station needs our urgent attention. A baby, Eva Fisk, went missing over a month ago and the Barrow team have drawn a blank." She turned to Ria. "Since Detective Inspector Sallow has her hands full, I want you to take the lead. An opportunity for me ... us to shine at the highest level."

"Yes, ma'am," Ria replied before Fenella got a word in.

Wants to be teacher's pet, Fenella thought. Then another thought struck: *One day Ria will run the place and I'll answer to her.*

Jeffery beamed. "Chief Constable Rae has taken a personal interest. A win on this and Civic Officer of the year for the fourth time is on the cards."

"You can count on that, ma'am," Ria replied.

"You will report your progress directly to me," Jeffery said.

This was way too sudden for Fenella. "We need to talk about this, ma'am."

"Chief Rae has rubber stamped the decision," Jeffery replied with a curt nod.

"But—"

"I do not have time for a deep conversation," Jeffery snapped. "It is out of my hands. Chief Constable Rae is also forming an oversight leadership team. A quick resolution with baby Eva Fisk and I might get a call. A win for us."

"Us?" Fenella asked.

"Our team." Jeffery spoke as if she was already practising her acceptance lines. "And our station, the wider Port St Giles community and Cumbria. Yes, a sharp focus will get results."

"Fine, but keep me in the loop," Fenella said through her teeth.

Jeffery nodded and marched from the room.

The briefing hadn't turned out as Fenella expected, nor she feared would the hours to come.

"Let's get going," she said, trying not to sound annoyed. "If anyone wants me, I'll be at Shirley Bickham's home. The family needs to know we are here for them, and I want to find out about Fred Bickham from the horse's mouth."

CHAPTER 11

Giddy with joy, Detective Constable Ria Leigh dashed from the briefing, jumped into her car, started the engine and floored it. As the car picked up speed, she clutched the steering wheel, grinning. She loved the attention of Superintendent Jeffery. Who but the very best gets picked for a special case? Civic Officer of the year four times straight was in her sights. Once she solved the baby Eva Fisk case, she was sure to receive the award. *Perfection*.

She blew a kiss in the driver's mirror, skidded onto the main road, roaring at twice the speed limit. Yes, she ought to drive to Barrow-in-Furness to speak with the parents of baby Fisk. Yes, she ought to stop at the Barrow-in-Furness police station to review the case files. There were a lot of things she ought to do, speeding home after the briefing wasn't one of them.

Ria pushed the car harder because she couldn't help herself. Curiosity had her in its jaws. The folded receipt in her handbag held the password to her secret bank account. She'd zip in and out of the house, log in, glance at the balance, then zoom on her way to Barrow-in-Furness. Who would ever know? Nothing could go wrong. *Sweetness*.

Even before Ria dashed along the garden path, she should have sensed trouble had her in its sights. She paused at the front door, key in hand, listening.

Something was wrong.

Cold black clouds swallowed the frowning sun. Shadows shrouded the entrance. The slow chime of the living room clock rung out the hour followed by a shriek.

Puzzled, Ria peered through the frosted glass. Her eyes scanned anxiously into the half-light of the hall. Was someone inside?

Oh God! Where did she leave her laptop? The laptop she used for her side hustle. The laptop with the secret bank account. She gulped deep lungfuls of air, thinking but could not recall where she left it. A thin sheen of cold sweat prickled her skin as she chided herself for being so foolish. Why did she take such a terrible risk? It was too painful to think about what would happen if anyone got their hands on her computer. It was in her bedroom, wasn't it?

Dizzy with fear, Ria fumbled the key into the lock. The door swung inward with an ugly creek.

"Hello. Who is there?"

Panicked screams filled the air. Stunned for an instant, Ria stood very still. More screams. From the garden.

She spun and scrambled along the path to the back of the house. At first, all she saw were sparrows flitting above the ground. They were screaming, beaks stretched wide.

It took two heartbeats to take it all in. The bird

feeder lay on the grass, sunflower seeds scattered. A gust must have blown it from the tree.

Annoyed, Ria stepped, stopped and blinked. Something large and grey stalked by the bird feeder. Rats. Three filthy sewer beasts. They twitched as her eyes grew wide. She stooped to pick up a rock but they scampered under the bushes.

This house is a disaster, Ria thought, troubled more bad news lurked around the corner. The first hint of the debt pit she'd bought pounced the day she moved in. Black mould lurked in the cupboard under the sink. Cracks snaked along the living room wall. Something to do with a shifting foundation the property inspector she had called to take a look said. "It will cost a pretty penny to fix," he added, deepening her woe. Then the house lights went out due to a bad fuse box.

When she phoned the estate agent who sold her the house, the reply came short and sweet: "Beat 'em down and beat 'em down again. You mashed the buyer to a rock-bottom price. Sold as is. Your problem now. Stay calm and carry on."

Within two weeks the groaning central heating failed. A nosy neighbour pointed out a ragged sheet of tarpaulin covered part of the roof. Staying calm was impossible. Ria panicked and used money from her secret bank account to pay for repairs. The old worn house sucked cash into a bottomless pit.

And now there were rats in the garden.

She glared at the bush where the rodents

vanished, swore and hung the bird feeder on a higher branch. Those squalid rats can't reach it now, she told herself, and suddenly recalled where she left the laptop. On the scrubbed pine table in the kitchen.

Sixty seconds later Ria peered at the laptop screen, gaping in disbelief. She pressed refresh.

"That can't be right," she said. "It can't all be gone."

But it was gone. The on-screen balance flashed red.

Ria had always had a firm grip on her life. Knew where her money came from and where it went. She loathed surprises and hated having to dip into her secret funds for house repairs. Now the damn screen was telling her she owed the bank money. And there was the last shipment of drugs for which she still owed a wad of cash to her supplier. They did not play nice with late payments.

Bile soured Ria's mouth. A shallow thud beat against her chest. With shaking hands she closed the laptop lid, walked across the kitchen and rifled in a cupboard. She found her burner phone, flipped it on and dialled her business partner.

"Hi ya Ria," came the cheery voice of Sloane Kern.

Sloane ran an anger management clinic for middle-class women. The horsy type who liked hunting and wine and tea with the vicar and were overwhelmed and stressed out by it all. Sloane supplied the clients. Ria supplied the drugs.

"How's business?" Ria asked.

"Slow."

"That's not good."

"Got one old gal, Mrs Stoke, who wants more, but I've sold her two lots this month. A third is excessive."

"Why?"

"Mrs Stoke has weak impulse control," Sloane replied. "I have to draw the line. I am here to help."

"Cash payment?"

"Of course."

"Sell it to her."

"I'm not some sleazy street corner drug pusher."

"Sell it," Ria shrieked. "We need the money, and cash only from now on. No more credit."

The demand from middle-aged women for under the counter drugs had not been as strong as Ria hoped. She thought she'd be raking it in by now, but there was not enough demand to pay for house repairs. Not even enough to pay Ria's supplier because Sloane gave her clients credit to sweeten the deal. Use now; pay later.

An upsetting thought struck and buried deep in Ria's brain. Was Sloane cheating her?

Sloane said, "I wasn't going to tell you just yet, but it is best you know. We have a huge problem."

Ria pressed the phone to her ear. "I'm listening."

"I need a large wad of cash. Unmarked notes. A client has turned the tables on us and wants money to keep her mouth shut."

"Blackmail?"

"If we cough up, we'll never hear from her again."

Unbelievable. Ria's heart battered against her chest. Blood rattled through her ears. This was absurd. They had been in business for only a few months and now they were being shaken down by some smart-arse addict. Or were they? Maybe it was Sloane who was shaking her down.

Stunned, Ria said, "But I vetted this woman, right?"

"You vet all my therapy clients."

And they all came back squeaky clean. Still, Ria had doubts about one woman. All sorts of rumours about her swindling men but no solid facts or police charges and therefore baseless. Ria's gut warned her, but she ignored it, blindsided by the rush for more clients. Not that she'd admit her birdbrained greed to Sloane.

Still, she couldn't be sure her gut was right, so she spoke with that certain bluster she used when bluffing over a cock-up. "Let me guess, runs a boarding house near the canal, Mrs Ruth Fassnidge?"

Sloane's sharp intake of breath convinced Ria she'd nailed it.

Sloane said, "You knew?"

"I'm a police detective. Knowing the corrupt and crackpots and cut-throat crooks is my job."

"Let's give her some cash and hope she goes away," Sloane said. "She can make a lot of trouble."

"No," Ria replied, thinking.

"Then what do I tell her?" Sloane asked.

"Nothing." Ria had enjoyed only two classes in college. First, police ethics. Second, mediaeval torture. "I'll deal with it."

Sloane said nothing.

"Oh, and I'll be over tomorrow," Ria said, cracking her knuckles.

"What for?"

"Review the books."

There was a long pause. "Tomorrow is Sunday. You know I spend Sundays with my kids."

"Your office at ten," Ria screamed. "I want to go over the numbers."

CHAPTER 12

It was a task most dreaded and few raised their hand to do. Fenella saw it as her duty. Shirley Bickham's house was near the canal, in a street of workers' homes, built back-to-back in weary grey stone rows.

Fenella parked her car and massaged the base of her spine. It felt sore and stiff and throbbed like a pulse. A low sun slanted between the rooftops and through the oak trees. The awful images of Fred Bickham played in her mind. A soul-crushing endless loop—the terrible cruelty of the attack; the violence, the stench of death curdled by the warm sun and the horror of Shirley Bickham finding her dad on her birthday.

Shards of sadness tore Fenella's heart to shreds and battered her nerves as she imagined how frightening an ordeal it must have been. She'd not find peace until she found out what had happened. And she wanted a nosy in Fred Bickham's things, convinced she'd find a clue as to why he died. She had to know the painful truth.

She steadied her breathing, cleared her mind, walked to the front door and pressed the doorbell. It echoed with a solemn toll. The slow shuffle of feet. A rattle of chains. The door opened.

She looked around fifteen with a delicate face, slender nose, wide eyes and black, shoulder length hair. Second glance revealed her to be slightly older, late teens or early twenties. She stared at Fenella through tear-stained eyes.

"I'm Fenella, pet. From the police. You must be Ginger."

The girl turned without speaking. Fenella followed her along a dim hallway into a comfortable kitchen with hard tile floor and cream walls. Thick net curtains blocked the May sunshine. A shroud of twilight gloom hung like fog and the air smelled of fried bacon and boiled cabbage. Shoes by the door. A vegetable rack by the wall near a stone jar. A broom, dustpan, brush, mop and bucket leaned in the other corner. Two women sat at a pine table in the semi-dark. One middle-aged and the other in her seventies. Ginger stayed by the door.

The older woman stood as Fenella made her way to the table. "I'm Ida Bickham," she said, squinting through pale grey eyes.

She had a deep voice, was short and slender with narrow shoulders and a friendly face. Her frizzy black wig meant one thing to Fenella—medical treatment. Chemotherapy, she thought, but would not bring it up.

Fenella introduced herself, expressed sorrow for their loss and waited. The sudden shock of Fred Bickham's murder needed space. She'd not crowd it out with her words.

Ida slumped back into her chair and placed her hands flat on the table. "We are all agitated right now. Death is torture, but this ... this is a nightmare. I am on the edge of despair."

She stopped. In the abrupt silence, the scent of stale food seemed to intensify to a rancid stink. Fenella's gut lurched but she said nothing.

"Forgive me." Ida's neck flushed. "Take a seat, please."

Fenella saw the room more clearly now, the scrubbed pine table, four chairs, gas stove, copper kettle. A farmhouse kitchen sink jutted out from the countertop. She eased into a chair, placing a hand on her stiff back. Three women around the kitchen table. One girl standing by the door. A conference of sorts, with the murder of Fred Bickham the only topic.

Ida held Fenella's gaze. "I suppose you are here to talk with my Shirley?"

At the mention of her name, Shirley Bickham glanced up. Anguish haunted her pockmarked face. Yes, she was the same woman Fenella saw wailing by the ambulance. A terrible shock to find your dad battered to death. Worse, seeing as the animals had been at him and the swarm of bluebottle flies.

Fenella softened her voice. "Aye, I'd like a word in private."

"Where is my grandad?" Ginger's voice throbbed with pain. She moved from the door to the kitchen table. "I want to see him."

Fenella softened her voice, knowing whatever

she said would not blunt the girl's sadness. "At the hospital and at peace now, pet. They'll take good care of him."

Ginger turned to her gran; voice feeble, childish. "Remember the games we played when I was little and came running into your bedroom on Sunday mornings?"

"I remember," Ida replied with pride. "We all remember."

New stirrings of sorrow captured the room. It held the three Bickham women in its unwelcome grip. Fenella's heart squeezed.

"And Grandad would pretend to be asleep," Ginger said. Her face appeared more childlike as she relived the past. "I'd call his name and, in the end, he'd get up and play."

Ida let out a soft sob.

Ginger glanced around and squeezed her eyes. "Come on Gran, grab your coat. He'll not want to be on his own in that cold hospital."

"No, honey, we can't go yet," Ida replied, eyes filled with sorrow.

"He'll wake up when he sees me Gran." Ginger took a deep shaky breath, her voice shrill. "He always gets up when I call his name. Oh, Gran…"

"It's all right darling," Ida was at the door with her arms wrapped around her grandbairn. "It's all right, honey. We'll be all right."

But Ida looked tired and defeated and suddenly old.

It was then Shirley Bickham spoke, her words

coming out in a slur. "Why don't you go to your room, Ginger?"

"Don't tell me what to do," Ginger said, fidgeting with a strand of hair. "I won't take orders from a bottle of cheap gin."

"No more, please Ginger," Ida said. She grimaced and slowly, with a gentle hand, led Ginger from the kitchen.

The door closed with a soft click.

Shirley waited until their footsteps faded before she spoke. "I haven't told her how I found him. His ... face ... someone did that to him, didn't they?"

Fenella didn't answer at once. The suffering in the room felt very real. Still, she was puzzled. She went to the stove, plopped tea bags into mugs added hot water, sugar and milk. She realised what was wrong. Ginger did not look at her mam. The two avoided eye contact. No matter—lots of parents have strained relations with their teen. She supposed Fred Bickham's murder had brought their crisis to the boil. But what family doesn't pull close together when a murderer strikes a loved one? What family doesn't ask what happened?

Shirley said, "Gin in the cupboard. Can you add a splash or two?"

Fenella found the gin, poured a dash in both mugs and returned to the table. "Get that down you, luv. Nowt like a mug of spiced tea in trying times."

It might help with her own back pain, and it would be easier to ask to search Fred Bickham's things with Shirley softened by booze. The part of the job she enjoyed best involved digging out secrets. If you did it well, it seemed like magic. One minute nothing, the next skeletons fell out.

Shirley's hand shook as she grasped the mug. Dark rings appeared under her eyes. She took a long sip. "I've been sitting here fretting over how much to tell my mam and Ginger. I couldn't tell them what I saw. We've been under so much strain since Dad moved out. If I told them what I saw, it would kill them."

Fenella kept her voice quiet but felt a wave of shock. "Mr Bickham does not live here?"

"Please call him Fred, everyone called my dad by his first name. And they call my mam Ida." Shirley looked down at the mug. "After thirty years of marriage they split. Three months ago, feels like years. Mam stayed in the house with us. Dad took his stuff and rents a bedsit. I hoped they might work things out, but now ... well, that chance is gone."

Fenella let that sit for a heartbeat. "What did they fall out over?"

Shirley shrugged. "Life. Dad loved growing veg and my mam spends her time with Ginger. They said they had some wonderful years together but the best was long behind them. It came as a shock."

"Did you see Fred often?"

"Once a week." Shirley paused, walked to the countertop and wrote on a slip of paper. "This is his address. He rents ... rented a grotty bedsit run by a horror called Mrs Fassnidge. Ginger visited him most Saturdays and slept over. I swear if he had been younger those two would have made a great couple. When will you visit?"

Fenella glanced at her watch. "Tomorrow most likely. Would you like to be there?"

Shirley shook her head. "Too many memories."

Fenella flashed a sad smile and picked up her mug. "What about your mam, did she visit Fred's bedsit?"

"Never."

The kitchen door opened. Ida Bickham glided in.

"Thought I overheard you talking about Fred. Shirley is right, since we split, I have not visited him. Can you tell me what you will do with the body?" She did not wait for a reply. "I must have his remains as soon as possible."

"What do you mean?" Fenella said, putting her mug flat on the table.

Ida turned and moved to the window so Fenella saw only her profile. "I want to put Fred's ashes on the mantelshelf."

"Stop it," Shirley said. "I hate to think of him as dust."

A cloud blotted the sun. The room darkened. Fenella could make out nothing of Ida's face now. Something about the way Ida hunched reminded her of a coiled snake.

"I want to put his ashes next to our wedding photo in the front room," Ida said softly.

The sun came back out, lifting the room to

its earlier gloom. Fenella blinked twice, saw Ida had turned full on and was watching her.

Ida's lips twitched into a broad grin. "Do you know why?"

"Stop it," Shirley said. "Please stop it."

Fenella didn't want Ida to stop. She was hungry for what Ida had to say. "Go on, pet. Get it off your chest. You will feel much better if you share."

Ida's pale grey eyes moved slowly from Fenella to Shirley. "I want him in the centre of the mantelshelf so I can…" She gazed at them. " … smile at him every day. He said I had a wonderful smile."

Fenella said nothing.

"Fred complained about groundwater pollution caused by graveyards," Ida said, as though in deep thought. "He'd be mad at me if I did not turn his body to ashes. For dust thou art, and unto dust shalt thou return."

"I'm sure your wishes will be met," Fenella said, staring at Ida and recalling the bible passage. "Did you see your husband recently?"

Ida's face turned the colour of bleached bone. "Why are you asking me all these questions?"

"Part of the job, luv. I'm a detective, we do nowt but ask questions."

"Good God, my husband has died and you have the—"

"Mam, please," Shirley said, rising to her feet. "Detective Sallow is here to help."

"Trust you to take their side."

"Me?" Shirley's face bloomed crimson. "What

about you?"

"What is that supposed to mean?"

Shirley paced to the window, her voice a low hiss. "Why do you always take Ginger's side?"

"She is my only Grandbairn. I want what is right for her."

"She won't even tell me who the father of her baby is," Shirley said. "But she has told you, hasn't she? Her bestie gran knows everything, while I am banned from asking my own flesh and blood daughter a question. I'm the one who carried her for nine months. My God, Ginger's father might be my own dad and I'd never know."

"Oh, and you are a living saint?" Ida snapped, waving her hands in the sign of the cross. "For dust thou art, and unto dust shalt thou return."

A tense silence fell over the room. An uneasy quiet as thick as the net curtained gloom.

One minute.

Two.

Three.

Fenella watched and waited, ignoring the dull thud at the base of her back.

At last, Ida said, "Have you been drinking?"

Shirley didn't answer.

"You always were a selfish child," Ida said, striding back to the table and slumping into a chair. "A ranting, complaining, amoral beast."

Again she made the sign of the cross with her hands. This time, more dramatic, like she was centre stage in a massive London theatre. Large sweeping movements so those at the back could see.

Shirley covered her face with her hands and sobbed. "I was a stupid teen when I had Ginger. A mistake that is now being repeated by my own daughter." Her voice rose to a shout. "I want to know the name of the lad that got my child pregnant."

"Your dad is rotting in the morgue and all you can think of is your own hysteric self," Ida yelled back.

Shirley fell silent.

Fenella waited, unsure whether the emotional fireworks were over.

"I'm your mam and should have been at Ginger's birth," Ida snapped. She turned to Fenella and her lips twisted into a mile wide smile. "So sorry, it is the stress. Please ignore our petty fights. We want to help in any way we can. We all loved Fred in our different ways."

Fenella's diaphragm lurched. She'd stepped into a snake nest where every move came with the potential for a nasty bite. This was not a happy family. She said, "Did Fred fall out with anyone recently?"

"No," Ida said. "He wasn't the type to argue, got along with everyone."

"What about friends?"

"He had a few mates at the allotment, that was about it," Ida replied. "He had a large plot at the back and spent much of his time working the soil."

"Let's talk about enemies." Fenella removed her notebook from her handbag, making a check of the ink with a scribble. "Do you know anyone who had it in for him?"

Ida blinked. "I must get back to Ginger. Goodness, she will wonder what has happened to me."

She dashed from the kitchen. The door clicked shut.

Fenella's gaze flitted from the door to Shirley. "Tell me about Fred."

When Shirley spoke, her voice was quieter than the tick-tock of the clock. "Dad wasn't one for confrontation."

"Really?"

Fenella found that single word often generated an interesting answer.

Shirley gazed at the closed kitchen door with a puzzled expression. "If there were a problem, he'd go around the houses to find a solution. Very private. You would never know he knew your business. You would never find out. For dust thou art, and unto dust shalt thou return. That was his favorite saying. And since we are dust it is best to do things on the quiet."

A silence. Fenella said nothing. She knew Shirley wasn't finished. The fridge gave a sudden shudder, its hum filling the void.

Shirley dabbed at her eyes. "Dad loved the garden, playing sports and enjoyed the outdoor life. He even forced me to play cricket when I moved back home. I hate the game but went along with it to keep him happy. I don't have much money and this place is rent free."

This was useful background, but Fenella wanted more. "Was he worried about anything?"

Shirley closed her eyes. "I got the sense there was something he wanted to tell me. Something important. Now I'll never know, will I?"

CHAPTER 13

It was three o'clock in the morning. Shirley Bickham slipped out of bed and padded to the window, her ears alert for any strange noises. She peeled back the edge of the patchwork quilt curtains and scanned the street, nervously watching the windows and doorways and gardens and the gaps between the parked cars. The light from the streetlamp cast such a feeble beam through the fog she couldn't be sure what lurked in the shadows. So, she watched, trembling with a sickening excitement at what she must do.

She tramped to the wardrobe, stubbing her toe on the bed. She held back a harsh howl of pain. Better to hobble around in the miserable dark cursing under your breath than to wake Ginger or her mam.

She stared at her shadowed face in the mirror and ran a hand over the loose skin and deep hollows in her face. It wasn't the booze, she told herself. She'd been born with bad genes into a life of bad luck. Slowly, she eased open the wardrobe door and fumbled through piles of clothes until she felt cold glass. Tense and impatient, she poured a long splash of gin into a shot glass, sipping it like fine wine. Her mind cleared. Did she have everything?

Yes, black yoga pants and matching top.

Yes, black gloves, so thin they didn't hamper your fingers.

And yes, ski mask.

From the bottom of the wardrobe she found the pricy trainers she'd bought from a posh sports shop. The salesman with the fake American accent called them midnight black sneakers, said they'd be good for her gym class, hiking, and running fast.

Shirley sat on the bed in the eerie quiet and brooded over her plan. She gazed at the bedside clock. Time to go on the wild ride, she told herself. Soon she'd be back in bed, under the thick covers and no one the wiser.

She tiptoed to the bedroom door, opened it, and heard snores drift from her mam's bedroom. She listened for Ginger, but her daughter slept like the dead and with the pills, she'd not stir till noon.

As she stepped out into the hallway, a noise came from downstairs. A creak. The front door closing. A shuffle of feet. Someone climbing the stairs.

Shirley crept to the stairs and peered down into the darkness. A figure detached from the blackness. It shambled up the stairs. She watched in horror until she saw the pale face and vacant stare of Ginger.

Her daughter climbed one step at a time, hunched like a bare-knuckle fighter, right hand carrying a bread knife, left hand grasping a cricket bat. Ginger reached the top of the stairs, turned and plodded to her gran's door.

"Oh God," Shirley whispered into the dark, shivering. "It has started again."

A loud clatter broke her desolate thoughts, and she sprinted after Ginger. Her mam's bedroom had a queen-sized bed shoved against one wall and a dresser under the window. An intense scent filled the chill air—fresh mint. Her mam swore it calmed the nerves. Shirley inhaled deeply as she took in the scene.

Her mam lay on the bed, snoring in great bursts of rattle. Ginger snuggled next to her gran with a blissful expression on her face. She held the bread knife loosely in her hand. The cricket bat had dropped to the floor.

Shirley sidled to the bed, eased the knife from Ginger's grip and pulled a sheet over her. She picked up the cricket bat and tiptoed from the room. What else could she do? Confronting Ginger by shaking her awake would result in a painful row.

When Ginger was six, she suffered from nightmares. They were so terrifying she would scramble from her bed in a sleepwalk. Most nights she'd go straight to the kitchen and return to her bed with a knife and a big stick. "The dream," Ginger would say in her small voice. "I had the dream."

The soft voiced doctor who prescribed the pills said it was normal for a child to wander in their sleep. Quite natural to dream about being chased. Shirley didn't tell the medic about the knife. Or how Ginger swung the big stick with brute force as she sleepwalked. Or how the dream always ended with Ginger wide awake and screaming about being sliced in two.

Shirley went to the kitchen, put the bread knife away and gazed through the window. Let's start the clock, she told herself as she closed the front door and crept out into the dark fog laden street. Her dad's bedsit would not take long to search.

CHAPTER 14

Shirley Bickham dashed along the quiet street unable to stop the alarm bells ringing in her mind. She urged her feet on, each step a dizzying fight against fear. There were so many things that could go wrong.

Was someone watching? The neighbours liked to meddle, fingers twitching their speed dial for the police when they suspected something odd.

She kept her head down, gloves and ski mask jammed in her pocket. No, she told herself, there was nothing to worry over. No one could see her in this mist, and she had a copy of the front door key to the building and knew where her dad hid the key for his room.

She turned left at the traffic light onto a cobbled road. Shops lined the street, their graffiti-stained steel shutters drawn down. The street lights faded to darkening pools of shadows. A wasteland ahead. Grim houses with boarded doors and alleyways smeared with brown stains. You had to keep an eye out for drunks and nut jobs and God only knew what else lurking in the alleys.

She slowed her walk, scanning for danger. A strange confidence gripped her as she touched the knife in her pocket. *Wrong night to mess with this lass. For dust thou art, and unto dust shalt thou return.* But as she turned onto the street of her dad's bedsit, she felt afflicted by doubts and misgiving.

"Can I go through with this again?"

She stopped at the steps of Mrs Fassnidge's lodgings and peered at the front door. It was vital now that she focus. First, chase away the doubts. Second, stick to the plan. She gulped and gasped and pictured herself dashing up the stairs, opening her dad's bedsit door, searching, finding, and galloping into the night. No need for the gloves. No need for the ski mask. No need for the knife.

"A brilliant plan."

Shirley climbed and hesitated, peering at the row of bell buttons, each with a nameplate. A chaotic mix of students, nurses and those down on their luck rented rooms in the glum building. Her finger hovered over the button marked in bold letters: *Mrs R Fassnidge—Landlady.*

She continued to scan, saw her dad's nameplate and became excited. That meant Mrs Fassnidge had not heard of his death. When the news broke, the witch would clear his room, dump his stuff in the alley and rent the hovel to someone else.

"Lady luck is on my side. In and out and no one will know. Ideal."

Shirley tried the door handle because you never knew.

Locked.

Not a problem. All the residents would be inside so there was no shock in a locked door. She reached into her pocket, pulled out the front door key, put it in the lock and turned, anticipating the magic click.

Nothing.

She tried again.

Shirley stepped back in bewildered shock. Only slowly did she realise what must have happened—Mrs Fassnidge had changed the lock.

She tried a dozen more times, then gaped in furious disbelief. Distressed, she tried again, feeling defeated as the key groaned and buckled. No point, it won't work she told herself and glared at the solid door fighting back hysteria. What if the police searched her dad's room before she got in?

"Hullo there."

Shirley whirled. A short figure scurried from the dark fog into the glow of the streetlamp and stopped at the bottom of the steps.

"Is this Mrs Fassnidge's place?" asked the woman with a faint Irish brogue.

"Aye, it is," Shirley replied, trying to stay in the shadows.

"May you live to be one hundred years. I'm new to town, just back from a hellish nursing shift and lost my way. If you had not been standing in the doorway, I might have missed it. Amazing luck, eh?"

She climbed the steps with great haste, door keys in hand and plunged the key into the lock. A quick shove and the door opened. She turned. "Going out?"

"That's right," Shirley replied. "Just thinking where I parked the car."

"Be careful there are sickos creeping about at this hour."

"I will."

The woman looked puzzled. "Day shift nurse?"

"Someone has to do it," Shirley said.

"Not me. I've dealt with vital signs, viruses and human waste all night. I'm knackered, time to purge myself with sleep. You ought to give it a whirl."

They both laughed.

"Good night," the woman said. "Or should I say good morning?"

She disappeared into the dark hallway before Shirley answered.

Pure adrenaline jerked Shirley's right hand to the handle before the door slammed shut. She stepped inside. The air reeked of damp clothes and beef stew gone sour. She waited until the woman's footsteps faded and she heard the click of a door then cast an anxious glance at her watch. The plan was taking much longer than she expected. But now she was in, she only had to climb the stairs and then she'd be at her dad's flat. Might take ten minutes and she'd be on her way back home.

Shirley crept up two flights of stairs and along an unlit hallway. She huffed with relief at her dad's bedsit door and savoured the moment. Her tough-mindedness got her this far. Now for the easy bit.

A coconut husk doormat lay by the door.

Shirley smiled. Dad kept a spare key under the mat. She stooped to lift the edge. A heartbeat later she staggered back in shock.

The key was gone.

CHAPTER 15

Fenella arrived at Fred Bickham's place anxious because of the early hour. It was six on Sunday, and her back still hurt. She wanted a nosy in his room before word spread to the public about the crime and asked Dexter to meet her. A sea mist hovered over the street, darkening the sky and threatening a cloud burst.

She peered through her car window at the run-down boarding house and grimaced. It was in a row of grand Victorian houses. Once picturesque and upscale, the rich had long abandoned the area, leaving landlords with rock-bottom room rates, their garish signs washed-out with age. She hurried through the mist, her car door shutting with a solid clunk.

Dexter hunched against the front door; his finger jammed on the bell. "Ain't got no reply, guv." He glared at the door. "The landlady is a heavy sleeper. I hear she is a bit of a hothead, heartless with it."

"Mrs R Fassnidge," Fenella said, reading the name below the button. "Having a Sunday morning lie in, eh?"

"That's what I reckon, guv," Dexter replied. "No

one has come in or out since I got here."

He staggered back, tilted his head and scoured the windows. There were no lights on in the rooms. No twitch of the threadbare curtains.

Fenella said, "Can't see much with all this fog."

"Think I should start ringing the bells at random, guv? Get someone up so they can open the door?"

"Nah, might cause havoc. We have enough on our plates without a stampede of complaints to Town Hall about the police ruining residents' sleep."

Fenella didn't want to waste time, neither did she want to face a rant from groggy renters grabbing a bit of shut eye after a gruelling workweek. They'd find the elusive landlady then search Fred Bickham's room. Minimal fuss was best on a Sunday at six in the morning.

"Think the door needs a good shove," Dexter said. "Looks rotten."

He grunted and threw himself, shoulder first at the door. He bounced with a painful cry. "Cor blimey, guv, think it is made of steel."

They stood in glum silence for a few minutes, then Fenella spoke. "Keep trying here, I'll have a nosy around the back."

A narrow alley ran at the rear of the houses. Everywhere hulking dustbins leaned against brick walls. The fog seemed to trap and compress their rotted contents to a hideous stink. Fenella walked quickly stopping at a pile of black bin bags next to an oversized dustbin. She wasn't certain why, but she lifted the lid expecting it filled to the brim. It was empty.

Why not put the bags in the bin? Curious, she jabbed the nearest bag with the tip of her shoe. Soft. She poked the second with her heel. Same. She swung her leg in a wild kick and whacked the third bag. More of the same. Not household rubbish, it felt like something else. She stooped, held her breath and opened the bag hardly able to credit what she saw. There was no doubt about it. She pulled out a pair of corduroy trousers and a broken pair of mirrored sunglasses.

From deep in the fog, there was a loud scurrying sound. Fenella listened. A door slammed. She straightened and picked her way around the black bags, feeling the slickness of the cobbles and noticing the stink of urine and dog waste.

A high brick wall ran the length of the alley with a gate at the far end. The gate had a latch but no lock. With any luck someone would see her as she entered the garden, she'd flash her warrant card, and they'd let her inside the building. All legal.

She pressed the latch and shoved, only hearing the hurried footfalls as it squealed open. Instantly alert, she shifted her body weight but it was too late. The gate creaked inward and she stumbled, sliding across the damp grass in the yard. A shard of pain burst around the base of her spine, causing her to gasp. As she lay dazed on the ground, a figure in black sprinted past.

Fenella struggled to her feet, fuming as her

hand squelched dog filth. "Hey you come back here. Stop. Police."

The figure didn't stop. They continued to sprint, slipping on the slick grass and stumbling through the gate. By the time Fenella scrambled to the alley, they'd vanished into the fog. Which way did they go?

She listened, heard only the rattle of a tin can and the soft hiss of the breeze. Vexed, she bent over her knees, huffing out ragged breaths of fury and wiping her soiled hands on the ground.

"Over here, guv. Quick."

Dexter's call came from behind. It carried such alarm Fenella spun and dashed back into the yard. Fog clouded her view as she moved toward his voice.

"God Almighty, guv." He stood in a doorway to the house and took a sharp breath. "Ain't seen anything like it."

A hollow pang bombed Fenella's gut. She opened her mouth to ask if he had seen the figure in black, then closed it, catching sight of his hollow-eyed stare.

Dexter said, "Gave the front door a shove and it swung wide. Went straight to Mrs Fassnidge's place and banged her door. It opened, so I went in and found myself in the kitchen. The door leads out here." He turned to point back at the house. "Guv, I found the landlady slumped over the kitchen table with her face smashed in. Mrs Fassnidge is dead."

CHAPTER 16

Shirley Bickham's heart battered her chest as she squatted on the floor in the nude. It was all going wrong. Who would have thought a key could bring so much hell?

A ragged pile of black clothes lay next to her. Great clumps of mud and muck and worse clung to her midnight black running shoes. The bedside clock ticked, then tocked.

She rocked to and fro, lungs wheezing with a gurgling sound. The patchwork curtains blocked out all light so it might have been midnight, except, when she turned to consult the bedside clock, it was close to seven.

On Sunday her mam and Ginger slept in late. Mam would rise at noon. Ginger after one. Time enough to rest and think and plan her next move.

Shirley stood and forced her gaze to linger on the smeared clothes, surprising herself with a clever idea. A shredder, better yet the furnace. Flame and fire and smoke and dust. For dust thou art, and unto dust shalt thou return. Ashes to ashes. *Brilliant*.

She rubbed her hands along her bare arms then padded to the wardrobe, knelt, fingers searching for the touch of cold glass. Only half a shot to get the zest of it and rouse her brain-dead mind. She downed two.

What next? A shower to wash away the filth. But blasting her body with hot soapy water would never cleanse the sins that stained her soul. She sat on her bed, emptied another shot glass and with renewed zeal promised to go to church, take part in Mass, speak with a priest, ask God to purge her soul.

The bedroom door flew open. Mam skipped into the room.

Shirley scrambled under the covers. "Knock before you come in."

"You've got nowt worth gawking at," Ida Bickham replied, adjusting her black fizzy wig and sitting on the edge of the bed.

Shirley didn't want to clash, not after the night she'd had. "Mam, I need my privacy. Please knock."

"You and your bleedin' secrets." Ida's eyes narrowed. "I didn't find out about Ginger until you were five months. Heartless. Why were you hell-bent on keeping me away from the birth?"

"Not now Mam."

"Your dad and I did our best and how did you repay us? By falling for a fool. It pains me to think of you being duped by a scrag end who ran off after the birth. We thought you'd gone half-mad when you hooked up with that seedy sicko. What was his name?"

"It doesn't matter."

"Sheesh, why did you ruin your life?"

"Mam, leave it."

But Ida wouldn't leave it alone. Her pale grey eyes narrowed, and she tugged at her frizzy black wig. "We had enough crap going on back then without being blindsided by your thoughtless actions."

The barrage sent Shirley's heart battering against her chest. She felt sick and turned away. "Okay, so I failed as a teen. Happy now?"

"Ah, so after all this time you agree he was a waste of space?"

Shirley said nothing. Her mam's morbid interest in the past always killed their conversation. Anyway, Shirley hadn't seen Ginger's dad in years. Didn't expect to see him ever again. The misery of the memory oozed like an old sore.

Ida's lips twitched into a mile wide smile, but her grey eyes were cold and hard. "The lad's name even sounded like a crook. What was it again? Ebenezer Scrooge or was it Fagin? No, no, no. His first name was Sewer, surname Rat."

Shirley seethed but did not speak. Arid years followed Ginger's birth. A blazing downhill slide to forty, heartbroken and living under the boiling glare of her mam. What did she have to look forward to? Fifty, under the same roof.

An acute urge for gin suddenly seized Shirley. The allure of alcohol always dulled the pain. But her mam had one thing right—she'd been a nut job as a young woman, falling for a snake who bewitched and then blighted her life. She thought she'd found her soulmate in that romantic way teenagers dream.

The spiteful truth was only learned with time and endless tears. Now she was older and wiser and toiled over her plans with an all-out zeal. Not a nut job anymore. A zealot intent of revenge.

Ida sniffed. "Have you been drinking?"

"I just got up," Shirley replied.

Ida padded to the window and drew the curtains. A slither of sunlight snaked across the room. "Been thinking about your dad. What happened to him at the allotments?"

"The experts are dealing with it."

"But who would want to murder Fred?"

Shirley shrugged and looked away.

"I'm worried about you, Shirl," Ida said in a whisper. "You've been acting strange these past few weeks. What is wrong?"

Shirley thought about her dad and she thought about his bludgeoned face and she thought about the child forming in Ginger's belly. "Nothing."

Ida looked at her daughter with sorrowful eyes. "No secrets, Shirl. I'm your mam."

They fell into a tense silence. The scream of a blackbird came from the garden. A blood-curdling shrill warning of deadly trouble.

Ida closed the curtain and skipped to the door, moving as quiet as a snake. She stopped. "Shirl, you can tell me anything."

"There is nowt to tell."

"No secrets?"

"No secrets," Shirley said, looking away. "I promise. I loved Dad as much as you. Miss him, too.

I've told you the truth."

"Last night I went to the bathroom and put my head into your room," Ida said, hand on the door handle. "You weren't in bed."

Shirley choked back the shock which bubbled up her throat filling her mouth with its bitter taste. "Must have been making a mug of hot milk."

Ida shook her head. "I went to the kitchen. I checked the downstairs toilet, living room and came upstairs and checked all the bedrooms. You weren't here. Where were you?"

"Here in bed."

Ida pointed to the floor. "Explain that pile of clothes and those filthy trainers."

Aghast, Shirley said, "Okay, so I went for a bloody stroll. Couldn't sleep."

Ida's eye's narrowed to slits. "Where?"

Shirley looked away. "Nowhere. I just walked."

Silence.

When Ida spoke, her voice came out in a bone-chilling hiss. "At three thirty in the morning? Absurd. Shirl, people don't go for a stroll at that time of night. Not in the dark and the fog."

"I had to get out. Dad's death ... it has all been ... too much."

"You argued with him last week."

"How did you know about that?"

Ida just shook her head. "What was that about?"

Shirley didn't reply. If only she could get away from her mam's glare, but there was nowhere to run.

Ida was still shaking her head. "You went to your dad's flat, didn't you?"

"No."

"To search for his medals."

"No."

"Before the police got their hands on them and God only knows what else."

"I went for a walk."

"Broke into your dad's room to steal his medals, didn't you?"

"Never."

Her mam's eyes blazed like hot coals. "And you wonder why Ginger won't talk with you."

She stormed from the room, slamming the door so hard the wall shook.

CHAPTER 17

The news which set Detective Constable Ria Leigh's Day ablaze came with the scream of a phone. It rattled with savage force at the bottom of a kitchen drawer.

Bang-bam-bam-bang.

Ria heard the awful noise as she walked to the bird feeder in the garden. A hideous sound bouncing through the open kitchen window. She hesitated, turned and dashed to the front door as her internal alarm bells shrieked.

It was her burner phone.

Apart from her secret bank account, only one person had the number—her business partner Sloane Kern. They were due to meet at Sloane's anger management practice to go over the books. Ria's gaze dropped to her watch. Nine-thirty. They had planned to meet at ten.

Bang-bam-bam-bang.

As she stumbled to the kitchen, her mind raced over the possibilities. Best case: Sloane called to say she'd be late due to Bren, her teenage daughter. *Bollocks to that*. She'd bawl Sloane out for always blaming the kid. Worst case: Sloane had sold more of their magic pills on credit. But Ria had made it clear—cash only from now on. Was Sloane's call a delaying tactic to stop her going line by line through the books? Did Sloane take her for a dimwit?

Endless questions drowned out the shrill of the phone. She swallowed the sourness rising up her throat, dragged the drawer open and riffled around for the phone.

Bang-bam-bam-bang.

Ria gripped the phone tight and peered at the screen. From force of habit she said, "You have dialled the wrong number. Whom do you wish to speak with?"

"Ria, it's me Sloane. We have to meet right now. Not at my office. Grub Pot Café in fifteen."

CHAPTER 18

Ria arrived early at the Grub Pot. The grease stained windows, protected by iron bars, looked out onto a row of tired shops. Twelve tables, all empty. Brown stains smeared the red tile floor. Damp wept from the walls. An intense smell of boiled peas and bleach did little to arouse her appetite. The all-day lunch specials and the free refills of hot drinks failed to pull in the punters. A safe place to chat without being overheard.

Ria chose a corner table. No tablecloth—salt, pepper and a bottle of ketchup with sauce congealed around the rim. It had a view of the door. She smiled at Frank, the owner, despite the almighty rage brewing inside. What the hell was going on? Was the change of plan a trick by Sloane to stop her reviewing the books? They kept them under lock and key in Sloane's office. Why did the drama queen insist they meet in this glum café?

She brooded over the questions, playing with the salt shaker. Blasts of steam hissed from a grimy coffee machine. Frank twiddled the gold hoop in his nose and dragged a rag along the counter in a ceaseless battle against the grease. He gazed mournfully across the café and turned to the door when it opened.

The hurried *clack-clack* of footsteps arrived seconds before Sloane. Ria sucked in a shocked breath. Her business partner's cadaverous face and anxious stare gave her the jitters. *Why does she always wear black? Looks like a spook.* They had worked together in their business for a handful of months. She had never seen Sloane so pale.

"Oh God," Sloane said, choking out the words and collapsing into a chair.

"What the hell happened to you?" Ria whispered. "You look like death."

"Oh God," Sloane said again with a sob as she picked up and put down the ketchup bottle. "You will think I'm crazy ... but we can't meet in my office to review the books. I'm haunted by the damn place. It's like we've been cursed."

Ria scowled. *Here we go, blowing smoke in my face.* "Did you bring the books with you?"

"Are you nuts? You know they never leave my office."

"Then we go to your office next."

"Don't be so damn cruel."

Ria swallowed. Why did she feel she was being taken for a fool? But she didn't want an argument. Not in this vile café with Frank pretending not to listen. She softened her tone, dropping her voice to a whisper. "I just want to nail down our exact numbers."

Sloane picked at the congealed sauce around the rim of the ketchup bottle. "We can't talk about the books now. Not after—"

Frank appeared at the table. "An early lunch for you ladies?"

"Yeah," Ria replied. "We'll have the special."

"Cabbage or peas?"

The café served roast beef with Yorkshire pudding drowned in brown gravy on Sundays.

"Two with cabbage," Ria said, without asking Sloane.

"A lot of folks go for peas," Frank said. "Our all-time favourite, grown on my plot in Seaview Allotments."

"You don't have cabbage?"

"I've got a green salad, but that will be extra."

"Peas, then."

Frank flashed a stained tooth grin; all car salesman dazzle complete with a fake gleam. "Can I tempt you with dessert? Peach cobbler or blackberry pie?"

"Is it part of the special?" Ria asked.

"There is a small additional charge."

"No thank you," Ria replied.

"Last of the bleedin' high rollers," Frank sneered.

He wandered back to the counter, shaking his head.

When Frank was out of earshot, Sloane said, "It is all too gory for me. I can't do it anymore." She let out a pained wail, eyes watching Ria's face. "That woman I told you about when we spoke on the phone. The old biddy that came back for more of our

... supplies."

"Mrs Stoke, wasn't it?"

"You said I must sell her more." There was a bitter lilt to Sloane's tone. "That is what you said, wasn't it?"

"Our business needs the cash. If they ask, give, and no credit."

"But I have a duty of care to my patients," Sloane replied. "That must come first."

Ria felt her jaw tighten. "I told you to sell her the bloody pills. If they want more, put the price up and sell it to them. You must beat them when they are down in this game. When they come back for more, you beat them down again."

Again, Sloane picked up the ketchup, squeezing and twisting the lid. "A bent cop can't tell me what to do." She wagged a finger and continued in a snarky tone. "I dread to think what the other cons will do to you in jail."

Incensed, Ria hissed, "Watch your lip you hypocrite. Your therapy business is a sham. Nothing more than a dope shop for flaky middle-aged women with fat purses. What makes you think you are any better than the sleazy sod peddling cheap weed in a slum doorway?"

"Oh, so now the self-important detective wants to tell me I'm lowlife? Well, I don't crawl the seedy snake pits of town buying drugs from violent thugs. Physician, heal thyself."

They glared at each other for a full thirty seconds.

Ria sighed. They had too much at stake to blow their business on a stupid fight. There were bills stacking up and drug suppliers to pay. When they were well in the black and her bank account bulged, she'd teach the stroppy cow a lesson. *Beat 'em down and beat 'em down again.* She pictured Sloane's horrified face when she turned the tables.

Ria smiled and let her voice soften. "Shift the pills I supply and the money will keep rolling in. We are not just business partners. We are friends."

Sloane closed her eyes quickly and looked away. "I just don't like it. Don't you feel dirty?"

Ria touched the salt shaker. "Let the cash wash you clean. You'd love more of it, wouldn't you?"

Sloane's lips were moving but it took a long moment before words came out. "Love? No. Need? Yes. I must have money to pay my bills."

Frank whistled a sad tune as he returned to their table. He hunched over the plates, sour breath reeking of cheese. "Voilà! Roast beef with a special sauce made just for you ladies."

Ria didn't like the sour gleam in his eyes or the slither of spittle trapped between his brown teeth.

Frank pointed at the plates, grinning. "A masterpiece of mind-blowing flavour created out of my hard work and sweat. Eat, savour, and enjoy."

Monstrous Yorkshire puddings poked from a morass of bullet-sized green peas. Glutinous gravy oozed over it all in ridges of brown sludge. It looked more like the noxious swill in the toilet bowl after a night on the town and an extra hot curry.

Frank made a slight bow. "Leave your jaw-dropping tip in the jar on the counter."

He slouched to the door and went outside. He looked both ways along the street then walked listlessly from their view.

Ria pushed the plate away. She didn't trust Frank's special sauce. "It is tough for everyone. Look at this place. We need to up our game, shift more pills. My new house is costing me a packet, and like you said, you need the cash." She flashed a thin-lipped smile. "Do you need another lot vetted? Give me the names and I'll run them today."

Ria used the police databases to check the criminal backgrounds of potential new clients. They only sold pills to women from the elite: Vicars' wives and the Women's Institute and the horsy type who gossiped as they guzzled French wine. No way would she make another mistake by selling to the likes of Mrs Fassnidge. That door was closed. Permanently.

Sloane ran a hand through her hair. "That is not what we need to talk about."

"Just tell me how many new clients we have? It's a risk forcing too many through the police system in one go. But I'll blaze through them, a handful at a time over the next week." Ria grinned. "Soon we'll be at full scale with a waiting list. A first-class problem, eh? Give me their details then we'll go over the books."

Through a friend who owed her a favour, Ria had access to the records in Cumbria police human resources. That gave her the names and photographs of everyone who worked in internal affairs. If they came snooping, she'd know. No need to worry about the National Crime Agency either. Her operation was too small to catch their eye. A perfect business. Her prized cash cow. *Genius*.

"Why don't you listen?" Sloane squeezed the ketchup. Sauce squirted across the table. "I've got terrible news."

The café door opened. Frank staggered to the counter and glanced around the empty café. His face filled with strife. "Sunday opening is a mug's game in this cut-throat business. How can I make a living when tightwads plague my café?"

He shook his head and went into the kitchen, slamming the door.

Sloane jerked to her feet. "We have to call a halt to our ... business. Mrs Stoke is unconscious in the hospital. She overdosed on our pills. When she wakes up, she'll point the finger and talk. We're screwed. I'm closing my therapy practice and leaving town fast."

CHAPTER 19

Den Ogden relished the hour ahead, ice-cold certain he'd win. He had been sitting at the counter in Quick Bet Bookie Store since they opened. Elfrid lay on the floor, his snout smiling although his eyes were closed.

They'd spent a wonderful night in the grand lobby of Fast Dough Pizza Shop, complete with food salvaged from a fridge. His superb skills in lock picking had paid off. They had scampered inside the pizza store as the man in the brown trilby strode past.

Den still felt very pleased. He had evaded the American's wrath while taking the blokes cash. A longshot for sure, but he was a betting man and longshots sometimes won.

Now everywhere men in flat caps and women in tight headscarves watched the huge screens. And the longshots were winning today—seven of ten horse races and counting. Den went with the trend. Not exactly science, but not a random pin in the race card either. If the gambling gods went with the longshots, so would he.

He grinned as he gave his last wad of notes to the clerk. He heard somewhere that less was liberating, but he didn't want less, he wanted more. He wanted a big win. He rubbed his dome shaped double chin for luck. Not that he needed it today. He felt the universe was on his side.

"I'll take care of me, if you will please take care of you," he said as he handed over his money.

The clerk stared at him for a moment too long. "You want to put fifty pounds down on Mister Dandy to win?"

"Aye, my friend," Den replied, half wondering if he knew the clerk. "I feel sunshine in my bones."

The beautiful thoroughbred would bring a thousand quid to his pocket, all thanks to the cash from the man in the brown trilby. He took a seat and tilted his head to watch the large television screen. Fascinated, he felt his heart pound as Mister Dandy entered the stall. A striking horse in exquisite form and the best looking of the lot. Why the hell was it twenty to one?

Den's bowels grumbled. He needed the loo. *I'll take a toilet break after the race.* The stalls opened.

"And they are off," the announcer said with a melodic twang.

The striking beasts leapt free in a firestorm of dust. They galloped along the straight with Mister Dandy tucked in nicely near the front of the pack. Den glanced at his betting slip never more certain of the win. As his gaze flicked back to the big screen, he suddenly had the feeling of being watched.

He turned and scanned the store. The frosted glass shop door was closed. A man with flat eyes slapped another man on his back. "On a losing streak again are you Fantam?"

"Ain't nowt to me," the other man replied. He had sunken eyes and a crack of a mouth. "The universe is getting me ready for my big win. They don't call me Fantam for nowt. One minute I'm down, the next I'm back. My luck is turning, I can feel it in my bones."

The man with flat eyes laughed. "Oh aye. You and me both."

A hooked-nosed woman with eyes as dark as coal waved her betting slip at the screen. Everyone else stared at the race. Gawking, gazing, smiling, frowning. Except a bloke in a flat cap with a gaping mouth who shook his head in sorrowful dismay. But no one was watching Den. Why would they? Nerves, he told himself, wondering if the man in the brown trilby had left town.

Den focused on the race, gleeful as Mister Dandy took the lead. "Not yet, hold the beast back. Don't make it look too easy."

A dark man with a gold earring yelled a bark of frustrated curses. The favourite struggled at the back. Two other punters joined in, screaming a chorus of foul words as it fell further behind. I'm a genius, Den thought, squinting at his betting slip and wincing at the firm grip suddenly on his arm.

"What's your game?" Den said, stunned to see the woman with the hooked nose at his side.

Bony fingers dug into his flesh and her charcoal eyes stared with menace. "Den Ogden?" she said. "That's you, ain't it?"

A pretty face once, Den thought, but in her early sixties now with blotched skin on the verge of dried prune. Where had he seen her before? A flash of recognition hit him. Jesus, it was her! What was her name? He couldn't recall, but knew she meant trouble. He tried to pull away but she held him with a gorilla grip.

"I've been dreaming of this day." She sneered. "Now my dream will be your nightmare."

"I no know what you mean," Den said, affecting a Polish accent. "I from Warsaw. Far away from here and no speak good English."

Her grip tightened. "Even after all these years I'd know you. Same cockroach eyes. Same slimy fat jaw. It's you ain't it?"

"You crazy woman. I Antoni. Mr Antoni Kowalski. I from Poland, Warsaw. I have passport to prove it."

"You're not Den Ogden?"

"Nie."

"Eh?"

"Polish for no."

She sniffed. "Let me see your passport."

"I leave it at home but have my dog with me. He from Poland too. Name is Elfrid. Did your Mr Ogden like doggy?"

"No," she said, loosening her grip. "He hated animals unless they were boiled, roasted or fried. He said pets wreaked havoc with his charm and got in the way of his job."

"I so sorry but I no eat meat. I not your friend." Den paused, holding his breath at the hesitation in her eyes. "I wish you find Mr Oggy and make peace."

"Not likely," she said, letting his arm drop. "Not after what that rat did."

Den watched her walk the length of the counter, toss a betting slip into the bin and head for the door. It clicked shut. He stared at the frosted glass for a long while, stunned.

He must finish his business and get out of this god-awful town before his lucked turned bad. But he refused to be rushed. Yes, pickings were slim in his line of work, and the years counted against him, but he still had enough vigour to cast ageist phobias to the back of his mind. He knew how to dazzle and wine and dine his way to a job. If only he could find the right person to let him in.

They were in the final stages of the race. The announcer spoke blazing fast. Den watched, mouth dry, fists clenched above his head. Mister Dandy led the pack as they galloped hard at the finish line.

"Twenty to one," Den shouted, leaning on the counter, clear-eyed and on the edge of delirium. "Twenty to bleedin' one!"

He blinked. The screen froze. He blinked again and collapsed against the counter. Mister Dandy trailed at the back. The horse limped across the finish line with the jockey lolling back in the saddle.

Dumbstruck, Den glowered at the screen, rage brewing at the freakish result. What were the odds? His bowels rumbled with fury. The gloom of the loser descended as he slouched to the loo, chose a stall and locked the lavatory door.

"I've lost it all on that bloody old nag."

He held his head and suddenly remembered the name of the pruned face woman with the hooked nose. Ivy something or other, and the cow was a witch with a gang of male friends with shaved heads and big fists.

Best get out of here fast. But his bowels moved before his legs twitched for the door. He gagged at the stink, finishing quickly, flushed and reached a hand for the latch. He hesitated. Through the crack in the door, he saw him—the man in the brown trilby. And he was scowling at Den's cubicle door.

CHAPTER 20

Shirley Bickham woke from an alarming nightmare, clutching the sweat-soaked sheets so tightly her nails shredded the fabric. As her head cleared, she choked back a gasp, glaring at the bedside clock—One-forty in the afternoon. She'd slept for six hours. How?

Bewildered, she closed her eyes and an ominous sense her day was about to get worse crushed the air from her lungs. Dammit, she needed a drink and staggered to the wardrobe, slipped on a dressing gown and felt around for the touch of cold glass.

Thwack-thwack-thwack.

The thumping came from the bedroom door. Stunned by the suddenness of the knock, and by its baffling clamour erupting into the silence, Shirley shoved the gin back in the wardrobe and stared at the door in shock. She tugged at the loose skin on her face, running a hand over the hollows. Who? Her mam didn't knock. Ginger never visited her room.

Thwack-thwack-thwack.

What did they want? An awful tightness throttled her throat. The door had no lock. Shirley pictured a uniformed policeman bursting in and firing off a round of cold-hearted questions. She remained motionless, tormented by the image of prison and the solid clunk of the cell door.

Thwack-thwack.

"Hello," Shirley said, dreading a reply. "Who is it?"

The handle creaked down.

Breathe, she told herself. Breathe.

The door eased open. Cool air rushed in from the hallway with an endless sigh. Ages. It felt like ages before Shirley heard the first *clack-clack* of soft footfalls. Her mam sidled into the room, face as pale as snow.

"What is it?" Shirley said, holding her arms tight around her body.

Ida slouched to the bed, adjusted her frizzy black wig, and stared at the window.

"What's happened?" Shirley asked again, voice screeching.

Mam could handle anything. She had battled disease laughing and singing and saying *To hell with death, I'll live life to the brim. Binge on it while I'm alive.* But Shirley had never seen her like this. Just sitting there, wide-eyed and trembling and suddenly very frail.

"I didn't take dad's medals," Shirley said softly.

Ida said nothing, but her whole body seemed to coil tighter like a snake trapped in a box.

Shirley swallowed hard to prevent herself from freaking out. Did her mam know? Had she told Ginger? *Oh God!* Somehow, she opened her mouth and quiet words tumbled out. "No secrets. Tell me what is up."

"Shirl," Ida screamed, springing to her feet. "I've called the police. Ginger is not in her room. She's gone."

CHAPTER 21

Den Ogden didn't like it, and he knew it was about to get worse. He crouched in a drab toilet stall, trembling with dread. When he snatched the cash from the man in the brown trilby, he'd snatched a wasp's nest of trouble. The American's accent might have been from Chicago. Didn't mobsters rule that city? Men who smiled as they killed and couldn't take a joke. And Den had crossed the man in a naïve jest. What if he demanded his fifty quid back?

Den cursed. He'd lost the lot on Mister Dandy.

The man in the brown trilby stepped toward his cubicle. Den's jitters blasted through the dial. His lungs expelled sour air. Blood surged in erratic spurts in his ears. A memory struck. Den was in another toilet, five years old, hiding, full of fear and confused. His mum had died in a car crash a month before. He never knew his dad. He was hiding because the woman with the fat face full of makeup told him he was to live with her. Her breath smelled of salt and vinegar crisps, her body of cheap perfume.

"A new and very happy home with lots of friends to play with," she had said in a sweet voice. "Your forever home."

But all Den saw was the rouge lipstick smeared like blood at the corners of her fat lips. He ran to the toilets, sobbing in huge bursts, convinced his life had been completely ruined.

Once, months later, the woman with the fat face full of makeup caught him watching *Dr Who* while licking the bottom of a packet of salt and vinegar crisps. He had found the empty packet under the sofa, but there were soft dregs worth eating stuck to the bag.

"We eat at the table," the woman with the fat face said. "One meal a day, no snacks. And the telly is for education not fun. Clear?"

He nodded, but she struck him with her fist. "Devil child," she had screamed as the blows battered his face.

They put in five stitches and fixed his nose. The woman with the fat face said he fell from a tree, that boys will be boys. When they got home from the hospital she beat him again, said it was his own damn fault, that no good would come of a boy more evil than the devil.

And five-year-old Den sobbed in heartbroken gasps because he believed every word—his fault his mother died, his fault he lived in hell. He was just born bad.

They took him and the other kids away from the woman with the fat face. She was the first of seven foster families. Each time the social worker smiled at Den and said they'd try again. He was nine and on his last home when he overheard the social worker complain they'd dumped a hopeless case on her plate.

He never found his forever home.

God, how he rejoiced when they tossed him out of the care system at sixteen. Den Ogden versus the world with the odds stacked against him. Longshots sometimes win.

Now, as the vivid memory faded, Den sat on the edge of a toilet in the Quick Bet Bookie Store with nowhere to run. Through the crack he saw the man in the brown trilby take another sinister step forward.

Den tensed. The man stood so close he fancied he heard the wheeze of his chest. *Maybe I've got it all wrong and he just wants to use the loo. A longshot, but longshots sometimes win.*

Then he saw the eye.

It peered through the crack in the door.

"Jesus Christ," Den said.

He threw the door open with a rush of feet and a savage yell, and then came a wail with an American twang, and the clunk of someone crashing into the cistern. Den snatched a glance over his shoulder, saw the man in the brown trilby struggling to his feet and heard the dry raspy voice call after him to stop.

But Den didn't stop. He dashed into the lobby, grabbed Elfrid's leash and sprinted from the store. He turned into an alley, crouched behind the dustbins, catching his breath in the foul air.

When he was certain he wasn't being followed,

he patted Elfrid on the head. "Good boy, but you ain't much of a runner. If we are going to eat, we need to get some cash."

Den exhaled a ragged breath. Mister Dandy had failed him, but the Russian with rag doll eyes would help. For a price.

CHAPTER 22

It was a thought that changed everything. It flitted at the back of Fenella's mind like a moth in a glass case. She called an emergency briefing to discuss the death of Mrs Ruth Fassnidge, puzzled at the sickening turn in events and stood at the front drained of energy and panicked at another death.

"You'll have heard about Mrs Ruth Fassnidge, Fred Bickham's landlady."

Most of her team sat in the first row, grim-faced. Shocking deaths required time to sink in. She'd give them as much space as they needed to process the toxic news, and had rustled up a tea urn and three plates of biscuits—custard creams, bourbons and a dozen sticks of Cumbrian gingerbread.

"This madness don't make any sense, guv," Dexter said pacing the edge of the room.

Detective Constable Jones balanced his laptop on his knee. "Agreed, it is senseless, boss. Wonder if we are in the midst of an all-out drug war. We must confront it now else all hell will break loose."

"A real tragedy." PC Beth Finn said. "Heartbreaking."

Detective Constable Ria Leigh chewed the end

of her pen. "Ruth Fassnidge, eh? The name's new to me. Not spent much time in that part of town. I hope she put up a fight."

Something niggled at the edge of Fenella's mind as raw and sore as her back. She watched Ria for a moment. The lass seemed fidgety. She wasn't the type to chew the end of her pen.

PC Woods was speaking. "Courageous of you to try to stop the killer, ma'am."

"Aye, I gave them a fright," Fenella replied. "But they were nowt but a shadow and darted away like a rabbit. They wore dark clothes. All black. Man or woman? I couldn't tell in all the fog."

She glanced at Ria's glum face and her heart squeezed. The lass looked defeated and rocked back and forth as though tortured by a complex decision. Was the baby Eva Fisk case too much for her?

Dexter stopped pacing by the plate of custard creams. "Ain't got no idea what type of scumbag would do in an old lass who ain't doing no harm." He paused, rage blazing in his eyes. "A lass in forensics told me that some evil bugger took a cricket bat lined with nails to her face like it were some bleedin' punishment. Reckon it's the same weapon that did in Fred Bickham."

"We can't be sure of that at this stage," Jones said, seemingly upset no one agreed with his gangland war theory. "Might be coincidence."

Dexter snorted, picked up a custard cream, swallowing it in three bites. "Don't be daft, lad. It were a bone-chilling bloodbath in her kitchen. The work of a crazy maniac killer with no self-control." His eyes squeezed shut. "They let loose such wild blows her blood smeared the walls. Ain't no chance in that, lad."

Fenella noticed a tremble at the corner of Ria's lip. She stopped rocking back and forth and sat very still as if she'd decided.

"Do you think we have a serial killer on our hands?" Jones rubbed his hands. "Could be the first blows in a killing spree. Psychos thrive on terror and wrong footing the police. Might send us a letter crowing about what they have done. Anyone checked the post?"

They fell into silence. Fenella massaged her back. Two dead in two days. What did Mrs Fassnidge know that caused her to lose her life? What dark secrets did the killer fear? Or was a serial killer on the loose striking folks at random? She thought back to the figure in black sprinting through Mrs Fassnidge's back yard. Why did she feel like she'd entered a towering inferno with flames hurtling toward her?

The tea urn gurgled. PC Woods waddled to the back, poured a mug and grabbed a huge stack of custard creams. For an instant, his munching and slurping were the only sound in the room.

Fenella cleared her throat and spoke in a brisk tone. "The link between the two deaths is our prime focus going forward unless anyone has a better idea."

A murmur of agreement.

She turned to Jones. "Have a sniff about for CCTV footage." She nodded at PC Woods. "You and PC Beth Finn are on the knocker. Door to door and rouse everyone. Someone saw something. And get a list of the residents of Mrs Fassnidge's boarding house. Did anyone see or hear anything?"

"Will do," PC Woods said, spitting out crumbs.

Fenella stared for a long moment baffled by his response. She'd expected a complaint about his back or a moan about wanting desk duty. Good God, she thought. A stack of custard creams and he is happy. He's not thinking about the fog or rain or scowling faces. He's focused on his gut. She wanted to clap but instead watched as PC Woods shovelled a handful of the said biscuits into his mouth. PC Beth Finn scribbled furiously in her notebook.

Fenella folded her arms. "What do we know about Mrs Fassnidge's life?"

PC Woods raised a hand. "She pulled herself up with cunning and penny-pinching." He paused, looking sheepish. "Ruth by name and Ruthless on the man hunt by nature. Successful, too—married thrice."

"We must speak with the ex's," Jones said. "Maybe she swindled them out of money. Revenge is a terrific motive."

PC Woods shook his head. "Can't. They all died." He slurped a mouthful of tea. "She enjoyed life as a widow, lived like a queen, posh cruises twice a year—spring and autumn. Rumour says she took to the high seas on the hunt for another man. Don't know if she found one, though."

"I heard she paid for the boarding house with cash," PC Beth Finn said. "Any truth to that?"

PC Woods nodded. "And she has a rental property in Spain, offered me a discount a few years back. Nice place, but I've never been to her flat here in town. She doesn't let many people near her rooms here. Close friends only, and tea with the vicar —Reverend Beasley. Shame some thug struck her down in her prime."

A vein throbbed in Fenella's neck. *Three husbands, eh? All dead. No shortage of secrets in that lot.* She felt a surge of energy and flashed a broad smile.

"Jones, find out about these deceased husbands. Natural causes? Have a poke in their medical records. I'll have a natter with her vicar, see if he can shed some light on what went on inside her rooms."

A splendid start to a squalid case, Fenella thought, feeling much better. She turned to Ria. "Update on baby Eva. Any good news?"

Confusion crossed Ria's face. Yes, her mind was elsewhere today. Fenella sneaked a quick glance at Jones. He leaned back in his chair, handsome and buff. Was Mr Charming the source of Ria's woes? Their private lives were none of her business, but she'd have a nosy anyway.

Ria gave the faintest of smiles. "Still working the files, ma'am."

"Keep me informed," Fenella said. She wanted

to work the case herself, but with two deaths in Port St Giles there wasn't time. "Do you need help?"

"Got it covered, ma'am."

The niggle at the back of Fenella's brain shrieked. She nodded at Dexter. "Tell me again what you saw in Mrs Fassnidge's flat."

"I walked in and found her at the table, guv. Pools of blood on the floor, some smudged on the walls. Then I went into the yard and saw you."

"It doesn't make sense," Fenella said and inched carefully to the whiteboard so that her back didn't twinge. "A stranger walks into your flat while you are having a cuppa. What do you do?"

"You approach them or you back away." This was Jones.

"Aye, but we found Ruth at the table," Fenella said.

"She must have known the attacker," Jones replied.

"Precisely," Fenella replied. "Possibly a friend."

Dexter said, "Aye, guv, my thoughts exactly. Focus on her relationships and we've got the bugger who did her in."

A new thought zapped Fenella's grey matter. "Jones, check if forensics found an address book or diary. A busy woman writes important stuff down. Impossible to keep track otherwise."

"You think she had a secret notebook?" Ria asked, face dough pale. "Surely she would use a laptop?"

"Mrs Fassnidge is a pen and paper lass," Fenella

replied. "I'd put money on her having a hidden notebook with details of all her dealings."

Ria looked shocked. Her mouth moved, but no words came out.

Fenella noticed but said nothing because she loved this part of an investigation. It was quite a feat to start with a blank page and find a direction. She pointed at the whiteboard. "Let's get a photo of Ruth on the board. Fred Bickham too. A nice snapshot where they are alive and smiling."

CHAPTER 23

Fog billowed on the slate roof, loitered in the gutters and swirled around Detective Constable Ria Leigh's feet. She crouched against a brick wall, a large black bag over her shoulder, watching the delivery bay of the Port St Giles Cottage Hospital. The steel doors, whitened by the moon, glowed with a smudged gleam. Dozens of trucks arrived during the day. Nothing moved at four in the morning. Nothing good came of that hour.

The delivery area, tucked in a back alley, was a different place in the fog and dark. A land of squalid blind corners where sinister shadows flickered. But it was the best time for Ria. An hour when tired workers near the end of their shift missed things they would catch when alert. Ria's stomach grumbled with the ache of hunger. When did she last eat? Ages ago. Food could wait. She must keep a clear head for the task ahead and keep out of sight. Recognition was the last thing she needed. Fog and gloom and dark. *Perfection*.

Her gaze swept over the area. It was very quiet. No voices. No light from the window above the bay door. The crash of waves carried from the beach and she fancied the scent of burnt wood hung in the moist air. An electric motor hummed, soft and faint and out of sight.

Whizz-click-whizz.

Ria slunk through the gloom to the metal steps that led to a side door. Deep inside, Mrs Stoke lay unconscious and bedridden. A helpless addict, dead to this world, but alive. For now.

Amazing how easy it is to get in and out unnoticed if you knew the back routes and where the steely eyed CCTV cameras watched. Like a ghost. Ria grinned. Tonight she'd become a phantom.

Whizz-click-whizz.

Ria gazed toward the sound. It might be a mechanical door opening or the internal grumble from the lift shaft. Swirls of mist danced in the shadows. She waited, but saw no one. Her gut twisted with a dread she could not put her finger on. Something about the cobblestoned alley filled her with doom. Something wasn't right. But she knew two things: There was no one in the alley and she wasn't being followed. So, what was the problem?

Might not be the alley, she told herself. *Might be my financial troubles.* Her eyes closed and she brooded over her problems.

First, her drug suppliers followed their own law with clients who didn't pay—a barbaric beating then concrete shoes and a ride in a rowboat far out to sea. Money, she needed cash to keep the buggers at bay. And that led to her second problem. House repairs. That damn house had plunged her deep into a pit of debt. How did payments pile up at such a dizzying speed? Bills are an awful beast, she thought. They choked life's joy and robbed you of peaceful sleep.

And now her business partner Sloane wanted to close her therapy practice and leave town. Ria swore. How did she end up in this insane mess? Sloane's clients were supposed to be high rollers living the ideal country life. Why the hell did they need credit? Why the hell did Sloane offer it? And once again Ria was struck by the distasteful thought her business partner was fiddling the books.

Ria exhaled a breath from deep down in her lungs. She hated the fear oozing from Sloane now things had become murky. But it was naïve of Sloane to think she could just walk away from their joint venture. She'd string the timid lass along for now and strike a fatal blow when fate gave her the chance. *Beat 'em down and beat 'em down again.*

Ria hissed out another breath and considered her most vexing problem. Sloane's client Mrs Stoke with her overdose and blabbing mouth. She presented an urgent challenge. The woman might be sitting up in bed now, telling the world who sold her the pills.

Sod it. She glanced at her watch.

Tick-tock.

Tick-tock.

Mrs Stoke would betray them when she awoke. Muscles twitched tight in Ria's shoulders. *It is not my fault the brain-dead hag binged on pills.* No doubt about it—when the poisonous witch woke up she'd pin them with the venom of blame. That meant the end of her career. Civic Officer of the year for four years' straight snatched from her deserving grasp.

"No."

Anger surged through her veins, savage and rotten and raw. Mrs Stoke made bad choices and must now suffer her plight. Ria snatched another sour glance at her watch.

Tick-tock.

Tick-tock.

"Action time."

She sprinted from the wall, stopping outside the circle of light cast by the lamps above the delivery bay. Her breath hissed in the dense air. For a while, she stared up the steps at the worker's door and listened to the pounding of her heart. When, at last, it beat at its normal rate she opened her black bag and checked her kit once more.

Check: doctor's white house coat.

Check: the mask with the evil Halloween scowl.

Check: the brown porter's jacket she'd slip into on her way out.

And check, the suffocation pillow. Press down hard for three minutes and done.

She smiled as she pictured herself creeping into the hospital room, placing the pillow on Mrs Stoke's face and pressing down, down, until the woman's breaths stopped and her body went limp.

Would there be a struggle? She'd never met Mrs Stoke but her name made her sound stout. Tree trunk arms and elephant legs infused with demonic strength. She'd thrash about with gasps and groans, refusing to die, fighting for the right to live. Ria imagined a bony arm stretching, fingers unfurling, pressing the bedside alarm. She pictured nurses and doctors hurtling into the room with Mrs Stoke pointing and screaming in outrage.

Ria's smile vanished. She shuddered and cursed and glanced at her watch. She'd check for snores at the room door. Best strike while Mrs Stoke slept. *Beat 'em when they are down and beat 'em down again.* The long nightmare was nearing the end. Twenty minutes in and out. Time to start the clock.

She looked at her black bag with the suffocation pillow and she looked at the metal steps rising up before her and she looked at the door at the top. The man with one eye slept in the room beyond the door.

Ria didn't know his real name, everyone called him One Eye. He'd been the night watchman for years. He never locked the door and did indeed have one glass eye. The other eye, clouded with age, read the newspaper and viewed late-night telly while he downed slow shots of rum. He was supposed to keep his good eye on the CCTV monitor, but the forty-year-old camera had not worked in a decade. No vans arrived before six. One Eye's shift finished at seven. He slept until five thirty.

She pictured a half bottle of rum on the table, One Eye curled in soiled bedsheets with a shot glass at his side. She'd used this door three times before. Every time he'd snored as she tiptoed by. Silently, Ria thanked One Eye for making her life a little bit easier. The dark hallways and corridors to Mrs Stoke's ward would be a breeze. A quick scan for nurses, doctors or cleaners and into Mrs Stoke's room. Blissfully simple after that.

Clear-eyed and filled with a cold-hearted urge to get the job done, Ria sprinted up the metal stairs, cursing at the sudden clang. Only as her hand reached for the door handle did she become aware of the damp clinging to her back. Sweat oozed from every pore drenching her in cold clamminess. She blinked away the salt stinging her eyes but could not shake the cloud of doom which squeezed her chest. Even though One Eye slept in a drunken stupor on the other side of the door, she shivered.

It got strange after that.

The door swung open before she touched the handle. Harsh lights blinded Ria and in that instant she sensed it was going wrong. One Eye wasn't sleeping. One Eye wasn't there. A figure framed in the doorway stared with disdain. And a giant gold hoop glinted. It hung from the man's nose. He wore a security guard's uniform and looked familiar.

"I've had my eagle eye on you," he said, stepping through the door. "What's your game?"

It's Frank, Ria thought. Frank from Grub Pot Café. He held a mobile phone in his right hand and a cricket bat in his left.

Ria's legs trembled. She shuddered out a panicked breath. Her mind worked at breakneck speed as her body fought off a mix of panic and flat-out fear. Had they set a trap? Sloane must have betrayed her. Snared like a sewer rat. Wait. Sloane did not know about her treat for Mrs Stoke. No one did.

Whizz-click-whizz.

Ria gathered her wits. "Where is One Eye?"

Frank leaned the cricket bat against the door frame. "He died last week. Can I help you?"

"Delivery."

"I don't see your van."

"Parked around the corner."

He had not recognised her. She relaxed a little and began plotting her next steps. But there was something else about the man. Something that bothered her.

Frank pointed to his left, to his right and straight ahead. "New CCTV installed yesterday."

A red light blinked above the bay doors. Ria's legs convulsed. She grabbed the cold railings, gut turning over in stress. The bloody thing had monitored her as she crept about in the foggy dark.

Frank continued. "Dazzling state-of-the-art camera. Scans the whole area for movement—whizz-click-whizz. Even beeps when a truck arrives. The thing is, it did not beep, but it did watch as you crouched by the wall. What the hell were you doing?"

"I ... I ... er ... came to speak with One Eye."

"Oh yeah?" He leaned forward, his eyes narrowed. A spider web of spittle glistened between his brown teeth. "What you got in that bag?"

"Nothing."

"Looks like a pillow." He grinned like the devil. "You One Eye's bit on the side?"

"We liked to talk."

"Me too, but times are hard and I ain't got much cash." The grin swelled and his tongue licked his cracked lips. "How much for the night?"

"Eh?" Even though Ria backed away she smelled his sweat. "What the hell ... I'm not some cheap tart."

Something flickered in his eyes. "I remember you now. You were in my café earlier. Last of the big spenders. And I wonder why I have to work nights in this hell-hole."

He raised his phone.

Click-click.

"Got your photo and I've got you on CCTV. Now sod off you penny-pinching whore or I'll call the police."

CHAPTER 24

Fenella sighed in frustration. Her day had started badly and she sensed it was downhill from here. It was ten in the morning and a monstrous pile of paperwork tottered on her desk. All urgent. All late. And her back pain hadn't gone away. A bad start to the day.

She pushed the mug of cold coffee away, tried to focus on the bland words of a form from the top of her pile with her pen grasped tight in her hand. Buckle down and do the work, she told herself. But she put the pen down and gazed around her tiny office. It's like a bleedin' cage. No wonder she felt like a mouse on a wheel.

There'd been no breakthrough in the Fred Bickham case. No word from forensics on Ruth Fassnidge, and a nauseating silence on baby Eva Fisk. Not even a call from a nut job claiming they snatched the bairn. Her heart squeezed at the misery of the parents trapped in a nightmarish hell. No news wasn't good news.

Focus, she told herself. Don't let your muse run free, it'll chase rabbits and waste the day. Focus on the forms. But she wondered what Dexter was up to, and whether Jones had any good news. What about

Ria? Were she and Jones an item? *They won't want me poking about in their business, best leave them alone.*

Then she recalled the slack jowled puppeteer from a management training course. One of Superintendent Jeffery's weird team building bright ideas. Fenella thought the whole idea was mad but, apparently, there was a lot to learn from puppets about how their masters pulled the strings. So they wrote notes while the puppet did a lot of the talking —an alcoholic wooden doll with a giant red nose and huge clogs for feet. Jeffery sat on the front row in a razor-sharp uniform next to Chief Constable Rae.

They clapped in astonishment when the puppet burst out in song. Not a nursery rhyme, opera—*O mio babbino caro*. They rose to their feet in applause when the puppeteer drank a jar of ale and ate a pork-pie then spoke with a friend on the phone while the puppet continued to sing. Fenella reckoned it was a recording played back through a hidden speaker in the doll's mouth. She'd taken a sly look at the puppet when the event was over. Its head was made from a solid block of wood. No sign of a hidden speaker or wires or batteries. No electronic anything, just a wooden marionette with strings. How had it sung with such clarity and gusto?

"It's your job to stay on top of things," the puppeteer's puppet had ranted as they neared the end of the day's training. "Ignorance costs money. Unsafe. Uneasy. Unwise. Superb leaders don't suffer from that blight. They know which string to pull to make the puppet dance. They must know what is going on in their world."

That's right. I must know what is going on in my team's personal lives. How else will I know where to poke my nose in? She snatched her mobile phone and scrolled to find Ria's number. She'd invite the lass for lunch and force her to spill the beans. Oh, and she mustn't forget PC Beth Finn. She'd invite her for lunch too. I'm pitiful Fenella thought with a gleeful smile. The door flew open before she pressed the dial key.

Superintendent Jeffery marched in, arms swinging at her side. She stopped at Fenella's desk, her face twisting into a wolfish scowl that might have been a grin. And she wore her full uniform with the gold tassels on the shoulders.

I should have run for it while I had the chance, Fenella thought, sensing her day was about to go from bad to worse. But given the state of her back, running was out. She glanced at her phone, willing the thing to ring so she could make an excuse and scarper. But it didn't ring. Not even the soft buzz of a text message. Where were her team when she needed them?

Jeffery said, "Thought I'd pop by to see how things are going. Team out and about?" She didn't wait for an answer. "And how is Ria Leigh settling in?"

"Busy with the baby Eva Fisk case," Fenella replied

"Excellent. She will make a first-rate detective." Jeffery leaned forward so her palms rested on the desk. "Hand-picked by me and plucked from the claws of the Regional Crime Team. A genius move, eh? Our win, their loss. Snooze you lose."

"Learn that from a puppet, ma'am?"

Jeffery stared for a long moment, jaw working. "I'm here to talk about visibility and waste."

"Eh?" Now it was Fenella's turn to look surprised.

"Visibility is the buzz word these days, Sallow. A waste if we don't use it to full effect." Jeffery's eye's twinkled with the zeal of a peasant at the head of a witch-hunt. Never a good sign when they glittered like that. "A word in your ear from a rock-solid source. Ready?"

"Yes, ma'am?" Fenella said, watchful and waiting for the first wallop of something nasty to drop.

"Chief Inspector Rae is all over the concept. He wants his leaders out in front. I have always worked that way, don't you agree?"

Fenella said nothing.

Jeffery snorted. "Our station is a vibrant model of modern policing. We lead the way with untiring steps and—"

"Can you get to the point?" Fenella said, cutting the boss off. "Don't want to waste time, do we?"

A flicker crossed Jeffery's face followed by a wolfish smile. "Good news. You've been selected to take my place in Cut the Strings: Visibly Moving Ahead leadership seminar. Chief Constable Rae has been called away and I ... can't attend either.

Starts in an hour and runs all day. The Chief is back tomorrow. Make notes and send them to me tonight."

"Notes, ma'am?" Fenella said thinking that filling out forms was a great deal better than sitting in a stuffy room listening to waffle and having to write it down. She pointed to the pile in her inbox. "Love to, but I have these forms to complete. They are already late."

Jeffery waved a hand. "They can wait. I have breakfast with Chief Rae at seven tomorrow and want to discuss the most important concepts from the day's training." She lowered her voice. "No need for him to know I had to skip out, eh?"

Jeffery turned, and with arms swinging, marched from the room. The *clack-clack* of her footsteps boomed along the hallway.

Fenella tilted her neck from side to side. Jeffery had organised a training session on visibility but would not show up in the room herself. Now hours of classroom torture stretched out before her. Was the alcoholic puppet back for round two?

Her heart sunk to a new low. She glanced at her desk looking for something to throw at the door. Instead, she picked up her phone. "PC Woods? Good... I've got a sit-down job for you ... my office in five minutes and bring a large notepad. Me? It is all about visibility. I'll be at the Seaview Allotments. I want to have a nosy around the crime scene."

CHAPTER 25

A moment before the strange encounter, Fenella parked her car on the main road and strode along the rutted lane to Seaview Allotments.

Sunlight glowed through the low clouds exploding glitter on the hills. Sheep grazed in the fields, their bleats erupting into the melodic rustle of the endless breeze. The sea lapped the distant shore. The walk filled her lungs with fresh air. Exercise worked her muse.

"Ideas required," she said, hoping for a glint of something new in the Fred Bickham and Ruth Fassnidge cases.

Although she knew the way, the remoteness made her uneasy. The quiet lane snaked across the landscape with lush hedgerows and steep banks on each side. The grim spectre of Fred Bickham's death hung over the place. If a crazy killer madman sprang from the bushes, no one would hear you scream. Thunderclaps thumped far out to sea. A blackbird shrieked from the hedgerow.

Fenella picked up the pace. Nowt like exercise to force the muse into high gear. Did the murderer hide in the thicket and stalk Fred Bickham along this exact path? Would anyone but a friend or family know where he hung out? And why strike down Ruth Fassnidge with such brutal force in her home?

As she huffed up a steep incline, her thoughts drifted to singing puppets and cricket bats lined with nails and the dull ache in her back. She rounded a slow bend to an area where the canopy thickened so the way ahead darkened. An unmistakable feeling traced its cold finger along her neck. Was someone watching her?

She looked behind expecting to see a grim-faced officer hurrying to get to the crime scene. The wind whipped dead leaves into a demented dance. But no one followed. Was someone hiding in the trees? She glanced up. The silhouette of a black-headed gull appeared through the branches, its shadow a shimmering dark blot.

Why would anyone be hiding in the trees? She felt like a fool. Yet, two deaths in as many days with a potential serial killer on the loose would jangle the nerves of a saint. She sucked in a breath and let the air out slow, but jumped at the ear-shattering scream of the black-headed gull.

"Nerves," Fenella said, hands on her back. "Just nerves."

The gull hovered, shrieked then bolted away. An eerie quiet filled the void. Fenella stopped to scan the area. What was that? A thin trickle of blue smoke whirled from behind a stand of hawthorn trees. She turned and scrambled through a gap in the hedgerow, curiosity driving her on.

In the dark recess of the tree trunks, a wizened

man in a flat cap with thick sideburns squatted on a child sized three-legged stool. In his sixties, he wore a rumpled brown short-sleeve shirt. His lips puckered around a bent stem pipe; eyes closed.

As Fenella approached, he inhaled, chest rattling like stones in a can. A hacking cough boomed as he exhaled. But the man's eyes remained closed, his weathered face as fixed as dried paint. She eyed his left elbow. Did he have some dreadful skin disease? Blotches streaked like paint splashed on a canvas and blistered in bubbles of puss. She waited.

Again, he sucked on the pipe, huffing out great acrid fumes with wild fury. His hand moved with surprising speed to his pocket. Fenella sensed he was much stronger than he looked. He pulled out a bulky black case the size of a book. With total focus, he fussed with the straps of the box, muttering under his breath and unaware a police detective watched.

Fenella's gaze turned to the direction he faced. She could scarcely believe her eyes. There, in the glitter of the sun, was a clear view across the fields to Seaview Allotments. A uniformed officer stood to one side of the crime scene tape. A white tent flapped in the breeze. Inside, arc lights lit the walls with a creepy glow. Figures in the tent looked like puppets in a Japanese shadow play.

With a chuckle, the man opened the black box and raised a pair of field glasses to his face, aiming at the crime scene.

Fenella stepped forward. "What are you up to?"

He rolled back almost losing his balance on the

stool. "Where did you spring from?"

"I heard coughing, thought you were choking and needed help," she said, feeling the throb of pain growing in her back. She should have taken her time rather than hurrying like a mad woman.

"Do I look like I'm on me deathbed?"

"What are you doing?"

"What's it got to do with you?"

"I'm with the police, luv." Fenella flashed her warrant card.

He peered at it for a long moment. "Keeping us safe, eh? I like that."

"Now what is all this about?" Fenella asked.

He looked away. "I ... er ... a spot of birdwatching."

"Don't talk daft. I saw you looking at the crime scene through those binoculars."

"It's me hobby."

"Watching crime scenes?"

"Birds."

Where had she seen him before? Had she interviewed him at the station? A perp she'd put away? Maybe she'd seen him at a do with her mam, Nan? He had that ladies' man gleam to his eyes. A randy old goat with a weathered face made up of hard angles and sharp edges.

He was still speaking. "Nowt wrong with a bit of fresh air with a romp through nature. Good for the soul. Sparrows, pigeons, black-headed gulls, blackbirds too. I love blackbirds." His voice had a sing-song lilt, like a cross between a barrow boy in a London Street market and a used car salesman. "I adore our feathered friends."

Fenella massaged her back. "Where is your notebook?"

He tapped the side of his head. "Full to the brim with brain cells is that. Genius memory. Pen and paper not required for this Albert Einstein bird peeper."

"Come off it pet. Twitcher or birder, aye. But no respectable bird watcher calls themselves a peeper."

Prickles of red bloomed on his cheeks. "Don't you have crooks to catch?"

A sea stink wafted on the breeze—rotted fish and dead seaweed. The air seemed to chill and the bleats from the sheep resembled the bellow of frightened cattle. At that moment, the alarm cry of an unseen blackbird screeched. Now Fenella recalled the exact place where she'd last seen him—screaming his head off in the town market. He sold fruit and veg from a stall.

She twisted from side to side to ease the throb in her back. "Are you George Rouge the greengrocer?"

"Well ... er ... my lad runs the full show now." He rubbed his left elbow. "I retired from that havoc five years back."

He had three sons. One worked in the town market. What did the others do?

Fenella eyed his arm. "What's wrong with your elbow?"

"Nowt."

"Looks nasty."

"Doc gave me some cream, says it will heal in a few days."

Fenella changed the subject. "How is business?"

"I only work Wednesdays to keep our old-time customers happy."

"And in your free time you spy on the police?"

"Keeping an eye out to make sure you lot don't trample me peas."

"Are you a member of the allotment?"

He laughed, all donkey bray and crooked yellow teeth with wide gaps. His gums were black and nasty looking. "I'm chairman this year and for the past ten years."

"You must be good."

"Only the best will do."

Now she remembered. One of his sons was a BBC journalist, the other a big shot lawyer in London. And George Rouge was known for his wild temper, taste for strong booze and boasting.

Fenella looked at his elbow and she looked at the field glasses and she looked back at the crime scene. And that's when she noticed it. What bothered her from the moment she spotted the thin plume of smoke. She cleared her throat, organising and ordering her next line of questions.

"Mr Rouge?"

"Call me George."

"George, can you tell me why none of your members discovered Mr Fred Bickham's body?"

Something flashed in his eyes and he half turned to peer toward the crime scene. "Someone had to find it. I guess Shirley Bickham was the unlucky lass."

It seemed he was full of fast answers. Fenella tried again, watching the man like a hawk. "We believe Mr Bickham's body lay exposed in the open for several days. Yet, no one spotted his body, not even you."

His dark eyes narrowed. "What? Oh ... well, our allotment covers a large area. Fred wanted a plot on the far side and the lots around his area are vacant. So, no surprise there, really."

"Don't you walk the grounds?"

"Once in a while, to check things."

"When?"

"What?"

"When was the last time you walked the grounds to check on things?"

"Hmm ... months ago." His fingers briefly caressed the field glasses. "Look, I'll do it more often from now on."

As the chairman of the allotment, he'd be expected to check the grounds weekly. The lazy sod hadn't done that and he'd been chair for years.

Fenella let that hang and changed direction. "Did you know Fred Bickham well?"

An odd quirk touched the corner of his lips, like he was trying to keep them straight. "It all started with Fred's gardening hobby, and now it has ended with his blood soaking into the allotment soil. It is awful. I can't stop thinking about it. Killing a man in his veg plot ... it's ... barbaric. The heartbreaking horror makes me feel helpless. It's Fred's wife my heart breaks for. And his granddaughter, Ginger. He was an idol to her. And now her idol is dead. Are you close to catching the fiend?"

Fenella pulled out a bottle of pain pills from her handbag and swallowed two without water. "Anyone from the police speak with you?"

"Detective Constable Jones asked for a list of members. I've got a chat with him later today." His gaze drifted toward the crime scene, hand twitching for the binoculars. "Fred was big on the show circuit and grew vegetables too nice to eat."

There was pride in his voice and something else. Resentment? A memory tickled Fenella's mind. "You do the show's as well, don't you?"

"Aye, started showing when I was ten. It was magical when I won my first prize. It was like a drug and I wanted more." His lips twitched at the edges. "Still is, although it has been a while since I got first place. But things change, don't they?"

Fenella thought he was hiding something. "How did you meet Fred Bickham?"

George Rouge tilted his cap so it covered his eyes. "Years ago. At a show. He told me he wanted to get into gardening." Again came the strange quirk to his lips. "I taught him everything I know about growing prize turnips, rhubarb, even bell peppers and English roses."

"Friends, eh?"

"Of course."

But there was something about the way he said

those two words that made Fenella push harder.

"Close friends?"

"Look, you'll hear it from others, so you may as well get it straight from the horse's mouth. Fred and I were good friends until we fell out five years ago." George glanced at his bent stem pipe and spat. "That's about when it started."

He snorted and turned away. His lips were moving but no sound came out. The wind murmured. A flock of black-headed gulls screamed. Their shrieks faded to nothingness. Fenella waited.

George Rouge continued in a quiet hiss. "You know how it is? All your life you think about retirement and when it comes, it ain't half as golden as you dreamed. Sure, I've time on my hands to work the soil. I thought it would be all glory—ribbons and trophies for my veg." He jabbed his bent stem pipe toward the allotment. "Then Fred Bickham came along and cleaned up. The bloke won everything and to think I was the muggins who showed him the ropes."

Fenella rubbed her back with both hands. It helped. "Do you happen to own a cricket bat, Mr Rouge?"

He thought for a long while before answering. An odd curve came to his lips. "What would a man of my age be doing with one of those? It's not like I'm spritely enough to sprint between the wickets. Now unless there is anything else, I'll be on my way."

He jerked from the stool to his feet, picked it up and walked with surprising speed toward the lane. Fenella watched as he clambered with the nimbleness of a gymnast through the bushes, vanishing from sight.

As the wind whipped up into a ghostly howl, she turned to face the crime scene thinking about George Rouge and unaware of the bizarre madness to come.

CHAPTER 26

By the time Fenella reached Seaview Allotments, the low clouds had turned dark and glum. She walked the short distance to the main gate feeling much better for the fresh air. Three tugs and the ancient iron gate screeched open. It closed behind her with a solid clunk. She couldn't have imagined the news that awaited her. Not in a million years.

With every step toward the crime scene, she felt herself gaining ground. Her chat with George Rouge made her wonder who else Fred Bickham rubbed the wrong way because of his winning veg. A lot of people have an interest in gardening, but how many show their produce at shows? There'd be rivalry and jealousy and a lot of peeping between the plant pots. They'd have closely guarded secrets on how to grow lush plants that won first prize.

She sent a text message to Jones:

Focus on Seaview members who work the shows, and get a blow-by-blow account of George Rouge's movements over the past few days.

Now she took in the ramshackle scatter of sheds, lopsided fences and plots infested with weeds and brambles. Everywhere green foliage.

Everywhere plants in full bloom. Trees shimmered in the gentle breeze; their soft rustling sound soothing. From the branches a young blackbird twittered. And yet, there was the sense of a graveyard about the overgrown tangle of plots. The knowledge that bad deeds had happened and the sixth sense of more bad deeds to come.

Her mind dwelled on the terrible violence that befell Fred Bickham and she once again made a promise to pursue the truth. Only then did she set out along the dirt track that wandered through the abandoned orchard to the crime scene.

A lone officer stood in front of the cordon. He stuffed a mobile phone into his pocket as she approached and held a clipboard under his arm, his slouch giving away the boredom of the job. Logging people in and out of a crime scene dulled the mind to mush. Far worse if you were on a double shift.

Fenella recognised the officer—PC Jon Phoebe. The sun had caught half his face so he looked like a striped lobster. She knew his wife well. Smart and beautiful and popular and Fenella enjoyed going out with her and a gang of other women for meals and bingo. They gossiped until their throats were sore. Always a fun night out. Always news about other people's lives. Fenella never missed a date because she was always curious. Always wanted to know. And it had been a while since their last gossip fest.

"Look at the state of you," Fenella said. "The wife's not going to be happy with a lobster in her bed."

"She'll not complain when I have her in me claws, ma'am." PC Phoebe grinned. "Wife's having a girl's night out next Saturday. You up for it?"

"Aye, I'm in," Fenella replied. "Double shift?"

"Nah, but I'm on night duty later this week. I reckon they'll be done by dusk, ma'am." He nodded toward white-suited figures crawling in front of the crime scene tent. "Fingertip search then a few more photos and we'll be able to go home."

"Any news?" Fenella asked, suddenly aware that her back pain was easing.

"Huge excitement when one of the white suits found a nail close to where Shirley Bickham discovered her dad's body. They are testing for fingerprints and DNA."

Fenella had no idea how they could tell where the nail came from, but she hoped they would find enough evidence to identify the murderer. They watched in intense silence as the figures in white continued their search.

The waspish buzz of a generator broke into their hush. It coughed out a black plume of smoke. The arc lights flickered. The buzz faded to a gentle hum.

PC Phoebe jabbed at the clipboard. "Going in, ma'am?"

She planned to have another nosy around the crime scene to see if anything new struck her. "Nah, I want to have a walk about the rest of the allotment first. Get a feel for the place. You're a keen gardener, aren't you?"

"Weekend warrior for what it is worth."

"Know this area well?"

"Have a plot here." He pointed to the far side, under a stand of beech trees. "Me and the wife have owned if for the past three years."

Fenella glanced at the neatly tilled soil and rows of runner beans. Beyond were the iron railings of the fence and fields dotted with sheep. In the distance the faint outline of the abandoned Port St Giles lighthouse was visible under the darkening sky.

She said, "Do many people use the lane?"

"A few dog walkers, but most of the time I only see one or two fellow gardeners. It dead ends at the allotments, so you are either lost or coming here."

The killer probably knew their way around the area, Fenella thought. Or scoped it out before they struck. "How well do you know George Rouge?"

"He's always here. Always poking about. Always watching."

"I take it you find him ... intrusive?"

PC Phoebe offered a quick smile. "My wife likes his fruit and veg. And anyway..."

His voice fell away as a blackbird fled from a tangle of bushes. The wind picked up to a howl carrying a noxious smell as sour as a stomach turned bad. Dark clouds crowded close to the ground. The start of a storm?

Fenella listened for the cry of the sheep and she listened for the rumble of thunder and she listened for PC Phoebe's next words. But he seemed content to let his voice drift away and turned back to watch the crime scene.

The figures in white suits continued their crawl. A fingertip search. Inch by inch, scanning the ground for clues. No excited shouts. No fevered huddle. Slow, with no guarantee of a find.

Impatience got the better of Fenella. She tugged PC Pheobe's sleeve. "And anyway?"

He looked confused. "Sorry, ma'am?"

"You were talking about George Rouge."

"He is the kind of man who irons his underpants. Set in his ways. At his age, I don't suppose he can help it. So, I don't blame him."

"How do you mean?"

An annoyed expression crossed PC Phoebe's face. "George is the captain of the Seaview cricket team. Twenty-five years in the role and no sign of stepping down. I've put my name down for the team. Not a sniff. Loopy if you ask me." His eyes flashed with a mixture of rage and sadness. "I suppose it is the type of crazy madness you find in men who retire and have nowt to do. Think they are young again and cling onto things they should let go. Cricket is a fast-paced game these days. I'm a leopard between the wickets, if I say so myself."

"George Rouge play's cricket?" Fenella asked.

PC Phoebe shook his head. "Look, he's a control freak, likes to head up the allotment, likes to be a veg stall man, likes to be captain of the cricket team even though he has not swung a bat in years. A man who must have his way." He stopped and studied the low clouds. "Brimming with pride is Mr Rouge. Even boasts about his prize veg. The thing is, his greens have not won ought worth shouting about for years. He laughs and smiles about it, but behind the crust of his mask it must make him mad. Not easy for a man who's worked with plants all his life when a newbie like Fred Bickham beats your prize veg babies into second place."

Fenella smiled. "And what type of man was Mr Bickham?"

"Kept himself to himself. The sort of bloke who won't be missed, not because he was bad, but because you never noticed him."

It hadn't been long enough for the breeze to lift the stink. It lingered in swirls of intense plumes.

Fenella said, "When did you last visit your plot?"

"Stopped by Friday after my shift. My wife joined me. Stayed until sunset then headed home."

"Anything strike you as unusual?"

He shrugged. "Not that I can think of. A few regular faces. Nowt else."

"Send me a list of their names."

He had his mobile phone in his hand as she walked away.

CHAPTER 27

The breakthrough came with a crack of thunder and a torrential downpour of rain. Not what Fenella expected. Not in a million years.

She walked on a dirt track that passed by a row of tomato plants, trying to block out the activity at the crime scene. All her brain cells focused on the allotment and where the attacker might have lurked. Someone must have seen something. Maybe a witness worked a plot nearby?

A dented pail collected water from a dripping hose. A sheet of corrugated iron flapped in the breeze.

Bam-bam-bam.

This is just one potential hiding place, she thought, gazing at the shacks battered down by the weather dotted around the allotment. And there were bushes to hide between, and trees where you could fade into the shadows. She did a slow three-hundred-and-sixty-degree turn. There were so many places to lurk it boggled the mind.

Biting back a burst of disappointment, she spotted a deck chair shaded by an oak tree. It was the type they charged for on a beach—sturdy, with bold red and white stripes made of tough waterproof material and hung between a wooden frame. She trudged gently to the chair and eased herself down, half thinking it might collapse with unseen rot. It took her weight with a slight clunk, but held firm.

It was comfy in the light breeze. Shady too. A nice spot to relax and steal a few minutes sleep. An oasis of calm and a great place to work the muse. If only she knew what she was looking for. Her eyelids closed.

It was the mumble of voices drifting from the crime scene that woke her. Stunned by the suddenness of it, and by the thought she'd been in a deep dream, she sat for a few moments listening. The back pain was almost gone, but she couldn't see much more than plant stems. And were you kneeling and working the soil, you'd see even less. Nor could she make out the words which ebbed and flowed on the wind. That's when it hit her. A witness was unlikely to come forward. They would have had their head down with the plants and would have seen nowt even if they had been next to the plot where the killer struck.

She stood and glanced around, trying to see the run-down buildings through Fred Bickham's eyes. Not an oasis of calm but a desolate land of despair. Fred Bickham met his death alone with no one nearby to help. A carefully calculated plan by the killer?

"Aye," Fenella said, feeling her body chill. "That about sums it up."

They faced a cold bloodied killer who'd struck

twice without mercy. Not a dimwit. A planner, despicable in their devious schemes. She'd seen a figure in the fog at Mrs Fassnidge's place. Man or woman? Boy or girl? She squeezed her eyes tight shut playing and replaying the images. Just a shadow in the fog. A blur of dark in the swirl. She slumped back into the chair, deeply disturbed, staring blankly into space.

Drops fell from the dark sky with a soft pitta patter. The first wave of rain. Ear-splitting thunder shook the sky. Fenella didn't move, rooted to the spot by her muse. What if Fred Bickham was murdered elsewhere and dumped here to make a point? Hadn't Jones mentioned gangland drug lords? She'd thought he was mad, been watching too much late-night American gangster shows on the telly, but now wasn't so certain and sent a text message to Dr MacKay, the pathologist:

Any evidence the body of Fred Bickham was moved?

She relaxed a little and ran a hand over her forehead, noticing the rain for the first time. She jerked alert at the sharp screech of a voice.

"Ma'am!"

PC Phoebe dashed along the dirt path and threaded his way through a patch of brambles. He skidded to a stop by the deck chair. His chest heaved for several heartbeats. "Ma'am, I've been thinking about your question." He sucked in a huge breath and let it out in a whoosh. "The question about anything odd when I was last working the allotment."

Fenella waited. She was good at the wait.

He lowered his voice. "I was just on the phone to the wife. Not what I do regular at work, like, but ... well, there ain't much to do guarding a crime scene out here in the wilderness, and she likes a natter. We got to talking about Fred Bickham's death. Well, she jogged my memory about a man. Never seen him before. He was hanging around the lane on Friday when we left. It was the wife who noticed him. Didn't look local. Who wears a brown trilby and pea green trench coat around these parts?"

CHAPTER 28

Something was not right. Shirley Bickham's eyes snapped open, body drenched in cold sweat. That dumb nightmare again. It always jerked her awake when the nurse with the flabby arms burst into the room and dragged the baby from the cot. Still, it was better than her other dream. The one where she smashed a man's face to pulp. She always had a bad day when she had that dream. A day filled with thoughts of dark violence.

Light dribbled around the edge of the patchwork curtains. The bedside clock glowed the noon hour. She eyed the calendar—Monday. Why couldn't she relax and enjoy a lie in like normal people?

She ran a hand along her pockmarked arm and picked at a scab. If she were normal, she'd be at work by now, or at least out on the street looking for a job. But she wasn't normal. Had never been normal. Not since the ... she closed her eyes and saw the nurse with the flabby arms. And then she heard the distant cry of a baby, the giggle of Ginger and the sly whisper of her dad.

Dad had worked as a part-time youth worker with vulnerable teenagers. It gave him so much joy.

He started as the repair man but it grew to much more. He'd come home late at night with a gleam to his face and snap to his step. He had even suggested she volunteer because it might lead to an offer of a job, but she'd declined. The kids he worked with were mostly girls. No. All girls. And she had enough on her hands with Ginger. But her dad had a way with teen girls. He got them to like him, trust him, love him. And he loved them, said they made him feel young.

Shirley pressed her hands to her head. Another Monday, but this was not the start of a lazy week. This was no holiday. Her dad was gone for good and the police were sniffing about. Oh God, if only she could turn back the clock.

Her thoughts dwelled on her dad for a few minutes more then shifted to Ginger and they shifted again to Ginger's unborn baby. She sat thinking in the darkened room, hands trembling. No one must know what she had done. Not her mam, not the police. No one must know her secret.

A drink. She needed a long slow shot of gin. She hated herself for using booze to drown her woes. She wasn't a drunk or an addict. Not really. Booze steadied her nerves better than pills, and after that dream, her dad's death and the truth behind Ginger's unborn baby, well, she deserved it.

Still, she hesitated, trying to recall the medical term her psychiatrist had used to say the chemicals in her brain weren't right. Well, unless she took the pills. But psychiatric pills and booze didn't mix well, and she felt better on the booze so she ditched the pills. Just until she felt better. It didn't do any harm, did it?

The outline of the vast oak wardrobe glimmered in the grey half-light of the bedroom. It kept her secrets secure. Only she had the key. But she did not move for some time. The week ahead seemed like a visit to the depths of hell. Who wants to rush into that?

With an almighty effort, she urged herself from the bed. Alcohol made her all powerful. She could do anything when it surged through her veins. Anything. She rushed to the wardrobe eager to surrender to the warm embrace of gin. Elated, she flung the doors open, kneeling on the carpet, reaching through the softness for the feel of cold glass.

"Doom be gone. Just a long slow sip."

When you live with your mam and your teenage daughter, you must be crafty to keep your secrets. Her hands knocked aside towels and tights and socks until her fingers gripped something hard and solid and square. She pulled out the object, eyes widening. Only now did the fug of the nightmare fully clear and she remembered with horror what it took to get her hands on the wooden box. It held a secret she'd take to the grave. A secret her mam must never know about.

Her breath sped up. A cold sweat oozed from every pore. With trembling hands, she opened the lid.

"Shirl? Are you up yet?"

Shirley raced to the bed and shoved the box under the pillow as her mam, Ida Bickham, skipped into the room.

"Good morning. Up already?" Her mam hustled to the curtains, pulled them back, opened the window and stared at the garden. "What a joyous day. No point living our lives in gloom and misery, eh?"

"I'm just waking up." Shirley adjusted the pillow so it covered the box. "But I had a good sleep."

Ida turned and squinted as she adjusted her frizzy black wig. For a moment, Shirley was certain her mam saw the box under the pillow.

Ida's pale grey eyes narrowed. "Have you been drinking?"

"I just got up."

"You look ... flushed."

"Um ... I might be going down with a cold."

"I heard you screaming in your sleep. Had that nightmare again, didn't you?"

"No ... I..." Oh God, she was such a terrible liar but she had to make something up. No way was she speaking with the woman in the white coat at the hospital. She didn't want the pills either. They turned her mind to mush and she needed to keep sharp. "It's Ginger. Why hasn't she called?"

Ida gave a tight smile. "That girl has a mind of her own."

Shirley's stomach churned. Why was she such a moron? Her mam knew where Ginger was hiding, knew she was safe. It was written all over her Mona Lisa smile.

"But where is she?" Shirley asked.

Ida said nothing.

Bloody hell, Shirley thought, trying not to lose her rag. Wasn't she the best mother in the world? Why the hell did they always keep her in the dark? Stay calm. Stay cool. If she lost it, she'd turn violent—throw things, scream, pick up something heavy and swing it. When the rage took her, the world became a crimson blur. She didn't want to go back to the hospital. Didn't want to end up in the padded room. She stared at her mam, body vibrating with deadly fury.

Ida said, "I know it is a shock that she is with child, but give the girl time."

"I must speak with her."

Ida sighed and shook her head.

The worst thing was how they kept their secrets out in the open so you knew they were there. Did they think she was some down-and-out tramp too wasted to care?

Another wave of rage ravaged Shirley. Her voice trembled. "What is she doing for money?"

Ida turned back to the window; face hidden in shade. "She has savings."

"From where? She doesn't have a job."

Ida shrugged. "Ginger is careful with her cash. Can't see her living at home and feeding off her mam when she is forty."

Now Shirley really needed a drink. "It is not

my fault," she said quietly. She didn't need another reminder that this hell-hole was her fortieth birthday week. "Anyway, you don't seem half as frantic as you were yesterday."

Ida kept her back to the room. "I don't know what you mean."

"It wasn't me who ran in here in a fluster and called the police."

"And why not?" Ida spun and her lips twitched into a snakish smile. "That's the first thing any mam worth their salt would do, honey. The very first thing."

Shirley said nothing. She was five when she stole the bag of cheese and onion crisps. The man behind the counter shouted. But she'd taken off, through the door and out into the street. She knew a quiet corner in the park where she could enjoy the crispy delights—a nook in the trunk of an ancient oak tree where only small kids could squeeze in.

It was the strength in the man's hand she felt first. Digging into her shoulder. "Caught ya," he said with a sneer, and marched her to the police station. They put her in a room with iron bars on the windows and she'd cried her heart out, confessing what she'd done. She thought she'd never see her home again. But her dad showed up, wrapped his strong arms around her and took her home. He never told her mam, but the smell of cheese and onion crisps still made her feel sick.

"I'm sorry, honey," Ida said. "Look, I'm not pointing fingers, just speaking my mind. I love you,

Shirl."

Ida hurried light-footed across the room, arms wide for a big hug. The wild fury which consumed Shirley vanished in the warm embrace. Her mam knew how to pull her strings.

"Poor thing," Ida said. "Your life's been a mess since Ginger's birth."

Shirley wondered if her mam would still hug her if she knew she had that box under her pillow. She snuggled deeper into the hug, knocking the pillow with her elbow. It tumbled to the floor. The wooden box followed, landing on the carpet with a thud.

Oh God no! Shirley wanted to throw up. It was all going horribly wrong. She knew what came next. She'd be marched to the police station, forced to confess. Oh no, she didn't want to spend another night in a police cell. What the hell to say? She tried to speak but no words came out.

Ida looked at the pillow and she looked at the wooden box and she looked at her daughter. "That is your dad's medal box. The box where he keeps his gold medals."

Slowly, she picked up the box and tenderly opened it. Her face crinkled as she peered inside.

Now there was only silence.

Ida closed the lid and sighed. "That woman detective wants to speak with me about your dad. She'll be around at three. Get dressed and clear off. Leave the talking to me. We are family, Shirl. We must stick together. Your mam will sort it out."

CHAPTER 29

The total collapse of Den Ogden's day began near the abandoned lighthouse on the Port St Giles Pier. He crouched on a bench staring at the pier entrance and the boardwalk beyond. The breeze held back the threat of rain. A watery sun glimmered through the clouds. A herring gull screamed.

In the twenty plus years Den had roamed from town to town, he thought he'd seen it all. From cockroach infested boarding houses to bed and breakfasts where five people shared a room. In all that time, he'd always had a roof over his head and a belly full of food.

But today was different.

Because there were no coins in his pockets and sod all in his wallet. He was flat broke, no job and living with a dog in a boarded-up pizza parlour. He needed money and he needed it fast. He waited patiently on the bench for his boat to come in. Not long now.

Elfrid lay by the feet of his master. The old dog gazed down through the slats at the waves lapping the pilings. Groups of teenagers roamed the pier, on their lunch break from the high school. They yelled and laughed with the joyous energy of youth.

And they ate from huge bags of fish and chips, the savoury aroma filling the air. Herring gulls hovered overhead, watchful. Den's stomach rumbled.

"We will eat like kings tonight, boy. I promise," Den said, eyeing a young lad wolfing down a slab of battered fish.

Elfrid glanced up with a snout full of teeth that looked like he was smiling. Something flickered in the dog's eyes.

Den said, "Don't nag. I haven't eaten either. I'm not to blame for this dumb mess. You do your job. I'll do mine. Our boat will soon be here."

A lad and lass, from the school, slipped from the lighthouse, hand in hand, leaving the door ajar. Den felt his heart tug. He'd never found love at that age. The girls he liked poked fun of his double chin and made puke noises when he approached.

The teenagers began to wander off to school. Within ten minutes, Den was alone on the pier. He glanced at his watch and felt the first stab of tightness in his chest. He was meeting the Russian with rag doll eyes. The man had a way of making you feel uneasy. Lots of menace behind those rag doll eyes.

Nothing will go wrong, he told himself, but the Russian had laughed when Den called. Told him cash was hard to come by, interest rates sky high and he wasn't sure he could help. Always the same act with Rag Doll Eyes: make them suffer. Den tried not to sound cheesed off at having to beg and grovel and plead for money with loan shark interest rates. At last, and with a cheery voice, the Russian agreed to meet him on the pier, but warned him not to be late.

"Sit on a bench near the lighthouse and wait," Rag Doll Eyes had said.

Den arrived early. Two hours early. He'd wait all day if that is what it took to get his hands on a wad of the loan shark's cash. He smiled at Elfrid.

"Wag your tail when the Russian arrives."

Soon he'd have a stack of money to tide him over until his next job ended. Nine months of bills is a long time, but the Russian with rag doll eyes had the cash. At a price. Den factored that into his venture. He'd always made a huge profit. He just needed to find the right job soon.

Two herring gulls squabbled over a fish and chip wrapper. Maybe he should snatch it from them, see if there was anything left for him and Elfrid to eat?

Instead of fighting gulls, Den stared at his watch—an hour to go. Might as well get some shut eye. Nothing like the sound of waves crashing against a pier to ease you into the land of snooze. His eyelids closed.

"What type of dog is she?"

The voice broke into Den's dream at the point where his plate brimmed with steak and ale pie and he was about to take a bite. Elfrid's bowl overflowed with prime beef strips. He wanted a bite of that too. Who? Where? Confused, he blinked, expecting to see the sneering face of the Russian with rag doll eyes. He blinked again.

She was in her late teens. Plump as a ripe melon even in an oversized neon pink puffer jacket which stretched over her wide hips. A dowdy pink skirt and pink ankle boots made up the rest of her wardrobe. Big boned and porky dressed in pink.

Den held back a grin at the lardy lass and continued to take her in. A mess of blue hair straggled to her shoulders in greasy clumps. Her top teeth jutted over her bottom lip, and her sharp, angular, nose flayed out at the tip. A smear of acne splattered her flabby cheeks. An angry red wart sagged from the right corner of her bottom lip. It was her small eyes that should have bothered Den—dark and quick, with trouble in their sharp gleam.

"Eh?" Den raked a slow hand over his chin, not sure of the question, but knowing there was one. "What did you say?"

Her small dark eyes darted from the dog to Den and back again. "What breed is she?"

"It's a he," Den said. "And I don't think he has much of a pedigree."

"Can I pet him?"

"Sure."

The girl sat crossed legged on the wooden slats next to Elfrid, whispering into his ear. The dog's tail began to thump.

A wave of joy surged through Den. His luck had turned. His idea worked. Elfrid, the ugly beast with the smiling snout, attracted teenage girls like fish bait. Oh Lord, he could kiss the dog. From now on, life would be easy.

"I got him from the town shelter, saved him from the vet," Den said.

The girl's eye's widened. "You mean they were going to put him down?"

Den nodded. Again, he snatched a sly glance at her body. Not much up top. Strong hips, broad thighs, face bordering on the ugly. Perfect. He had a system that worked like magic. Pull on their heartstrings and watch them dance.

The girl's gaze fell back to the dog. "What's his name?"

"Elfrid," Den replied, placing a hand on his dome shaped double chin. He waited a heartbeat, knowing his next move might end the game.

"And your name?"

She poked at the wart on her lip. "Penny. Penny Adcock."

"Nice to meet you, Penny." His thin slitty lips curved into a smile. "I'm Den."

"Den as in Dennis?"

"Denizio. It's Italian."

Penny said, "Hiya Denizio."

"Hiya Penny."

Stick to the well-worn plan, Den told himself. Yes, it might take several days, but he'd have Penny Adcock on his hook. Smitten. Deeply in love. His to do with as he pleased. He'd work her like a farmer works fertile soil. Hard and steady until it bears fruit. Today, he thought, my luck has turned.

"I'm new to town," Den said. "Do you work near here?"

"Part-time at Logan's bakery."

Joy of joys, she had a job. Den couldn't believe his luck. The gulls continued to squabble over the fish and chip paper. His stomach grumbled.

"You hungry?" he asked.

"I'm vegan."

"Me too," Den replied.

God this was easy. He'd suggest lunch somewhere nice, make out he'd lost his wallet, and get the lardy lass to pay. Not a vegan place. No way. He'd order steak and ale pie with lashings of gravy and no veg. A bowl of steak strips for the dog. Not a big ask. Nothing to break the bank. Not at first.

But he had a question. The same hook bait question he had used for years. He rubbed his dome of a chin. "I'm going to take a wild guess. I'm betting you are … twenty-five. No, twenty-three."

She grinned exposing a mouth full of teeth. They always grinned. Always wanted to seem older. He knew how their minds worked.

"What has it got to do with you?"

"Just asking," he replied, his hand still stoking his double chin.

My God, he was on his game and feeling good. He liked them plump and fresh and stupid. Eighteen, he guessed. Fertile soil. His girls had to be at least seventeen. No older than twenty. Older girls gave too much trouble. They'd lived a little and knew the score. Younger led to trouble from the law. He'd learned the hard way, got away by the skin of his teeth. Were they still looking for him? That's why he moved from town to town, staying in each new place for no more than a year. People forget your face if they don't see you every day. Den preferred it that way.

He gazed at his watch—forty minutes before his meeting with the Russian with rag doll eyes. Plenty of time for a little side business.

Penny was still considering his answer. He snatched a sly glance at her flat breasts. Oh, how he loved teenage girls. Not the confident ones. He sought the weak-minded and feeble and those who thought they were no good. The spotty and bloated and those with bad teeth. Runaways were best, or girls from broken homes where money was an issue. Plain and dowdy Penny Adcock fit the bill.

Penny smiled, but did not speak.

Den licked his cracked lips as he savoured his first bite in a long lean while. No way he'd throw roly-poly Penny back. Eighteen was just the right age. He'd haul her in with his biggest net.

He tried to hide his impatience. "Come on then, how old are you? Don't tell me you are thirty?"

"Do I look like an old fogy?"

"No, but I can see you are a woman of the world."

Penny giggled. "I'm thirteen, and have the day off school because I went to the doctor." She lowered her voice. "Twelve right now, but thirteen this August."

"Jesus Christ," Den yelled. "Leave off the dog or I'll set him on you. Tear off your face, he will. Savage it, so it doesn't look so damn ugly."

Penny sprang to her feet and faced him squarely. Her eyes blazed in fury. "What did you say?"

"Bugger off you fat cow." Den's thin mouth stretched so wide his front teeth jutted out. "Else I'll have you on the butcher's slab and feed your bones to the pigs. Except your fat head. I've got a bleedin' big hook for that and will roast it on a bonfire. See, me and the dog ain't eaten for days. Think we'll enjoy the meat feast."

Den lurched from the bench snatching at her face, fingers curled into claws. Just to frighten her away. A twelve-year-old! What the hell did she take him for?

Penny screamed and took off in a splay-footed waddle. At the entrance of the pier, she turned left onto the boardwalk, her pink puffer jacket merging with the crowd. It was then that Den became conscious of a short figure weaving through the throng. A fat meatball of a man with toothpick legs.

Den squinted. Yes, it was him. The Russian with rag doll eyes. And he was early.

"Money," Den whispered to Elfrid. "Here comes cash on two legs."

The Russian with rag doll eyes stopped at the entrance of the pier. He fooled around with a mobile phone, although his head swivelled owl like. You don't rise through the loan shark ranks without being damn sure you are not being followed.

Den shoved his shaking hands into his pockets.

This was it. Pay day. Steak and ale pie and steak strips for Elfrid.

He considered climbing on the bench so he was easy to spot, but thought it would draw too much attention. The last thing he wanted was some sharp-eyed police officer accusing him of hooliganism and peppering him with questions. He shuddered. If they nabbed him, found out about his system, they'd toss him behind bars and throw away the key.

The Russian looked back along the boardwalk. Past the ornate lampposts lit on bonfire night. Past the row of wooden stalls which served as gift shops during the summer. If Den had been closer, he'd have been able to follow the man's gaze. Impossible from where he sat.

As Den was thinking about how much to ask for, the Russian with rag doll eyes took off at a fast walk. Away from the entrance of the pier. Putting as much space as possible between himself and Den. Almost sprinting now.

"Hey," Den yelled, clambering onto the bench. "Over here."

A flash of pink on the boardwalk caused his heart to skip a beat. Penny Adcock was jabbing and pointing and striding toward the pier with two policemen at her side.

CHAPTER 30

When Shirley Bickham scurried from the house in her pink headscarf, she had no idea where to go. The air was cool and crisp with black clouds hanging so low the street took on a grim sheen. A storm was brewing. A bloody big one. She couldn't shake the unnerving sensation that she should run back home and slam the door tight shut.

But the last thing she wanted was to face the woman detective coming to speak with her mam. If she went back, she might leave the house in handcuffs.

The front gardens in the street seemed to shimmer. The sodden lawns and dark net curtained windows danced. Shirley's gut spun in sour angst. Foul-tasting acid crawled up her throat. Why did she hide her dad's medal box under that damn pillow? That was bonkers. Why was she such a fool? There was something off about the day from the moment she opened her eyes. More nasties to come, though she didn't know what.

From behind, came the grumble of an engine. She looked back. A blue Morris Minor crawled to a stop outside her mam's house. A slender woman with shoulder length grey hair climbed out. The woman slammed the car door and strode with zeal to her mam's front door. She exuded a strange confidence that told the world she knew what she wanted and would get it.

Shirley watched in horror. No screaming sirens. No flashing lights. But that was the detective. What was her name? Sallow. Fenella Sallow. She knew a busy body when she saw one, but this woman was nosy above and beyond the blue uniform. This woman would grab at a secret and shake it until everything lay exposed. Oh God, she needed a drink.

Shirley tightened her headscarf, turned in haste and hurried away, not wanting to draw the detective's eye. Mam would take care of it. She always did.

It wasn't until Shirley was around the bend and huffing for breath at the bus stop that the first stirrings of fury grumbled. Why was she running like a convicted crook? They had nothing on her. She should go back to the house to hear what they were saying. The detective would talk about Dad. How he died. What they'd found. There would be questions about what he did in his free time. His hobbies. Shirley frowned. Dad was either digging his veg or down the Hope Haven shelter with the teenage girls. His two loves, she supposed. And of course, he doted on Ginger.

As she slumped on the metal bench at the bus stop, Shirley's heart pounded uncomfortably, and she began to have the uneasy feeling that the detective's questions would turn to her.

She cursed. "I must go back to the house and stand shoulder to shoulder with my mam. Together, we'll face down that detective."

The sound of the voice made her jump. It seemed to come from far away, but when she glanced around, she realised it came from her throat. It was one thing to think words, another to say them out loud. She'd been doing a lot of that lately. Jabbering away like a child with a secret friend. Was it the pills? Was it a good idea to go back home?

Her mind flipped to the detective. Yes, she, Shirley Bickham, could exude just as much confidence once she had a drink to steady her nerves. She'd go back to the house and stand side by side with her mam.

She set out flushed of dread and full of fury. She'd give that detective what for, beat her at her own game. What family lets an outsider into its private affairs?

The slip-slop of her footsteps echoed in the silent street. Anger surged through her veins. She picked up the pace. This wasn't nuts she told herself over and over. What she did, had done, would do, made sense to her and that meant she wasn't crazy.

"You are a careful planner with a fine eye for detail," the psychiatrist had said.

She recalled the grey medical eyeballs watching her, assessing her condition, writing in a notebook, nodding as they explained. They must have prescribed half a dozen pills.

Mam pestered and pushed until Shirley promised to take them. Still thinks she swills them down daily with a mug of tea. Shirley knew better. Who wants to be a walking zombie? But part of her was scared of what happens when she does not take them. The blackouts. The wild rage. The violence.

And she hadn't taken them for over a week. Not since she asked her dad why Ginger always spends her weekends with him in his single room bedsit. There is only one creaky old bed. Where does she sleep? Dad's Adam's apple bobbed. He flashed his sly smile. But he didn't say a word.

Slip-slop. Slip-Slop.

She tried to walk with less sound, but her legs were heavy. She slowed, thinking about her late-night visit to Mrs Fassnidge's boarding house. What a bloody mess! It was not as quick or as clean as she would have liked, but the dark and the fog helped. *A careful planner.*

A nasty twinge pulsated in Shirley's neck. A thought slammed her brain. She stopped. What did she do with the black clothes she wore on the night she went back to her dad's flat? The plan was to burn them to ashes. *For dust thou art, and unto dust shalt thou return.*

Shirley clutched her head with both hands. The clothes were still in her bedroom, and the detective was in the house.

"Oh God, what have I done to deserve this?" She was shouting now, screaming at the top of her voice.

"I'm a great mam. A caring person who is trying to do her best."

She needed a drink, couldn't very well knock back shots of gin with the police in the house. And there was her mam's beady eye and sharp nose. No, she had to push on to wherever it was she was going. She must keep her head down, get on with the rest of her life and hope her dark secret never came out. Mam knew what to say.

Shirley wandered back to the empty bus stop, mind whirling. Black wisps of cloud danced in demented swirls. She sat on the metal bench and considered her next steps. There were two parts to her problem. First: where to get a strong drink? Easily solved—take the bus to the beach, find a pub then burn off the toxic effects with a stroll on the sand. Second: she had to purge herself of the guilt and shame. The Irish priest in the black cassock with lemon breath had said, "Talk it out to lift the burden. A problem shared is a problem halved."

And it worked. Shirley's pent-up rage withered when she shared. The urge for violence faded when she prayed. Not that it did much to quell her desire for revenge. Vengeance always burned wild and hot in her breast, even when she took the pills and told everyone they helped.

A quick glance both ways. No sign of the bus. Not a soul in the street. She ripped out her mobile phone from her handbag, telling herself what she was about to do wasn't a sign of madness. She hesitated, preparing herself. Then she dialled.

"Hello?" The deep voice sounded groggy like the call jerked him from deep sleep.

"It's me Shirl."

"Shirl!"

"I'm sorry Dad, I had to call. I hope you understand. See, I'm not nuts. God wanted it this way. His plan, not mine. Mam will help us and your medals are safe." Shirley was speaking faster now, spitting out words like sparks of fire. "Pray for me, Dad. Yes, we'll give the body a good send off. Weeping and moaning and gnashing of teeth. And I promise to plant geraniums on the grave. Wine red, with lots of mulch so they grow with thick green leaves. Make you proud."

She hung up, shuddering with raw excitement, lungs oozing out heavy breaths. She pictured her dad's sly smile, his strong arms around her ... around Ginger. Life and death and babies growing in their bellies. She laughed. Dad dead? That's crazy talk. He wasn't dead, just hiding in a place where the police couldn't find him. She'd go there too if they came after her. She didn't know who the bloke was she found in her dad's allotment on her birthday. She didn't know why the poor sod's face had been battered to mush.

Shirley picked at a scab on her arm. She must remember to take her pills. But not yet. Not until after the funeral and they had buried the body, and the police had gone away. How long would that be? Weeks? Months. She longed for things to go back to the way they were. She longed to be normal.

The wind picked up, snatching leaves from the trees and tossing them along the street. It hissed with a haunting howl.

Oh crap, she forgot to mention she'd found out about Ginger's baby. She swallowed. Call him back? Her finger twitched toward redial. Before it touched the screen, the nurse with the flabby arms popped into her mind with a baby cradled against her breast. *Tell them nothing* the nurse said, eyes glowing like hot coals.

"Purge me," Shirley whispered. "Purge my nasty, lurid soul."

She squeezed her eyes shut, but she stifled the instinct to bow her head like when she was in church. She was not in church. She was not kneeling in a pew. She was at a bus stop with her eyes closed and God knows who else watching.

Her eyes twitched open and blind rage surged through her chest. For an instant, her world was swamped by ragged fury. She'd wipe the grin off that bloody nurse's face. In her mind she was an animal now. A rabid dog. Manic. Pure savage mania. Barking like a thug. Spitting venom at its master. Lunging, teeth bared. Quiet Fido turned into a devil dog. Tearing. Slashing. Biting. Blood everywhere. She'd make the nurse with the flabby arms pay. Make them all pay.

Lost in her toxic thoughts, in her vile dreamworld, in the tearing of flesh and gushing of blood, Shirley didn't hear the low wheeze and mechanical sigh.

"Hop on lass," the bus driver said, eyes dropping to her right hand. "You can chat to your fancy man on the way."

Dazed, Shirley gazed at the phone gripped so tight her knuckles were white. She smiled at the driver then peered at the screen, focusing on the number she'd dialled. Her eyes grew to saucers and her head thudded as though bombs were exploding in her brain cells. Because it was not her dad's number. It was some random number. She had dialled the telephone number of some bloke she didn't know.

CHAPTER 31

Fenella flashed a broad smile when Ida Bickham opened the front door, partly to be friendly and partly because her back pain was gone and partly because it was always a challenge when a loved one dies, even worse when it is murder.

"Come in." Ida's voice, light and airy, could not hide the abject misery in her face. She adjusted her frizzy black wig, turned and moved with such light-footed speed she might have been a twenty-year-old.

They entered the front room that smelled musty like the tang of a used bookshop. The curtainless windows were closed, lattice panes smeared with grime so the sunlight died on the way in. A walnut bookshelf stood next to a corner bar. Swirls of mauve speckled the deep pile carpet, and a glass-top coffee table stood between two grey-brown wingback armchairs. There was something churchlike about the room, something of the solemn glumness of a shrine. And there was something else about the place. Something that bothered Fenella.

Trinkets cluttered the mantelshelf—a dancing black rabbit with a white collar, family photos, a cow bell and a horse shoe. Laid out like an altar, Fenella thought. That black rabbit with the white around its neck might be a priest. A watercolour of the Port St Giles lighthouse hung on the wall above the fireplace.

They stood for a minute in the middle of the room and listened to the soft hiss of the wind in the fireplace.

"I thought it best if we speak in here," Ida said, watching her through pale grey eyes. "We'll have more privacy here."

This room is for posh guests, Fenella thought as her eye travelled over the photos. She would have preferred to sit in the kitchen with the hissing kettle and humming fridge. To get people to share their secrets you have to make them feel at ease. Much harder in this glum space. She shivered at the cold chill of the room, wishing she had some good news to warm up the atmosphere.

"That you and Fred?" Fenella asked, studying a framed photograph in the centre of the mantelshelf.

"Taken on our wedding day," Ida replied. "Old-style film where you never knew what would come out. We had to pose for ages to get it right. No digital snapshots in those days. Please — take a seat. I've brewed a pot of tea. I know you like custard creams."

"Aye, that will be champion," Fenella said, wondering how Ida knew she had a taste for the sandwich biscuit.

Ida didn't move. There was something she wanted to ask. She cleared her throat. "Have you caught Fred's killer?"

There was such hope in her voice it broke Fenella's heart. She considered her response and realised it was more than hope in Ida Bickham's voice. It was desperation. The woman wanted the killer caught and she wanted the killer thrown behind bars. Like yesterday. So she could breathe easy and relax, presumably. But policing didn't work like that. They'd got so few leads they were still grasping at straws.

Fenella said, "No, luv. How about that tea?"

Ida returned with a silver tray, the type you use for the vicar. She placed it on the coffee table between the wing-backed chairs and nodded Fenella to a seat. Ida eased into the opposite chair, poured. They sampled the custard creams in silence.

When the plate was almost empty Fenella said, "I'll not beat about the bush. I've no news on your Fred. But we do have forensic teams working the allotment and his room at the boarding house. There is a good chance we'll have something to go on when they are done."

Ida sat up straight. "Is Mrs Fassnidge's death related to Fred?"

So, she'd heard. Not a surprise. Foul news leaks out fastest. "We must consider all possibilities at this stage," Fenella said. "Tell me about Fred's relationship with his landlady."

Her grey pale eyes blinked. "Relationship?"

"How did they meet?"

"I've no idea."

Again Fenella waited.

Ida clasped her hands together. "Fred found the room on a noticeboard in a café—the Grub Pot. He said the place was a bit of a dive, but he felt it best if he moved out of ...this house."

"Why?"

Ida picked up a custard cream and nibbled. "Is this necessary?"

"Aye, luv. We have to build a full picture."

Ida frowned. "No. I won't talk about it until I've seen Fred's body. I must speak with him in private first."

Not much Fenella could say to that. Not without going all stroppy and raising the temperature in the room. She'd wait, wasn't sure it was material anyway, but it didn't hurt to pry.

She changed the subject. "I saw your daughter in the street."

"Shirley?"

"In a pink headscarf. She was hanging around like she wanted to come back home but wasn't sure. What was that about?"

"It has not been an easy week for her." Ida's voice sounded strange. Formal. Like a lawyer clearing her throat before she started the defence. "She just turned forty, and finding her dad ... dead..."

Her voice trailed off.

Fenella said nothing.

Ida said, "I guess Shirl is on her way to the job centre."

Fenella glanced at her watch. Almost one. "Shouldn't she be there at nine?"

Ida didn't speak for a long time and when she did, her face seemed very old. "We've never been able to find Shirley's natural talent. She has had a difficult time holding down work being a single mother."

Fenella recalled Shirley's grainy breath. The tell-tale smell hovered over the lass like a shroud. No point beating about the bush. "Does she have a problem with drink?"

Ida's face became a mask. "She is clean for a while and then she lapses. I suppose it has to do with the..."

She stopped, her face flushing as though she'd given away a family secret. As though she had said too much.

Fenella waited, hoping the silence would tickle Ida's tongue. She'd turned the wait into an art. Never rush. Be patient. Give them time to spill their secrets. It was amazing how many detectives failed to use time to their advantage.

Ida took a deep breath and became very still. It was as though she were going back in time. Searching a pocket of memory. At last, she spoke. "Shirl is an amazing daughter. Whenever she lost a job, she'd speak with incredible hope about her dreams—college, a profession, a big house in the country. We always hoped for the best. It was only as the cracks widened that we saw things for what they were." She stopped, glanced around, eyes clouded and in the past. "Alcohol is the bane of our Shirley's life. A bogeyman who keeps coming back to ravage and destroy."

"It can't have been easy," Fenella said and waited for more.

"I refuse to go into the gory details. Hell and fury will have to suffice. Enough to say that we support Shirley as best we can. I can't deny that at times Fred and I felt we'd failed her. That is why he made such a fuss over Ginger. Fred doted on the girl. Swelled with pride."

Again she stopped and frowned.

Fenella said, "Go on, luv. I'm listening."

"Those two had a special relationship. His death has hit Ginger hard. Maybe he should have married her." Ida laughed without mirth. "He loved Ginger so much. We all do. And now my Fred is ... dead."

Her voice fell away, hands flying to cover her face. If she sobbed, the sound was so quiet it didn't reach Fenella's ears. And the way her body shook might have been mistaken for laughter.

Fenella watched Ida closely, waited for the shaking to ease, then cleared her throat. "You look as frail as a fawn, but I reckon you are a tigress."

Ida's hands dropped from her face and she looked away.

Fenella waited a heartbeat. "Mrs Bickham, do you play cricket?"

"No," she replied, turning to gaze at Fenella with a huge smile. "Can't abide the game."

"What about Shirley?"

Her smile became a straight line. "Shirley is the last person in the world who'd be seen in cricket whites."

"On my first visit, she said her dad forced her to play the game when she moved back home."

"Did she?" Ida rolled her eyes. "It didn't last long, only a few weeks, really. She gave away her gear ages ago. She won't even watch the game anymore." Ida touched a finger to her lips. "Fred was great at the game, won awards. Lots of them. He was a fantastic bowler and good with the bat. Good in the field, too. An all-rounder. I think he took his kit with him or gave it away. It's been a few years since he played. Ten years … no … twenty at least. Is it important? Would you like me to search the loft now?"

"No, luv. That won't be necessary."

A whip of cold air blasted from the fireplace into the yawning silence. Fenella's gaze drifted to the clutter of the mantelshelf, focusing on the photos. They were like a memory going back in time. Deeper and deeper. Snapshots of life captured and gone. Next to the dancing rabbit was a photo of a woman in a black leotard. She stood on the tips of her toes, arms raised above her head, a grin as fat as a melon. A giddy snapshot of a fun moment. A faded photograph of Ida Bickham.

Fenella tilted her neck from side to side. "I see you were a dancer."

Ida's gaze travelled to the mantelshelf, lingering on the photo in the way a tourist gorges on the view. She rose from her chair, walked to the mantelshelf, picked up the photo and eyed it with a sad frown. She placed it to her lips. Kissed it.

"I was a whizz in ballet," Ida said, placing the photo next to the rabbit. "I got selected to tour with a dance troupe. The best five years of my life. After, I learned to act and took to the stage. Musicals. I never quite made it to stardom, but in my last show I played the lead."

"Oh aye," Fenella said. "What show was that?"

"I played Fantômas in an all-woman cast of the show with the same name."

Fenella smiled. "Cat burglar, wasn't he?"

Ida's eyebrows rose. "I see you know your French shows."

Fenella grinned. "I saw the show in London. Years ago. Inspector Juve, journalist Jérôme Fandor and Lady Beltham, eh? It stayed with me."

"Really?"

"Aye, luv. And you played the ruthless and cunning Fantômas?"

"I wasn't very good at it." Ida gave a tight smile, eyes as watchful as a priest. "The show only ran for two weeks. I've given up the acting lark, not a first love. But I still dance a little, not quite as delicate on my feet as I once was, but not too bad for a woman of..."

Her voice trailed off, and it seemed her eyes were in the past.

No one likes to feel old, Fenella thought. The years pass in such a whirl the best we can do is hope we don't notice until the very end. She completed Ida's sentence with her own spin. "For a woman of any age, eh?"

Ida smiled; her eyes gleaming like pearls. "Most youngsters can't hold a candle to my moves."

"I can see you are fit."

"Very."

"And Fred, was he into sports these days?"

"If you count drinking in the Navigator Arms and darts."

"Not sporty then?"

"Not like he was in the past. You never are when you get old."

"Did he own a cricket bat?"

"If he did, he took it with him when he moved out. Why do you ask?"

Fenella ignored the question. "Did Fred rent a lock-up or storage shed?"

Ida made a humming sound as though she were rummaging around in her mind. "No, I don't believe he rented a lock-up. He was mad about his veg and would get irate if the buds didn't show or the weather was off. Not that bad weather should come as a shock to those who live in this town. That allotment turned him into a right old grumble wart. But he was good at it. One of the best in the county. Won all sorts of awards—"

"Including the Johnny Dew's Organic Garden Centre gold medal," Fenella said. "Four years in a row. A record isn't that?"

"Fred was proud of his veg," Ida said. "Very proud indeed."

Fenella gaze fell to the plate of custard creams. Three left. She picked one up, took a bite. "Those medals."

"What about them?"

"Must be worth a lot of money, being gold."

Ida said nothing.

Fenella took a bite and munched for a moment. "We've not been able to find any of them. Did he keep them here?"

Ida held Fenella's gaze for a long moment, then she gave another tight smile. "Fred took everything. Plant pots, shoelaces, his medals and his trophies."

Fenella glanced back at the plate but decided she'd have enough. "What do you think happened to his medals?"

"I suppose he might have sold them." Ida was quiet for a moment. "Or perhaps the killer stole them. I wish I could help, but I can't."

Fenella flashed an encouraging smile. "You have already been a great help."

"I have?"

"Aye, luv. Now, have you seen anyone hanging around? A stranger?"

"I don't think so."

"What about a man in a pea green raincoat wearing a brown trilby, does that ring any bells?"

Ida's eyes glittered. "Oh my God, yes. Certainly. When I met him, I fell instantly in love. It was the hat and coat. He dazzled me and looked so professional. I'm a sucker for a man with good tastes."

Fenella said, "I'm not with you, pet. Are you telling me you have met the man I've just described?"

"Of course I have! My Fred wore a pea green trench coat and a brown trilby when I first met him. He wore them for years, even when they fell out of fashion. But that was decades ago. How on Earth did you find that out?"

CHAPTER 32

When Fenella left Ida Bickham's home, she thought the strange feeling about the room where they had talked might have been due to the closed windows. The place needed a good airing and the glass panes scrubbed clean. But a lot of homes she visited could benefit from the same treatment, including, alas, her house. What was it about that room?

As she settled into her car, the oddness of the room struck her harder. The cluttered mantelshelf with the dancing black rabbit and the aged photos of Ida adorned in a black leotard doing ballet was somehow odd. It felt like she'd stepped into the secret shrine of a weird cult. A holy place where joy lived in the past and the bold vigour of youth glowed from faded photos. Ida Bickham adored dance and mourned a life that died with her final stage curtain. And Fred Bickham wore a pea green trench coat and brown trilby when he was younger.

What did it mean? Fenella sensed it wasn't good. But one thing she knew for sure, the anguish on Ida Bickham's face was real. Mrs Bickham wasn't the person she used to be. Fred Bickham's death had changed her.

Fenella reached into her pocket, searching for her car keys, when her fingers stumbled across the eggplant brooch. She pulled it out, looking at it as it sparkled. *It will bring you luck*, the young girl, Cherry Dew, had said. But the more she looked at it, the more expensive it appeared. She'd give it back when she got the chance.

She dropped the brooch in her pocket and saw her car keys. She'd left them in the ignition. A police officer ought to know better, she told herself, lowering the window and looking back at the cottage. Ida Bickham stood in the doorway, watching.

Her phone buzzed—Dexter.

"Guv, anything come from your meeting with Ida Bickham?"

He was like a radar, always on the lookout for what was coming, always in the know about what was happening. A gift, she thought with fondness. Her detective sergeant's deft skills made her life a little easier.

She said, "Mrs Bickham is a dancer, light on her feet, rabbit fast, retired now."

"Wonder if she knows my Priscilla?"

Priscilla, his ex-girlfriend, sang in nightclubs and had recently gone to America to pursue her career.

Fenella said, "Mrs Bickham is more upscale than the nightclub scene. She danced in posh theatres and also trained as an actor."

Fenella turned to watch the Bickham house.

Ida was still on the doorstep, fists resting on her hips.

"A bonny belle of the stage," Dexter said. "A star, eh? Has she won any awards or been on the telly?"

"Don't know, but I reckon she could charm the legs off a flea, and be as brisk as a chill sea breeze. Fluid is the way I'd describe her, and alert with a vibe I can't quite catch."

"All them stage folks have a bit of flair, guv. Their talent is like fog. You can see it but can't catch it in your hand. They ain't like us normal folk. One night my Priscilla stands up in the middle of bingo and sings. I saw the fog that night."

"Did they clap?"

"Guv?"

"When she finished her song at bingo?"

"Oh aye. She had them on their feet with a Diana Ross number. The bingo place invited her back, paid her too. It turned into a regular gig."

He began to sing the opening lines of *You Can't Hurry Love*.

Fenella hummed along for a few bars. How on earth did they end up singing? Focus, she told herself, clapping her hands. "We can enjoy your silky tones at a later date. Put yourself down for the staff karaoke night."

"Got carried away, guv."

She could hear the grin in his voice, quelled the urge to laugh and said, "Ida Bickham is hiding something."

"Worth my while having a follow-up chat with

her, guv?"

"Nah. Once we get the preliminary report from Dr MacKay we'll have a better handle on the exact time frame to home in on. But she knows something."

Dexter went quiet for a moment. "Might be nowt, guv, but the duty sergeant, Len Moreland, recalled a Mr Fred Bickham visiting the station last Wednesday. He asked to speak with a detective. An appointment was made for the following day, but Mr Bickham never showed up."

"Any idea what he wanted?"

"Nope."

There was a moment of silence, the background grumble of a car creeping along the street.

Dexter said, "Do you think Fred Bickham's death might be a marital tiff gone wrong?"

"Not your regular tiff," Fenella replied. "Not with a cricket bat full of nails. The killer knew Fred Bickham's routine. Knew he would be at Seaview Allotments. Knew the place would be deserted. It might have been brewing for years. Time enough to plan for revenge. We've seen it before and we'll see it again. I'll not rule Ida Bickham out just yet."

She glanced at the Bickham doorway. Ida was gone.

Dexter said, "Been rooting around for this bloke in the brown trilby."

"Oh aye," Fenella said and waited.

"Shook the trees hard and nowt came out."

Dexter paused, and she heard him suck in a breath. "But on the second shake I struck gold in the form of a bloke called Fantam, real name Harry Clark. Heard of him?"

"Aye, he's got a taste for drugs no right minded doctor would prescribe," Fenella said, hands on the steering wheel. "Likes a pint, too."

She'd crossed paths with Fantam over the years. Most often she'd find him slumped behind dustbins in a cobbled alley. When he needed cash, he played tunes on his banjo in the town market with a large upturned hat. He was one of the regular faces in the homeless crowd.

Dexter said, "Fantam likes a flutter on the horses when he's flush with cash. He was in Quick Bet Bookie Store on Sunday when a man dashed out of the toilets. Fantam said he might not have taken much notice, except the man spoke in a soft American accent. Fantam reckons the bloke is from Chicago or New York City. Says he'd heard that accent before."

"Where?"

Dexter snorted like a horse reluctant to go on. "In the movies, guv. He said something about *The Godfather*."

Fenella sighed. Fantam wasn't the best class of witness. The word of an addict must be treated with caution, hence Dexter's hesitation to share. Still, Dexter had a knack for finding things out. She trusted his judgement, and Jones had suggested Fred Bickham's death might have been at the hand of mobsters. Fenella considered it again, rolling the idea around her mind.

Dexter said, "Bit of a long shot ain't it, guv? But with Jones going on about gangland this and gangland that. Well, it makes you think. I've got a bad feeling about it."

Fenella's neck muscles tightened. "What did this American bloke look like?"

There was a long pause. Two, three, four heartbeats. Was he reconsidering whether his information might be legit? Better to hear it, though. Might be the missing piece of the puzzle. Fenella waited.

"Like a..." Dexter cleared his throat." ... shadow, guv."

"Eh?" Fenella peered at her phone as if it wasn't working properly. "Like the shade cast by a tree type of shadow?"

"That's how Fantam described the bloke. One minute he was there and the next he was gone. Fantam also said the bloke wore a brown trilby. Sounds like the same man who was hanging around Seaview Allotments."

Fenella's hands' dropped from the steering wheel. "Aye. I want a word with Mr Brown Trilby. Did you get a name?"

"Nope, but I spoke with the clerk who didn't see or hear anything. You know how that goes. So, I asked for their CCTV footage. Nowt doing. The camera wasn't active on Sunday. Hasn't worked in months. They have a contract with Scroop Security, but Seth Scroop, who runs the show, has not been out to fix it yet."

"What about the surrounding businesses?"

"Already checked guv, but no joy."

Fenella tilted her neck. "Whoever this bloke is, I reckon he is still in town on unfinished business. But what?"

She turned to stare at the empty front door of the Bickham house. Whatever Mr Brown Trilby's intent, there was no doubt the clock was ticking. Fenella's mind worked over the deaths of Fred Bickham and Mrs Ruth Fassnidge. A man in a brown trilby had been seen hanging about Seaview Allotments. Did anyone see him near Mrs Fassnidge's boarding house?

It seemed Dexter's mind was working along the same lines. "It don't look good, guv. If this bloke came all the way from the States to hunt folks down, it means trouble. Big trouble."

CHAPTER 33

Shirley Bickham had downed a half pint of milk stout and a shot of gin before she found herself on the Port St Giles boardwalk carrying a small white bag in her left hand. When your first meal of the day comes in a glass called booze, you must fortify your stomach soon after. The white biodegradable bag contained her lunch—battered cod and chips.

The dull grey morning had given way to sun with scudding clouds and it was wonderful to be strolling along the boardwalk with the gentle splash of waves lapping the shore. Already the edge of fear was fading in the pleasant warmth. The fug had lifted from her mind and her dire predictions of imminent doom retreated to the shadows. *Her mam knew what to say.*

The boardwalk was crowded with tourists and locals and high school teens straggling back to school. Not to mention the pensioners. This time of day attracted the grannies like flies. They clustered around the food trucks with their bright coloured headscarves. They browsed the gift shop windows. They sat on benches eating ice creams and chatting. Traffic moved at a crawl on the road, but you could tell most were out-of-towners looking for a place to park.

At last, her day had turned. Uphill from here, Shirley told herself, prodding the sore on her lip then adjusting her pink headscarf. She'd visited the lows, and now, with the booze in her belly, awaited the highs. She felt confident her secret was secure and wanted to enjoy lunch in the open with the wind rustling through her hair. She paused at a large sign posted on the railings:

Protect and preserve our beach wildlife. Put your rubbish in a bin.

The town had hired wildlife protection workers who patrolled the beach in plain clothes and issued instant fines to those who damaged nature. About time, Shirley thought. If it were left to her, she would fling people who harmed nature into prison and throw away the key. And as for those who littered, hanging was too good for the buggers.

Why not eat her cod and chips on the beach? There were benches at the far end where few people strolled. A great place to sprawl and watch the dark heaving water flecked with foam crash against the shore. A chance to let the food work nature's magic while she sprawled out on a bench. How long had it been since she was one with nature? Yes, time alone on the quiet beach would do her good. Might throw in some yoga chants for world peace and harmony. She was a good person at heart. A kind woman. A loving mam. A nature lover. She set off for the sands with a bounce in her step.

A few minutes later, she was on the beach, all alone and thinking of her food when her gaze went back to the boardwalk. Something about the view was off. The railings followed the curve of the shore. People milled about—early birds at the start of a long tourist season. But something made her uneasy.

She suddenly felt very alone. The hustle and bustle on the boardwalk might as well be a million miles from the lonely beach. If something happened and she cried for help, would anyone hear?

A savage scream sounded a moment before a ball of feathers crashed from the sky, clawing at the white paper bag, screeching in fury. A herring gull. Just some gaunt bird with filthy feathers. It wanted cod and chips, and it wanted them bad, and it wanted them right then. It let out an ear-splitting cry.

That the gull had made a big mistake was clear with its next shriek. I will not let it steal from me, Shirley thought. *Not a single scrap of fish.* A vein pulsed in her neck. Her eye's narrowed and filled with the darkness of cold bloodied vengeance. She fired off a salvo of vexed cursing, her right hand snatching at the bird's neck. She grasped the gull by the throat, shaking the feathered fiend with the savage force of a dog.

The bird, squawking in panic and squealing in fear and thrashing about, wriggled from her grip. It slammed onto the sand, legs in the air, giant wings fluttering, body twitching in spasmodic shock.

A passer-by might have seen a woman crouching like a tiger, then pouncing on something small and feathered. They might have heard the clamour of terrified squeals. And the dead silence that followed. But there were no passers-by. No one strolling on this section of the beach. The throng stayed on the boardwalk with the ice cream parlours, the fish and chips shops and pubs which sold local ale.

Shirley attacked with rabid zeal. A beast in the grip of mania. She raised her foot, yoga style, heel aimed at the bird. Higher. Higher still. And she saw, as the gull lay on its back twitching, the soulless eyes of the nurse with the flabby arms. She raised her foot an inch higher, intent on smashing it down so hard the bird's guts burst through its arse.

With a shiver of pleasure, Shirley's heel came down. Gale force fast. Vengeance fast. Stomp until you are mushed gull fast. Straight at the twitching bird's gut.

Couldn't miss.

Not this close.

Not with such foot speed.

For an instant Shirley imagined stooping down and picking up the bloodied corpse by the legs. In her mind's eye the bird twitched and shuddered, fighting against the claws of certain death. Then, it went still.

Now, as her foot came down, a gust of wind whistled along the beach with the hollow moan of a graveyard. The gull shrieked, rolled, scrambled to its legs and ran. It took to the air, wings flapping furiously.

Shirley remained there for some time filled with hatred and shame and loathing. She doubled over, huffing and puffing as malice drained from her veins. Sometimes it felt like she had a split personality. She flipped from easygoing to violent thug so rapidly. What had she just tried to do to that bird? She told herself she didn't remember anything. That her mind was a blank. That it was the pills. But it wasn't. She had wanted to kill that bird, beat it to a bloodied stump.

"Purge me," Shirley said. "Purge my nasty, lurid soul."

The beach seemed as silent as a grave as she trudged back to the boardwalk, left hand still gripping the white paper bag. No way was she eating her lunch here with vicious gulls stalking her every move.

She was huffing up a dune when she noticed the strange man leaning on the railings. He wore a pea green trench coat and a brown trilby. He peered through binoculars. Were they trained on her?

Oh Christ, did he see her trying to kill the gull? What if he stormed the beach and demanded to know what she was up to? What if he was a wildlife protection nutter?

She'd deny it, tell him she loved all creatures great and small, had a bird feeder at home, was a member of the Port St Giles conservation society. None of which was the slightest bit true. It didn't matter. She'd turn the tables, call him a sicko. Why was he creeping up to women on the beach with his pea green flasher coat and face hidden by a sinister hat?

But the man in the brown trilby didn't rush to the beach. He wasn't looking at her. He seemed mesmerised by something on the pier.

Shirley tightened her pink headscarf and squinted at the abandoned lighthouse. The silhouette of the pier reminded her of the long tentacle of an octopus. If there were people milling about and enjoying the view, she was too far away to make them out. When she turned back to the railings, the man in the brown trilby was gone.

CHAPTER 34

I'll binge my cod and chips in the warming sun on a bench by the lighthouse, Shirley Bickham thought. She'd keep an eye out for greedy gulls and relax to the ebb and flow of the vast sea.

As she approached the arched entrance to the pier, a fierce-faced police officer stomped toward her. His boots clacked on the wooden slats with an angry snap. He was after her, she was sure of it, and there was nowhere to run. She didn't deserve to be locked behind bars; she was a mother with a pregnant daughter to look after. She thought of her dad and Ginger and her mam and wanted to cry. It wasn't her fault. None of this stinking mess was her fault.

Then she noticed the plump girl, twelve or thirteen, at his side, and beyond another uniformed officer followed.

"Now we'll be havin' no more of your bleedin' lies," Shirley heard the officer say. "And I'll be having a word with your dad. You ought to know better, Penny. You are going straight back to school."

Shirley strolled to the end of the pier and leaned against the railing. No one sat on the benches. The two police officers and the girl waited on the boardwalk. A patrol car skidded to the kerb. They climbed in. The patrol car didn't move for a full five minutes, then drifted into the traffic.

Feeling suddenly elated at having the pier to herself, Shirley slumped on a bench near the lighthouse. The building rose to the heavens like a strange castle in a fairy tale. Painted white, it had a huge dungeon-style door made of wooden slats and held together by giant iron braces. The door might once have been black, but had weathered to faded grey. And it looked thick and Victorian solid. If you were locked inside and trying to get somebody's attention, nobody would hear your pounding fists. You could scream until your throat was raw, and nobody would know.

She recalled a story about a castle with an evil ogre inside or was he hiding under a bridge? She shrugged away the half-remembered memory, stretched out under the warming rays of sun and started on the cod and chips. They were still warm and delicious.

She chomped on the last of the battered fish, crunching the bag into a tight ball and tossing it onto the ground.

"Biodegradable," she grunted as a gust of wind blew it along the slats.

It clattered to a stop by the railings, tottered for a moment then plunged off the edge.

Overhead, gulls screamed. They hovered over the lighthouse looking down with beady eyes. If she'd been in a woo-woo mood, she might have taken their shrieks as a warning. She'd eaten her food without yielding a scrap to the flying rats. She closed her eyes and relaxed as her stomach digested the meal. Good things were coming her way, she could feel it. Only one question. When?

Shirley heard the low scrape first. A sound above the slush of the waves and below the racket of the gulls. Like a sigh or a moan. A whoosh and a creak. Her eyes snapped open.

The sound came from the dungeon door of the lighthouse.

It was moving.

A thousand thoughts flashed through her mind, none of which made any sense. She'd only had a half pint of milk stout and a shot of gin. Was she seeing things, again?

The door continued to move.

Freaky.

Didn't the wind blow in strong gusts along the pier? Maybe it worked the door open. Only one problem, the wind was hardly blowing. And it would take a storm to shift that weighty door.

Shirley watched expecting someone to step out, but the gap was too narrow for anyone but a child to slip through. Perhaps council workers were fixing something inside? But council workers always put up signs. And there was no one hanging about in the shadows smoking or drinking tea. Definitely not council workers.

Her eyes strained to search the darkness in the crack. Was that the outline of a face? The flash of watchful eyes? A ball of dread formed in the pit of her stomach. Something wasn't right. She clutched her mobile phone as if it were a talisman and bit back fright, her throat dry. Where were the police when you needed them?

Inch by inch the door moved. Sigh and moan. Whoosh and creak. Waves crashed against the pilings. Gulls screamed from the heavens. Shirley exhaled a shocked gasp as a creepy man sidled through the crack.

She froze. Couldn't be, she thought, eyeing him with alarm. Could not possibly be. Same rat shaped face. Same domed shaped chin. Same glint in those doleful eyes which promised you the truth, the whole truth and nothing but the truth. Same slit of a mouth that spat out a never-ending string of lies. Except this time he had a dog with him rather than a bunch of roses swiped from a recent grave.

What the hell was Den Ogden doing back in Port St Giles?

CHAPTER 35

Shirley Bickham always knew, in some nightmarish way, Den Ogden would spin back into her life. Now he stood by the lighthouse door, running a hand over his double chin, gaze darting from her to the entrance of the pier—the entrance where the police had taken away the young girl in their car.

Shirley's blood turned to ice. She thought he'd died. No, she hoped he'd died. Cried tears of joy at his imaginary grave and kicked his headstone down in vivid dreams. Why was he back in Port St Giles? Gulls circled the lighthouse, their cries urgent and shrill.

Shirley tugged at her pink headscarf and her mouth worked a little before she said, "What are you doing here?"

"I'm from the Lighthouse Preservation Board." He cast a quick glance at the entrance of the pier. "We check old lighthouses to make sure they are safe and sound. This building is sound. Nowt wrong with the internals of this old girl."

He didn't recognise her. She picked at the sore on her lip wishing she'd put on some face powder and lipstick. "You work for the Lighthouse

Preservation Board?"

It sounded like a good job. A job that paid well. Now there was a turn-up for the books. Maybe he'd done well for himself since she'd last seen him. Maybe he'd made a little money.

She thought about taking her headscarf off but her hair needed a good brush, so she smiled. "Sounds important."

"It is an honour to service the ancient buildings of this great country," he replied, tugging at his dome shaped double chin. "I was selected from a shortlist of five thousand. This job is my life's devotion."

Yeah right, Shirley thought, watching his slit of a mouth as it moved. Every word that man said was a lie, including hello and goodbye. And then she doubted herself. Maybe he'd changed. God, why didn't she slap on some makeup?

She touched the knot in her headscarf, loosening it a little. "What did you say your name was?"

He blinked. "Clive. Clive Fremlin at your service."

"Clive?"

"Yep."

"Fremlin?"

He bowed. "At your service."

He hadn't recognised her yet. Or was he playing her for a fool?

He straightened, crack of a mouth turning up at the edges. "Where are your friends? I know you ladies like to work in packs. Nice weather for you grannies, eh?"

What did he just call her? Granny? Yes, he looked better than he should after the twenty hellish years she'd faced since she'd last seen him, better than she'd aged in that time. But she was no granny.

He patted the dog at his side and watched the entrance of the pier, a slow smile spreading like a curved slit. "This old boy is great for sniffing out ... mould and ... er ... damp. Nothing to worry about here. This building is as tough as old boots. A passing grade for the old maid. Not bad for an old biddy of a lighthouse."

All the while he was speaking Shirley had the unshakeable feeling he was laughing at her. Not in the straight line of his lips or the eyes shrunken to dots or even the stillness of his body. It was in his sing-song voice. He was laughing at her because she was ugly, laughing at her because she looked old, laughing at all women over forty. And his laughter stirred a rumbling of poisonous fury which tasted bitter in her mouth.

He patted the dog on the head. "Like I said, this lighthouse is solid. It'll stand for another one hundred years. Safe and sound for your grandkids, eh? Now I..."

It dawned on Shirley that he didn't recognise her because he wouldn't recognise her. Had she changed that much in twenty years?

" ... how's about that for a nice treat for an old lady? Must cheer your heart to know the future is secure. Not that I do it for the money, but it pays well enough..."

Would he be so chatty if he knew who she was? Should she let him know? It would be worth it to see his face freeze and his eyes go wide. She imagined smashing it with a bat. Pictured his face bursting open, a ripe water melon with red flesh and black seeds everywhere.

" ... always said you grannies are more than welcome on the..."

The muscles in Shirley's neck tightened. As she forced out a sour breath, she noticed the ragged wrinkles in his clothes. Stains too. Her nose twitched at the dank odour seeping from him like bubbles of pond mud exploding their stink. She considered the hunch of his shoulders as he held the dog leash and knew what had happened.

Den Ogden was back in Port St Giles because he needed cash.

He was down on his luck and here to shake someone down.

And he knew her secret.

Above the lighthouse the gulls screamed.

Den Ogden clucked his tongue. "Must be on my way. Cheerio."

He tugged on the leash and strode with quick steps toward the pier entrance. The dog limped a few paces behind.

Shirley watched until he turned onto the boardwalk and joined the swaying crowd. Then she raced after him, thinking about her black clothes—

ski mask, yoga pants and gloves. She made a solemn promise to wear those clothes one last time before burning them to ashes.

CHAPTER 36

It was not yet six in the morning and Fenella was in her small office in the Port St Giles police station sipping a mug of tea and trying to clear her mind. But her muse kept going back to baby Eva Fisk.

There had been no time to review the case files. All her focus had been on the deaths of Fred Bickham and Mrs Ruth Fassnidge—her major investigation. And they were in a holding pattern as far as those deaths were concerned. Detective Constable Ria Leigh had been assigned to the baby Eva Fisk case, but Fenella felt guilty for her lack of support. She'd had five bairns of her own, wouldn't want to lose one and couldn't imagine the abject agony the parents were going through. A living hell. Fenella's heart squeezed. Tension gripped her neck but she was grateful the bruises on her back no longer hurt.

She glanced at the clock on the wall and she glanced at the inbox on the computer screen and she glanced at her closed door. She decided. In the two hours between six and eight, she'd make a start on the baby Eva Fisk files. The mam and dad deserved that much from her, probably more.

She massaged her neck then sent a text

message to Ria Leigh asking for an update. Her eyes closed as she went over what she knew about missing babies.

When a baby went missing, it was a toss-up if you got them back. Fifty-fifty they would get the bairn back. Maybe less. An irate parent or relative snatches the child and disappears, often overseas. Less often there might be a ransom note.

Whatever the circumstances, the parents were always under siege from all sides. Questions from the police. Questions from the news media. And worst of all, questions from their conscience—could they have done more to protect their bairn? Even with a good outcome, the parents carried that terror to their grave.

Fenella eased back into her chair, took a long gulp of tea, tapped her keyboard and started reading. Mr and Mrs Fisk loved nature. Keen to continue their environmentally friendly life with their new baby, they had one car and Mr Fisk cycled to work. But on the day in question he had a business meeting in Carlise. He took the car, while Mrs Fisk and the bairn rode the bus for her weekly shop. They'd purchased an American pushchair, a three-wheeled stroller designed for joggers which collapsed with the click of a button and was easy to carry. The weather had closed in with fog and drizzle, so Mrs Fisk didn't hang about Frescho. As she waited for the bus home, the only person at the bus stop, she stepped into the road to watch for the bus. When she returned to the kerb, the push chair was empty—baby Eva Fisk was gone. Mrs Fisk collapsed, screaming hysterically by the empty stroller.

Fenella turned away from the screen and stared at the fogged window. Years ago, she'd made a promise—she'd not let a bairn come to harm on her watch. A heartfelt promise. An emotional promise. An impossible promise to make. An impossible promise to keep.

Police officers scoured every inch of the surrounding streets. In the fight against time, they flew drones with thermal cameras above the buildings. They imaged every lane and alley.

No baby Eva Fisk.

Fenella's phone buzzed. She glanced at the screen—a message from Dexter. She swiped but the text was empty. That meant one of two things. He might resend the message in a few seconds, or it was a warning. She waited several seconds then her eyes drifted back to the report. Her mind absorbing the details like fingers exploring a scar.

Mr Fisk, wild-eyed with terror, collapsed in shock at hearing the news. He was rushed to the hospital with heart tremors. Mrs Fisk fared a little better—tranquillisers quieted her screams. Fenella felt their agony, saw the streets of Barrow-in-Furness through their eyes—an alien land of sinister alleys and stifling fog. A land which had ripped their bairn from their life.

Over the following twenty-four hours, locals were drafted in to search the surrounding area. Two detectives from the Barrow in Furness station worked the case. Shoppers visiting Fresco were quizzed. No one saw anything. No one heard a thing. No hint of abuse by the parents. They adored Eva, were devoted to their only child.

Everyone was baffled, but one thing was clear to Fenella. Someone snatched baby Fisk. Someone who knew what they wanted. Someone who knew what they were doing. *Fifty-fifty. Maybe less.* She closed her eyes against the glare of the screen as the cruel reality set in. Not fifty-fifty. Not after all this time. Not forty percent. Not twenty. Not ten. Certainly less.

A timid knock sounded from the door. It did not open.

"Come," Fenella said.

PC Beth Finn shuffled in; her face twisted in a troubled frown. "Sorry to disturb you, ma'am."

"Take a seat, pet," Fenella said pointing to the chair on the opposite side of her desk.

PC Beth Finn eased into the chair and let out a long sigh that sounded like air from a deflating balloon. "I'm putting in a request to move to another station, ma'am. Thought you'd like to know."

Fenella leaned forward. "Where do you have in mind?"

PC Beth Finn looked at her hands. "I hear Whitehaven is nice."

"Any particular reason?"

"I … er … I need a change."

Fenella thought about PC Beth Finn's on and off relationship with Jones. They'd tried to keep it a secret, but she knew. Or at least she thought she knew. She'd had a poke about but Jones and PC Beth Finn's lips were as tight as superglue. But now ... she smiled, hoped she didn't look too eager and took a wild guess to get the ball rolling.

"What happened last night, pet?"

PC Beth Finn's eyes grew wide. "You know about that!"

"Spit it out, luv," Fenella replied. "You know how these things get twisted when they come to you through gossip."

For an instant Fenella felt ashamed at the thrill of excitement racing up her spine. Only for an instant, though. She'd joined the police so she could poke about in other people's secrets. Same reason she'd wanted to be a priest as a teen. It wasn't that she was nosy. Well, no more than anyone else. She was just born curious. Anyway, when dark corners of the closet are aired, it is easier to see what you've got. Best to hear it from the horse's mouth. Whatever it was. She smiled and nodded at PC Beth Finn to continue.

"Oh, it is nothing, really," PC Beth Finn said.

"Are you sure?"

"Well, I suppose it is something..."

Her voice trailed off. Was she having second thoughts?

"Go on, I'm listening," Fenella said, voice warm with giddy anticipation. "And don't spare the details. You will feel better once you've shared it all."

For a moment Fenella feared she sounded too

eager. Sounded too much like a nosy parker or that neighbour whose curtain twitches when a stranger appears in the street.

PC Beth Finn swallowed, looked like she was about to cry and said, "It's about me and—"

The door flew open. Superintendent Jeffery marched into the room, arms swinging at her side. Her stiff uniform was starched so hard it made a creaking noise. And she looked thrilled.

"Ah, there you are Sallow. No need to stand."

But PC Beth Finn was already on her feet, dashing for the door before Jeffery pegged her with some nasty task.

Jeffery said, "Ah, PC Finn, just the person. My office in twenty minutes. I have a rather interesting administrative task. How are your alpha numeric sorting skills?"

"Fine, ma'am," PC Beth Finn replied, then hurried through the door.

Jeffery waited until the door clicked shut. She cleared her throat and flashed her wolfish grin. The grin that told you that whatever came next wouldn't be good for you but benefited the boss in some way.

Fenella waited.

Jeffery said, "I won't beat about the bush. I have some rather important news."

CHAPTER 37

Fenella leaned back in her seat sensing a bombshell was about to go off. There was a moment of silence, footsteps beyond the door.

Jeffery cleared her throat. "I've had a rather nice chat with Sir Kiku. Do you know of him?"

Everyone knew Sir Curt Kiku. A big shot businessman who pulled political strings. He liked his bread buttered on both sides, giving huge donations to whoever occupied Town Hall. Sir Kiku paid for campaigns. He watched in the shadows as 'his' politicians kissed voters' babies. He shaped their speeches. He was influential, and an upstanding chap on first sight. Except for the rumours he'd grown rich on booze, drugs and the sweat of sex workers. You name it, Curt Kiku had his fat fingers in the pie, allegedly.

There was another silence. Fenella had the impression there was more. "I hear Sir Kiku has quite a cult following in Town Hall. Our political all-stars cling to him like drug addicts."

"Indeed," Jeffery replied, clearly not listening. "Sir Kiku is somewhat of a local hero."

"An idol, ma'am," Fenella said, thinking of the evil kind. "With a mob of grateful friends. Has Sir

Kiku been up to mischief? Do you want me to have a quiet word? Bring him in?"

Jeffery sniffed. "Let me remind you that he is the largest donor to the police widow's benevolent fund. It is not people like him who need a word from the police. Do I make myself clear?"

"Ah yes, sorry about that, ma'am," Fenella replied. "Are they giving him the keys to Port St Giles, again?"

Jeffery ignored the question. "I'm pleased you understand the importance of the reassignment."

"Reassignment, ma'am?"

Jeffery's phone buzzed. She pulled out a pair of reading glasses, placed them on the tip of her nose and swiped the screen. After a moment, her lips began to move. Fenella craned her neck, but the boss held her phone at an angle that made it impossible to read the screen.

"Speak of the devil," Jeffery muttered, eyes glued to the phone. "We shall have to cut this short, Sallow."

Fenella knew better, knew it wasn't the done thing, but she couldn't help herself. "Is it a message from Sir Kiku? You might want to mention my cooking circle, we can always use large donations."

Fenella ran a group that cooked for police officers with unwell spouses. A way to keep up with the gossip. A way to help those in need. Let them know they are not alone. When you are dealing with an ill partner, it can be a long and lonely road.

A knock came from the door. It flew open.

Dexter raced into the room. "News guv. Big news. Just heard that—"

He pulled to a halt, gazed at Jeffery and edged back toward the door. Whatever it was the boss was about to tell her, Dexter already knew. He kept his ear so close to the ground it was as if he had a spy inside Jeffery's office.

Jeffery took off her reading glasses and rubbed her nose. "I see your informants are on the ball as always Detective Sergeant Dexter. You may as well stay to hear it from the horse's mouth."

But she didn't share the news. Instead, she gazed at her phone with a wolfish grin.

One second.

Two.

Five.

Ten.

Fenella coughed. "Perhaps you'd like to enlighten us now, ma'am. Noon is only six hours away."

Jeffery snorted and waved her phone. "Sir Kiku's sister-in-law, a Mrs Eudora Stoke, was rushed to hospital on Sunday. She may not survive. Sir Kiku believes it is foul play and has asked me to investigate. This is our chance to help a local hero. It will elevate my ... our standing. A win-win."

So that was it. A chance to shine in front of Sir Moneybags Kiku. Dexter made a show of sniffing as though a foul stink had suddenly swamped the room.

Fenella didn't like it either. "Why does Sir Kiku

suspect foul play, ma'am?"

"That is what I want you to investigate," Jeffery replied.

"We are at full stretch, ma'am. We don't have the resources to chase after allegations and rumours."

Jeffery nodded. "Yes, you are right. That is why I want our newbie, Detective Constable Ria Leigh, on this. Mrs Stoke takes priority. One hundred percent of her effort until I say otherwise."

Again, Dexter sniffed.

Fenella said, "I can't accept that, ma'am."

"Pardon?" Jeffery's voiced hummed like bees. "What did you say?"

Dexter gulped. Fenella got the message. He was warning her to stay well back. Nowt good came from Jeffery when her voice buzzed like that.

Fenella slammed her hand on the desk. "I can't leave the parents of baby Eva Fisk hanging."

"Baby who?"

"Eva Fisk, ma'am. The case from the Barrow station you asked Ria to work on."

"Oh, that!"

Jeffery's mouth worked a little but no more came out for several seconds. It was as though she were performing some difficult career calculation. Baby Eva Fisk or influential politician?

When at last she spoke, the buzz in her voice seemed louder. "Yes ... well ... it is not your problem."

"A bairn has been snatched from her mam's arms," Fenella replied. "That is everyone's problem, ma'am."

From the courtyard came the slam of a door, the mumble of voices, the sudden wail of a patrol car. Dexter cleared his throat. Fenella waited.

Jeffery exhaled a snarl of breath. "We'll move the baby Fisk case back to the Barrow-in-Furness police station. Let them deal with it."

"But you are in charge of both stations, for now," Fenella said. "And Barrow is shorter staffed than us. That's how we got the case in the first place, ma'am."

"I am well aware of that, Sallow," Jeffery replied. "We'll put the Fisk case on the back burner until we have more capacity."

"I'll let the parents know you want to speak with them, shall I?" Fenella said, folding her arms. "Tell them to warm up their teapot so you can share the good news over a mug of tea and a plate of custard creams. I think baby Eva would have quite liked custard creams when she got older. Bairns do, don't they?"

Jeffery's skin drew tight over her jaw and her nostrils flared. If she were a volcano, the villagers would be running for the caves.

Fenella let her lips quirk at the edges. Best to get in before the fireworks. "Ma'am, I recommend my team keep the baby Eva Fisk case active. I'll take the lead from now on. It will be my responsibility. I'll see it through." She lowered her voice. "I'm thinking about your image with Chief Constable Rae, ma'am."

"My image?" Jeffery said, unable to hide the

hint of alarm in her voice. "What about my image?"

"When he learns your team are working all three cases with very limited resources, he'll want to know more. Have you thought about your answers to how you drove such efficiency?" She took a breath, might as well lay it on with a thick trowel. "He might even put you on a board or two in Carlisle. Didn't you say he was forming an efficiency oversight leadership team?"

Fenella stopped and waited, holding her breath. Had she over-egged the pudding?

Jeffery blinked rapidly. "My thoughts exactly. Efficiency is how I'd define my leadership style. Yes, go ahead and look at the baby Eva Fisk files. And have Detective Constable Ria Leigh work with Mrs Stoke. In fact, I'll tell her myself. Efficiency gets more done. Carry on, Sallow."

She spun, and with arms swinging at her side, marched from the room.

"I've a bad feeling about this," Dexter said, rubbing his temples. "It doesn't smell right, guv."

"Aye, happen you're right," Fenella replied, tapping her fingers on the desk. "And I reckon the stink is about to get worse."

CHAPTER 38

When the call came through, Detective Constable Ria Leigh went straight to the Port St Giles Cottage Hospital, knowing what she must do.

The nurse in the blue uniform signed her in and walked her to Mrs Stoke's private suite. Now she stood alone inside the hospital room, bitter and determined, staring at the unmoving figure on the bed.

So, Superintendent Jeffery wanted her to investigate the illness of Mrs Eudora Stoke. She'd almost gone berserk with relief at the jaw-dropping news. Brilliant, was her first thought as Jeffery explained. *Bloody brilliant.* Lady Luck was back on her side. A large black bag rested on her shoulder, left hand gripping the straps.

The room was larger than she expected with the decor you'd see in a luxury hotel. Lush furnishings and oil paintings of the beach hung on the peach walls. Six vases, vibrant with colour stood in a cluster on a broad table by the curtained window. Sweet pea, peonies and white roses were a few she recognised. The fruit in the crystal bowl caught her eye. It wouldn't be out of place in a still life drawing class. There must have been fifty cards of all shapes and sizes. The largest with giant red and gold balloons: *Get Well Soon Mummy*.

Ria's second thought, as Jeffery droned on, was less knee-jerk celebration and more thoughtful. She needed a new plan. When the call ended, she packed the black bag which now rested on her shoulder. No need for the doctor's white house coat or the mask with the evil Halloween scowl. She'd left the brown porter's jacket on the kitchen table. Only one thing rested soft and easy inside the black bag. Only one thing needed. The suffocation pillow.

Mrs Stoke lay under a thin white sheet. A mask covered her nose and mouth. Her face was the colour of uncooked pie crust. Dark sunken sockets marked her closed eyes. But Ria could make out the lines of her thick arms and fat legs. Tubes and wires led to unknown machines. My, how still she seemed. How vulnerable.

Ria took a step closer, opened the black bag, hand reaching inside, feeling the softness of the pillow.

Mrs Stoke was more popular than Ria expected. All those cards, the flowers and this private room. And she was a mam with kids.

Ria sniffed. No harsh tang of antiseptic, disinfectant or rubbing alcohol. Just the sweet scent of the flowers and a faint trace of pricy perfume. She wanted to believe Mrs Stoke was a neurotic drug addict but now she had a nasty feeling it was more complex than she first thought. This cow had class and money to go with it. And that meant she knew someone who knew someone. The cow had influence.

Ria hesitated, calculating her next move.

Her business partner, Sloane Kern, sold pills to middle-class women in need of more than anger management therapy could offer. Discreet women who paid top whack for illegal supplies. A far cry from the pond scum Ria used to shake down on the streets of Whitehaven. Pond scum never grassed even when the police stole their supplies. But Mrs Stoke came from another type. Who did she know? Would they cause trouble? Ria was too new to town to know and superintendent Jeffery had held her cards close to her chest. What did Ria know about the woman's background?

She glanced at the flowers and cards: *Get Well Soon Mummy*. Women like Mrs Stoke had friends who might arrive at any moment with bunches of flowers and more cards. Maybe Mrs Stoke's children would show up to check on how she was doing.

Ria turned to the door, cocked her head and listened. Only the constant beep of a machine and the thud of her own heart. The beeps piqued her interest, and she listened for a while.

Beep-beep-beep.

So precious. So precise. So plentiful. The digital sound of Mrs Stoke's life. And then Ria thought of what she must do.

Thud-thud-thud.

She took another step to the side of the bed. Up close, the woman's face swelled with ugly blotches and her narrow nose flared as though trying to suck in more air. She had brown hair which faded to white at the roots. Deep lines like cracked earth snaked across her forehead. Mrs Stoke looked ancient. Like she belonged in a glass case in the British Museum. A breathing mummy fetched up from the tomb. What bloody right did she have to live and spill the beans on Ria's business?

Beep-beep-beep.

Ria took out the pillow, holding it firm in both hands. She tried to control her breathing. In through the nose. Hold. Out through the mouth.

In. Hold. Out.

In. Hold. Out.

Thud-thud-thud.

A shrill beep sounded. A jarring wail. Ria turned to the wall of instruments, unsure which had made the noise. Would the nurse in the blue uniform come running? Her fingers squeezed the pillow as she waited, alert, listening. Ten seconds. Twenty. Thirty. One minute. Two. No more shrill beeps. No nurse on the run to help.

In. Hold. Out.

Thud-thud-thud.

In the silence as quiet as snowfall, Ria leaned over the bed.

"Mrs Stoke, can you hear me?"

Nothing.

"I'm a friend of Sloane Kern. You know Sloane, don't you?"

Mrs Stoke's face remained blank and pale. Her

chest rose and fell.

Beep-beep-beep.

"Sloane gave you pills to help you out. Do you remember?" Ria spoke in a soulless monotone. "Sloane told you how to use them and gave you detailed instructions. But you got greedy, didn't you Mrs Stoke?"

Ria's hand's twitched as she eased the pillow close to the woman's pale face.

In. Hold. Out.

Thud-thud-thud.

Breathy breaths now from Ria. Short breaths. Shallow. In. Hold. Out. Eager to finish the job.

"But you didn't listen to Sloane, did you, Mrs Stoke? Instead, you overdosed and ended up here. Have you any idea of the problem you have created? I'm Detective Constable Ria Leigh, Civic Officer of the year three times in a row. This year will make four. A record. I'm a legend, Mrs Stoke. They'll talk about me in history class one day, use me as an example of what girls can do. I can't let your greed for pills stand in the way of that, can I?"

Ria was in the light now. Bright and white with no hint of shadow. All she had to do was drop the pillow on Mrs Stoke's face, press and wait. And then she'd crawl back to the dark. The glorious dark where her underhand dealings went unseen. Freedom from worry. Freedom from fear. Release.

Beep-beep-beep.

It would all be over in a handful of minutes. Her mission complete and the misery lifted. A handful of heartbeats to freedom. Mrs Stoke's heartbeats. *Beat 'em down and beat 'em down again.*

"Next time we'll be more careful who we sell our happiness pills too," Ria said, fingers squeezing the pillow. "Suicidal maniacs are a curse on society. A blot we must wipe out."

Ria closed her eyes, gripping the pillow with strong hands, heart kicking hard against her chest.

Thud-thud-thud.

Earlier she'd wandered the hospital, checking the location of CCTV cameras. The nurse in the blue uniform had been good enough to tell her there were none on this ward. Once they know you are with the police, they'll tell you anything. Now she knew where the CCTV cameras were, she knew how to avoid them. She looked down on Mrs Stoke's peaceful face.

And then, suddenly she lurched forward, face grimacing, hands firm on the pillow.

Thud-thud-thud.

The mask! Mrs Stoke's mask was still on her face.

Ria stopped, dropped the pillow on the bed and shoved the mask to one side. It left a red indentation. She picked up the pillow with both hands.

Thud-thud-thud.

Mrs Stoke must never wake up. Never tell what she knew. Never give Ria's business cause for concern. The dead don't speak. Only the living lie.

The door opened. The nurse in the blue

uniform marched in.

"That's ten minutes. I'll have to ask you to leave. Mrs Stoke needs her rest." She turned and headed for the door. "This way, please."

Ria quickly replaced the mask and leaned so close her lips were an inch from Mrs Stoke's ear. "If you push a person to the brink, they will do terrible things. This is a dry run to get the lay of the land. No one will see me when I come back tonight to finish the job."

CHAPTER 39

Fenella didn't want to stop, but when her stomach growled, she realised she had not eaten all day. It was noon. Tea Jug was the nearest café, at the end of Marsh Street, Barrow-in-Furness. She parked her Morris Minor and went inside.

There were six tables scattered about the small space, brown tile floors and a high counter where a fat man in a chef's garb which might once have been white sat on a stool reading a newspaper. An American soap opera played on the large screen TV with the volume turned down. A faint trace of fried food hung in the air, remnants of what they served at breakfast. The glass case on the counter caught Fenella's eye. It was filled with fresh tarts and cakes and pastries.

"Welcome," the fat man said. He put down the newspaper. "Ain't from around here, are you?"

"No, luv," Fenella replied. "Port St Giles."

"What I thought. We don't do much business between noon and three. An early rush and a late rush is how I make ends meet. So, I figured you are not from here. You've got the place to yourself. What is your pleasure?"

"Those cakes fresh?" Fenella asked.

"I trained in France, Paris," he replied. "Them cakes are made fresh every day, and those I don't sell go to the homeless shelter. No reason why folks down on their luck shouldn't eat good food."

Fenella ordered a pot of tea and a giant custard slice: two crisp flanks of flaky pastry with a dollop of custard sandwiched between; the top flank was layered with sweet icing with brown swirls added for an artistic touch. She took her food to a table by the window. She wanted time to think about the questions she would ask baby Eva Fisk's parents.

The fat man went back to reading his newspaper. She took out her notebook and read for a while then stared through the glass panes at the street. A young woman, twenty at most, in a floral dress and flyaway black hair held a toddler in pink shorts by the hand. Was she the mam? Or the big sister? An aunt? A child snatcher?

The bairn looked in the café window, planted her feet and pointed at Fenella. The young woman with the flyaway hair, turned, followed the toddler's gaze and waved.

"You from the police?" The fat man placed the newspaper on the counter and was regarding her with curiosity.

"Aye, pet," Fenella replied.

"Thought so."

He picked up the paper and continued to read. Fenella nibbled the custard slice, closing her eyes to savour the delicious vanilla flavour. Moist and sweet and crisp and crumbly. Perfect.

The café door pinged. Fenella opened her eyes and took a gulp of tea as the woman with the flyaway hair strode in. She was laughing. The toddler tapped her arm and pointed at Fenella.

"I want one of those," the toddler said, voice carrying across the empty café.

Again, the woman waved at Fenella. "Sorry about my niece pointing," she said, and went to the counter to order a custard slice. Fenella's eyes dropped to her notebook.

When the café door pinged again, she looked up expecting to see the girl and bairn out in the street. Instead, she saw a dark green beat-up Ford parked by the kerb. It wasn't in the street a moment before. No way. She'd have spotted it and left by the back door. Her eyes bounced from the Ford to the café front door as a sinking feeling flooded her gut.

A rat-faced man in a scruffy duffle coat dashed into the café. He paused, nose twitching, eyes darting around. What did Rodney Rawlings want?

He was a reporter for the *Westmorland News*. One of the last from the old school who drank hard, chased stories like a fox and foxed around with women like a hound. If he had a crooked bone in his body, Fenella would have tossed him behind bars by now. But he was on her side of the law. The right side. The side that puts bad people away.

"Ah, there you are," he said, scurrying to Fenella's table. He glanced through the window, his eyes darting along the street. "We need to talk."

He shuffled to a chair on the opposite side of

the table, so his back was to the window. Fenella supposed it gave him a wide view of the café like a secret agent in a spy novel. Or a crook watching out for an old enemy intent on revenge.

She wrapped both hands around the mug and took a sip. "How did you track me down?"

"I have my sources." His nose twitched. "That custard slice looks good. Is it fresh? Not something I can afford on my salary. People think the newspapers are glamorous, they aren't. Not these days."

"Wait here," Fenella said.

She went to the counter. The woman with the flyaway hair held a custard slice in one hand and was grinning at the toddler. The toddler grinned back, a smear of custard on her lips.

"I got what you got," the toddler said. "And it is good."

"Aye lass, can't beat a custard slice when the mood strikes. And it strikes me often."

The woman with the flyaway hair laughed. Fenella watched them leave, ordered two custard slices and a flat white coffee and returned to the table. Whatever Rodney Rawlings had to tell her it was worth at least that, probably more. He tracked her down for a reason.

She slid the coffee and one custard slice across the table. She kept the other for herself. A jog on the beach tonight would soon burn it off. Rawlings sniffed the custard slice. He took a bite, yellowed teeth like fangs. He turned to the coffee, sniffed and took a gulp. His nose twitched, pointy face and dark eyes unreadable.

Fenella said, "So?"

Rawlings glanced around as if someone in the café might be watching. The man with the fat face was reading the newspaper. There was no one else in the place.

"Heard something that might take your interest," Rawlings said in a half whisper. "I'm writing a feature on baby Eva Fisk. I hear you are working the case now."

Fenella said nothing.

Rawlings pointed his sharp nose at the counter. It twitched. "Snatched child, tearful parents, that sort of thing. The sad sob shifts a lot of newspapers. We will sell a ton because the story is local."

"You are losing me," Fenella said. "What do you want?"

"Give me a chance."

"I want the headline version, not the feature."

"Okay, okay. Now where was I?"

"Baby Eva Fisk. You have news?"

"That's right." He took a bite of the custard slice. His pink tongue slid from between his lips, mopping up the crumbs. "The thing is, I'd like to share. But I mean, I have costs." Again, his nose twitched. "This job is like running in a sewer full of rats. Not sure how long I can take it."

"Twenty years isn't bad, pet."

"Almost thirty."

"I'm sure you will survive until paper is a thing they keep under a glass case in a museum," Fenella replied. "They might even wheel you out to tell the kids what it is."

He grinned. "Damn right. Now, how about a deal?"

"Tell me what you've got and I'll have a think about it."

He took a long slurp from his mug. "Look, those other journalists are a pack of bleedin' rats. One whiff of cheese and they will be all over it. This is for your ears only."

"You will always be king rat in my book. I won't share your cheese. What have you got for me?"

He stared, biting his lip. "I've tried every trick in the book to get in contact with the parents of baby Eva Fisk."

"Let me guess," Fenella said, finishing her custard slice. "They won't speak with you. It might be that your tatty duffle coat is putting them off."

"Do you think so?"

"No."

"What then?"

It was hard to trust a rat-faced man, but Fenella didn't say that. "I suppose they've got so many requests they don't know where to start."

He was too old a hand to believe that. He grunted. "The police record shows there has not been a ransom request."

So that is what he wanted. The police hadn't confirmed or denied that fact. The entire case was confidential, wrapped tight in bureaucratic red tape. Rodney Rawlings wanted an affirmative answer. Why?

Fenella sipped from her mug, considering. "I cannot deny that, but I can't confirm it either."

She put special emphasis on the word *confirm*.

Rawlings stared at the remains of his custard slice like he was lost in thought. "I see. Then you'll want to know..." His voice trailed off and once again he glanced around. "I'm writing a story on human trafficking. Baby Eva Fisk is no longer in the country. My sources reckon the bairn was shipped to Turkey a few days after she was taken. I have solid information that she met her new family in Istanbul. They are Canadian or American. The Yanks buy their kids on demand with three easy payments. Look, I'm sorry to tell you, but I'm certain the bairn is gone."

Fenella's chest heaved in disappointment. "How certain is certain?"

"My feature is due on Friday. It will run in the Sunday paper."

That meant he was pretty certain. He'd double-checked his facts and was filling in the gaps. Fenella was silent for a long while.

She said, "I'll want to speak with your source."

Even journalists as seasoned as Rodney Rawlings got it wrong sometimes. She'd triple check, get it from the horse's mouth, provided he revealed his source. She folded her arms and waited.

"Oh come on, you know the rules of the game.

I can't give you that." He smiled, bearing yellowed teeth. "I heard there was an incident at Seaview Allotments."

Again, a statement with hidden meaning. He wanted to know what had happened and in return, he'd tell her what he knew. Not the name of his contact, she was sure of that, but something useful. She considered. Fred Bickham's death would break soon and she saw no point in denying it. Time to trade.

Fenella told him the details, missing out two important facts. First, the suspected murder weapon was likely a cricket bat lined with nails; second, the death of Mrs Fassnidge. No point showing all her cards.

Rawlings rubbed his hands. "My God this is juicy. I can see the headline—Man Slayed in Town Turnip Patch." He glanced over his shoulder. "What do you think?"

"You might have to work on that title."

"What was the murder weapon? Please tell me it was a bunch of prize-winning rhubarb."

Why did she feel, whenever he asked a question, she'd been sprayed in farmyard muck? She said nothing.

His nose twitched. "Got a name for John Doe?"

"Fred Bickham," Fenella said. "He was a husband with a teenage granddaughter. Write that down and spell it right."

He grunted, pulled out a notebook and made a show of writing the name. "Did he have a dog?"

"No."

"Shame. A photo of Fido pining by his master's armchair does wonders for sales. How tasty is the teen? Is she a good looker? A weeping beauty on the front page might be better than a flea-bitten dog."

Fenella placed her hand flat on the table and leaned in. "Tell me about baby Eva Fisk and tell me now." Her lips quirked. "Or would you rather share at the police station?"

Rawlings raised his hands, palms out. "Like I said, my article is about mail order babies where the client makes a choice from a checklist down to the eye colour and blood group." He glanced around the café once more. "A Russian gang operating out of Barrow-in-Furness have moved into people trafficking. The gang steal babies to order."

"That is good to know, now give me a name."

His body language changed and he hunched as if trying to make himself very small. "You didn't hear this from me, okay?"

Fenella waited. There was more, and by the twist in Rodney Rawlings lips she would not like it.

"I can't confirm what I am about to tell you," he said, voice guarded. "But Sir Curt Kiku's fingerprints are all over this."

CHAPTER 40

Rain pelted from low clouds as Fenella pulled her Morris Minor to the kerb outside the Fisk house. The gravity of baby Eva Fisk's situation had sunk to a new low. Rodney Rawlings might be wayward regarding women, but his nose for a news story was as sharp as the stench from a broken sewer. The press man knew his job and he knew it well. She couldn't be certain, couldn't be sure, but felt more bad things were coming. And they were coming fast.

Fenella stared through the car window at the faded street. An abandoned canning factory stood on one corner; its walls stained by graffiti. On the opposite side was a row of red brick houses. The Fisk household was a one-story bungalow with an extension built on the side and a dormer added in the loft. There was a low brick wall with a small gate and a gravel yard. No grass. No trees. No plants of any kind. Not a style Fenella liked. Too barren. Too dead.

She spotted the CCTV camera as she opened the garden gate. A small device above the bell button. There was a brass knocker with a huge lion's head. Too grand for such a small place. Still, it told Fenella the Fisk's were ambitious, eager to improve their status. The door opened before she touched the bell.

"Yes?"

The question came from a slim woman with a deep tan and short cropped brown hair. Her oval face had wide eyes and broad lips and a flat nose which curved up at the tip. She wore a black suede skirt and cream blouse, both as expensive as her perfume which swirled in an aromatic cloud.

"I'm Detective Inspector Fenella Sallow. Are you Mrs Jill Fisk?"

"Yes. Have you found her?"

Mrs Jill Fisk looked every bit the Paris fashion model, only better. A pang of envy stabbed Fenella's heart. She didn't look half that good when she was a teenager, and Mrs Jill Fisk was thirty-two. Then she thought about baby Eva Fisk and felt another pang of guilt for her mam. She'd not tell the lass that her bairn had been taken overseas, not until she confirmed it as fact. And there was the Sir Curt Kiku connection to consider. This case became more tangled with every step she took.

She said, "Can I come in, luv?"

Mrs Fisk hesitated.

Fenella gave the woman her identification.

Mrs Fisk peered at it, smiled and handed it back. "Oh, you are the boss of that nice Detective Constable Ria Leigh?" Her voice sounded excited. Hopeful. "Please forgive me, we've been pestered by a ratty faced reporter these past few days. I won't answer the phone and always use the camera to see who is on the door step. Please come in."

She led the way to a lounge with expensive furniture and rosewood panelling. Framed photographs of buildings hung on the wall—all modern design and eco-friendly and looking like they would do well on Mars. The oak floorboards screamed aspiration, as did the Persian rug. The Queen Anne fireplace was an original from a demolished house and fitted into the old hearth to up the lush factor. The second hand of an antique wall clock jerked with a sharp click.

They settled in deep leather armchairs which smelled new. On a low coffee table was a home design magazine, tablet computer, a pair of knitting needles and a ball of pink wool.

"I haven't cried," Mrs Fisk said. "I'm staying strong for Eva. Sorry about the mess."

She picked up the knitting needles. The object she'd been working on took form—a pink baby cardigan, almost done. The bairn had been missing for weeks and would have grown. How did Mrs Fisk know what size to knit?

Fenella said," Keeping yourself busy?"

"This is for when we get Eva back." Mrs Fisk sniffed, her eyes filling with moisture. "It is the size she wore when she left us. I'll put it in her bedroom with the others I've made. One each week since she went missing. I don't suppose they'll fit now, do you?"

Fenella said nothing.

Mrs Fisk began to work the needles.

Click-clack-click-clack.

No point rushing, Fenella told herself and waited.

"We lost our old cleaner and the new one has taken a fortnight off to visit her family," Mrs Fisk said without looking up. "That is why the place is such a mess."

But it wasn't. Not to Fenella's eye. It looked like a photo from a fashion magazine. She said, "Gone down south?"

"Moldova."

"Chișinău?" Fenella asked, recalling the capital of the European country.

Mrs Fisk put down the knitting needles, eyebrows raised. "That's right, well almost. She is from a small village ten miles from the capital. Don't ask me the name, I can't pronounce it. Once you get past Dover, it's all foreign to me."

Fenella warmed to the woman. Not a stuck-up snob who looks down her nose at the world. More like a lass who'd come from poor stock and wanted to do better. Nowt wrong with that.

Fenella eased back in her chair. "What is the cleaner's name?"

"Sofia Rusu, and she does a fantastic job," Mrs Fisk replied.

Fenella recalled the name from the files on baby Eva Fisk. "Mrs Fisk, I should have called ahead to make sure you and your husband were home."

But she hadn't because she wanted to surprise them. You got more out of people when you came at them raw.

"Max is at the office," Mrs Fisk said. She spoke in a soft voice where emotion threatened to break free with every word. "He is an architect. It won't take him ten minutes to get here. I'll call him."

She thinks I've got news Fenella told herself. Good or bad she wants her hubby to be here to hear it. But there was no news. Well, no good news, and the bad she didn't want to share just yet. Not until she was absolutely certain.

"No pet," Fenella said, "Best not disturb him. It's you I want to speak with."

"I thought you came here to tell us..."

Mrs Fisk's voice trailed off. In the silence came the tick-tock of the wall clock. Outside, a car rumbled in the street. Rain pelted against the windows with the force of a fistful of gravel.

Mrs Fisk said, "Will I get Eva back?"

Fifty-fifty when a bairn is snatched. After all these weeks and the news from Rodney Rawlings, five percent, maybe less. Fenella wanted to cry. "You will be the first to hear when we have news we can share. Good or bad, I promise to tell you myself. Right now, I'm here to follow up on a few loose ends."

Mrs Fisk picked up her knitting needles.

Click-clack-click-clack.

"Max is a marvellous hubby," Mrs Fisk said. "We met in college. Not one of those fancy universities, just the local college here in town. We fell in love and the rest is history. We love each other and we love our daughter and she loves us. With all that love, how could anyone take her?"

Fenella said nothing.

Mrs Fisk stopped knitting and stared at Fenella with eyes much older than her years. "They say in despair, hope anchors the soul, but I knew you didn't have any good news about my baby. I knew it when I opened the door. I didn't want to say it, hoped I was wrong, but I knew. We trust the police, don't we? We have faith they'll come through for us when we need them. Max and I need you now. So does our Eva. And you are the boss, but you've come here with no news. I'm not a fool, it's not looking good, is it?"

She dropped the knitting needles and smiled. It was a ghost of a smile which flickered for an instant before her lips turned down and her face crumpled in anguish. She held her head in her hands and rocked from side to side weeping.

Fenella wrapped her arms around the woman and held her tight. Until the sobs subsided. Until the only sound was the slow tick-tock of the wall clock. And still Fenella kept the lass in her arms. Sharing her loss. Sharing her grief. Sharing her fear of what was to come.

CHAPTER 41

When Mrs Jill Fisk eased from Fenella's hug, it was clear she wanted to talk. Her mouth opened and closed and she crossed her hands in her lap. And she smiled at the detective with a smile of a mother who'd experienced deep loss. Rain continued to drum against the windows.

Fenella returned to her armchair. Although she had read the police files, there was nothing like hearing the story in person. Body language conveyed much more than ink on the page. And there was always something left unsaid. Something you'd think was nothing. But police cases often turned on nothing.

Mrs Fisk sniffed. "Are you a mother?"

"Five. All grown."

"Ever lost one?"

"No, luv. But I've lost my sister."

"What was her name?"

Fenella smiled. "Eve, and she went missing from the Port St Giles Cottage Hospital over seven years ago. Never found."

"Then you know how I feel."

"Aye, lass. I know."

The wall clock ticked, counting down the

seconds. Outside, a voice shouted in the street. Rain continued to drum on the windows but with less force. The storm was moving on, over the beach and drifting out to sea.

Mrs Fisk rubbed her eyes. "I lie awake at night thinking about Eva, and when I fall asleep, I dream about her, about the day she was taken." She picked up the knitting needles and put them back down. "You have questions?"

"Tell me what happened," Fenella replied. "Start with the weather, if that helps."

Mrs Fisk closed her eyes and her breathing slowed. She was back in time. Back to that day when her only child was taken. "It was one of those days when the drizzle never stops and the air is so cold you hustle to get back home for a cup of tea by the fire. I remember the fog the most. A sea mist swamped the town, thick and yellow like the smog they used to have in London. I had Eva with me, tucked up snug in her pushchair, an American model. They call it a stroller over there."

She stopped. Her eyes snapped open. She didn't want to be in the wretched past. She didn't want to be in the present, either.

Fenella leaned forward. "Go on, luv."

Mrs Fisk drew a deep breath and her eyelids fluttered shut. "Max works on green buildings, and we have an electric car which we share. He cycles to work most of the time, but on that day he had a business meeting in Carlisle. The trains are unreliable, so he took the car. I didn't mind, I enjoy taking the bus, even with our baby and the pushchair. It makes going to the shops a bit of an adventure." Her eyes opened. "Oh, I'm meandering, talking about nothing. None of this is relevant, is it?"

"Keep going, pet. Take your time. No rush, I'm listening."

"I was on my way home from shopping at Two detectives from the Barrow-in-Furness station worked the case.; at the bus stop on Brown Street when it happened."

Fenella knew the street. "The bus stop opposite the Sweet Rainbow café?"

Mrs Fisk nodded. "Yes. Have you dined there?"

"Aye, pet. I've sampled their Grasmere gingerbread."

"Me too!" Her face lit up with an effortless smile. "Not a dish I'd wish on my worst enemy."

They both laughed.

All of a sudden, from outside, came a loud clatter followed by a boom. A soft crumbling sound came next, like the slow collapse of a wall.

Mrs Fisk hurried to the window. "They are knocking down that old factory and turning it into a green park with energy efficient houses and locally owned shops. Max reckons prices will boom with the redevelopment. He said we should get in early, convert one of the old bungalows and wait it out. So, we bought this place with our savings. Neither of us factored in the noise of living on a construction site, but we can't sell up and leave this house. Too many memories of Eva. If we leave, I'm frightened they'll fade away."

"Come and sit down, luv," Fenella said. "When the time is right, you and your hubby will make the best decision."

Mrs Fisk shuffled back to the armchair. Another crashing sound thundered. The walls of the bungalow shook. It was like being trapped in a biscuit tin with someone throwing pebbles at the lid.

Fenella ignored the shudder and let the noise fade to nothing. She said, "So, you were at the bus stop opposite the Sweet Rainbow café when it happened?"

"Yes, I was waiting for the bus. Because of the fog I had to step into the road to see if it was coming. They don't always stop and with only two buses an hour, it can mean a long wait if you miss it. With the fog and the cold and the drizzle, I didn't want the bus to whistle past without stopping. But when I stepped back on the kerb, the pushchair was empty. Eva was gone."

Again, Mrs Fisk began to weep. This time Fenella let her cry. It was distressing to watch. She felt angry but knew Mrs Fisk needed the release. Needed to let the pain out. Needed to do that in front of a stranger so she could keep a stiff upper lip at home. Fenella understood and waited.

Mrs Fisk said, "I'm sorry, I haven't been able to cry and today I'm all tears." She dabbed at her eyes and sniffed. "I've told you what I told the original detectives who worked the case. I've told you it all."

And she had. Her words matched those written in the files, but something did not add up. There was a gap in there somewhere, like a hole filled with nothing because you can't see the air. Fenella sensed it, felt around the edges for the shape of it, listened intently for the soft swish of air. If something came from nothing, she was going to find it.

She said, "Did anything unusual happen that morning?"

"Not that I can think of," Mrs Fisk replied. "It was our regular routine. Nothing special."

"Baby wasn't grumbling?"

"She was fine."

"Notice anything unusual on your shop?"

"Nothing."

"Did you see anyone watching you?"

"No."

"Following you?"

"No."

Fenella considered. Sometimes you got your best answers when you asked questions based on feelings. "Tell me how you felt that day."

"Pardon?"

"Happy, sad, filled with energy? How did you feel when you woke up?"

Mrs Fisk sighed. "What do my feelings have to do with it?"

"I don't know," Fenella replied. "Just try your best."

Mrs Fisk rolled her eyes, but to her credit,

she was up for Fenella's game. She said, "Happy, I suppose. No, not happy, content. I felt a deep sense of contentment as a first-time mother, do you know what I mean?"

Fenella nodded. "So, when you woke up you felt content?"

"Yes."

"And when you dressed the baby?"

"That's right."

"What about at the shops?"

"It was busy and cold and foggy and I was in a hurry to get back home, but I was at peace with the world in a strange way."

Fenella said, "How did you feel on your walk to the bus stop?"

"The same."

Not what Fenella expected. "The same?"

"Yes."

"You didn't feel as if someone was following you?"

"No."

"Watching you?"

"No."

"Did you feel threatened at any time during that day?"

"No."

Fenella glanced at the wall clock and she glanced at the Queen Anne fireplace and she glanced at Mrs Fisk who sat upright in her chair. She'd shaken nothing new from the trees.

She tilted her neck from side to side and

tried again. "Did anything unusual happen between leaving Fresco and arriving at the bus stop?"

"Nothing." Mrs Fisk closed her eyes and crossed her right hand over her left. "Except..."

Another boom shuddered the house. The sound echoed into nothingness.

Mrs Fisk opened her eyes and said, "Probably nothing but someone asked me the time as I left Fresco."

Fenella sat up straight. That detail wasn't in the reports. She kept her voice steady. "You were asked the time on your way out of Fresco?"

"Yes. I'd just left the doorway and stepped into the street when I was asked the time."

"By who?"

Mrs Fisk shrugged. "Not someone I recognised."

"Can you describe this person?"

Mrs Fisk shook her head. "I'm sorry, I'm not a detective. I don't take in every detail when a random person asks me the time."

"Please try."

"Is it important?"

"I don't know."

Mrs Fisk closed her eyes, clearly trying to recall some details. The wall clock ticked. One second. Two. Five. Ten. She shook her head.

"It is a blur."

"Man or woman?" Fenella asked.

Silence, apart from Mrs Fisk's long sigh. It took Fenella some time to realise that it contained a single word—a word she never expected. A seemingly impossible word. And it came drifting from the woman's lips in a wisp which twirled in the warm air of the room, spreading slowly into meaning.

"Neither."

The wall clocked ticked then tocked.

"Neither," Mrs Fisk said again, her eyes snapping open. "Neither man nor woman."

A jangle of nerves tightened in Fenella's neck. "How'd you mean?"

"I ... I ... thought he was a boy. I suppose that is why I stopped, but he was a man. A short meatball on toothpick legs." She laughed and then her face took on a serious tone. "He spoke with a strong Russian accent, and there was something unnerving about his doll-like eyes."

CHAPTER 42

Shirley Bickham hunched over the bench in the semi-light of the garden shed, bitter and out for revenge.

The shed was a wood shack with a rusted iron roof and a thick metal door. Her dad, Fred Bickham, built it before she was born, plank by plank, with thick walls and a small window with glass fortified by steel wires running through it. Layered with years of grime, it let in a smear of sunlight which shimmered off the boxes and tins scattered about the dirt floor.

"A grand old place," her dad had said. "Private and secure."

It smelled of tobacco and was crammed with implements that might have been found in a mediaeval torture dungeon. A shelf ran the length of one wall packed with crates filled with nails, screws and an odd assortment of hammers. Shirley studied the collection of barbaric looking saws with clawed teeth so sharp they could slice through bone. Outside a blackbird shrieked.

The shack had everything she needed.

She tugged at the loose skin around her neck and took a sip from her hip flask; a quickie to lubricate the mind. A full twenty-four hours had passed since she had seen Den Ogden sneaking from the lighthouse on the pier. Twenty-four hours since he denied who he was. But Den Ogden was back in town. That was him with that grinning dog, she was one hundred and one percent sure of that. And he didn't recognise her as she followed him and watched where he went. *Good. Bloody Good.* Twenty-four hours to stew. A lifetime to plan.

The shed was her dad's hidey-hole. The place where he bolted when he wanted to be on his own or when he was working on one of his secret projects for the Hope Haven shelter and their gaggle of teenage girls. Ginger spent hours and hours in here with her grandad. Shirley scowled at the memory. Her dad's face beamed when he and Ginger returned from the shed. Positively glowed.

Shirley dusted off cobwebs, cleared a space on the bench and stopped. A small blue packet lay on the dirt ground under the workbench. It must have fallen between the slats. She bent down to pick it up, staring at it in silent shock. Why did her dad keep an open packet of condoms in here?

All of a sudden, a thud smashed against the window. Something screamed. She dropped the blue packet, gaze darting to the smeared pane. She exhaled. A bird had flown into the glass, probably a blackbird that had lost its way. For a moment, she was cast back into the past. She sat around the hearth with her dad and Ginger. "A blackbird in the house is a bad omen," he had said, his mouth a lipless slit. She remembered him watching her with beady black eyes as his arm snaked around Ginger's shoulders. Her daughter must have been twelve back then, growing rapidly into a woman. But it was her dad's next words that now sent a cold bolt of fear through her body—*If a blackbird beats upon your door, a child's death is for sure.*

Outside the birds began to shriek. Shirley moved in a feverish rush, she sure as hell didn't want to find out what that screaming meant. She grabbed the tools she needed. All she wanted was a few minutes peace to finish her project. She picked up a claw hammer, rolled it in her hands, feeling its weight. Her dad bought quality tools that lasted a lifetime and beyond.

What would he say if he knew of her plan? She banished that question from her mind but her dad's lipless smile stayed and his mouth began to move. No. She wouldn't listen. Her heart pounded with almighty thumps. No way in hell would she abandon the plan now. Not after all her anguish. She took another sip from the hip flask, told herself she didn't have a problem with drink and continued with her project.

Tap-tap.

It was important to get it right. She worked in spellbinding silence, labouring hard and grimacing as she went. The barrage of tapping went on for some minutes peaking with an inferno of hammer blows.

Tap-tap-tap-tap.

The panic-stricken rage at stumbling into that blockhead, Den Ogden, on the pier had long faded. Was it an accident that they met? Or the hand of fate? She decided the fickle finger of fate had pointed him out and instantly worked the hammer harder.

Tap-tap-tap-tap-tap-tap.

She'd felt a deep sense of shame when Den Ogden didn't recognise her. The man had bravado. The sheer scale of his lies boggled the mind. *Lighthouse inspector my arse.*

It was laborious work but she went at it with a joyousness fuelled by her alcoholic fug. Did Den know her dad was dead, murdered? No point wondering, she told herself. He would find out soon enough.

She put the hammer down and took a ragged breath. Moisture oozed from her palms and collected on her brow. She thought about her dad and she thought about the baby growing in Ginger's belly and she thought about her dismal life as a single mother. Ginger, her daughter, hadn't returned home. No interest from the police because, in the end, her mam had not reported the girl missing. *Why didn't I do it anyway? I love my daughter.*

Then she remembered she was the last to hear about Ginger's new baby. She took a long slug from her hip flask. Why waste time going to the police when Ginger is twenty-one going on twenty-two, and her gran knows where she is? No one looks for an adult runaway even if their belly is full with a growing baby. Anyway, adults can do as they please.

The police have more important things on their plate. *I've done the right thing.* She took another swig. *No one will ever find out. No one will ever know.*

"Shirley, are you in there?"

Shirley froze at her mam's voice. Why had she been thrown into a hellish soup where doom lurked around every corner? Her mam must never set eyes on the project. Never see what she was doing. Never know what she'd planned. It would kill her.

"Be with you in a minute," Shirley said.

The door handle rattled. Shirley stared in horror as the knob turned. Her mam was on the way in. She was coming inside to see what Shirley was doing; coming inside to see what she had done.

Shirley took off at a sprint. Her feet pounded against the dirt floor, kicking away boxes and tins. She hit the door with her shoulder, shoving it with all her weight.

"It's stuck, Shirl," her mam, Ida, said. "From the inside."

"Out in a few minutes," Shirley replied.

"What are you doing in there?"

"Tidying Dad's tools."

"Leave that until after the funeral."

"Got to keep busy."

The door handle rattled.

"Come out now," Ida said.

"I'll be done soon. I need some space to remember Dad. This was his special place where he built things for Hope Haven shelter. I just want to spend time in his cave."

Silence, apart from the thud in Shirley's chest. She leaned against the cold metal door, sweat running freely down her cheeks. Slowly, at the edge of her hearing came the barely audible rustle of footsteps. Her mam was on the garden path and walking back to the house.

Relief washed over her like rain. She let out a breath and leaned her back against the door. She gasped in stupefied horror at the creation lying on the workbench.

"A wickedness," her mam would have called the Frankenstein created by Shirley's hand.

Shirley pressed her back against the door trying to get as far away as possible from her creation. As though a bolt of lightning might strike and jolt the bloody thing to life.

"Oh God," she cried, suddenly filled with sorrow. "What am I doing?"

She wanted to believe it was the booze. She wanted to believe it was the pills. But it wasn't. She'd been planning this for years.

A shadow blotted the window and the shack went from dim to dark. The shadow twitched and jerked and turned into a familiar shape. The dim outline of her mam's face pressed against the glass.

"Mam, leave me be," Shirley yelled, gasping back fear.

"Are you drinking in there?"

"No."

The shadow vanished from the window. It's impossible to see inside the shed, Shirley told herself. Too much grime on the window, and those thin wires in the glass added to the blur. She let out a choking breath, hands clenched into tight fists. She had not expected it would be this difficult to find a few minutes' peace. In her mind it was easy. An hour to build. A moment to use.

She waited until the house door slammed shut then walked slowly to the workbench and put on a pair of gloves. For some time, she stood, staring, worrying the sore on her lip with her tongue. It wasn't until she picked it up with her gloved hands that she began to laugh. Chortling like a mad woman. Like she'd dodged the orderly and escaped from the asylum into the countryside beyond. Like she was running through a meadow with her hair blowing wildly. She rolled it in her hands, satisfied at its weight. *For dust thou art, and unto dust shalt thou return.*

The detectives were tight lipped over how her dad died. Not so the uniforms. She'd overheard an officer saying he'd not want to die by being clobbered by a cricket bat lined with nails; said he'd rather jump from a burning building or take his chances in the icy sea as a cruise liner went down.

Shirley gazed once more at the small window to make sure nobody was there. Then she took a long, hard, slug from her hip flask and swung the cricket bat, freshly cleaned and lined with nails.

CHAPTER 43

At five thirty in the morning, the Port St Giles police station was quiet. It was too early to be at her desk, but Fenella couldn't sleep. She sat in the half-light of the desk lamp, her chin resting on her hands. For some time now, she'd been staring at the still image on her computer screen.

The low hum of a vacuum cleaner carried through her closed office door. A cleaner was already working the hallway. Soon the station would spring to life and with it the clatter and jumble of another day. She'd be at Carlisle Crown Court most of the day; then meetings with senior management until six in the evening. With a bit of luck, she'd be home and tucked in bed by nine.

She picked up her mug, slurped lukewarm tea and put it down without taking her eyes from the screen. It was a blurry image taken from a CCTV camera inside Fresco. It showed Mrs Fisk a few moments before she left the store. She pushed a dark blue pushchair with the hood folded down and blue material draped down the sides. A three-wheeler with oversized tyres and an easy grip handle designed for runners. But Mrs Fisk wasn't moving at jogger pace, more at a leisurely amble. A handful of seconds from inside the store to outside and then she was gone. Except, there was no way of confirming the bairn was in the pushchair. The CCTV footage wasn't that good.

A tuneful whistle carried from the hallway. In rang out in time with the swish of a broom. As Fenella tried to recall the name of the tune, she realised something was bothering her. It concerned the bloke who'd ask Mrs Fisk the time as she left Fresco. Mrs Fisk claimed he was the last person she spoke with. Her description was vague—short, Russian, doll-like eyes. But the man was going into Fresco and the baby vanished at the bus stop.

Fenella clicked her mouse and replayed the CCTV footage. Over and over she played the grainy images, eyes unblinking and fixed on the screen. At last, she was certain, clicked pause and drummed her fingers on the desk. There was no footage of a short man going into the store in the minutes after Mrs Fisk left. Women in headscarves. Yes. Men in flat caps. Yes. Toddlers and teens and boys and girls. Yes. But no one fitting Mrs Fisk's description.

Fenella considered. Who asks the time at the entrance to a store and doesn't enter? Two possibilities. First the man didn't exist. Fenella had seen some strange things over the years. Could it be the pushchair was empty? Did Mrs Fisk go through the motions to create an alibi?

Second possibility. The man turned around and followed Mrs Fisk to the bus stop. But that meant he knew where she was going. Knew the store had CCTV. Knew the streets well. Had someone been watching the Fisk family?

She sent a text message to Dexter:

Baby Eva Fisk: Need review of CCTV footage from streets around Fresco in Barrow-in-Furness. Person of interest a short man who stopped Mrs Fisk to ask the time. Possibly Russian or Eastern European. Looks like a child. No mention of him in the files.

She wondered if he'd think her batty for sending such a request so early in the morning.

A second later her phone pinged.

On it, guv.

The office door swung open. A woman in a brown apron danced into the room. She wore headphones and pushed a vacuum cleaner, singing at the top of her voice. She plugged it into the wall socket, straightened and gasped. "Oh so sorry, I didn't think anyone was in this early. I can come back."

The woman was in her early twenties with thin arms and plump legs and that worried look which told you she was new.

"Nah, keep going," Fenella said. "Haven't seen you before, have I?"

"Started this morning, agency worker."

"Is that right?"

"Yeah, pays better than regular cleaning. Might get a full week here as three of your cleaners are off sick. I go all over town and see all sorts."

She flipped on the vacuum cleaner and went to work.

Fenella leaned back in her chair, mind darting between Fred Bickham and Mrs Ruth Fassnidge. Why did she feel, whenever she thought about their deaths, that she was on the never-ending road to nowhere? Her eyes closed and, once again, she conjured up the image of the figure in black dashing through the back yard of the boarding house. Man or woman? She squeezed her eyes tight and blocked out the hum of the vacuum. She must have focused for a full five minutes. The figure wasn't tall. That is all she got. She sighed and opened her eyes. At least she could rule out a serial killing giant.

"Ta-ra," the cleaner said, wheeling the vacuum from the room.

Fenella waved but her mind bounced to Fred Bickham. The attacker had more time in the remote allotments. No one would have heard Fred's screams. Except the blackbirds. Her phone rang. She gazed at the screen—Gail Stubbs, a long-time friend.

They'd met years back when Fenella was a rookie and Gail was at the start of her career in nursing. Recently, Gail's husband had left her for a younger woman, and she moved to Port St Giles to work in the hospital and rebuild her life. Not an easy task at any age, difficult when you've turned fifty.

"Thought I'd go straight to voicemail," Gail said in a happy tone.

"Wide awake and ready to go," Fenella replied, pleased at the interruption.

"You at work already?"

"Aye, a heavy day ahead."

"Well, lucky me, I've finished and my weekend starts after I've had a shower and a long sleep."

"But it is only Wednesday," Fenella said. "How come you get the rest of the week off?"

"I've worked double shifts because we are so short-staffed. Oh, don't forget tonight."

"Tonight?"

"My place at seven for a girls' night in. I've found this fish dish I want to try out. You haven't forgotten, have you?"

She had, but said, "I'll be on time."

"Good because I've got some big news."

CHAPTER 44

Den Ogden knew he'd have to bow, knew he'd have to grovel, but he had no idea how low he'd have to go.

Arranging to meet the Russian with the rag doll eyes for a second time wasn't easy. It was like trying to speak with the Pope from a coin-operated payphone. Good luck on finding one of those these days. Good luck on having the right coins. So, Den went through the long process of contacting the Russian, and waiting and waiting and waiting. Until on this Wednesday at the end of May, he got the nod to show up at a disused industrial warehouse at six in the morning.

He waited on a metal landing in a cavernous hall, so high up it made him giddy. There were wide gaps between the metal grid flooring. You could trap your foot and no one would hear your cries for help. Daylight seeped through gaps in the roof. It cut through the gloom and splattered the red brick walls. Overhead pipes snaked off into the distance. Iron hooks hung from chains strapped to giant girders. The air smelled of damp and rot and something sweet.

Den inspected the nearest hook. It was oiled

and primed and clearly still used. Wasn't this place supposed to be abandoned? He eyed the hooks again, brow growing damp with sweat. No. He didn't want to know their purpose.

He turned away and considered what he'd say. He'd borrowed cash from the Russian before. At loan shark rates. He needed a few thousand quid to see him through to his next big pay day. With any luck, he'd triple it with a few wise bets on the dogs. Optimistic. That was Den. He'd heard someone say shoot for the moon, if you miss, you'll end up amongst the stars. Screw two grand, he'd ask for ten. A nice round number in crisp fifty pound notes.

A door opened in the metal wall. A shadow beckoned Den inside. He entered an inner chamber with no windows. It smelled of rum and cigars mixed with a sweet odour he couldn't quite identify. He blinked. Why was it dark? He blinked again. Still no light. He shifted from foot to foot as his eyes adjusted to the gloom. Then it hit him, and it hit him hard.

Thick metal walls.
Soundproof.
One door.
No lights.
Giant hooks.
And that smell? He'd caught a whiff of it at the morgue.

He turned to run.

Two Neanderthals appeared behind him, blocking the door. They had razor blade short hair, cauliflower ears, flattened noses and colourless eyes. The Russian's henchmen. They might have been identical twins. And they looked at him as an underfed cat looks at a shivering mouse.

Den held his hands up, palms out. These men had iron fists and knew their way around a fight. Both men stepped in his direction. Both men grinned.

They enjoyed dishing it out, Den thought with a growing sense of panic. Where the hell was Rag Doll Eyes? They did whatever the Russian commanded. He had his men trained like Pavlov's dogs. One click of his fingers and they'd be slavering. Another click and they'd pounce like wolves. He had to speak with the Russian before these men got it into their heads that he was their latest toy.

Den turned around and faced the darkness of the room. At the far end, an orange glow swayed in the dark. It moved from one side to the other as something unseen creaked. Goosebumps pricked his neck when a hand from behind shoved him forward.

It was only then that Den made out the huge executive chair. The oversized desk came next. A dim light flickered on. Very dim. No brighter than a candle flame. And then he saw the diminutive figure. The Russian was dressed in black like a Japanese ninja. Except he wore a fat silk tie printed with frolicking dogs. The little man held a thick cigar in his right hand and rocked from side to side in his chair. The tip of the cigar glowed hot but the Russian's breath was loud and raspy. Like he was breathing hard and wasn't happy.

Den shuffled from side to side, waiting for a gesture to move forward and feeling very uneasy at what was to come. Maybe he should have brought Elfrid, the grinning dog, with him, but it was too late for that.

"Ah, you are here, my friend," the Russian said, still rocking. His accent was thick like he'd just stepped off the plane from Moscow. "Come nearer. I want to see your eyes."

Den shambled to within three feet of the desk.

The Russian sucked on the cigar, exhaling a plume of foul smoke. "If someone makes a careful plan to meet with a contact on the pier and the police show up, what would you do?"

Den said nothing. It hadn't started well and he feared it was downhill from here.

The Russian spoke again, his voice void of emotion. "One might think you told the police about our plan to meet. One might also think you discussed with them my money-lending business. Isn't that so?"

"No." Den said. "No way."

"It makes one wonder if the police have been told other things." There was still no emotion in the Russian's voice. "Things that could bring a hard-working man like me a lot of, as you like to say in England, bother."

Den heard feet shuffle behind him. The henchmen had stepped closer.

"I didn't call the police," Den said.

"Then, why my friend, were they there?"

"I don't know."

"You don't know?"

The Russian chuckled. "Ha-ha-ha. Funny, eh? Ha-ha-ha."

The henchmen joined in, only they cackled like hungry hyenas. Den swallowed the lump in his throat. He squeezed his hands, wondering how he got into this mess and trying to figure a way out.

The Russian clicked his fingers.

The goons stopped laughing.

The executive chair creaked.

Slowly, the Russian placed the cigar in the ashtray. He sprang to his feet. He was short with skinny legs, had a meatball wide body and was as light on his feet as a dancer. His rag doll eyes stared at Den without blinking.

It was a bad idea to come to the man's lair for money, Den thought. A very bad idea.

The Russian leapt in front of his desk, spider fast. He folded his arms and tilted his head, regarding Den like he was a fly.

Den stepped back. He didn't want to move too close to the Russian. The man had large hands and took unnatural pleasure in squeezing things until they were dead. He'd seen the bloke in action. Fast for a little bloke. Lethal hands. And his legs might look like toothpicks but they delivered a mighty kick.

I should run for it now, Den told himself. He'd dodge past the two goons and make his escape. But he didn't think he'd get as far as the door, not with the tremble in his legs.

The Russian stepped forward, dropping his arms so they swung loose and easy at his side. He bounced on the tips of his toes. His fingers clenched and unclenched.

Now, Den told himself and turned to run but felt the sour breath of a henchman in his face. The big man was grinning like he'd found an extra chicken nugget in the carton and was ready to chomp it down.

Den turned back to face the Russian. A hollow pang hummed in his gut. It fluttered like the fast beat of bluebottle wings, bringing a fresh wave of dread.

Now or never, he told himself as he sucked in a ragged breath and rolled the dice. "I want to ask a favour. I need two thousand in cash before I leave today."

The Russian flexed a leg and adjusted his position.

"Granted."

It took Den some moments to realise the meaning of the single word. He opened his mouth but no words came out. *Longshots sometimes won.*

The Russian smiled. "I hope the usual terms will be acceptable. Do unmarked fifty pound notes work for you?"

"Deal," Den replied, stunned.

A wave of relief washed away his tension. Next time he'd meet the Russian in a café with bright lights and surrounded by a horde of people. But he felt good now. With the cash he was back in the game. I'm not too old, he told himself. I've still got the magic touch.

The Russian was smiling, his rag doll eyes like black beads. The henchmen shuffled back to the door. Den grinned now. It was easy. Too easy. He should have asked for more.

The Russian raised his right hand to shake on the deal. They shook, long and hard.

Too long.

Too hard.

The Russian held Den's hand in a solid grip. "You will get the cash after you have done a small favour for me."

CHAPTER 45

The favour was bigger than Den Ogden expected.

When the Russian with rag doll eyes asked for help, he did not take 'no' for an answer. It was not the first time Den had been asked to help out. Not the last time either. And every time Den found himself deeper in a quagmire from which there was no escape.

The Russian watched Den with a steely gaze. His rag doll eyes were jet black and flecked with yellow specks. They reminded Den of a spider.

The Russian clicked his fingers and the two henchmen retreated from the room. The door closed with a solid click.

They were left standing in front of the executive desk, less than two feet from each other. Close. Too close for Den, but he didn't want to step back now the goons were gone, didn't want to give any ground. The odds, he thought, were moving in his favour.

The Russian touched his silk tie with the frolicking dogs. "Tell me, what happened to that hound?"

"Hound?"

"I saw you with a dog on the pier."

"Oh, that was Elfrid. I took him back to the animal shelter. Told them he was always barking and that I couldn't stand the noise. They said they'd give him till Friday."

"What is important about Friday?"

"That's when the vet comes to put the old-timers to sleep."

"Shame," the Russian said, waving a large hand, his fingers as fat as cigars. "He suited you."

"That is what I thought at first, but he was attractive to young girls."

"How young?"

"Twelve."

"You hound dog." The Russian clicked his teeth. "You want to get a schnauzer; women go wild for them. Eighteen-year-olds. Nineteen-year-olds. Twenties. Throwing themselves at you because of a dog. All legal. Trust me, I know."

"Schnauzer," Den said, wondering if he'd seen that breed in the animal shelter. "Thank you for the tip."

The Russian stepped closer, tilted his nose and sniffed the stale chamber air. His black beady eyes shone as though he liked the reek and wanted more of the foul pong. He sniffed again, keeping Den in his yellow specked gaze. It gave Den the creeps.

The Russian adjusted his silk tie with the frolicking dogs. "Now that favour you will do for me."

There was something wild and unpredictable

about the way the man watched you. Still, Den held his ground, to step back would be a sign of weakness.

"Go on," Den said, voice guarded, massaging his dome shaped double chin. "What type of favour?"

"A small one."

"That's what you said last time."

"You got the money, didn't you?"

"And I paid back the loan with interest."

"That is why I am asking you. You are reliable, have shown yourself to be a trustworthy friend over the years. I value that."

Although the Russian's dark eyes were hard to read, Den thought he saw a predatory flash in them. Like a spider creeping up on a fly.

Den frowned. "It has to be something big to be worth two grand. I'd like to know what I am getting involved with."

"Nothing you can't handle," the Russian replied. "Unmarked fifty pound notes to do with as you please. How does that sound?"

Den considered. The task might not be too bad this time. It might be something easy. Hadn't the Russian's jobs always worked out well for him in the past? Yes, he was certain the job would be easy.

He touched his double chin. "Ten grand."

"We have already shaken hands," the Russian replied.

"Eight."

"Three."

"Seven, with no interest and a year to pay it back," Den said.

"An interest-free loan?"

"That's right."

The Russian began to hum. A melancholy tune. Den tried to make it out. *The Funeral March*. My God, he thought. Is Rag Doll Eyes trying to unnerve me?

Although they were in a sealed metal chamber Den wasn't about to flake. He needed cash and he needed it now and his stomach rumbled with hunger. He would not back down. Not a chance now the henchmen were gone. If the midget got shirty, he'd grab the silk tie with the frolicking dogs and strangle the bugger. The odds were in his favour. The little meatball of a man in his black ninja suit didn't stand a chance.

"Deal," the Russian said, reaching out his hand for the second time.

Den shook, wished he'd asked for more and said, "What do I have to do?"

"I have a slight problem with an item stolen to order. The buyers didn't come up with the money. I want you to keep it for a few days until I shift it on."

The last time it had been guns. The time before that, drugs. Den didn't like guarding either. "What type of item?"

"A small baby. You like those, don't you?"

Den said nothing.

"You will look after it until I can sell her. A week at most. All expenses covered."

Den wondered why he had not seen this

coming. He'd heard the Russian was dabbling in the people trafficking business, and there was always an eager buyer ready to snap up a stray child. Good news, for the Russian, he supposed. And good news for him, except he felt uneasy. Selling babies came with hiccups, and it would hinder his own business in Port St Giles.

He said, "I don't have a place to stay."

"Already sorted."

"Wouldn't a woman be better?"

"You'd think so, but the last one took an overdose and ended up in the hospital. I can't take a chance. This time I hire a man. And that means you will be living with the child until I get things sorted at my end."

For all his menace Den knew then the Russian was in a tight corner. He puffed out his chest, cockerel style, thin lips stretched into a smile over his crooked teeth. He had the upper hand. His luck had turned. The odds were on his side now. He'd squeeze every penny from Rag Doll Eyes. Squeeze him for all the loan shark interest he'd paid over the years. Squeeze him for enough cash to finish his business in Port St Giles and get back on his feet. Then he'd go back to the animal shelter and get himself a schnauzer.

"Twenty grand," Den said, folding his arms across his chest. *I'll take care of me, if you will please take care of you.* "I won't do it for less, and I want half up front. Take it or leave it."

Den heard the crack of his jaw a second before

his face hit the floor. He didn't see the fist. As he lay on his back struggling for air, he became conscious of the sweet, fishy, gaseous stench which hung in the windowless chamber. He tried to slow his breathing.

In-out.

In-out.

Waiting for the next blow to land.

It never came.

And it was in those few moments when dazed relief gave way to joy at being alive that Den felt knees pressing against his chest; strong hands around his neck; felt the first nauseating wave of choking rise in his throat as thick fingers squeezed and squeezed and squeezed.

CHAPTER 46

It was that pleasant period a couple of hours before sunset when the day's work is over. Before Fenella knocked at the door, it flew open and Gail Stubbs let out a shriek of joy.

"Welcome," Gail said, with a smile, ushering her into the flat.

"Here is something for us to enjoy," Fenella replied, handing over a bottle of wine.

She'd splurged on a pricy Pinot which went well with fish. Tonight, her friend had big news.

Gail eyed the label, her smile stretching wider. "God, this is good stuff."

It was a small flat with a tiny kitchen. Soft jazz music mingled with the aroma of cooking. The living room served as a dining area. A blue and white floral table cloth covered the scrubbed pine table. Two place settings with wine glasses and silverware polished to a shine.

Fenella sniffed the delicious aromas wafting in from the kitchen. Nowt better than hearing news with a plate of good food. She didn't want to rush her friend to spill the beans, so she slipped into an armchair by the window. Her stomach rumbled. She craved food after a long day in court and endless meetings with senior management. She also craved Gail's news. Her friend was a superb nurse and an excellent cook whose food was well worth the wait. And so were her secrets.

Fenella nodded toward the kitchen. "What have you got in the pot?"

"Guess."

"You said fish, earlier, so I'll go with that."

"One point Sherlock. Guess the name of the dish and you'll get three."

Fenella made a show of sniffing. "Not fried in batter?"

"No."

"Or grilled to a crisp?"

"Do you smell burning?"

"Baked, then?" Fenella sniffed again. "Baked haddock in garlic sauce?"

Gail grinned. "Close. It is Cajun cod in garlic butter, a dish from Louisiana."

"Oooh," Fenella said, rubbing her hands. "You are a genius with food."

Gail threw her head back and laughed. "Got the recipe from your mam."

"Nan?"

Gail nodded. "And she got it from Priscilla, Dexter's..." Gail searched for the right words. " ... long time ex-girlfriend."

Fenella said, "Priscilla lives in New York City and travels all over as a backup singer. I guess she must have visited the Bayou State. What a life, eh?"

"Exotic," Gail replied.

"Like what you've got in the pot," Fenella said, "I'm dying to hear about your fish dish."

"Tender cod fillets baked in a buttery Cajun seasoning with crushed garlic cloves, a splash of extra virgin olive oil and a dash of cracked black pepper." Gail looked radiant, glowing. "All served with a fresh garden salad and cob rolls with local butter."

Fenella stared at her friend. Anyone with a face that radiant over baked fish had huge news to tell. If they hadn't been friends for donkey's years, she would have demanded to know right away. But she knew Gail. Knew things had to be done in their own time. Food first, then drinks and then a chat to share secrets.

When they had finished the cod, which was superb, and Fenella was enjoying the last spoonful of dessert, homemade bread pudding, Gail said, "How about I whip up a hot buttered rum? We can sip and chat while relaxing in the armchairs."

"Let me help you clear up the dishes," Fenella said.

The sooner they relaxed in the armchairs by the window, the sooner their conversation would turn to Gail's news.

They laughed and chatted about the latest soaps on the telly as they washed the dishes—Coronation Street, Emmerdale, and EastEnders. After the last dish was dried and stacked away, Gail whipped up two hot buttered rums and they sank into the armchairs by the window. It was a picture of contentment. Two friends, bellies full of fine food, slowly downing strong drink. Not a care in the world. Nothing to worry about, except discovering Gail's news.

And they had the whole evening ahead of them.

Time enough for a long natter.

The sun had sunk behind the rooftops, but this late in May it remained light outside. At last, it was time for Gail's news.

Fenella sipped her toddy, licked her lips and said, "So?"

The phoned jangled from the kitchen. A *cock-a-doodle-doo* which jerked Gail to her feet. "I'd better take that," she said, hurrying from the room.

Fenella looked at Gail's empty armchair and she looked at the fading light through the window and she looked at her rum toddy. She rose, glass in hand, and followed Gail to the kitchen.

"It's Olivia," Gail whispered. "Olivia Clemens."

Olivia Clemens was a mutual friend who worked as an emergency room nurse. The three had been friends for over twenty years and hung out when time allowed. Not so much these days with their busy schedules, but once a year at least.

Gail pushed a button and the speakerphone came on. "Fenella's here with me as a witness. Are you calling to say you have won the lottery and are giving me half?"

Fenella giggled. When the three got together, all hell broke loose. Was it too late for Olivia to pop over? When they were younger, they often met up midweek for an all-nighter. As they got older, with bairns and family, they reserved that luxury for the weekends. Fewer as the years went by. Nowadays, it took the weekend to recover.

"If only life were that easy," Olivia Clemens said with a sharp and anxious lilt to her tone.

Troubling.

Something terrible had happened. Fenella stared at the phone as if it were a hot poker. "What is wrong?"

A moment of silence. A sharp intake of breath. "An unusual spate of emergency admissions to the hospital," Olivia Clemens said in a frantic rush. "Seven at the last count. Gail, can you come in?"

It took three seconds for her words to sink in.

"On my way," Gail said, already moving toward the hall.

Fenella loved that about her friend. Nursing wasn't a career. It was a vocation. Tonight she was on a mission. Tonight Gail Stubbs would save lives.

Olivia Clemens was still talking. "Just had word of two more sick women. They are on their way in. This is so strange. They have all come in unconscious, and they are all middle-class women from the villages. Fenella, you'll want to be part of this."

Fenella kept her first aid skills up to date and had just renewed her CPR training, but nursing in a hospital was another level. "Oh aye," she muttered, feeling a knot of tension in her neck. "And why would that be?"

"Sir Curt Kiku has just arrived and is spouting off about a drug overdose and tainted supplies. The news media will be all over this." The phone went quiet for a heartbeat. "Oh my God, I've just got word of another one."

CHAPTER 47

Detective Constable Ria Leigh slouched at the table in the kitchen as the last of the sun's golden rays disappeared beyond the horizon. Not that she saw the majesty of the setting orb. The room was pitch-black. The curtains drawn. A bottle of rum and a shot glass rested on the table. The perfect place to plan a murder.

For some time now, she had been replaying her route to Mrs Stoke's hospital room. Tiptoeing to the bed. Pressing the pillow down.

Holding.

Waiting.

Counting.

She'd timed it to the second.

By midnight, Mrs Stoke would be dead.

A murmur from the fridge crept into the darkness. A nervous hum and splutter. The savoury smell of microwave food hovered in an intense cloud. A more promising scent than the bland flavour the frozen meal offered up to Ria's taste buds. She poured rum into the shot glass and took a long slug. Five minutes max, she told herself, letting the rum roll over her tongue. Five minutes holding the pillow over Mrs Stoke's face. Five minutes and her problem would be gone.

Her burner phone began to ring. Outside an owl hooted. The trees rustled in the breeze. Ria wondered about the blackbirds and refilling the bird feeder. The blackbirds had young and needed good food. There was one other item she'd take with her. A hand mirror to check for breath. It lay next to the rum bottle.

Only now did the clamour of the phone sound at the edges of her mind. A mass of bells and clangs. Even then, she did not at first respond, her mind navigating the labyrinth of hallways as she made her escape from Mrs Stoke's room. The route free of CCTV. And then she was out in the hospital car park, punching a fist in the air and home free. A masterpiece. Civic Officer of the year for the fourth year straight was a certainty.

Ria heard the burner phone then.

Its manic ring set her heart beating in dread. Don't be ludicrous, she told herself. She'd planned it out. Solved the problem. *Nothing will go wrong.* Still, as she stared at the trembling phone, a lick of fear reared up in her gut.

Her hand stretched out, hovered for a moment and she glimpsed herself in the hand mirror. Two bottomless hollows stared back. The skin sagged under her eyes. She didn't recognise the grim face and looked away.

The phone continued to ring.

A cold sweat broke out on her palms. Something was wrong. Her business partner, Sloane

Kern, only called when there was a cock-up. Christ, what had the cow done now? What cesspool did she want Ria to clean up? There were limits to what a genius could do.

Ria cursed.

Their joint business, only months old, was already more work than she expected. It had turned into a nightmare. And the profits were nowhere near what she needed. Splitting the meagre earnings in two whittled it down to almost nothing. All this risk and for what? Once she'd dealt with Mrs Stoke, she'd kill Sloane Kern.

Decided, she snatched up the phone, gritted her teeth and swallowed hard. "What now?"

"Ten of our clients have been taken to the hospital," Sloane Kern said. "It is all your fault, Ria. You gave me tainted pills."

CHAPTER 48

Fenella drove to the Port St Giles Cottage Hospital and gasped in shock at the sight. A thin line of ambulances waited at the receiving bay. Their lights flashed in a solemn beat. A mob of nurses and doctors appeared at the entrance and raced to the first ambulance. A momentary pause. The back door opened. A whirlwind of action followed. In seconds, a trolley was rushed through the front doors with an unmoving figure strapped tight. It was a grim scene made more upsetting by the wails and shouts of family members.

Fenella pulled the car to the kerb. "What on earth is going on here?"

Gail Stubbs said nothing, opened the car door and strode to the entrance, disappearing inside. It should have been a girl's night in with hot buttered rum and a natter about Gail's big news. And now this ... whatever it was.

Fenella parked her Morris Minor and raced to the entrance. A large crowd jostled in the main lobby. They clustered in clumps on the white-tiled floor, muttering and moaning and wailing. An endless crush of grief-stricken families, medical staff and members of the public. No signs of the news media, thank goodness. But it wouldn't be long before the likes of Rodney Rawlings sniffed it out.

"Over here, guv."

Dexter hunched in the shadow of a doorway. He wore a rumpled brown suit with a creased shirt that might once have been white. A plump man in an orange tweed blazer, cream shirt and black bow tie had an arm around Dexter's shoulder. It took a moment for Fenella to recognise Dr MacKay, the pathologist. He drank, gambled and speculated in equal measure. The man's face glowed warm and rosy as though he'd downed a dram or two of fine whisky.

Dr MacKay said, "I was having a rather nice supper with the wife when the call came through. We didn't get to dessert, a rather delightful French Fig Tart." He touched his bow tie and grinned. It twirled. "At least I got to try out a new magic trick before the alarm call went out."

A crowd of staff rushed by, hauling a fat woman on a trolley. They worked with speed, shouting and pressing buttons. A medical device beeped. Dr MacKay's eyes gleamed like a raven who'd spotted something that glittered.

He twirled his bow tie. "She is still alive, by the looks of it."

Jones showed up with a tray of coffee and a box of doughnuts. "Picked these up on my way here, boss."

Fenella slurped coffee and ate half a doughnut. Dexter scoffed two. Dr MacKay took a cup and waved a hand at the doughnuts. Jones wandered off to collect the names and addresses of those who'd been brought in.

"What do we know?" Fenella asked.

"Ain't got a clue, guv," Dexter replied, rubbing crumbs from his lips. "Just got here myself. What do you think, Doc?"

Dr MacKay tilted his head back, drained the cup and crushed it with one hand. His bow tie twirled. "Can you believe it? Every person they've brought in so far has a rather strong heartbeat."

"That's not what I was asking about," Fenella said. "What can you tell me about these women? What have you heard?"

Dr MacKay's bow tie continued to twirl with a soft hum. "It reminds me of the time when I worked as a volunteer in Kenya. Lamu, a port town on an island off the coast. Damn hot. Great crab soup. They make it with ginger."

"I'll put it on my holiday wish list," Fenella said.

"Don't know about ginger and crab," Dexter added. "It don't sound like it would taste right. Now, a splash of malt vinegar or a squeeze of lemon and you've got a right tasty dish."

"Can I get back to Lamu?" Dr MacKay asked. "I was enjoying the said soup when I was informed that seven women and seven men who spoke in a strange tongue had been rushed to the hospital."

Dexter said, "They weren't local, then?"

"Germans," Dr MacKay replied. "From the city of Hamburg."

"What were they doing in Lamu?" Fenella asked. She knew she shouldn't. Knew it might set Dr MacKay off on a rabbit trail, but she couldn't help herself. She wanted to know.

Dr MacKay shrugged. "Something to do with the moon and aliens."

"Eh?" Fenella wasn't certain she'd heard correctly. "Aliens?"

"They were part of a new age religious group," Dr MacKay replied, pressing a button on his bow tie so it twirled faster. "They'd overdosed on a local potion in the hope of getting beamed up to paradise on the mother ship. I pumped their stomachs and sent them on their way. I do save lives as well, you know."

A trolley stopped less than ten feet away. A woman with white hair and as pale as a ghost lay very still. Her eyes were wide but unblinking. Dr MacKay raised both hands, stepped toward the trolley, lips twisted into a gargoyle grin. His bow tie was twirling faster, humming, buzzing. The trolley began to move, picking up speed as the medical team trundled the woman away. He followed for several paces, stopped and retraced his steps.

He clasped his hands and spoke in a whisper. "I've sent word to the ward."

"What for?" This was Dexter.

"Any corpse must be sent straight to my studio." He made a sort of snipping motion with his hands. "These things are easier if you get the body fresh."

Fenella blocked out what he did in his lab and focused on her questions. "Any other thoughts?"

A shade of unease crossed Dr MacKay's face. "My best guess is that these poor women took some tainted potion ... yes ... a poisoned pill. I take it you haven't ruled out the cult angle? Anyone up for a bet of a good bottle of Glenmorangie whisky on that?"

Dexter's mouth opened. He glanced at Fenella and seemed to change his mind. He said, "It don't bear thinking about what might happen by tomorrow morning. It'll be a miracle if one of them don't cop it."

"Let's hope they all make it," Fenella said. "For the sake of their families."

"Of course." The uneasy look was back on Dr MacKay's face. "Well, it promises to be a long night of waiting. If you want me, I'll be in my studio awaiting news."

He strode away with the high-tipped skip of a young man excited about a date with a lass. Lights from the overhead lamps shone on him in a devilish orange gleam.

More people surged into the hospital lobby. Still no reporters. And no sign of Sir Curt Kiku.

Fenella said, "We don't have much time before things kick off with the press and politicians. Do you think Dr MacKay might have a point?"

"About the cult?" Dexter asked.

"Nah, tainted drugs."

"Aye, guv. It might be the link that ties these women together. Once we find the source of the pills, we'll have our answer. And there is Mrs Eudora Stoke too. That don't smell right, neither. Didn't I hear she took some dodgy pills too?"

Fenella nodded. "Ria is working that case. I called her on my drive in and told her to get here fast. She should be here by now."

CHAPTER 49

The sky had turned midnight blue with clouds crowding out the moon. Detective Constable Ria Leigh drove in a blind panic to the Port St Giles Cottage Hospital. The phone call from her business partner, Sloane Kern, sent her world into a tail spin. The call from Detective Inspector Fenella Sallow blew it to pieces.

"This can't be happening to me," she said, over and over as though the very utterance of the words would make it true.

One moment she was within a pillow squeeze of setting her world right. The next moment, this. And it wasn't her fault. This mess was down to Sloane bloody Kern. She took a corner hard, tyres screaming.

Ria thought of Mrs Eudora Stoke on her hospital bed, and she thought of the women taken ill. Now the clock was ticking at double speed. She tried to think of a new plan to make things right, but her brain cells were empty and she drew a sour blank. Bile brewed in her gut, bubbled and crawled up her throat in acid agony. How had her day turned so nasty?

Darkness grew around her as she plunged on,

gripping the steering wheel tight and cursing the day she met Sloane Kern. That damn hag had brought a huge wave of crap on Ria's life. It hung over her with its foul stink about to burst. Now doom awaited. She sensed it deep in her bones. Police officers convicted of selling drugs lived a hellish life in prison.

Her saving grace, she thought, was that Mrs Stoke was still unconscious, mouth shut. With a bit of luck, the woman might not make it through the night. She let that idea roll around her mind and liked it. But what about those other women who'd been hauled in by the dozen?

The tyres groaned against the gravel as the car lurched into the hospital car park. Ria blocked out the flashing lights and the crowd by the entrance. She must settle her mind. Must come up with her best plan. Must douse the blaze of self-doubt which threatened to ruin everything. She inhaled for a count of ten, then let out a breath as cool as dawn.

I can do this, she thought. She'd shaken down drug addicts for their supplies without mercy. She'd outfoxed her police superiors for years, wheedling her way into their confidence and accepting their awards. And she was on target for Civic Officer of the year, four times straight. Yes. She would get out of this hole and then she'd make Sloane Kern pay.

She cut the engine, held her head in her hands, willing her grey matter to fire off an idea. One minute. Two. Three. Five. No answer came. No plan formed. Nothing but the hurried pulse of blood through her ears and the sour gurgle in her gut.

Douse the blaze of self-doubt. At least she had … what did she have? Time. Not much, but a slither was all she needed. First, figure out what the hell is going on. Second, use it to inform her new plan. Third, and maybe this should have been first, get a status update on Mrs Stoke. She felt more convinced than ever that Mrs Stoke wouldn't make it through the night. A sixth sense, she supposed with a flicker of excitement.

She got from the car, mind still working on the best order, but firm on the status update of Mrs Stoke first. Her sixth sense told her the woman was a goner; that she might already be dead. A gust of wind whipped across the tarmac, throwing grit into her eyes. She stopped under the glow of a streetlamp, blinked, wiped and blinked again. For the first time since she arrived, her gaze fixed on the hospital entrance.

At the flashing lights.

At the madhouse activity.

At the figure standing in the shade to one side of the receiving bay door.

Detective Inspector Sallow was speaking to a nurse and jotting the answers in a notebook. Ria thought she had more time. She ought to be the one asking questions. How had Sallow got here so fast?

Then it struck her, Sallow must have been on her way to the hospital when she called.

"Oh God," Ria said as though only now fully realising the hell-hole she'd stepped into. "This cannot be happening to me."

Ria began to walk with little mincing steps, feeling like a new dog approaching the food bowl and uncertain what the old dog will do. *Do they know about my sideline business? Jesus. Has Sloane Kern cracked and confessed the truth?* She swallowed, edged into the deepest shadow she could find and pulled out the burner phone.

"Got ya."

The voice came from behind; from out of the shadows. Male. Ria spun.

Detective Constable Jones flashed a broad grin. "Thought it was you. We should stop meeting in places like this."

Ria said nothing.

Jones was at her side now. "What's wrong with you?"

"Me?"

"You look like you've seen a ghost."

"I'm fine."

"You sure?"

"Really, I am."

Jones didn't seem convinced, but said, "You've heard about this lot, then?"

He pointed at the entrance.

"Inspector Sallow called me," Ria said, tugging at a lock of hair. "Shocking. I can't understand it. I hear it might have to do with tainted pills."

Jones nodded. "That means gangland drug dealers have invaded our town. They'll be a turf war if we don't get a grip."

"Do you think so?" Ria replied, shaking her head. "That is horrible. Makes me sick. I transferred from Carlisle to Port St Giles for a quieter life. And now this!"

"Thought it would be right up your alley, pet." The words came from Fenella.

Ria couldn't believe it. How did the woman get so close without her noticing? She must have sprinted from the entrance on the tips of her toes.

"Yes, ma'am," Ria replied with a slight rattle in her voice. "But I didn't expect this in Port St Giles. What happened?"

"It is our job to find out," Fenella said. She turned to Jones. "I've asked PC Beth Finn to go to the ward and gather information. She could do with a hand. And look smart about it, Superintendent Jeffery is on the way."

"Yes, boss," Jones said and turned to leave.

He got about three paces and stopped. The sound of footsteps came from the pavement. A figure galloped toward them. And now, without warning, Dexter was among them.

"News, guv," he said, face grey and panting hard. "Big news."

He doubled over, gasping for breath and Ria knew that Mrs Eudora Stoke was dead. Her sixth sense. She blew out a breath of relief and prayed the woman had faded from this world in a cloud of sweet dreams. Oh God, she was so thankful for the hand of fate taking her side. Her mind drifted to the other women, brain cells firing with such intensity she almost missed Dexter's next few words.

"Mrs Eudora Stoke is awake, guv. And she's talking."

CHAPTER 50

Fenella glimpsed the pale face of Detective Constable Ria Leigh as they hurried to Mrs Stoke's ward, but it didn't register. She had other things on her mind. She was curious to meet the sister-in-law of Sir Curt Kiku. Eager to hear what Mrs Stoke had to say.

It was a private ward with floral scents and fresh flowers in giant blue vases. Pink orchids and white roses and bunches of saffron crocuses. Their petals glistened under the ceiling lights with shining droplets of water. Classical music played through unseen speakers. Low and soothing.

Fenella felt giddy and wanted to blame it on the wine and rum toddy, but knew better. It was excitement. A great chance to speak with Mrs Stoke on her own. No politicians present. No lawyers, either. No point telling Superintendent Jeffery, well, not until after her little chat. All she needed was a few minutes and she was sure she'd get the woman to natter. Impossible to stop the river once the dam burst.

The nurse at the reception desk was dousing a vase of mauve tulips with a spray mister. A slender woman, dressed in a dark blue uniform and an old-fashioned cap. She glanced up, a tiny smile kissing the edges of her lips and placed the mister on her desk. She knew they were from the police.

"Well, hello there," the nurse said, somehow working her Irish accent so it sounded like a smile. "To be sure, Mrs Stoke is awake and chattering away like a morning lark. No need to call the priest out of his bed for that one. Strong as an ox. Sir Kiku was here earlier but left. The doctor just went in. Room thirteen, second on the left."

A gasp came from behind Fenella. A dramatic dry throated rasp, surprisingly harsh against the soft music. It seemed to suck the melodic notes out of the air, replacing them with something toxic. Fenella turned as Ria staggered back two steps and placed a hand on the wall to steady herself.

"What's wrong, luv?" Fenella asked.

Ria's right hand shaded her forehead. The whites in her eyes seemed very bright. Was she on the verge of an epileptic fit? Fenella dashed to her side and held her by the left arm. Dexter had moved, and now stood behind Ria. If she fainted, he'd catch her.

"I'm ... f... ff ... fine," Ria said.

But something moved behind her eyes. Something deep and dark and full of dread. Fenella saw it and recalled how pale Ria's face was in the car park. And now the lass had turned a shade of green and her nostrils flared as though trying to suck more oxygen from the sweet-scented air. Ria Leigh didn't look right.

"You are trembling, pet," Fenella said, "And look at that sweat on your forehead. You are not okay."

She walked Ria to a row of plush leather armchairs, each separated by a coffee table and scattered with upmarket glossy magazines.

"Sit here, pet," Fenella said, easing Ria into a seat. "Catch your breath."

"I'm fine," Ria said again, but it came out weak and feeble like the voice of a frightened child.

And like a frightened child Ria's eyes had grown wide and her bottom lip quivered. She thrust her head forward, shoulders stooped, hands clenching her knees. Her body jerked in tiny spasms despite her stiff posture.

"Let me look at you," the nurse said, the sing-song lilt gone from her voice, replaced by a coarse Belfast working-class tone. She hustled from her desk, took Ria's pulse, blood pressure and temperature. "Sweet Jesus, your heartbeat is high and so is your blood pressure. Are you on any medications?"

"None," Ria replied, voice a childlike squeak. "I passed my last medical with flying colours. I'm fit and strong. There is nothing wrong."

"Not what the instruments say," the nurse replied. "Sit here for a while, we'll see if things change, and first thing in the morning you must see your doctor."

"That is an order," added Fenella, again eyeing the lass with concern.

They waited five minutes. The nurse retook

the readings. The blood pressure monitor hissed as it squeezed Ria's arm. The nurse stared at the numbers, shook her head, then turned to Fenella. "I'm sure the doctor is finished by now, why don't you two go ahead and visit with Mrs Stoke? I'll stay here and keep an eye on Ria."

Fenella stared at Ria and she stared at the nurse and she stared once again at Ria. She hesitated. Was she mistaken or did a shadow of fear cross Ria's face at the mention of Mrs Stoke?

"That okay with you, Ria?" Fenella asked, watching Ria closely.

Ria nodded but her eyes were cast down.

The nurse said, "Please go. We'll have a nice relaxing chat, won't we, Ria? I'll send for a mug of tea, and we'll see if those numbers improve."

If they were anywhere else, Fenella would have demanded an ambulance pronto. But they were in the hospital with medical help on tap. Still, guilt at her eagerness to speak with Mrs Stoke pressed deep fingers into her neck. She tilted her head from side to side, but it did not ease the tightness. Why had it not registered with her that Ria was ill?

"Any change in her condition, I want to be the first to know," Fenella said, hand massaging her neck.

"Of course," the nurse replied.

"Want me to stay here, guv?" Dexter asked.

"Nah," Fenella replied. "We'd best both go. Less chance of missing anything and I want all the details down to names, addresses and dates. Come on, let's have a natter with Mrs Stoke and find out what all this is about."

CHAPTER 51

Outside Mrs Stoke's hospital room Fenella said, "I'll sit by the bed, but if I get an inkling she goes for the grizzled type, you do the talking."

"Aye, guv. Got my questions lined up and ready to fire." Dexter jabbed at the gold plate to one side of the door. "Number thirteen. I ain't superstitious, but I don't fancy them medics whipping me into a room with that number. Private ward or not."

"At least it isn't Friday," Fenella said, staring at the number as a bell tolled in her gut. It rang with a solemn tone—the clang-clang of anticipation mixed with curiosity at what she'd find beyond that door. Always the same stirrings when she was about to meet a person in her search to find things out. She imagined a gaunt faced woman pointing the finger of blame. But at who? Or would Mrs Stoke, pious faced, put her illness down to the cruel hand of fate?

Fenella knocked with a soft clunk, pushed the door open and stepped inside.

It was cool, and the air was thick with the fragrance of fresh flowers. Soft lighting and floral wallpapers. Leather armchairs. An executive desk with a banker's desk lamp. Plush furnishings everywhere. If it were not for the *beep-beep* of some hidden machine, it might have been an upmarket hotel suite. A buzzer which looked like a room service brass bell rested on a table. The ceiling fan toiled with a pleasant hum.

Fenella thought the furnishings were over the top. The only thing missing was a dour-faced butler. Sir Curt Kiku's family expected the best, but this was crazy.

"Top of the range," Dexter said, letting out a low whistle. "Quiet, too. When my grandad came in for his heart, the medical devices beeped like crazy. The general ward is like a shanty town compared to this lush lot. They'd riot if they saw this. How the other half lives."

For a moment, neither of them said anything more. A breeze of sweet air from the fan pressed in on their faces as the unseen medical device continued to chirp. Fenella wondered why it was beeping. Mrs Stoke's heart? Or the measurement of some other vital organ? Or was it like the time her bedside clocked chirped because it needed a new battery?

A mauve velvet curtain with gold beading shielded the bed. It shimmered and parted. A familiar figure in a green dress and with a massive afro poked her head through the gap and smiled.

Fenella said, "Dr Kendi, how is the patient?"

Bishara Kendi, from Kenya, had lived in Port St Giles for less than a year and was already rated as one of the best doctors. Fenella met her through her nurse friend, Gail Stubbs, and gave her one of Nan's blackberry pies. They weren't quite friends — yet. Fenella would work on that.

Dr Kendi stepped from the curtain, closing it behind. "I heard the police were on site, didn't expect two detectives. Mrs Stoke is doing well."

"I hear she is singing like a bird, Doc," Dexter said. "Did she say anything about who sold her those pills?"

"I don't know anything about pills," Dr Kendi replied. "But Mrs Stoke has made a strong recovery, although there is still some way to go. Anyway, I'm finished here."

Fenella could sense the relief in Dr Kendi's voice. She must be at the end of her shift, she thought. *And I'm still on duty for who knows how long.* Then, right away, she felt foolish. She loved her work, loved the hunt for clues, and was now more eager than ever to speak with Mrs Stoke. She wanted to hear what the woman had to say. Eduardo, her husband, called it her curious gene. Her mam, Nan, called her a nosy parker.

Fenella glanced at the shimmering velvet curtain. "Knocking off for the night?"

"Oh no," Dr Kendi replied. "Double shift. Next comes my favourite —the general ward."

She scowled, but in a happy sort of way. Fenella remembered she'd scowled like that when they first met. She had seen her scowling on the ward and with the nurses and with the cleaners. Not in a bad way, either. In a happy, contented, 'I love my job' scowl of someone who will get the work done. And everyone loved her for it, including Fenella, hence the gift of Nan's tasty blackberry pie.

Now Fenella focused on her work. "Mind if we have a few words with Mrs Stoke?"

"Now?" Dr Kendi's gaze bounced from Fenella to Dexter. "At this time of night?"

From somewhere in the room came a rapid beeping. An electronic alarm. A high-pitched alarm. One fast *beep-beep-beep* alarm.

"It might be her heart, Doc," Dexter said, faced creased in concern. "It'd be just our luck for it to give out before we had a chance to have a word. Same thing happened with my grandad."

Beep-beep-beep.

Dexter stepped toward the velvet curtain like a medical man who knew what he was doing. He stopped and rubbed a hand over the back of his neck. "It's her heart, ain't it, Doc? It's about to pop."

Beep-beep-beep.

Dr Kendi threw her head back and gave an easy laugh, her Kenyan accent more pronounced. "Not Mrs Stoke's heart. Not to worry. It will stop in a second or two."

It did, and the room was suddenly filled with a sweet-scented silence.

Fenella once again eyed the velvet curtain, eager to go inside. "Mrs Stoke asked to see us. We've a few questions to get the ball rolling. Not a formal statement, mind you, we'll get to that when Mrs Stoke is ready. Tonight we'll keep it quick, in and out in ten minutes."

Dr Kendi folded her arms. "I'm afraid that is out of the question. I ordered a sedative for Mrs Stoke. It was administered five minutes ago. She is now sound asleep and resting peacefully."

CHAPTER 52

Den Ogden thought things were bad until they really began to fall apart.

He touched his neck and shivered. It took the two henchmen to drag the Russian with rag doll eyes off him. If they hadn't burst into the windowless room, he'd be nowt but a sweet-smelling vapour. He recalled those giant hooks, well oiled and primed for use. He pictured himself hanging from one, limp and dull-eyed, and shivered. The fishy stench of death still curled deep in his nostrils. The henchmen saved his life.

It was the dead of night and he stood by the door of the tiny bedsit, up three flights of stairs at the end of a windowless corridor. It was a small wooden dormer added to the roof. A single room. One electric outlet on the wall, and a camper's double ring stove on the counter by the sink. The light switch was in the corner, high on the wall, like it was placed there to be difficult to find. A low wattage electric bulb hung from a thin wire. No lampshade. The sour reek of unwashed clothes mingled with the stench of the blocked toilet. Home for now, and better than the pizza shop floor.

The only real furniture was a television on a

pine table, a narrow fold-up bed next to a crib, a built-in wardrobe, and a full-length mirror nailed to the front door. It was clouded and cracked and chipped at the edges, but you could see your reflection if you leaned in close.

Den sucked on the last of his cigarette and dumped the butt into his beer can. The dull sizzle made him think of food. A curry and a fresh six-pack of ale. That's what he needed to see him through. He crushed the beer can and tossed it at the bin. It missed, clattered and rolled along the bare floorboards coming to a stop by an empty pizza box.

A twenty-four-hour café occupied the ground floor. The first-floor rooms were rented to people who minded their own business and never talked to the police. Shadowy folks who worked jobs which paid cash. Men who had something to hide. Women that didn't want to be found. And the rooms on the floor below were all empty. The dormer was the only room at the top. A place where no one came. A safe house.

Only Rag Doll Eyes and his henchmen knew he was here. Well, except that nosy cow with the pale face and blood-red lipstick who lived on the lower level. She had that fearful look like she was hiding from the police and was checking he wasn't a cop. She'd not bother him again. Whatever her gig was it wasn't totally legal. He'd steer clear of her.

Den walked to the cracked mirror on the door and gazed at his face. Yes, the swelling on his neck was going down, but it was still sore to touch. When he spoke, his voice croaked with the rasp of a frog. It had been that way since he'd nodded a terrified acceptance of the Russian with rag doll eyes terms. Five thousand pounds at loan shark interest rates paid in full once he'd done the man a 'favour'.

"You look after the baby and I look after you," the Russian had said. "Feed baby. Change baby. Put baby to sleep. All will go good. Fifty pound notes, unmarked, no? Now, you do what I say, okay?"

They shook hands on the deal. Not that Den had any real choice. Not with the possibility of the Russian's thick fingers back around his neck. Of course, he had no idea of what he was getting into. No idea of the boatload of trouble to come.

He reached in his pocket for the packet of cigarettes, realised it was empty and swore. How had he smoked the entire packet since walking through the door? How had he drunk a six-pack of ale for that matter? His stomach grumbled. He was starving, tired and needed a smoke.

He went to the window. The view wasn't much to write home about either. Just the rooftops of buildings on the opposite side of the street. Red chimney pots and grey slate roofs. Satellite dishes and long abandoned television aerials. If he poked his head through the window and looked down, he had a clear view of the street below. Parked cars, a bus stop and the front gardens of the houses which backed up to the road. Nothing spectacular. An ordinary seaside street on an ordinary night in May. Except that Den had the sinking feeling he'd made an irreversible deal with the devil.

But that wasn't his biggest problem.

It was almost midnight and the baby wouldn't settle. It had begun as a soft whimper. A small hiccup in the road to a quiet night in. A curry and a smoke and a few beers in front of the telly was all Den wanted. Not a big ask, and after the past few days, he deserved it. But the baby's whimper had blossomed into a non-stop wail.

Wah. Wah.

Den squeezed his eyes tight to fight back the headache. It did nothing to block out the noise. He walked slowly to the cot, jabbed at the covers, tucked the baby in to make it comfortable, and jiggled it onto its back. The bairn was a strange moonlight pale with blue under the eyes and mouth turned down at the edges. *Something wasn't right.*

Den clawed at the covers and leaned closer. The baby coughed, then screamed. All out. At the top of its lungs. A high-pitched siren that set your teeth on edge. A wail which told you it didn't want to be in this grim room, didn't like this man, wanted to be back home with its mam. Or at least that is how Den interpreted the wail. He'd done a deal with the devil and now there was hell to pay.

Wah-wah.

His head throbbed. He glared at the cot. "All right!" he snapped, "I've had just about enough of this."

Wah-wah-wah-wah.

His nostrils flared as he eyed the brat. It would

wear itself out and fall asleep, wouldn't it? He just had to give it time. But he'd been in the flat for six hours without a moment of relief. *Something was terribly wrong.* He wanted to call the Russian, tell him the baby wasn't right. But he'd been told not to call. Rag Doll Eyes or one of his henchmen would contact Den when the time was right.

"A few days," the Russian had said. "And lie low in case the police are still looking for the child."

Den stepped back from the cot and turned away unsure of what to do. He'd changed the brat. Fed the brat. Even rocked it in his arms. But pale faced and small-eyed, it screamed and screamed and screamed.

"Stop it," he hissed. "I don't want to be here either."

The thing was wriggling about, moaning, trying to roll on its side. Was it trying to look at him? No, he told himself, that was mad. A bairn knows nothing and can't speak. Still, a terrible fear gripped him. The same fear he'd known in the windowless chamber with the Russian's thick hands squeezing his neck. The fear that death lurked in the shadows and was lurching nearer. *Something wasn't right.* He didn't want the infant to roll over, didn't want the bleedin' brat to look at his face. He wasn't a religious man, but no way in hell would he be the last thing it saw.

"Stop it," he yelled. "Stop it. Stop it. Stop it."
The baby howled.
Den ambled to the window, stretched and

yawned. He wouldn't be rushed by the brat's howls. Kids had to learn that they weren't the centre of the world. They needed to know who was master. And anyway, what were the odds the brat was really sick? He gazed at the child and didn't know. He wasn't a bleedin' doctor.

Still, he waited a full three minutes before deciding what to do next. If he'd had a packet of cigarettes, he'd have had a good smoke to let the brat wait longer. He was in charge now. He was the boss. At least in this tiny grim slice of the world.

He opened the window a touch, hoping a blast of fresh air would help settle the brat. The night seeped through the open crack, soft and sweet with a hint of the tang of the sea. It thinned the reek of soiled nappies, the pong of baby formula, and the pungent odour of fast-food cartons piled to overflowing in the bin. It cut through the cigarette stench and the stink of stale ale, and with it, from the street, came the rumble of tyres mixed with the screech of a police siren.

Den swung the window wide inviting in more of the warm breeze. It flowed like an unseen liquid, sweeping away the dankness. He leaned through the frame and peered down at the street. Blue flashing lights streaked the buildings. The siren continued its mournful wail, growing distant as the police car continued on its way. *A safe house.*

Den's gaze swept the street and fixed on the lone figure at the bus stop. They've missed the last bus, he told himself. *I've had hell tonight, let the bugger walk*. He cursed as a taxi pulled up to the bus stop, then turned and glared at the brat, wondering if his idea of 'fresh air' would work. All he wanted was for it to stop crying so he could enjoy a six-pack of ale, curry and a smoke. So, he waited now, not knowing what else to do.

One minute.

Two.

Three.

The baby's wail became a dry gasping croak.

Four.

Five.

Its eyes glazed over. Its skin turned pigeon wing grey. Den didn't move. After another five minutes, it shuddered and gave a thin sob which faded to a soft whimper. And to his relief, the whimpering soon died and the baby became still. Very still.

CHAPTER 53

Shirley Bickham stood five paces from the bus stop, head tilted up, staring at the top floor. A thin dribble of light shone from the dormer window. It was after midnight and she knew Den Ogden was home. She clutched a canvas bag with gloved hands. This was the night hellfire broke.

Her gazed darted to the blackened panes on the level below the dormer. The rooms on that floor had been in darkness since she'd been watching the building. Many of the windows were boarded up. Others had their glass panes smashed. No one lived on that level. On the ground floor, a yellow glow seeped through the clouded windows of the all-night café.

Shirley had followed Den Ogden when he slithered out from the lighthouse on the pier, but lost him in the boardwalk crowd. Quite by chance, as she rode the bus, she saw him again. He was scurrying along this street. By the time the bus stopped and she clambered off, she had once again lost him. She fumed for a while, then decided to take positive action. Why not watch the street from the bus stop? Who takes much notice of people waiting for the bus?

And today, at dusk, she spotted him. Pure luck she supposed. Or the hand of fate. He kept to the shadows, moving like a sewer rat. He paused at the alley by the café, cast a rodent glance over his shoulder and disappeared into the darkness. He must have used the side door to enter the building, she thought. When the light clicked on in the dormer, she had him.

Footsteps sounded on the other side of the street. Shirley became instantly alert, tightened her pink headscarf and waited. Who would be walking around at this time of night? She eased into the shadow of the bus stop, making herself as small as possible, watching.

A wizened man scurried along on the other side. He had thick sideburns and wore a flat cap tilted over his face. She recognised George Rouge without getting a good look at his face. He stopped in front of the yellow glow from the Eggshell Café, peered through the window, then hurried on.

Shirley moved from the shadows as his footsteps echoed away. Air rattled in her chest. Excitement. Her breath, she knew, smelled of booze. She'd downed two shots before she set out and another, from her hip flask, when she set eyes on Den. She adjusted the bag on her shoulder. Time for Den Ogden to get a full measure of what he deserved.

The building had four floors in total, with peeling paint and rotted window frames. The café on the ground floor was a flea pit greasy spoon which smelled of fried food and served tea so strong it tasted bitter. Low prices, cash only and everyone watchful of strangers. A late-night dive for taxi drivers working the graveyard shift. A place to do a deal for those who crawled the midnight streets. A safe house for the criminally minded.

Shirley scanned the building again and reckoned most of the rooms were empty. Only those down on their knees would choose to live in the place, or those who enjoyed crawling around in the gutter. That wasn't the Den Ogden she knew which meant he was out of cash and in Port St Giles to work one of his diabolical schemes. The sooner she got to the bugger, the better. A surprise visit in the dark.

Shirley focused on the dormer. Why was his light still on? Something was happening up in that room. Something dark and nasty and dreadful.

A shadow moved in the dormer window. The silhouette of a man. Although Shirley couldn't be certain, she sensed it was him. And he was looking down into the street. She dashed back to the bus stop and sat on the bench. Did Den Ogden see her?

Shirley took a swig from her hip flask, and for the first time, admitted that their relationship felt off from the start. She fell head over heels, but he always had the shiftiness of a used car salesman. It was a fleeting affair. Intense. Passionate. A candle flame which soon burnt out.

It changed her life.

She started drinking when it was over, broke out in sores, body infested with sexually transmitted diseases. That is when she started having the dreams, found she couldn't even hold down a job, and the doctor gave her psychiatric pills. A long slide which led her here tonight. But it had left Den Ogden unscathed. The bugger.

It wasn't fair.

It wasn't right.

But life wasn't fair. No one said it should be. The universe had rolled the dice and she'd been given her lot. A fine lot indeed! A room in her mum's house because she couldn't afford better. A dad who'd died a vicious death. A pregnant daughter on the run from home. And now she was forty. Oh God, her life was a living hell.

She blinked and the image of the nurse with flabby arms flashed before her eyes. The nurse's head tilted to one side, her face glowing with vengeful delight. She cradled a still newborn in her arms. *Tell them nothing.* She held the child out with both hands and walked backward, eyes blazing with flames.

Shirley squeezed her eyes, clapping her hands over her face. Firm and tight and blocking out the street light. Pressing down until her eyeballs hurt. The booze was doing her head in. Or was it to do with her pills? Delusions is what the psychiatrist called it—visions and voices that appear when awake. She hadn't taken her pills for quite some time.

"Go home now," she heard the voice in her head say. "Take the pills because they will calm your nerves and make you fall into a deep sleep."

No. She would not give up and go home.

Tonight she'd get answers to a question which burned in her gut. Tonight she'd get justice.

Lost in bitter thoughts, Shirley didn't hear the rumble of tyres, or the sharp creak of the handbrake.

"You all right there, darling?" A hooked-nosed man with a thuggish voice leaned from the car window. "The last bus has gone."

The words 'last' and 'gone' seemed to join to make one long sound. What made him pull over? Concern for a lone woman at a bus stop? Worry Shirley might not know the last bus had gone? Or was it like the time she hitchhiked home and bounced into the rancid arms of Den Ogden?

"Hop in and I'll give you a discount," the hooked-nosed man said. The taxi sign on the roof buzzed off.

Shirley remained very still, except for her right hand. It snaked inside the shoulder bag and squeezed the cricket bat handle. A thrill of anticipation danced at the pit of her gut. A feeling of stepping into something dark and wanting to go there. Again.

The man leaned further out of the window, eyes rolling over her body. "How much?"

Sweat prickled her forehead, slithering down her cheeks. And there was a moment, as brief as a sigh, when she wanted the man to step from the car and amble to within her reach. The cricket bat. Grip tight. Swing thrice. Head. Chest. Balls. But the moment passed in a sour huff of words.

"Suit yourself," the hooked-nosed man said.

The car window eased shut, and the engine roared as he sped away.

Now, as Shirley waited in the shadow of the bus stop for the dormer light to go off. Her hand gripped the hip flask, raising it to her lips. She swigged a mouthful and then another and one more for good luck. The clock was ticking. When the time came, she'd swing the bat. Fast and hard. Repeated blows. Teach Den Ogden a lesson he'd never forget. Then, when the bugger was a quivering heap of flesh, voice wailing with remorse, she'd ask her question. The question which had burned a hole in her soul for more than twenty years—what did you do with my son?

CHAPTER 54

Den Ogden eased the door shut and crept down the darkened stairs. He wanted a curry and he wanted it bad and he wanted it with a six-pack of ale. But he didn't want to chance disturbing the baby, so he left his door unlocked.

The stairway was dark and the air still and dank with a strong whiff of mould. No bulb to light the way. No handrail, either. The walls were damp to the touch. Den picked his way down with the beam of his phone's torch, taking care not to trip on the worn carpet.

As he entered the hall on the ground floor, he glanced at his watch. Plenty of time. He'd order a takeaway—beef vindaloo, extra hot, with soft naan bread and saffron rice.

A pot bellied Welshman and his skinny Pakistani wife ran the local curry house. They closed at two, sold cheap booze under the counter and didn't do delivery. Ten minutes on foot wasn't too bad a walk, even this late at night. And it was much better than calling a taxi. Taxi drivers asked questions and remembered faces.

Den crept through the ground floor lobby and out onto the step at the side of the building. The sky was midnight blue and the night growing misty. A breeze whistled along the empty street bringing a blast of salt air from the sea. The light from the all-night café splashed the pavement in an orange glow. A taxi rumbled to a stop outside the café. The hooked-nosed driver looked at the bus stop, scratched his head, glanced his way for a long moment and strolled into the café.

Den's eyes swept past the bus stop and along the parked cars. There was no one in the street now. Why did he have the feeling he was being watched?

He placed his back against the brick wall and gazed at the buildings across the street. A shabby row of Victorian mansions converted into bedsits. Boarded doors with iron shutters and dark windows, some smashed. He studied each window but saw no one watching.

An alleyway snaked between the buildings. Littered with dustbins and black bin bags, it led to the canal path and a shortcut to the curry house. He watched it for several moments but saw no one there, either.

A police car trundled along the street. Den backed into the shadows. They were always patrolling this part of town. He watched until the sound of the engine faded away.

He was about to dash across the road and into the alley when his eyes flicked to the line of parked cars. A blue Toyota truck. A silver Honda hatchback. A brown Ford car and a blue Citroën van. He'd seen that brown Ford car before, hadn't he?

He dropped to his knees and stared at the car for a long while. Slowly, his eyes traced the outline of a person inside. A man. He couldn't be certain, but he thought the person was looking his way.

Keeping low to the ground, Den scurried across the street and into the alley on the opposite side. It was a cut through to the canal, and the quickest way to the curry house. Black bin bags leaned against overflowing dustbins. Slivers of broken glass glistened in the blue light. Everywhere piles of rubbish clustered in festering mounds.

Den sidestepped a brown smouldering pile of what could only be human in origin. He eased the sharp shards from broken beer bottles to one side with his shoe. Holding his breath against the stink, he crouched between two dustbins. Like a rat. And like a rat he watched. If he was being followed, he wouldn't have long to wait.

A car door slammed. Rapid footsteps. The footsteps stopped and there was a flicker of shadow across the alley entrance. The person stood on the threshold of darkness and appeared to be thinking or waiting or planning.

Den thought he heard a grunt, but couldn't be sure. At any rate it was a man's voice from deep in the throat. Like a gulp or a gasp. A moment later, the footsteps started again. Slow and hesitant. The man had decided and was coming Den's way.

This was bad. Very bad. The odds didn't look good. Take shallow breaths, Den told himself as his mind raced. He pressed his limbs in, lowering himself further into a rat crouch. His heart drummed against his ribs, and it struck him who the man was and what he wanted.

Years ago, the dad of one of his conquests tracked him down. A full three years after he'd pleasured himself with the man's school-aged daughter. A lass whose face he could not recall. But he remembered the babies—maggot fat twins, each with a wild mop of curly black hair and eyes the shape of pearls.

The dad cornered Den at the end of a windowless corridor on the top floor of a cheap motel in Whitehaven. A sodding awful night where rain lashed down from the heavens. He was a big bloke with the square jaw of a boxer, tree trunk legs and cannonball biceps. Six-foot-nine and almost as wide. A nightclub bouncer type who dished out the law with his fists.

Den tried to reason with the man as he backed away. When that failed, he ran. Square Jaw was quicker, grabbed Den by his shirt collar and hauled him through the emergency exit. There was no doubt what he had in mind, and it wasn't a gentleman's handshake.

That's when Den got lucky.

As they struggled on the metal steps, slick with rain, Square Jaw slipped. He tumbled over the railings taking Den with him. From the top floor. A long way down. Nowt but an empty car park below. Square Jaw hit first, his head bouncing off the tarmac like a basketball.

Thud.

His huge body broke Den's fall.

Den didn't wait for the police to arrive.

Much later, Den discovered the man died from his injuries. And his teenage daughter? She committed suicide. Not Den's fault. No one's fault, really. *I'll take care of me, if you will please take care of you.*

Now, in the dank alley, the wind moaned with the mutter of a graveyard. Footsteps. Soft and careful and cautious. The man came into view. He wore a brown trilby hat. And yes, Den had seen the bugger before. Definitely the man in the brown Ford from outside Mrs Fassnidge's boarding house. The same man who peered through his toilet stall in Quick Bet Bookie Store. Den was certain now. Trilby Hat was searching for him. Trilby Hat wanted revenge.

Den pressed himself down another inch, squatting the way no man of his age should. Everything folded in, flattened so that his chest almost touched the soiled cobblestones. He breathed in a long stale breath of stink and leaned his forehead on the bins, peering through the crack. Was the man holding something? A knife? A gun? It was too dark to tell. But any second the man would turn his head and see him squatting amongst the filth.

There was only one thing to do, and Den did it then.

He sprang from behind the bins, screaming at

the top of his lungs, his heart pounding fit to burst, adrenaline surging. He smashed a fist into the back of the man's head, swung him around and plunged a knee deep into his groin. The man stumbled back, arms flailing, howling like a wild hog. Den landed another volley of blows, low to the gut. The man half turned trying to run but skidded on the smouldering brown pile. He fell, arms flapping furiously like some giant bird trying to gain height. He hit the cobblestones, face first. A solid, bone shuddering thud.

Trilby Hat didn't move.

The brutal suddenness of the end caused Den to freeze.

One heartbeat.

Two.

Three.

He stared at the fallen man through a veil of red mist and with such intensity there was nothing in the world except the stink of the alley and the moan of the breeze.

Four.

Five.

Den's whole body twitched in a mixture of excitement and fear as he squatted by the man's side. Search his pockets, he told himself. Find his wallet. Two reasons—Identity and cash. Maybe the bloke had a photo of his daughter to jog Den's memory.

Moving quickly, he rolled the man over, opened the trench coat but stopped. The gush of blood pooling around the man's head didn't look good.

"Oh Christ," Den whispered, staggering to his feet and backing away.

If he'd been less focused on the body, he might have noticed the blue flashing lights. He might have heard the drum of boots. It was the shout of the police officers that jerked him alert.

Adrenaline gave way to fear.

Den Ogden ran.

CHAPTER 55

Much later, Fenella would wish she didn't, but would remember everything about that cursed night and the following days; the unspeakable things, the tragedy that changed everything and the unhappiness which resulted.

It was almost one in the morning as she sipped from a mug of decaf coffee in the hospital canteen. The air smelled of boiled cabbage and bleach. A handful of late-night workers sat at tables scattered across the dining area. They nursed mugs and stared at their phones. Under the dim overhead lights, their faces seemed to glow.

Fenella and Dexter sat by the huge windows, neither speaking. After the pathetic night they'd had with Mrs Stoke, there was nowt more to say. A glum doom filled silence hovered over them. From the kitchen came the clatter of pots and pans and the rattle of silverware. By the swing doors, a cleaner worked a mop.

Suddenly tired, Fenella drained her mug. "Time to call it a day."

Dexter said nothing. He'd been drowning his thoughts in a huge mug of hot chocolate. Sipping it as though he had something heavy on his mind.

He put the mug down. "That lass ain't right, guv. Something is up but I ain't got a clue what."

"Ria Leigh?"

"Aye, guv."

"She'll see the doctor later this morning," Fenella replied. "Nowt we can do but wait until then. I don't suppose she'll want to share what is wrong, but I'll get it out of her."

"Ain't what I mean, guv."

"I know," Fenella replied, staring through the window at the rushing clouds in the black sky. She had her doubts about Ria. Nothing she could put her finger on, but there was something sick and terrible and nasty about the lass. Not just the savage greed of pure ambition, something more. And that something made Fenella uneasy. A sick feeling bubbled in her gut. But she said nothing more.

Dexter said, "Whatever is wrong with the lass, won't stay secret for long, guv." He gazed at the enormous swirl of clouds blowing in from the sea. "A storm's brewing."

The clanging echo of footsteps broke the silence. It skittered across the canteen with the sharp crack of pistol shots.

"Boss, over here," Jones called from the swing doors. "That bloke in the pea green trench coat and a brown trilby hat. We've got him."

His words crashed through the room like an explosion. They were on their feet and at the doors before Jones uttered his next sentence.

"Come on lad, spit it out," Dexter said, rubbing

a hand over the back of his neck.

"Two minicab drivers who work for Hodge Taxis saw a man in a brown trilby leap from a dark Ford car and dash along Shrimp Street," Jones said with strangled joy. He pulled out a notebook and glanced down. "I don't have their names yet, but the minicab drivers were on their break in the Eggshell Café. Not much to see at that time of night, I suppose. They went outside and heard shouts. PC Crowther and PC Phoebe were already on Shrimp Street and arrived a few moments later. They found Mr Chuck Baker unconscious in a side alley. A cut through to the canal. They saw someone running away and called it in."

Earth-shattering news. Unforgettable. A crack had opened in the Fred Bickham and Ruth Fassnidge murders. They had the man in the brown trilby in their charge.

Fenella's heart ticked up a beat. "Did they get a description of the runner?"

"No, boss. Too dark. He looked like a man."

"And Mr Chuck Baker is here, at the hospital?" Fenella asked.

"That's right, boss." Jones said, his face flushed with excitement. "He's an American. Do you think he is here on holiday?"

"Ain't no one comes to Port St Giles for their holiday, lad," Dexter said, massaging the back of his neck. "Not from America any roads."

Fenella agreed. Tourists stayed on the well-worn paths. Buckingham Palace. The Cotswolds. A dip in a seaside town in Wales, or a long weekend in Edinburgh. If Mr Chuck Baker came to town, he was here for a jolly good reason. And it wasn't to admire the disused lighthouse at the end of the Port St Giles Pier.

Fenella was wide awake now and glanced at the cleaner working the mop. "They found Mr Baker in an alley on Shrimp Street?"

"That's right, boss."

Which only confirmed Fenella's suspicion. Shrimp Street wasn't the ritziest part of town. Not a place you'd visit for sightseeing. Not a place to go walking in the dead of night.

Fenella closed her eyes. "We'll need a statement from Mr Baker as soon as he wakes up. Find out about his recent movements and have forensics look at his clothes. If he is living in a hotel, we'll need to search his room." Her eyes snapped open. "And we'd better get an officer to guard his room."

She was thinking about the deaths of Fred Bickham and Mrs Ruth Fassnidge. Cricket wasn't big in America, but she was damn sure they knew how to swing a bat. Her thought process stalled at the motive. Why would Chuck Baker travel thousands of miles from America to kill a retired bloke in his vegetable patch? What did Mrs Ruth Fassnidge have to do with it?

She only half noticed as Dexter eased through the swing doors and out into the hallway. Her mind was on her next question which she directed at Jones. "What do you know about the attack?"

"Looks like Mr Baker got into a fight and lost a lot of blood, boss."

"Any signs the attacker used a cricket bat?"

"Don't know, boss." Jones shifted from foot to foot. "But it was a vicious attack in a dank alley after midnight where no one in their right mind would go. Might have been a gang of thugs waiting to jump him."

Fenella wasn't buying. "But the officers only saw one man, and he fled."

Jones made a small nod. "Well, the attacker might be a friend of Mr Fred Bickham, out for revenge. I still think we ought to consider the drug gang angle. If we don't take control of this; they'll be a drugs turf war."

He sounded excited, almost joyous, and the pitch of his voice reminded her of a blackbird marking its territory. There was no shifting the drug gangland idea from his mind. Jones turned his head to gaze across the canteen.

Fenella followed his gaze to the windows where the dark clouds billowed like a rough sea. "Fred Bickham grew turnips not cannabis. But, suppose you are right, what is the link to Mrs Ruth Fassnidge?"

Jones smiled and leaned forward. "Trophy killing, boss."

"Eh?"

"People will go all out for a trophy. When I was in detective school, I studied a case where a grandmother learned martial arts. She went on the hunt for a fourteen-year-old boy and attacked him with kung fu kicks to his legs. Only his legs. No kicks to the head. No kicks to the body. Just the legs, boss."

Fenella knew better. Knew she shouldn't ask. Knew this was nowt but a wild goose chase. But she couldn't help herself. "Why on earth would a grandma do that?"

"Football, boss." Jones appeared pleased he had her attention. "The youngster she attacked was the best player in the school team. He scored forty goals that season. When the school team reached the final, he was certain to play. The granny wanted to hobble the lad as her grandson was on the reserve team bench. With the key player out of the way, her grandson would receive a finalist medal. Boss, some people will do anything to wrap their fingers around a trophy. It might be the reason why Mrs Fassnidge got knocked off."

Fenella was thinking of a suitable response when the swing doors opened. Dexter hustled back into the canteen.

"Had a word with Hodge Taxis, guv. They cover Shrimp Street, have done for years and their office is only five minutes away. The boss is an old friend. We help each other out."

He stopped as the cleaner worked the mop around them, picked up the bucket and strolled to the kitchen. And Fenella knew then Dexter had something important to say. It wasn't just the strange gleam in his eyes, but the way he stood. Legs planted wide, crouched forward with his arms swinging at his side.

"Go on," she said. "I'm listening."

Dexter lowered his voice. "Got lucky, guv. I called in a favour and spoke with both drivers. You know what they are like, don't want to put anything on the record. Don't like to speak with the police, neither. But I have me ways."

"Oh aye," Fenella said. "I'll not ask about that. Just tell me what they said."

"Neither driver had seen the American, Chuck Baker before. But one, Mr Tony Bass, recognised the man who entered the alley a few minutes before." Dexter grinned. "You remember Tony, don't you guv? Hooked nose like you see in those horror movies."

Fenella had crossed paths with Tony Bass. He'd worked the streets of Port St Giles in his minicab for as long as she could remember. Always at night. Always after dark. He might be named after a fish, but he had the eyes of a hawk and memory of an elephant.

Dexter was still speaking. "This bloke who went into the alley ahead of Chuck Baker goes by the name of Den Ogden. He's got form, guv. Shoplifting, drunk and disorderly, fraud."

He tapped a few keys on his phone and handed it to Fenella. She stared at the screen. A colour photo of Den Ogden. A thin, smug, oily face with a mop of black hair and a fat chin. He'd be older now and his hair a bit thinner.

Fenella had seen and heard enough. "Put the word out to patrol to bring him in for a chat. We don't want our American friends to think Port St Giles isn't a safe place to visit, even if they wander around dark alleys at night." She turned to Jones. "Find out everything you can about Mr Ogden. Focus on his last known address and work from there."

Dexter bounced on the tips of his toes. "Mr Bass says Den Ogden is staying in a room above the Eggshell Café. He saw him hiding in the doorway."

"Do we have a flat number?" Fenella asked, mouth dry with anticipation.

"Aye guv. Mr Bass reckons it is the dormer at the top as he saw a light on when it is usually dark."

"Then we'd better pay Mr Ogden a visit," Fenella replied, pushing open the swing doors. "Like now."

CHAPTER 56

The moment Fenella pulled her Morris Minor to the kerb in Shrimp Street a sense of dread overcame her. She stared at the dismal row of Victorian houses, most with boarded-up windows and padlocked doors. The clouds were much lower now, carrying with them swirls of mist from the sea. It danced around the bus shelter and rolled across the street mingling with the yellow glowing lights from the Eggshell Café. Rain beat down in thin sheets of fine spray, collecting in brown pools, and dribbling into the gutter. A miserable place in the dark early morning. A street full of doom and gloom.

They sat in the car, watching the quiet street for some time.

"Let's hope Mr Ogden is in bed when we knock at his door," Fenella said, watching the empty street and feeling uneasy. "Tucked up tight and fast asleep."

Dexter stared at the demented swirls of mist. "It's half-past one, guv. My grandad called it the Witching Hour, where the veil between life and death is the thinnest. A time when the Grim Reaper walks about looking for souls to snatch. Old Grim don't care who he takes. It might be an old man watching late night television with a can of ale. Or a lass deep in sweet dreams about her young man. Even a bairn wrapped up tight and settled for sleep ain't safe from his grasp. That's why they call him the Reaper. The bugger chops down everything in sight." He turned to Jones. "Prepare yourself lad, God only knows what we'll find tonight."

For once, Jones was quiet. No laptop on his lap. No fingers dancing across the keyboard. Just a stony face looking out at the rain and fog and dark.

Dexter was shaking his head. "The things the old-timers said and believed would scare today's kids to death. Still, I've never liked this time of night, it always brings trouble."

A sudden blast of thunder rumbled across the sky. The neon sign of the Eggshell Café flickered. If the weather were a sign of woe to come then the next few hours would be downright disturbing.

Fenella massaged the sudden bolt of tension in her neck. It was late and she was tired. All this talk of ghosts and death put her nerves on edge.

"Sod Mr Reaper," she said, tilting her neck from side to side. "He will have to go somewhere else to reap tonight, we've got work to do. Jones go around the back and keep watch. If Ogden darts out nab him. Me and Dexter will take the stairs. Let's go."

It was the smell of death that Fenella would remember most about that night. It hit her nostrils hard as she hurried to the alley at the side of the Eggshell Café. The sour tang of refuse and the stink of burst black bin bags—a bubbling brew of rotted veg and thrown away meat and milk gone sour. It clung to the thickening fog in a reeking dense odour. It was captured by the raindrops and scattered in exploding stink bombs.

And there was a strange stillness at this hour. A quiet as though the rising mist captured all sound and the rain damped it to nothingness. Only their footsteps disturbed the air. Galloping hooves of weary soldiers on ancient Roman cobblestones. On the march to the alley which led to the side entrance of the last known address of Den Ogden. Jones, head down against the rain, disappeared around the back. Fenella and Dexter climbed the steps to the entrance.

A sturdy oak door, recessed between two ornate pillars, indicated it had been an entrance of importance back in the glory days of the street. The days when Queen Victoria reigned and Port St Giles grew from a seed of a village into a bustling town. Now the steps were slick with slime, cigarette stubs littered the stoop, and posters, most faded, splattered both pillars.

A handbill on top of the others looked newer. A grainy colour image of a middle-aged woman. She wore huge gold hooped earrings and an oversized white turban, and her small eyes stared with the intensity of a cobra snake. Thick makeup plastered her face. Dark eyeshadow and pale powder on her cheeks. Blood-red lipstick lined her thin lips. Fenella leaned in to read the flyer:

Are you worried about tomorrow? Wonder how

you'll pay your bills? Worry no more. Let Mystic Marge tell you your wonderful future. Cards and palm and (for an extra fee) a foolproof crystal ball. Know what tomorrow holds. You deserve it. Satisfaction guaranteed.

Dexter jabbed a finger at the woman's face and chuckled. "Think I know that lass, used to work the check out at Fresco. She liked to chat more with the customers than ringing up their bill. Donna ... Donna Fipps. She didn't have mystical powers back then, only her hand in the till. She got caught and fired. Mystic Marge, eh? Wonder how much business she'll drum up advertising here?"

"Slim pickings by the looks of this place," Fenella replied, turning to gaze at the empty street and again feeling uneasy.

Dexter grunted, then fell silent for several seconds. When he spoke, his words came as a complete surprise. It was the last thing Fenella expected.

"Might give the lass a try, guv. See what she has to say."

"About what?"

He took his time in answering and cleared his throat. "You know me and my Priscilla were supposed to wed, but with her moving to the States it was called off. Well, we've been speaking on the phone and it might be back on."

Fenella's mouth opened and closed twice before he spoke. "You thinking about moving to New York City again?"

"No, guv. Priscilla says being a backup singer on the road is tough going. She is thinking about coming back to England. I don't want her to give up on her dream, though. Ain't no harm in seeing what a mystic has to say, is there?"

Fenella said nothing. He and Priscilla's relationship had more twists and turns than a funfair ride. At times it churned the stomach. At times it made you laugh with joy.

The fog grew suddenly thicker, but at least the rain eased to a slight drizzle. In the distance, waves crashed on the Port St Giles shore. A night for the lighthouse to guide ships on their way. But it hadn't been used for that purpose in years. The rocks which sunk vessels were still there, but ships navigated by other means these days.

Fenella turned back to the solid door, reached out for the handle and hesitated. Whatever the night held, whatever they found inside, there was no debate about the next step. Once they were in the building, they'd climb the stairs to the dormer, knock and when the door opened, they'd take Den Ogden in. Her mind leapt three steps ahead to the moment she asked him why he attacked the American, Chuck Baker. That will be the key moment, she told herself. The moment when she will have clear insight into what went on and why.

She yanked the door handle and pushed. "Locked."

Instinctively, her hand fell to her pocket, searching for a key. She pulled out the eggplant brooch given to her by Cherry Dew. *It'll bring you luck.* She placed it carefully back in her pocket and stared at the door.

Dexter gave it his shoulder. The door didn't budge. He tried again, grunting this time. Nothing. They stood back, looked at the door and then the dungeon shaped keyhole.

"They don't make locks like that anymore, guv." Dexter rubbed his shoulder. "Doors neither. Looks like it would do a grand job guarding the crown jewels."

"Aye," Fenella said looking at the sturdy door and solid lock. "If we can't get in without force, we'll have to seek a warrant and come back in daylight."

"That might take until tomorrow, guv. You know how slow the paperwork is since they started counting the number of search warrants."

They took a few paces back, staring at the entrance. A huge clay flowerpot stood to one side of the door. If it had once been filled with blooming foliage, there was no sign of plant life now. Brown dirt and cigarette butts and burnt-out matchsticks spilled from the top. Dexter moved it, searching for a key.

"Nowt but filth and muck," he grunted.

On the left side of the door were a row of bell pushes, most broken or taped over. The few in good working order had no names. Fenella pressed at random, holding each down for a count of ten.

"That'll wake the dead, guv," Dexter said, grinning.

But no one answered.

When Fenella peered through the letterbox, no light shone inside. Only dark and deathly silence and an oddly sweet smell. Strange. Again she jabbed at the bell pushes. No buzzing or ringing. Nothing.

They were about to go back to the street when footsteps, light and fast came toward them through the fog. Not Jones, he was waiting around the back. Who? Fenella placed a finger to her lips. A shadow appeared through the mist. At first a ghostly shape, then the outline of a woman, and at last, a dropped mouth and small cobra eyes staring at the detectives in shocked disbelief.

"Coppers!" the woman said, stepping back, left hand going to her gold hooped earring. "What the hell do you lot want?"

"That's right, luv." Fenella showed her warrant card. "We're the police. I'm Detective Inspector Sallow, and this good-looking gentleman is Detective Sergeant Dexter. We'd like a word. Mystic Marge, is it?"

Something moved in the woman's eyes. "I don't know who that is. Never heard of that person. You lot better check your computer; it wouldn't be the first time you got it wrong."

She spoke with the soothing tone of a doctor. A soft and sweet and convincing voice. Most would have believed her.

Fenella said, "I almost didn't recognise you without the turban. That's you on the flyer, isn't it?"

"I ain't done nothing wrong."

"You just lied to a detective."

"I ... er ... well, it's dark and foggy, ain't it? How did I know you were pointing to the picture of me?"

Fenella waited a heartbeat, smiled and said, "What is your full name?"

The woman's eyes darted from Fenella to Dexter and she seemed to realise the game was up. "Donna. Donna Fipps." Her eyebrows arched. "Look, is this about the complaints? They are nothing but bleedin' lies."

But she said it in a way which told the detectives the opposite.

Fenella became curious. "Come off it, pet, I wasn't born yesterday. We'd best hear your side of it."

Donna Fipps folded her arms. "So, a few people have complained about the spirits not getting the future right. Why should I take the blame? Its dynamic is the future, always changing. Anyone who has studied the art of the crystal ball will tell you the same. I'm only a clairvoyant, a channel. You know what I mean? Like a channel in the ground where water flows. It ain't my fault if the spirits fill it with sludge. There are no guarantees and no refunds in this game. I've bills to pay just like the rest, and in this line of work anything can happen."

"Never know what tomorrow will bring, eh?" Fenella said.

"Damn right. If I knew that I'd be a millionaire." Donna twiddled with her hooped earrings and her face suddenly took on a strange gleam. Her snakelike eyes widened, voice dropping to a dry rasp. "The aura isn't right tonight. I sense death."

"We didn't come here for a reading, luv," Fenella said. "How long have you lived here?"

"About three months."

"So, you've a key to the front door?"

She glanced at the huge clay flowerpot by the side of the door and looked quickly away. "Of course, I have. I ain't lying when I say I live here. Who would about this dump?"

Fenella's lips quirked. "Do you know a Mr Ogden? Den Ogden?"

"What has he done?"

"I can't tell you that, pet."

"I don't know him."

"Are you sure?"

"Look, most of the rooms are empty. I'm only here until I get back on my feet."

"So, you've never heard of Den Ogden?"

Donna Fipps glanced at Dexter as if seeing him for the first time. She smiled, left hand touching an earring. "There's this new bloke who just moved in, not half as good-looking as your sergeant."

"Oh aye," Fenella said, and waited.

"Right at the top, in the dormer. I told him it is bloody freezing up there in the winter, but I suppose the rent ain't much. Still, I'd not want to climb all those stairs every day. It'd be murder."

CHAPTER 57

They left Donna Fipps at her first-floor flat with instructions to stay inside. Fenella and Dexter climbed the dark stairs to the dormer. No lights on this part of the stairway, broken steps and no handrail. They took their time, pausing on each level, looking backward from where they had come and forward to what lay ahead.

At last, they were on the final flight and peering down a narrow gloomy hallway. The smell of mould and damp and something sickly sweet clawed at their nostrils.

"Wonder if Den Ogden is the type to leave a key under the doormat," Fenella said.

But at the dormer door there was no doormat under which a key might lie. No flowerpots either. Just the flat wall with a solid white door with paint peeling in giant slithers and a peephole which looked like a clouded eye.

Dexter's voice dropped to a low hiss. "A bit too still, guv. The place is like a bleedin' graveyard."

A hollow pang buzzed in Fenella's gut. Like the persistent ring of an internal alarm, soft and quiet and warning of trouble. Always the same feeling when she stepped into the unknown. And on this dark night with the rain and fog she sensed what lay behind that door might lodge so deep in her mind it could never be purged.

She knocked. "Mr Ogden, this is the police, Detective Inspector Sallow. Open the front door now."

She waited sixty seconds and pounded the door again. No stirring from inside. No angry mumble of voices. Nothing.

"He ain't home guv," Dexter said, eyeing the door. "Or he's knocked out in a drunken stupor with a dozen ale cans at his side."

"That means he might be in danger and in urgent need of medical help," Fenella said, knocking again. "We'll have to break down the door."

"Aye, guv," Dexter replied. "Wonder if it is as solid as the one downstairs."

It certainly looked sturdy, made of the type of thick wood used to guard a tomb. Fenella reached for the knob and twisted. The door swung inward. A gust of stale air rushed out.

"Police!" Fenella waited in the doorway for a heartbeat. "Mr Ogden are you here?"

The answer came in a soft whistle of wind. She stepped through the dark doorway. Where was the light switch? She couldn't find it and it took several more seconds for her eyes to adjust to the gloom.

The curtainless window was the source of the breeze. It let in an orange glow of town light. Fenella scanned the room. An electric outlet on the wall. A camper's double ring stove on the counter by the sink. A television on a pine table. Against the wall, a narrow fold-up bed. Then she saw the cot.

Driven by some primaeval instinct, she ran toward it. Behind, she felt Dexter move into the room, heard his gruff voice curse. They'd worked together for so long she understood his frustration. Den Ogden wasn't in the place. But in that instant, as her legs carried her forward, she no longer cared about the man. She cared about what was in the cot. What lay hidden beneath the covers?

From the edge of her vision came the hazy orange glow from the street. It lit the two ringed stove and the counter littered with baby formula bottles. In that instant, the heavy scent of the room crept up her nostrils, hitting her memory banks hard. A pungent aroma of soggy nappies and the sweat of sleepless nights. A memory from long ago when her bairns were small and new. Fenella hurried.

As she reached the cot, Dexter grunted. "Found the lights, guv."

They flickered on. A thin weak ray from a single unshaded bulb. It hissed and spluttered as if at any moment it might go out, and lit the room with the brightness of a candle in a tomb.

Fenella peered into the cot, blinked and looked again. Cold horror crawled from the base of her spine. Bolts of tension tightened on either side of her neck; a mass of sinew and veins pulsating in ghastly horror. The bulb flickered out for a moment then spluttered back to life. A weaker glow this time, ghostly pale.

Fenella gasped. A baby lay tucked between the sheets. On it's back. Face blue and unmoving. Hands, winter day grey. Eyes clouded and wide. And Fenella knew it was baby Eva Fisk.

"God Almighty," Dexter said. "Jesus Christ."

Fenella had no memory of scooping the bairn into her arms. But she felt the coldness of the tiny body against her warmth and the eternal stillness.

"Oh God," she said. "Oh God."

With care, she lay the limp bairn back in the cot. Dexter was already on the phone, shouting fast, demanding medical help right now. His furious voice faded from Fenella's hearing. She was in a tunnel, dark on all sides, a speck of light in the distance. Nothing mattered. Nothing but that speck of light. Her training kicked in, everything on automatic. She eased the bairn's head back and lifted the chin, checking the mouth and nose for obstructions. *All clear.* She blew steady breaths into the bairn's mouth and nose. Slow rescue breaths, counting, watching, as the small chest rose and fell. Keeping the bairns head tilted, chin lifted, she eased her mouth away, two fingers on the chest, pushing down, watching for the chest to fall.

Again and again.
Soft and slow and steady.
With the care of a mother who'd had five.
Not lost one.
Would never lose one.
Not on her watch.

She didn't hear the wail of the ambulance. Didn't hear feet pounding up the stairs, the mumble of urgent voices in the room. Didn't hear any of that. Only felt the soft hand of Dexter on her shoulder, easing her away from the bairn as the medical crew went to work.

CHAPTER 58

They brought in the big guns to track down Den Ogden. Officers with snarling dogs which yanked at the leash. Patrol cars, out in force, scanning the streets, searching the places where a man on the run might hide. And as the night-time mist receded back out to sea, a helicopter hovered low over the town, watching with an eagle eye. Meanwhile, a tech team were on site, to tear his room apart, searching for anything they might find.

It was the waiting time now. Time for a breath between the action. Everyone expected news of some sort, but when it came, it wasn't what anyone expected.

The three detectives sat at a window table in the Eggshell Café, eating bacon rolls and sipping from mugs of steaming hot coffee. The café owner, a short greasy-haired man with a huge forehead, shocked at what they found, offered them a free breakfast to show support.

"It is terrible," he said, accent clearly French. "C'est terrible. C'est horrible. And it takes place above my head!"

He returned to the counter, shaking his head and looking up at the tiled ceiling as though wishing for X-ray vision. The mood was sober, air filled with fried food. Outside, three patrol cars waited by the kerb, blue lights flashing.

Fenella poured milk into her coffee which she normally drank black. "Not an easy night. I thought the bairn had left us."

She had called Mrs Jill Fisk and told her the news. Mam and dad were at the child's bedside.

"Didn't look like she had much life left in her guv," Dexter replied squeezing ketchup onto his third round of bacon rolls. "Any longer and she'd not have made it."

Jones took a vicious bite from his bacon roll. "I wish Den Ogden was in his flat tonight, boss. Wish he'd tried to escape so I could have clobbered him. A couple of blows to his head and half a dozen to his gut. Might even have slipped in a few low strikes to his groin just for the hell of it."

That wasn't like Jones, Fenella thought. The terrible find of baby Eva Fisk, the long night, and the wait for news was getting to him. It was getting to her too. The coffee didn't help, made her edgy.

Den Ogden was on the run and lying low. There was no debate he was aware of the police presence at his flat. He'd have seen the flashing lights and ran into the shadows and the alleyways. To where? The more time passed, the greater the chance he would escape their tightening net. They had a matter of hours before he slipped from town and vanished in the throng of a big city. The clock had started and was ticking fast.

Fenella took another sip, noticed Dexter's lips beginning to work up to say something and waited.

"Knocking people about ain't what we do these days, lad. But it is a sodding good idea for the likes of Den Ogden."

Jones was nodding. The lad's knackered, Fenella thought. Tiredness has taken over his brain. Jones followed the rules, black and white without a hint of grey. And Dexter was, well, the opposite. But they both agreed Den Ogden would benefit from a good kickin'. A visceral reaction to a tough night. And how did she feel? Huge relief that they'd found the bairn. Horror at the conditions in the dormer. Joy that the bairn survived. Now her entire focus was on Den Ogden. She'd nail the child abduction case tighter than the lid of a coffin ... once they'd got him.

And anger stirred in her, too. Hot and wild, a giant rolling ball of rage. But she clamped it down, breathing slow. "Our job is to catch the bugger. Justice is for the courts. The good news is baby Eva is in safe hands with her mam and dad at her bedside. She'll recover and have no memory of what happened."

They fell into silence. The warm smell of fried food swirled up their nostrils with grease laden fingers. Black pudding and bacon and fried things from the past. And their minds were all focused on one thing. When would they hear news of Den Ogden? Today? Tomorrow? Or months from now would the data be transferred in digital bytes to the cold case files in Carlisle?

The café owner, aware of the sudden stillness moved from behind the counter. The tea urn hissed with a long high-pitched blast of steam. And the detectives' phones pinged. All three at once. A nerve-jangling buzzing sound like wasps about to attack.

News. Big News.

Fenella scrambled her mobile phone from her handbag. She read with speed, then leaned back, folding her arms. Dexter grinned. Jones took another savage bite out of his bacon roll and chewed with his eyes wide and wild.

Fenella dropped her phone into her handbag. "So, they've found a cricket bat in Den Ogden's flat, eh?"

"A bloody big one," Dexter added, rubbing his hands. "Lined with bleedin' sharp nails."

CHAPTER 59

Fenella woke at six thirty the next morning from a deep and restful sleep. Not eight hours. Nowhere near as her head hit the pillow after three. But all the tired brain fog had lifted and the events of a few hours ago seemed a lifetime away. Morning light shimmered at the edge of the curtains. She eased from the bed not wanting to disturb Eduardo who kept artist hours. He was working on a comic strip for a firm in Beijing. An ancient tale based on Chinese myth with a white snake as the hero and an icy turtle as the foe.

Fenella padded to the window and pulled the curtain back at the edge. The overnight rain had long stopped and the mist lifted. The countryside glistened under a deep blue cloudless sky.

She inhaled, held her breath, then exhaled for a count of ten. The past few days had been one huge ball of mad tension. A wild ride on an epic adventure. An adventure which was far from over. She exhaled the last of her yoga breaths, refusing to foul her mind with thoughts of Den Ogden.

The last anyone had seen of the man was in the dank alley on the opposite side of the street to the Eggshell Café. Not yet, she told herself. Not at home.

Save work for work. The only thing she wanted right now was to enjoy her time at home. She let her mind empty and slipped out of the bedroom, easing the door shut.

In the kitchen, her mam, Nan, fussed at the stove, humming a little snatch of a song. She boogied to the sink, did a twirl, saw Fenella in the doorway and smiled.

"You came in very late last night, Fen."

"Aye," Fenella replied. She never talked about work at home, preferring to keep those lives separate. "The cock was about to crow by the time I drifted off."

Nan did a pirouette on the tips of her toes. "Bacon and eggs with toast?"

"What's got you so merry?"

"I'm always joyful."

"Righto," Fenella replied, watching her mam closely.

Nan was humming, her whole body vibrating with joy. She cracked an egg into the frying pan, spun in a tight circle and gave a howl of laughter.

Fenella said, "What are you howling about?"

"Coffee? I've some fresh beans from Grainbowl café. Their Kenyan roast must be the best coffee I've had the pleasure of drinking."

"Are you going to tell me what all this joy is about?"

"Eat first."

They ate their breakfast in peaceable silence. Well, apart from Nan's humming which Fenella thought she was doing deliberately to ramp up her curiosity. And it worked. She had to know what all the joy was about.

When they finished, Nan cleared a space on the table and flipped on her tablet computer. She used it for surfing social media sites, watching internet videos of cats and looking up recipes of exotic dishes to cook.

"Now then," she said, swiping the screen. "Here it is. Everyone is talking about it Fen, and I mean everyone."

Her eyes glittered, and she grinned so wide it reminded Fenella of a friendly Halloween pumpkin.

"What are you on about?" Fenella said, unable to hide the curiosity in her voice.

"Oh, you just go back to your daydreaming. You were always a big daydreamer even when you were a nipper."

"Who's a big daydreamer?" Eduardo stood in the doorway wiping sleep from his eyes.

"None of your business, you nosy sod," Nan replied as her smile broadened.

Eduardo ignored the jab and sniffed. "Is that sausages?"

"You are on a diet and can't have fried food," Nan replied, wagging a finger. "I'll mix up some porridge made with water like they do in Scotland. One or two pinches of salt?"

Eduardo gazed at Nan with wide puppy eyes. "Oats block my tubes. What about two small rashers of bacon? A bit of fat helps to get things moving."

"You are a crafty sod," Nan said, on her feet and heading for the stove. "I was just saying to Fen that she was always a big daydreamer."

Eduardo said nothing.

Fenella folded her arms. "Are you going to tell us what everyone is talking about?"

"Yeah," said Eduardo, rubbing sleep from his eyes. "What's the news?"

Nan, who loved drama, did a little shuffle of a dance. Eduardo was on his feet and joined in, lips twisted in a sly grin. He was trying to butter up Nan so she'd cook him a fry up of bacon and eggs. Fenella knew her husband well. She'd confiscate half for herself. She watched them twirling around the kitchen and laughed. Her mam was nuts. And so was her husband. She wondered if drawing comics had made him that way, but he was like that when she met him. An artist, with his head in another world which wasn't quite this one. Not that she minded. She, too, was mad, in her own way. And she knew her mam was playing with her curiosity, drawing it out like chewing gum stretched into a fine string. And it worked. She had to know now.

"Come and sit," Fenella said. "Don't want you so out of breath you can't talk."

Nan sat at the table opposite Fenella. Eduardo joined them, huffing. He had pounds to lose and wasn't winning that battle. He gave a drum roll on the table. "Now for the news."

Nan said, "Everyone is saying you are a hero, Fen. The hunt for Den Ogden is all over the news.

All my online friends are talking about you saving baby Eva Fisk. Of course, I let them know you are my daughter and I would expect nothing less."

Fenella felt her face flush, opened her mouth to protest but her mobile phone rang. A familiar ring tone. She picked it up, placed it to her ear, knowing her work day had just begun.

"On my way over to your place, guv," Dexter said. "The American, Chuck Baker, is awake. Didn't think you'd want to wait until visiting time to speak with him."

CHAPTER 60

When Fenella arrived at Chuck Baker's hospital room, she was surprised to find him sitting up in bed digging into a plate of fried bacon, eggs, beans, black pudding and toast.

He did not look up; instead, he jabbed a forkful of black pudding into his mouth, then went after the fried bacon.

A medical device beeped in soft low tones as she stood in the doorway. "Hello, pet. How are you doing?"

He glanced up, his mouth working a chewy strip of bacon. He raised his hand beckoning her further into the room, but did not speak. He swallowed the bacon and went after a fat slice of black pudding.

A wave of relief washed over her. He wasn't as badly beaten as she'd feared. She would have been even more pleased if they had Den Ogden, his attacker, in custody. That thought faded into the background as she regarded him closely. She was struck by his youthfulness. He had dark intelligent eyes and a crop of thick black hair. He couldn't be over twenty-five, possibly younger. And he was twiglike with everything thin including the bruise face and the sunny smile upon it.

And it was his face she focused on.

There was something familiar about it, but she didn't know what and wished Dexter or Jones were with her to put their finger on it. She'd left Dexter at the hospital reception where he'd gone to check up on Mrs Stoke. Jones wasn't due in at the station until eight, and Ria Leigh was off sick. It was ten past seven.

She sent a text message to Dexter to join her, then walked to the bedside and sat in a chair. "Sorry, I didn't mean to disturb your breakfast. I'm Detective Sallow, but you can call me Fenella. Can we talk?"

He waved his fork. "Not a problem at all. This black sausage is fantastic, never had it before. Is it made of beef or pork?" He spoke in a soft accent. Educated. New England. Boston, maybe.

"Aye, can't beat it for breakfast," she said.

Did it matter what went into black pudding if he enjoyed it? Anyway, it was too early to be talking of boiled pig's blood and fat and oatmeal. *Best let him eat and digest it first.* She changed the subject.

"What part of Boston are you from?"

"Not Boston, but Wayland, a town not too far from the big city. Have you been to Boston?"

"Aye, for the marathon. Not to run in it mind you, just to watch and wonder. How can anyone run for that many miles?"

Chuck laughed. "I could have done with faster legs last night." He dropped the fork on the plate.

"Might have saved me, how you say over here, a bit of bother. And to think, I'd spent the whole night watching that street in my kit."

"Kit?"

"My brown trilby and green trench coat. I watch a lot of old British movies. Thought I'd wear the get-up for my adventure over here. Never thought I'd get into a, as you say, punch-up."

Fenella smiled. Chuck brought up the attack rather than her drawing it out of him. A good sign that he'd be all right once his physical wounds healed. Now to find out what happened. All of it.

She said, "Do you own a cricket bat, Mr Baker?"

"Of course. It is one of the benefits of going to a private school founded by an English man and his Welsh wife. We played the game. I still do, and picked up a couple of custom-made bats to take back with me. Newbery's. Do you know the brand?"

"Aye, luv. I've heard of them." She kept her voice bright and cheery and changed direction. "Did you see anything unusual last night?"

"What do you mean?"

"I don't know. Anything unusual while you were watching the street. That is what you said you were doing?"

She'd get to why, later. First, she wanted to keep him talking. Once the words started flowing, it was hard to stop them.

"It was dark and not much traffic on the road," Chuck said. "A few taxi drivers visited the café. I thought one of them, a man with a hooked nose, saw me. But if he did, he didn't say anything."

He became silent. Fenella wondered if he had told her everything or he needed another push. She decided to push. "Anything else?"

He frowned. "No, not really."

There was something about the way he said those three words that bothered Fenella. "I'm sure you are probably right about that, but have a little think, will you?"

He sighed. "I don't know how important it is, but there was a woman at the bus stop. Middle-aged, dark coat, large bag, might have been canvas, not very tall. She wore a pink headscarf." He paused. "I thought she was a bit odd. The bus came, number 26. When it left, she was still there. Twice. And then the last bus came and she was still there. Even a taxi pulled up but soon drove off. I think she might have been waiting for someone. Not a nice way to treat a lady. I hope she dumps the guy."

A knock sounded from the door and Dexter strode in.

"Sorry to interrupt, guv." He glanced around, taking it all in. "Mrs Stoke is doing well. The nurse says we can speak with her around four this afternoon."

Good news, Fenella thought. Another mess they'd soon sort out. First things first. "Mr Baker, this is Detective Robert Dexter."

"Cor blimey," Dexter said, seeing the same thing Fenella first saw. He stepped closer to the bed. "You look familiar, lad. Is this your first visit to

England?"

"First time outside the states," Chuck replied with a broad smile. "And it's been a wonderful adventure, well, except last night, but that will make a good story in a few years, I suppose."

Dexter rubbed the back of his neck, staring at the lad as if he were a ghost. And like a ghost Chuck Baker lay there, thin and pale faced with an unworldly story to tell. There was something odd about the lad. Something wasn't quite right.

Fenella glanced at Chuck Baker and she glanced at Dexter and she glanced at the lad again. "Wayland is a long way from here. Why are you in Port St Giles?"

"I came as a twenty-first birthday present. I've always wanted to travel to the British Isles." He stopped, and his face became sad. "I'm getting ahead of myself."

"Take your time, pet."

They waited in momentary silence as Chuck's mouth opened and closed and opened again. He squeezed his eyes tight and turned away. When he looked back, his face was twisted into a frown.

"My mom and dad died in a car crash five years ago. I'm an only child." He cleared his throat. "I went to live with my uncle. He is a straight shooter and told me things I needed to know about my parents. It was my uncle who gave me the cash to travel here. As a birthday present."

"You came here alone?"

"I'm a bit of an introvert, like my own company

and figured I was old enough to take care of myself. Wayland might be a small town but I've been to Boston enough times to be street savvy. I didn't think I'd get knocked about in a quaint English seaside town."

"But you were out late at night, in a rough area, why?"

Chuck blinked. "Because that is where I knew I'd find him."

"Who?"

"Den Ogden."

Fenella glanced at Dexter. He leaned forward as though mesmerised. She, too, was eager to hear more. And there were so many questions. But neither interrupted. Not this time. Not with Chuck Baker in full flow.

"I tracked him down to Whitehaven and from there followed the trail to Port St Giles," Chuck said. "It took some time to pinpoint his rough location. I heard he was staying at a boarding house run by a Mrs Fassnidge. That was my first port of call, but he'd moved out. Then, quite by chance, I stumbled across a man I thought was him. I was in Quick Bet Bookie Store and was told by the clerk that a man of that name was in the toilets."

Again he stopped, flushing brick red.

"Go on, lad." Dexter spoke this time, eyes glued on Chuck Baker. "What happened?"

"I'm ashamed to say it."

"We want to hear it, pet," Fenella said. "All of it."

Chuck glanced at his hands. "I went to the

men's room and ... peeped through a stall. Not for anything lewd, just to check. You see, I wasn't sure I could trust the word of the clerk even though I gave him fifty pounds for his trouble. The stall door burst open and I was knocked to the floor but I got a good look at the man."

Again he paused, his mournful gaze on the breakfast plate. Fenella waited. Dexter cleared his throat.

Chuck took the prompt. "The next day I was strolling on the boardwalk birdwatching when I glimpsed the man I saw in the toilet stall. Of course, I couldn't be certain it was the same man, but I followed him, convinced he was Den Ogden or knew of him. I lost him on Shrimp Street. All I knew was that the man was living somewhere along that road. So, I parked my car in a high foot traffic area, close to the bus stop and near the Eggshell Café, waited and watched." His eyes glowed. "Not that I'm a detective, but I'm proud of myself. Another night of watching and I'd have had him. Instead, he got me."

Fenella let his words settle for a moment. "Go on, luv."

"Then, last night while on my watch, I saw him coming out of an entrance at the side of the Eggshell Café. He hesitated at the top of the steps, looking around and stared at my car, but I didn't think he saw me. I planned to sit tight, but in the excitement I went after him when he dashed across the road and went into an alley. I was afraid of losing him." Chuck paused for a long moment, eyes pleading Fenella to understand. "That's why I went into that alley."

"I'm not with you, pet," Fenella said. "Why were you looking for him?"

Chuck shook his head, tears welling in his eyes. "I didn't want to lose him again, not after all these years, all this time searching. I just don't understand why, when I called out his name, my dad attacked me."

CHAPTER 61

In the stunned silence of the hospital room came the soft low tones of a medical machine. Fenella's chest tightened in a mixture of excitement and panic. Dexter's breath erupted in sharp rasps. No one spoke for so long the air seemed to crackle with static.

Den Ogden was Chuck Baker's dad.

It was a strange sort of news. A sudden bolt of shock. It seeped into the ears and crept like rising damp into the brain. And it wasn't the last stunning revelation. There was plenty more to come.

A never-ending stream of questions blew at gale force through Fenella's mind. She opened her mouth but saw the slim silhouette lying on the bed with the echo of Den Ogden on his face. That, she reflected, was what was familiar about him. Her mouth closed with a soft click.

Chuck Baker leaned against his pillow, wiping tears from his eyes. As he spoke, his voice floated across the room, ghostlike. "When I was eighteen, my uncle told me a secret I promised never to share."

He stopped as though weighing things in his mind.

Fenella said nothing. If Dexter was breathing,

his chest barely moved. The beeps on the medical device lowered as if in anticipation.

Chuck said, "But I must now break my word."

Again he stopped. And again, he seemed to be weighing his response.

Fenella waited. Dexter shifted his weight. The beeps faded into nothingness.

Chuck exhaled a sharp breath. "My parents adopted me. At first, when my uncle told me, I didn't want to know. But the truth gnawed at me. The people who raised me were not my biological mom and dad. Can you imagine?"

"Ain't your fault, lad," Dexter said, watching Chuck as though he understood. "Mam and dad ain't a biological thing. Plenty of kids live with folks who ain't their blood parents. Must have spent more time at me neighbour's place than at home. Nowt wrong with that in my books."

Chuck glanced at the scraps on the breakfast plate. He cleared his throat. "I tried to shove the truth of who I really was into the locked vault of my brain's lost memories." He looked up, a faraway gleam in his eyes. "Like the time when I was three at the aquarium and I decided to swim in one of the fish tanks. I half drowned. That's what my dad said. I don't remember, must have put it in the lost memories vault. So, I tried to forget I had another family. But that sort of thing gets into your psyche. Burrows deep down and festers."

"Aye," Fenella said, voice a soft whisper. "It ain't easy, is it, luv?"

Chuck sighed. "I had so many questions. Questions my uncle couldn't answer. I wanted to know where I came from, who my biological parents were, and if they were still alive. At first, my uncle was reluctant to tell me anything other than my mom died in childbirth."

Fenella said, "I understand, pet. A nice lad like you must have been horror-struck by the news."

Chuck let out a soft choke. A dry primordial rasp of pain from wounds still weeping. "I... I can't go on."

"Yes, you can, pet," Fenella said. "You've started so you may as well finish. You will feel so much better when it is all out."

"No ... I can't."

Fenella watched him for a moment, realising he needed a push.

"You must, luv. Your psyche is starving to tell it all. Don't bottle it up. It has festered for too long and needs a good airing. I'm here, pet. I'm listening."

Had her nosy gene pushed her mouth too hard? She wanted to get the grim details and felt giddy as she peeled away the secret. But she had to contain her zeal, tread with care for the last shuddering drops of truth.

Dexter walked to the door. Fenella smiled. Her second in command was razor-sharp. He didn't want this conversation to end by way of an interruption. If anyone knocked on the door, he'd shoo them away. Very good, she told herself. Now we'll have it all, to the very last drop.

"Go on Chuck," she said. "It is time to tell us the rest."

He hugged himself and half closed his eyes. "About a year ago my uncle took me aside. He told me he believed I came to my parents through illegal means. He didn't have details on my biological mom, but he believed my dad was a man by the name of Den Ogden from Northern England."

Fenella said, "How do you mean, illegal?"

"My parents could not have children the usual way. My uncle said my parents showed up with me one Christmas. No paperwork from an adoption agency. No forms. No trail of papers to follow. Uncle knew my mom couldn't have children, so he dug until he uncovered the truth. He argued with my dad, his brother. They came to blows. It turns out my dad handed over a large sum of money, and a few weeks later they got me. 'A Christmas gift,' my uncle said."

A knock thudded on the door. The handle turned.

"Go away, we are busy," Dexter said, and shoved the door shut.

Fenella expected they'd knock again, harder, and push the door with more force. That's what she'd have done, and screamed bloody murder in the bargain. And she wondered who they were and what they wanted. But Chuck Baker was still talking.

"My mom and dad lived in fear the people whom he paid to deliver me would come back and ask for more money. Or worse—blackmail him. He was a lawyer, you see; worked for the state in a high-profile job."

Fenella reached out and took his arm. "Is that what happened, luv, blackmail?"

Chuck shook his head. "My parents never heard from them again. No calls for more cash. No blackmail requests. Nothing."

Another fist thudded the door. It flew open before Dexter moved to jam it shut. PC Beth Finn hurried into the room, her face flush with excitement. PC Woods shuffled two paces behind.

PC Beth Finn said, "Sorry ma'am, but PC Woods knocked earlier and didn't get in, but I thought it best to interrupt. Thought you'd like to hear the news. We've got him, ma'am. We've got Den Ogden."

CHAPTER 62

The news brought a wave of excitement to the hospital room with everyone talking at once. Except Fenella. She said nothing, thinking.

One second.

Two.

Three.

She clapped her hands for silence and turned to the twig thin man in the hospital bed. "Mr Baker, you are to do exactly as the nurse's request. Later today I'll send over an officer to take a formal statement."

"I'm not pressing charges," Chuck replied. "And I want to see my dad as soon as I get out of this place."

It was clear he had no idea his dad was on a charge of child abduction. It wasn't the time to tell him about that. Not with him bruised and bandaged in a hospital bed. There would be plenty of time once he healed for the truth to sink in. The courts moved slow. Plenty of time for Chuck Baker to reflect on what his dad had done. Plenty of time for the lad to change his mind. Yes, Den Ogden was his biological dad, but he'd put nowt into the lad and couldn't expect more than nowt out.

Fenella touched his arm. "Of course. Now rest, your body needs to heal." She made a shooing motion with her hands. "Everyone out."

The team gathered around a water fountain in the hallway. PC Woods, PC Beth Finn, Dexter and Fenella. A young man in a white house coat jogged past the water fountain. A dark smudge of stubble smeared his thin chin and his bloodshot eyes bulged in a panic-stricken glare. A junior doctor overworked and underpaid and running from ward to ward.

When his footsteps faded, Fenella glanced at the closed door of Chuck Baker's room. "Details on Den Ogden, please."

PC Beth Finn cleared her throat. "We found Mr Ogden hiding in a derelict factory by the canal."

"Near the Navigator Arms pub," added PC Woods.

"Wait till I lay my hands on the bugger," Dexter hissed. He wasn't grinning. No hint of a joke, not when it came to kidnapped bairns. "He'll not walk right when I'm through."

PC Beth Finn coughed. "You'll have to wait in line, sir. Behind the medical staff, sir. Mr Ogden tried to run and took a nasty bite from one of our German Shepherds." She turned to Fenella, a gleam in her eyes. "Made a meal of his private parts, ma'am. He's here in the hospital recovering. We picked up a Russian national, a Mr Boris Ivanov. He and two other men are now at the station."

Dexter rubbed a hand over the back of his neck.

"I know the bloke, guv. He's got form as a small-time drug dealer. Eyes like an evil rag doll." He gave a twisted grin. "Putting that bugger away will be fun. Mind if I have a go at him now?"

"Go right ahead," Fenella replied.

"Are you coming to grill him with me?"

"Nah," she said.

She had never told anyone. Her strange idea, if it could be called that, had brewed for days, in the back of her mind, and she'd never breathed a word about it. She had kept quiet because she knew it was a weird one. None of it could be proved, not then. Not when she stared at the body of Fred Bickham in Seaview Allotments. Not when a figure in black darted from Mrs Fassnidge's boarding house and vanished into the fog. But now? With Chuck Baker and that hideous cricket bat found in Den Ogden's flat, the pieces had fallen into place. Now she had the shape of the puzzle and would work quickly toward the solution. Still, what she planned next was a chance. A big chance. There was absolutely no guarantee it would pay off. And if it backfired? She'd keep Dexter out of the line of sight. It was her idea. She'd take the full weight of blame if it went wrong.

"Guv?" Dexter stared at her with surprise.

"There is one more thing I want to do," Fenella said. "Then I'll join you at the station. PC Beth Finn and PC Woods, with me."

CHAPTER 63

The front door opened on the first knock.

Mrs Ida Bickham stood in the entrance wearing black silk pyjamas with her hands on her hips. She wore a yellow silk headscarf tight around her head. No frizzy black wig. Too early. But she looked fit and strong. It was a little after seven in the morning.

Fenella said, "Can I come in for a chat?"

Ida peered through the doorway; pale grey eyes fixed on the patrol car in the street. "It's early, everyone is asleep and I'm in the middle of my tai chi exercises."

Fenella followed her gaze. A wizened man in a flat cap and thick sideburns hurried along the street and stopped at the garden gate—George Rouge. He glanced at Ida and he glanced at Fenella and he raised his flat cap. "How do, lucky ladies. Keeping us safe, eh? I like that."

He let loose a donkey bray laugh and hurried back the way he had come, with startling speed for a retired man.

"Bloody nosy parker," Ida said. "This street is like living in a zoo."

"I can come back later, if you prefer," Fenella said, lips quirking at the corners.

"That would be best." Ida began to close the door. "I'm sorry you have wasted your time."

"It's just that you didn't ask," Fenella said into the gap.

Ida widened the door. "Ask what?"

"A detective shows up on your doorstep at seven in the morning and you'd think you would want to know why. Especially since the detective is the lead investigating officer into your ex-husband's death. But you didn't ask if I had news. Didn't pester me with questions about progress. Didn't even ask why I was at your door at this ungodly hour. That makes a detective wonder about things."

Ida was silent for a moment. "So sorry, Fred's death has been such a strain I get muddled. I don't know what I'm doing these days. Please come in."

They walked through a silent hallway to the front room. The same room where they chatted on her second visit. Same musty tang of the used bookshop. Same lattice panes smeared with grime which damped sunlight to dusk. Same walnut bookshelf and swirls of mauve speckled deep pile carpet and cluttered mantelshelf. Same solemn glumness of a shrine. Or a tomb.

Fenella strode to the mantelshelf and studied the dancing black rabbit, cow bell, horse shoe and scatter of photographs. Yes, she was certain now. Absolutely sure.

She turned to face Ida Bickham. "Is Ginger still missing?"

"She is an adult and can do as she pleases."

"Not worried, then?"

Ida said nothing.

Fenella said, "I think you know where she is."

"Don't be silly." Ida moved to the mantelshelf and touched the horseshoe.

"I'm a police officer, luv, don't lie to me. I wouldn't want to have to haul you to the station for a formal interview."

"Is that a threat?" Ida adjusted the dancing black rabbit then ran a finger along the cow bell.

"Just a statement of fact," Fenella replied, gaze dropping to the photos.

Ida was silent for a long moment. She exhaled. "Ginger has moved in with her boyfriend. The lad is her baby's father. They want to marry." She stared off into the distance. "Fred was keen on the lad and introduced them. He'd be pleased they are together. He encouraged them to meet in his shed, as Ginger didn't want her mam to know. I turned a blind eye. My Fred worked with all those teenage girls and saw enough misery at the shelter to know what real love looks like. I think it will last. Look, I haven't told Shirley because Ginger told me not too. Not yet. Ginger and I are rather close. We keep each other's secrets. Alas, Ginger is distant from her mam."

"Still, Shirley must be worried sick," Fenella said. "Any mam would be if their only daughter went missing."

Ida shrugged. "If only Shirley had the same feminine intuition as the rest of us. She never quite clicked with her daughter. Oh my manners! Please take a seat."

They sat in the wingback armchairs by the unlit fireplace.

Fenella eyed the mantelshelf. "You used to be a dancer?"

"That's right." Ida gazed at the dancing black rabbit. "I often wonder about my choices. Life might have been so much different if I'd found success. I was good. Good enough, but lightning didn't strike."

"Light on your feet, eh?"

"Goes with the job."

"What about Shirley?"

Ida shook her head. "When she was a child, I thought she had promise, but she never showed any real interest in dance or the stage." Her voice turned bitter. "Men were her thing. And booze."

Fenella sighed. Now came the difficult part. The part her mind had raced over again and again. The part that involved the cricket bat, the death of Fred Bickham and the slaying of Mrs Ruth Fassnidge. The murder part that had kicked this whole case off.

She said, "I'd like a word with your daughter, Shirley."

A hiss of breath escaped Ida's lips. For a fleeting moment she reminded Fenella of a cobra curled tight and ready to pounce.

Ida's body gave a sudden jerk and she sprang to her feet. "I'll put on a pot of tea," she said before dashing from the room.

Ten minutes later, Shirley Bickham shuffled into the front room rubbing sleep from her eyes.

"You want to speak with me?"

There was an element of night-time slumber rudely disturbed in her voice, and something else too. Something deep and primitive and difficult to hide—fear.

Fenella, still sitting in the armchair, now with a pot of tea and toast, wished they'd light the fire. The room needed warmth because there was only chill in what she had to say. But she waited for Shirley to settle into the armchair and pour a mug of tea from the old brown Betty teapot. She's preparing herself, Fenella thought, for the game of cat and mouse.

Shirley clutched the mug tight, took a long sip and half turned to glance through the window. A slanting sheet of drizzle speckled the pane. Ida Bickham hovered in the doorway as though uncertain whether to go or stay.

Fenella said, "We need to speak alone."

"I have a right to hear what you are going to say to my daughter," Ida replied.

"Mam, don't be ridiculous. I'm forty not four," Shirley said, mug in hand. "I'm sure it won't take long, will it Detective Sallow?"

Fenella said nothing.

Ida padded through the door. "I'll be in the kitchen if you need me."

The door closed with a hard click.

Shirley took another gulp from her mug. With care, she placed it on the coffee table next to the teapot. "So?"

Fenella looked at the defiant face and she looked at the thickening drizzle and she looked at the solid door which Ida Bickham closed on her way out. She said, "We are going to have a chat about the murder of your dad."

Shirley rose. "I should light the fire."

"Leave it and sit," Fenella replied.

Shirley glanced at the dead fireplace. "Okay," she said as she slouched back into the armchair. "Let's do this your way. But I've told the police everything I know."

"Everything?"

Shirley poked at the sore on her lip. "Yes, everything."

"I see. Well, I have a few routine questions to help fill in the details."

"Oh come on, how much more taxpayers' money are you going to waste?"

Fenella ignored the question. "Where were you last night?"

Shirley picked up the mug and became watchful. "At home as usual."

"All night?"

"Look, what is this about?"

"I was hoping you might make things easy on yourself. Tell me why you did it, pet. Tell me what happened."

Shirley picked at the sore on her lip and she picked at a scab on her arm and she picked at a fleck of dandruff on her shoulder. "I don't know what you are on about."

Fenella pulled out her phone, swiped and dabbed and studied the screen. No point rushing now. Not when she was so close. She stared at the flickering phone saying nothing.

A hollow wind echoed in the fireplace. A dry high-pitched whistle which ended as quickly as it began. The sudden silence compressed to a needle point of stillness.

Shirley shifted in her seat. "What are you looking at?"

Fenella continued to study her phone. Another hollow blast of wind howled through the fireplace. Another high-pitched whistle. The drizzle would soon be hard rain.

Shirley placed the mug to her lips, but did not drink. "I've done nothing wrong. I was here all night. In this house. In my bedroom. In my bed. Under the covers and sound asleep."

In the rush of words, Fenella caught the sour whiff of alcohol on Shirley's breath. She looked up and scrutinised the pockmarked face blotching with smears of red. Slowly, she held out her mobile phone and turned it around.

"Can you tell me what this is, Miss Bickham?"

Shirley didn't answer, her face a frozen mask of horror. Slowly she placed the mug on the coffee table.

Fenella said, "What's wrong, luv?"

Shirley leaned away as if the phone were a red-hot poker. And she was breathing hard. Her mouth opened but no words came out. She raised fluttery hands to cover her face. A tragic wail hissed from her lips as her eyelids closed and she sagged forward in the armchair. She slipped, in slow motion, to the mauve speckled deep pile carpet. Knees. Hips. Whole body prostrate on the soft flooring. A faint that would have made any stage actor proud.

"Get up," Fenella said. "I don't fool that easily."

Shirley scrambled to her knees and crawled back to the armchair, watching Fenella through narrow slits.

Fenella jabbed the phone at the lass. "Do you recognise it?"

"Of course not." Shirley clutched her hands together and placed them in her lap.

Fenella said, "Have you seen it before?"

"No."

"Are you sure?"

Nothing.

Fenella eyed the screen. "I wonder who it belongs to. Not you, you've said as much."

Nothing, except the twitch of Shirley's left eye and the whiteness creeping across her clutched hands.

Fenella said, "Do you know a Mr Den Ogden?"

Shirley's mouth opened. The only sound a dry gasp.

Fenella waved her phone. "See that cricket bat? It was found in Mr Ogden's bedsit. At the bottom of his wardrobe. Nothing unusual about that except for the nails and—"

"What has it to do with me?" Shirley sprang to

her feet and hurried to the window. "No. I've never heard of Den Ogden."

Fenella leaned forward, her voice dropping to a dangerous low. "Sit down, sunshine. I haven't finished."

There was a tense silence. Something rattled in the fireplace with a thin tinny sound. Shirley shuffled from the window, dropping into the arm chair with a heavy thud.

Fenella smiled. "You were on Shrimp Street last night."

"No."

"Sitting at the bus stop with a large canvas bag."

"No. No. No."

"The thing is, the bus came and went and you were still at the bus stop. Why?"

"It wasn't me."

"You were seen, pet. We have an eyewitness."

Shirley said nothing, but she watched Fenella like a fox who'd been to the hen house and hoped some other bugger got caught.

"I think you were waiting for Den Ogden last night," Fenella said, eyes fixed on the woman. "At some point you got inside the building and went to his bedsit and left that cricket bat. The one thing I can't figure out is how you got in."

Shirley laughed. A harsh cackle with no humour in it. "I'm in the dark about what you're saying. Have you gone mad?"

"But then I remembered the flowerpot to one

side of the door. I reckon the front door key was under it and you took it but forgot to put it back in your rush to leave. Didn't you see the sick bairn in the cot?"

"What baby?" Shirley hissed. "There was no baby in that flea pit."

And they both knew Fenella had her then. A sudden burst of rain splashed against the window. A howl of wind blasted through the fireplace. The dim gloom of the room shimmered as though in anticipation.

Fenella took her time now. "You were too drunk to notice, eh? Well, the bairn is in hospital getting medical treatment. She'll live, though, no thanks to you."

Silence, except the soft splat of drizzle on the window.

Shirley squeezed her hands, her lips moving, speaking in a soft hush. "Purge me. Purge my nasty, lurid soul."

"What was that, pet?"

"I want to call my solicitor."

"You haven't been charged with anything."

Those words seemed to rally Shirley. "That's right because you have no evidence. None whatsoever. Anyway, everyone knows eyewitnesses make mistakes. I don't know who the person saw, but it wasn't me. Mam will back me up that I was here last night. You have nothing but empty words. Now, unless you have hard concrete facts on which to base your wild speculation, I must insist you leave our house."

The steady beat of rain drummed on the window. A sound like tiny pebbles dashed against glass.

Fenella made to stand up but didn't. "What bothers me, pet, is what you did with that key. They are funny things when you think about them. We tend to use them without thinking. Open a door, close a door, put the key in our pocket or handbag without thought." Fenella glanced around the room. "Wouldn't take my team long to search a house like this. It's what we do for a living, pet. Search places to uncover the truth. Let's start with your handbag, where do you keep it?"

Shirley's eyes widened. "You need paperwork for that."

"Can get it within the hour. Where'd you put the key?"

"Look, I didn't kill my dad." There was an edge of dread to Shirley's voice now. A creak like wood about to crack. "I didn't kill anyone."

"You put that cricket bat in Den Ogden's flat."

"Stop it. Stop it. I've never heard of the man. Why can't you understand that I'm innocent?"

"Because of that cricket bat, pet. It doesn't belong to Den Ogden. See, it is a woman's bat. Your bat. Lined with nails and placed in his wardrobe by your own hand. We'll find fingerprints and DNA, no doubt."

Fenella held up the phone again then eased to her feet. She felt one hundred years old and tired of it all. She paced to the scatter of photos on the mantelshelf and exhaled a long slow breath. Shirley Bickham's cold eyes followed her, guilt smeared across her pockmarked face.

Fenella didn't want to do this, but there was no other way. She picked up a photo of Ginger. She wore a school uniform, cream blouse and blue blazer. Big smile. Fourteen or fifteen at a guess. Twiglike with everything thin, including her slender nose.

"You had twins with him, luv." Fenella waited a heartbeat. "Den Ogden is Ginger's dad. And her brother is a lad called Chuck Baker."

"Liar!" Shirley Bickham exploded in a flood of tears, her hands covering her ears. "No. It is not true."

"Your son is in the hospital, luv. He came over here from America to find his dad. He thinks you are dead. They've done the blood work; won't take long to confirm you are his mam. It is all over, luv." Fenella tilted her neck from side to side. "Revenge. That was your motive for leaving that cricket bat, wasn't it?"

Shirley wiped her tear-stained cheeks, sniffing with miserable sobs. "I ... I need a drink."

A wave of sorrow crushed Fenella's heart, but she had to keep digging until the truth lay fully exposed. She'd not leave fragments buried in the dirt. She had to have it all. "How much did Den Ogden pay you for your son?"

Shirley squeezed her eyes tight. The nurse with the flabby arms smiled and counted out fifty pound notes. *Tell them nothing,* she had said in a thick Russian accent. *Tell your parents you only had one.*

Shirley's tongue flicked out to moisten her lips. "I ... I always wanted a girl, couldn't care for twins. I needed the money."

"How much?"

Shirley said nothing.

Fenella shook her head. "Greed is a fat demon with a small mouth. Whatever you feed it is never enough." She touched Shirley's arm. "I bet you didn't make half as much as Den Ogden made on the deal, luv. Did you?"

Shirley remained mute.

"It doesn't matter," Fenella said, removing her hand from Shirley's arm. "I'll find out. When I'm finished, I'll have the details down to the last penny."

Voices came from outside the room. The door opened. PC Woods and PC Beth Finn came in.

CHAPTER 64

It was almost nine when Fenella pulled her Morris Minor into the Port St Giles Cottage Hospital car park and strode across the wet tarmac. The rain had eased, but under the low clouds, drizzle slanted in great sheets, drifting in mist like swirls. She wanted to tie up a few loose ends before formally interviewing Shirley Bickham at the police station.

Jones met her at the hospital entrance. From his inside pocket, he took a folded paper. "Details on what I've been able to dig up, boss."

She accepted and read, then folded it, slipping it into her handbag. "Let's go."

They hurried through the warren of corridors to the ward where Den Ogden waited.

PC Jake Kent stood guard and nodded them into a room with drawn curtains and the smell of antiseptic and soap. Not much to see. A table bolted to the floor. Two orange plastic chairs and an array of ancient looking medical devices. Even the bed looked like it came from another era. All iron and twisted slats. White blinds hung on the small window, shuttered against the morning light. Not as lush as the private ward of Mrs Stoke. This was a room used only for those in the custody of the police or the prison service. One way in. One way out, and a barred window which didn't open.

Den Ogden lay on the bed with his eyes closed. He wore a white medical gown which disappeared beneath the covers. An instrument beeped at regular intervals. He appeared frail and weak and pale. A very ill man, on first sight, who wouldn't hurt a fly. But then Fenella thought of baby Eva Fisk and knew he had ice running through his veins.

Jones pulled up a chair and sat to one side of the door. He took out a notebook and waited.

Fenella stepped closer to the bed. "Den Ogden?"

Den opened his eyes. The stunned glance he gave her told her he expected a nurse. "You look like a copper."

"Detective Fenella Sallow."

"I'm in pain." He spoke in a weak voice.

"Can't help you with that."

He squeezed his eyes tight shut. "I want to see a nurse. I need more pills to numb the pain. Please call the nurse."

Fenella wanted to help, but she hesitated. Was it the domed shaped double chin or the slit of a mouth? Something about the man was off. She sensed it tingling in the air like static. He let out a soft moan, more whimper than words, and she realised what it was. Den Ogden had a temper on him. It vibrated below his pale skin.

She moved a plastic chair to the bed and sat. "I've a few questions, Mr Ogden."

His eyes remained shut, only the narrow

mouth moved. "Call the nurse. Now."

"After our chat."

"Look, I didn't have anything to do with the kidnapping of that child."

It seemed Den had been thinking, planning, working the odds and making up his mind what he would say. It wasn't his fault. He was an innocent man.

Fenella said, "But you had the bairn in your room. It was your room, wasn't it Mr Ogden?"

He opened his eyes and turned to face her. "Yes, I was living in that place, but I've been duped, made a fool of." A sudden anger flared and his voice became strong. "It had nothing to do with me."

Fenella wanted to hear it all, right now, this instant, but she had to take her time with a man like Den Ogden. Prod, poke and tease it out. Use his rage against him.

She said, "Tell me about it."

His gaze turned to the door, his eyes filling with some sort of calculation. "I'll give you my full cooperation if you will please ask the judge to take it into consideration. I've been a fool. Look, I'm not a bad person."

So, he wanted to do a deal. This pleased Fenella. "Aye pet, they will take that into account. Now let's get something down for the record."

She beckoned Jones. He put away his notebook, took out a voice recorder and moved his chair to the bed. Fenella nodded and Den Ogden began. He told her about the Russian with rag doll eyes; that something had gone wrong with the original buyer of baby Eva Fisk—they did not want the lass and he didn't know why. He was not involved in the kidnapping, by the way. He was only the muggins at the bottom of the totem pole. He spoke about not wanting to take the job, but needing the cash to see him through. He had to eat. Who would blame him? And he mentioned the Russian had stolen other children, but he didn't know from whom. Then he told them how he was strangled by the Russian and almost died. He spoke his words in a feeble voice, but underneath lay real fury. He'd been wronged and he hoped the police would help put it right.

When he finished, he collapsed on his pillow. "So, you see, I'm a pawn and as much a victim as any child. I'm an innocent man who has been tricked into this mess. An innocent man, Detective Sallow. Write that in your notebook and underline it with red ink."

There was a self-satisfied pride in the way he said his words, almost boastful. He'd been wronged and was now on their side. A team, eh?

Fenella shifted in her seat. "Baby Eva almost died."

"I would have gone to the doctor in the morning."

"Really, because it looked like you'd done a runner."

"Come on, see it my way. Yes, I panicked when I saw the blue flashing lights. But wouldn't you? Your lot hasn't exactly been a lucky charm for me, so I thought it best that I scarper. I planned to call a doctor. That is the honest truth."

Fenella let that hang in the air for several seconds then steepled her fingers. "Why did you attack that lad in the alley last night?"

He stared with sly eyes. "I've no memory of last night. I hit my head when that bloody police dog pounced. Don't get me wrong, I love dogs, but that bleedin' hound ought to be put down. A bullet to Fido's brain. Happy to pull the trigger."

Fenella glanced at Jones. A thick vein pulsed in his neck; his eyes narrowed to slits. She changed track. "Do you know a lass by the name of Shirley Bickham?"

He shook his head. "It doesn't ring any bells. Shirley? Nope."

"You were in a relationship with her twenty or so years ago."

Again, he shook his head. "Too much water under the bridge. What about her?"

"It was her son you attacked in the alley on Shrimp Street."

"Look, it was self-defence. The sod got what he deserved."

"He is your son, Mr Ogden."

Den jerked back on his pillow. "I ... er ... my son?"

And then, suddenly, Fenella understood the final piece of the puzzle. Her heart skipped a beat and slammed against her chest. *Dear God, the man is more than a monster. He's a bleedin' devil with it.*

She'd have to be careful to get it all out. Needle him. Trigger him. Burst his bubble of pride.

She massaged her neck. "I bet you didn't think you'd see your son again, not after you sold him off to America. Remember Shirley Bickham now?"

Silence. The rain started again. It fell in torrents, pounding against the window with sodden thuds.

"Shirley Bickham," Den said, drawing out her name. "What has the old slag been saying?"

For the first time there came a hint of menace in his voice. A hint of the real man. A hint he had been playing Fenella for sympathy. A hint something inside had long ago snapped and could never be repaired. A hint of anger bubbling just beneath the surface. And Fenella smiled.

She ignored his question and smoothed the edge of his bedsheet. "How much did you get for the lad?"

Den threw his head back, laughing. "I've always believed in a simple philosophy. I'll take care of me, if you will please take care of you. A simple way to live that brings a man everything he desires." Again, he laughed. "Everything."

"How much, Mr Ogden? Were you short changed?"

"Me cheated? No bloody way." He pounded a fist against his chest. "I'm the victim here. I'm the one who has been savaged by a mad dog."

Fenella leaned in a little, picking her words with care. "So, you sold the child you had with

Shirley Bickham?"

"Is that what the cow said?"

"I'd like to hear your side."

Den stared with small dark eyes, hard and mean and greedy. "Yeah, I got cash and gave a wad to his mam. It was her idea. I only went along with it because she said it was what she wanted. Our relationship was never going to last. Look, the boy got the good life in the land where the sun always shines. A win-win."

"Selling kids is a win-win?"

"It is a job and as good as any other." He spat the words in a blaze of fury. "They leave the dark and go to the light. That is what we want for them, isn't it? A better life."

Fenella sensed from his answer, Chad Baker wasn't the last bairn he'd sold. She was on to it immediately.

"A job?" she said. "Getting young girls pregnant is a job?"

"Same as farming." He was grinning now, the thin slit of a mouth turned up at the edges. "That is what I am. A farmer. Till the soil and plant the seed, tender and reap the harvest."

The man was a mass of contradictions, and yet Fenella marvelled a little at his brazenness. The stone-hearted fiend had no shame or compassion.

She tapped a finger on the bedframe and jabbed him with a needle-sharp question. "You are a bit old for that lark these days, aren't you?"

"I've enough to go around."

He was boasting now. A cockerel at dawn. Crowing and puffing out his chest, lips stretched over his crooked teeth in a sinister smile. Never once had he turned his gaze to Jones. If he had, he would have seen the furious glare and shrank back between the covers, pulling them over his face.

Again, Fenella jabbed the needle and twisted. "Can't be easy to meet lasses who find skinflint meanness attractive. Not at your age, anyway."

Den's grin broadened and there was boastful pride in his voice now. "The ugly ones are easy pickings. Runaways and girls from broken homes. Teens. Sensitive and supple and stupid. They are eager for it. Love they call it." He laughed. It wasn't pleasant. "Easier to rob than a blind man's wallet. More fun, too. When I get them up the duff with my child, I make an offer. A very nice wad of cash for the sprog. Plant the seed and harvest."

The cold calculation in his words sent Fenella's nerve ends tingling. No remorse. No regret. Only selfish greed and stupid boasts. Repulsive. How many girls had the man got pregnant? How many bairns had he sold? She'd find out and nail the bugger for every last one.

Another silence. Longer. Den's chest heaved with violent jerks. He sucked in air and spat it out. He was trying to control his mouth, but he'd already said too much.

Fenella forced her voice to remain even. "Mr Ogden, thank you for telling me your side of the story. Very helpful. But I'd like to come back to

Miss Shirley Bickham."

"Like I told you, I've no idea what the lass looks like. I have not seen her in years. I didn't even recognise her son, and that is God's truth."

Fenella nodded. "Do you know Mr Fred Bickham?"

"Who? Don't tell me, is he Shirley's husband? I'm no detective, but I see where you are going. Well, I've never met him. Don't want to meet him neither."

"Oh come off it, you don't fool me." Fenella leaned back in her chair, crossed her arms and smiled. "We know Mr Bickham came to the police station to speak with a detective, but changed his mind. Maybe you and he met, and you persuaded him not to return to the police station. Maybe you told him you would turn yourself in. It doesn't matter. What does matter is that you killed Fred Bickham because he found out his daughter, Shirley, had twins and that you sold the boy child for profit. You killed him because he was going to speak with the police. But we know all about your seedy secret now, don't we Mr Ogden? So, you killed Fred Bickham in vain."

A sudden flash of fear oozed from Den, draining colour from his face. His jaw worked for a while but no words came out.

"And you killed Fred Bickham with a cricket bat because he was a fine player in his day," Fenella said. "I asked myself about the nails in the bat. Now I've met you, I understand. You put them in the bat out of pure spite, to cause the greatest damage, to make sure Fred Bickham would never talk."

Sweat pimpled his brow. "You've got no evidence I met that man." His voice was harsh now. As hard as nails. "You'll never make it stick."

And he was right. There were no CCTV cameras at Seaview Allotments. None on the way to the place. There was no visual evidence that Den Ogden and Fred Bickham had ever met.

But Fenella went with her gut, rolled the dice and twisted the needle again. She opened her handbag and took out the sheet of folded paper, read for a moment and sighed. "It says here you were a resident of Mrs Fassnidge's boarding house."

"Yeah, what of it?"

"Why did you kill Mrs Fassnidge?"

Den Ogden said nothing.

"I think it was because she asked you to leave," Fenella said in a sharp voice. "You killed her out of spite."

Among the blandness of his face, where Fenella and Jones focused, something moved: a shadow crossed his baker dough pale skin. Dark on light. Fenella held her breath. She counted, dead certain of what she had briefly glimpsed. Blind rage.

It took two heartbeats.

"The cow deserved it," Den yelled, eyes like two blackberries on a vine. "She threw me out on my ear without a moment's notice. She stuffed my belongings into bin bags and tossed them in the alley. No flea pit landlady does that to Den Ogden. I am somebody."

"That's right, but you've forgotten one thing. We are all somebody and nobody has the right to take the life of those folks that get in their way; that includes you Mr Ogden." Fenella turned to Jones. "Caution him. I need to get out of here and breathe some fresh air."

CHAPTER 65

At exactly four in the afternoon, Fenella and Dexter went into Mrs Stoke's hospital room. Within five minutes, Mrs Stoke was comfortable enough with Fenella to begin to speak freely, to admit mistakes, to explain what happened as best as she knew. They chatted for a full hour and a half, Mrs Stoke going over it all in a miserable rasp. She told Fenella about the other women involved, counting them off on her fingers and naming them one by one. All middle-class. The horsy type who liked hunting and downing bottles of wine and going to tea with the vicar. Women of influence with husbands who were part of the elite.

Fenella had her go over her answers again and again, asking her questions from different angles. Mrs Stoke slumped against the pillow as a medical device beeped. Fenella cooed and soothed and encouraged her on so that she talked steadily, never noticing the scratch of Dexter's pen on paper or the soft click of his recording device.

When it was over, Fenella shook Mrs Stoke's hand and planted a kiss on her cheek. She had it all now, every last bit, in black and white on paper and in bits and bytes on a recording device.

They left Mrs Stoke with a smile of relief on her worried face. Then Fenella gathered her team and they drove to Ria Leigh's home.

CHAPTER 66

Ria Leigh heard the screaming and thought the rats were back in the garden and trying to get at the bird feeder. But she hesitated a fraction of a second longer than normal, realised it was the screech of brakes and dashed to the window in the front room.

Acid churned in her stomach and surged up her throat. Detective Inspector Sallow was out in front, striding along the street. PC Beth Finn, PC Woods and Jones hurried behind. They were headed for her house, coming to her door.

This is it, she told herself, feeling her body wilt in shame. They'd cart her off and toss her in a cell and throw the whole bloody book at her. For a moment she remained frozen to the spot, thinking about all she had won and now lost. And where was her business partner, Sloane Kern? Fled from town? On a beach in the Costa Brava? Chugging sangria and eating calamari with a bronzed Spanish waiter? Or was she already in a prison cell blabbing her mouth and pointing the finger?

The room swirled around her. She grasped for the wall, turning away from the window like a cockroach frightened by light. She glimpsed her pale reflection in the glass, a shadow of herself. A ghost.

She wondered if she knew the person looking back at her.

And like a cockroach, she scurried across the dark shadows of the front room. There was a chance she could get away if she dashed along the garden path and out through the back gate. Then what? She didn't know, all her focus was on getting away.

She ran hell for leather through the hall, her heart pounding fit to burst, sprinting the way a criminal scarpers from a crime. She skidded to a stop in the kitchen, staring at the back door in shock. Two eyes peered through the glass. Dexter's face pressed against the pane.

"Oh God save me," Ria cried as she felt her legs give way and her world turn dreamy then black.

Much later, as Ria sat up in the hospital bed, heart monitor beeping and in that mental fug induced by drugs, she could do no more than listen.

Dexter sat at her side, rubbing his unshaved chin. "Just as well we arrived when we did. You passed out, lass, and hit your head. That's why they had to bring you in. Same wing as Mrs Stoke. Private suite, eh? Fancy that."

Ria opened her mouth but no words came out. Her head throbbed with a dull pain and she felt too weak to move her limbs. What the hell had they pumped into her?

Dexter was still speaking. "Funny thing that. Same wing, I mean. But Mrs Stoke is in the upmarket bit. I suppose that is how it goes sometimes."

He looked around the room as though

checking no one was listening. "You'll find out in due time, lass. Me and Detective Inspector Sallow had a chat with Mrs Stoke. A good long chat. We got it all down, even got her to sign a statement. So it is over."

Ria felt her eyes widen, jaw drop, but only a dry croak came out.

"Doc says you are to take it easy," Dexter said, turning to look at the heart monitor whose beeps had increased to an alarming degree. "Try not to move, don't want your heart to pop."

He turned to watch the heart monitor for several moments, then turned back to Ria.

"Beef stroganoff," he said with a flourish. "Who'd have thought a bunch of middle-class women would have got food poisoning from that? Never knew bad beef stew could lead to paralysis, respiratory failure and unconsciousness. Severe, it were too. Knocked half of them ladies for six, and the other half weren't much better. Poor Mrs Stoke is blaming herself, since she provided the dish for a pot luck. She ate a big bowl of it and got sick the day before their social gathering, but was in hospital knocked out and couldn't warn anyone. It were her cook who stored the food at the wrong temperature and then took the dish to the party. Two giant pots of it. They all ate it. Still, no one died and there are no charges."

He rocked to his feet and strode to the door. "Like I say, it is just as well the team came to your house to see how you were doing, ain't it? Get well soon, lass."

CHAPTER 67

It was seven in the evening on the following day when Fenella and her team sat around a table in the Sailors Arms pub. A popular spot for serving and retired police officers. They'd finished a meal of beefeater chips, steak and green peas and were now enjoying a pint, except Dexter who sipped from a glass of orange juice.

Fenella took a long slug from her half pint of lager and lime, mind going over the day. She'd popped into Johnny Dew's Organic Garden Centre in the early evening to return the eggplant shaped brooch to Cherry. She had been surprised by two smiling faces. Cherry Dew, and at her side a black dog with pointed ears, a green headscarf tied around its neck and a snout so filled with teeth it gave the appearance of smiling. Her dad had got him from the animal shelter—Elfrid. Two cute faces sell more plants, Fenella supposed, but she knew better than to say anything.

She took another sip from her lager. "That meal hit the spot."

"Ain't nowt like pub grub, guv," Dexter replied.

"Can't beat it when the mood strikes," PC Woods said, mopping up the last of his gravy with a wad of chips. "Think I'll have a smoke once I've downed the blackberry crumble with custard."

Jones and PC Beth Finn sat next to each other, arms touching, saying nothing.

The barman ambled over to shake Fenella's hand and slap Dexter on his back. He was a retired desk sergeant and had heard the news.

When he returned to the bar, Fenella took another sip from her lager. "That Den Ogden was a cool one, but we got it all, eh?"

"Brass neck is what we used to call it, guv. Not an ounce of shame." Dexter picked up his orange juice and sipped. "He'll go down for so long that when he gets out the world will be in a new century and he'll be in a box."

Jones raised a hand like he was in school. "What shocked me most was Shirley Bickham's confession that she went to her dad's flat dressed in black."

"That weren't the shocking part," Dexter said, unable to stop himself from butting in. "It were the reason why she went to his flat in the first place. To put her dad's medals back. But she couldn't find a key and so took them back home. It seems her daughter, Ginger, had stolen them to pay for the wedding with her lad."

There was a moment of silence.

Fenella picked her words carefully. "Ginger cried her heart out over stealing his medals. Blames herself now her grandad is dead. The young don't think, do they?" She took a long pull from her lager.

"Shirley Bickham discovered what her daughter had done, knew we'd ask about the medals and tried to put them back before we discovered they were missing. Mams protect their bairns."

"What about her son, Chuck Baker?" Jones sounded indignant. "She sold him for cash. What type of mum does that?"

"Naïve actions of a young girl." Fenella put her glass on the table. "I reckon she has long regretted it. Shirley is an alcoholic whose life has been one downward spiral of misery. Selling her son ruined her life. They'll be charges, though. It is with the Crown Prosecution Service now."

PC Beth Finn edged closer to Jones. "I can't understand why people get themselves in such a tangle. I mean, in the end it was Shirley Bickham's choice."

Fenella didn't respond. She was thinking about planting the tray of eggplants out in the garden rather than the greenhouse. They had predicted a hot summer and she thought the fresh air would yield a bumper crop. Plenty for salad. Plenty for gifts, and the remainder she would store in the freezer.

The barman began to whistle, dragging a rag across the counter. Two men in flat caps clinked glasses and downed their pint mugs of ale in one swallow. A slender woman carrying a canvas bag came through the main door, and sat at a table in a corner, waved at the barman and gazed at her phone. The dessert came. Steaming bowls of blackberry crumble with dollops of hot custard. And Fenella decided. She'd visit Chuck Baker again in the hospital, just to find out how he was doing and to watch his face when she told him what went into black pudding.

The Detective Inspector Fenella Sallow series continues with Tell-Tale Bones.

AFTERWORD

If you have enjoyed this story, please consider leaving a short review. Reviews help readers like you discover books they will enjoy, and help indie authors like me improve our stories.

Until next time,

N.C. Lewis

PS. Be the first to hear about new releases by joining my **Readers Newsletter or visit** https://bit.ly/NCLewis.

Made in the USA
Monee, IL
17 September 2024